ICE SONG

ICE SONG

KIRSTEN IMANI KASAI

BALLANTINE BOOKS
NEW YORK

Ice Song is a work of fiction. Names, characters, places, and incidents are the products of the author's imagination or are used fictitiously. Any resemblance to actual events, locales, or persons, living or dead, is entirely coincidental.

A Del Rey Trade Paperback Original

Published in the United States by Del Rey Books, an imprint of The Random House Publishing Group, a division of Random House, Inc., New York.

DEL REY is a registered trademark and the Del Rey colophon is a trademark of Random House, Inc.

ISBN 978-0-345-50881-2

Printed in the United States of America

www.delreybooks.com

2 4 6 8 9 7 5 3 1

Book design by Christopher M. Zucker

Dedicated to the memory of Kirsty M. Brown,
her British Antarctic Survey colleagues,
and Gary Hicken, as promised.

Acknowledgments

My thanks to the women of the San Diego Writers Group, especially Sharon and Ondine, for their invaluable encouragement and advice. Thanks to Professor James Corbett, for reintroducing me to Homer's *Odyssey*, the seed for this story. Thank you Jen, B-1, and Skyler, for feedback on early drafts. Thanks to my agent, Helen Breitwieser, for plucking me from obscurity, to Otis, for soundscapes and endless discussions about the meaning of art, and most importantly, to my wonderful husband, for everything.

"The Story of the Seven Ravens" is based upon the Brothers Grimm fairy tale of the same name.

Characters

Ayeda	(Eye-a-da)	*Sorykah's daughter, twin to Leander*
Carac	(Care-ak)	*a par-wolf, Sidra's aide-de-camp*
Carensa	(Ka-ren-za)	*a maid in the House of Pleasure*
Chen		*Matuk's son*
Daoud	(Dah-ood)	*Matuk's father*
Dunya	(Dun-yah)	*the dog-faced girl, Matuk's housekeeper*
Elu	(Ell-oo)	*Chen's patissier*
Kamala	(Ka-ma-la)	*Elu's mother*
Kika	(Kee-kah)	*a sled dog*
Leander	(Lee-an-der)	*Sorykah's son, twin to Ayeda*
Marianna	(Mar-ee-ah-na)	*matron of the House of Pleasure*
Matuk	(Ma-took)	*the Collector, an evildoer*
Meertham	(Meer-tham)	*a somatic, Matuk's number one henchman*
Nels		*Sorykah's nanny, a devotee of the Blessed Jerusha*
Radhe	(Rod-ah)	*Matuk and Tirai's daughter*
Rava	(Rah-va)	*an octameroon*
Shanxi	(Shanks-see)	*the witch, Matuk's sister*
Sidra	(Sid-ra)	*Queen of the Erun Forest*
Soryk	(Sor-ik)	*an artisan glassworker, male alter to Sorykah*
Sorykah	(Sor-i-kah)	*an engineer, mother, and female primary to Soryk*
Tirai	(Teer-eye)	*Matuk's first wife*
Zarina	(Za-ree-na)	*a jealous rival in the House of Pleasure*

"Why should I mourn at the ultimate fate of my people?
Tribe follows tribe, nation follows nation, like the waves of the sea.
It is the order of nature and regret is useless.
Your time of decay may be distant, but it will surely come."

CHIEF SEATTLE, DUWAMISH

ICE SONG

1

SONG OF THE SIGUE

THEY TOUCHED THE SIGUE COAST AT DUSK, just as the ice was cracking. Standing on the slippery top deck as the massive ice-drilling submarine churned toward shore, Sorykah Minuit inhaled, taking the cold ocean air deep into her lungs. It felt so good to be outside after weeks below sea, working cheek by jowl with sixty filthy, sweat-stained miners and their collective, tactile reek. The air sang down her throat and pierced her lungs, but she welcomed the discomfort. It helped to clear her head of melancholy and milk-fog. For a moment it seemed that the cold would solidify around her and crack apart her carefully wrought shell, releasing her from the prison of her secrecy—but it did not.

The helmsman sounded the docking horn. A long, low peal vibrated the metal deck beneath her feet. Frigid brine sluiced over the *Nimbus*'s hull as it rose, its imposing bulk breasting the waves like the body of a sleek black orca. Afternoon light the color of apricots glistened atop the water; heat splayed against an icy sky.

Soon, the color would fade and night emerge, liquid indigo turning the snow to charcoal. Southern sunsets lingered for hours. Siguelanders said the sun bled to death each night; this dazzling show repeated the story of Sun's grisly murder by his lover Moon, who stabbed him while he slept, jealous of his affection for a mortal woman.

The noise of the ocean penned in by the icy harbor was terrific. Ice groaned, squeaked, and bellowed. Water droplets froze in midair and fell toward the wooden pier, bouncing upon its snowy crust like scattered, shining stones. Nearer the surface, one long sheet of ice groaned deep within its white skin, a sound like a woman birthing, or so it seemed to Sorykah, still sentimental from the memory of her own children's birth but a lunar skein behind.

The Sigue was the Land of Ice Song, a surreal pole formed from ice that sang, juddered, and moaned. Ice plates ground against one another with subarctic cricket legs, keening shards and frosts that played the most primitive and abstract melodies yet had shaped the culture of this tiny nation. Musicians and singers attempted to capture the eerie, haunting songs but could not repeat the melancholic strains. Sound technicians embedded microphones deep within the ice plates in an effort to record the music, chart the notes, pitch, and timing of the songs, but the recordings replayed a mishmash of disconnected sounds, discordant and chaotic. The melody was lost in translation and the mocking ice refused capture by human whim. Hearing it now—angry, plaintive, sorrowful—Sorykah remembered why she had volunteered for this frigid, outlandish post, for the Sigue song replicated her own bitter tune. Perhaps the ice could sing to drive out the ghosts within her, banish the image of that deceitful Trader as he climbed from her bed, the smug, careless grin he'd offered as he wiped himself clean and slid into his trousers.

Sorykah licked the salt from her lips as she watched the harbormaster signal from the dock, his bright orange flags lost among the colorful clouds. She would live on the Sigue for the next two years, drilling the ice to extract iridescent tubes of microbe-rich frozen seawater. Northern processing stations would melt, distill, and bottle the fossil water for sale in nightclubs and restaurants, to be guzzled by sensation-seeking holidaymakers. The Company claimed that fossil water was the first nonaddictive substance to create recreational altered states. Touted as a panacea, the burgeoning fossil water trade rapidly had become the fastest-growing market segment of free-trade capital. Water had finally replaced gold and oil as the world's most valuable commodity.

Even with modern conveniences, ice mining was rough work; Sorykah eagerly anticipated a reprieve before the sub's giant bits and rigs were pressed into service on the morrow. To maintain a competitive edge, the Company drove them in recycling, fourteen-hour shifts. They pushed hard; the rig cut ice nonstop to harvest as much as possible during spring thaws, when the polar ice sheets thinned enough to blast through without crumpling their ships in the process. Furloughs were meant to be savored; a vacation day was an oasis promising warm hotel rooms, a soak in the famed Sigue sulfur springs, and perhaps a willing companion, bought for a few hours from one of the dockside bars—a brief respite of heat and haze in the midst of a cold black ocean.

The ice was no more of a challenge for Sorykah than bedrock and granite. She was a miner by trade, an engineer and a doctor of ecology. However, she lived as a woman most of the time and the controlling, misogynist Company culture did not allow women to do anything more mentally taxing than the most rudimentary work aboard the *Nimbus*. Tucked among the books and data of her dry profession in the progressive city of Dirinda, she could have played the university professor were she brave enough to weather the few prickly questions and stares that sometimes accompanied her public outings. Aboard the *Nimbus*, she was just a grunt—another core-drilling drone servicing the hive. She should have been navigating the sub from the engine room instead of being buried in one of the tiny miner's cells, but she had deferred to the omnipotent Company, happy to have a job that paid enough to support her two children and their nanny, Nels.

A burning sensation flared in Sorykah's heavy breasts and milk dampened her cotton bra. She had a sudden image of her twins curled like commas in her lap, their chubby hands roving over each other's hair and Sorykah's gown the morning before she departed to join the mining crew. Drowsy and warm, the three lay in Sorykah's small bed, cozy within a nest of protective arms and fluffy down duvet. She had fed them one last time, stroked their heads, memorized the whorls of their soft, waving curls and the texture of their skin. She had inhaled their scent; no matter what they ate, they smelled of apples, amaranth flour, and sticky-sweet mother's milk. Ayeda's forehead was as smooth as a polished egg while short, almost invisible hairs furred Leander's. They were small ships seeking the safety of a familiar and welcoming harbor. How was it possible to find such satisfaction, such pleasure in their care?

The pregnancy had destroyed Sorykah's life but the birth of her children had restored it, breaking open her detachment's careful façade and sending her reeling into sensation and wakefulness. At the very beginning, adrift and alone, she had wished them away, or rather wished the experience away, back to less encumbered days. The thought was but a flickering spark, and guttered out as it should.

She missed them very much.

Her breasts ached. She was surprised to find tears welling as she emerged from her reverie. She hated how fragile the babies made her feel, like a teacup balanced atop a precarious, swaying block tower.

That such a rash act had brought her those two! The babies had split her open, leaving her raw and bared to experiences both sensual and deeply emotional, and bullied her into feeling with their incessant demands for acknowledgment and nourishment.

With the funds from her governmental maternity grant, Sorykah had hired a nursemaid. Generous and superficially stern as all good nannies should be, Nels was a plump, blond devotee of the Blessed Jerusha, matron saint of mothers, children, and outcasts. Religious devotion was foreign to secular, math-minded Sorykah, but even as she marveled at Nels's rigid and unyielding faith, she admired her constancy.

Nels had remained in Dirinda with the children while Sorykah completed her assignment. Now Nels was en route to the Sigue, bringing both children and luggage via the overland train to Ostara. Once established in their new Company-built home, Nels would keep the twins during Sorykah's tours, teaching them their letters and numbers, how to gauge the thickness of pack ice for walking or skating, or how to tease the occasional egg from the warm underbelly of an island bird.

The sub plowed inland through the frozen, slushy sea. Solid ground loomed behind crackling ribbons of ice churned up by the sub's advancing nose. Her back firm against the *Nimbus*'s conning tower, Sorykah clutched the railing in excitement as she strained toward shore, attempting to view the town through obfuscating swirls of blowing snow and vapor. Ramshackle tin sheds and concrete block storefronts lined Ostara's harbor, their weather-ravaged façades slumping against each other like tired old men huddled together against the cold.

Ostara was a dirty little place thrown together by a steady surge of transient workers on get-rich-quick missions. Hunters, poachers, and pirates on the lam populated its rough fringes. Bars, brothels, and hotels of questionable virtue crowded the harbor, jostling for space and patrons. Crude wood-framed houses, their walls stuffed with insulating hay and dung, and aluminum Quonset huts spread inland away from the sea, forming concentric rings of increasing squalor. A few small families from the decimated indigenous population clung tenaciously to their ancestral homes, the last stragglers of the ice-dwelling tribe that had ruled the Sigue for a thousand years. Their igloos dotted Ostara's perimeter, small snowy mounds lost against the vastness of the frozen wastes. The town offered few comforts but it was land, steady and beloved after the rigors of drilling far below on the ocean floor.

The quay tightened into view. Sailors, miners, and soldiers appeared as dark clumps moving through sparkling clouds of airborne snow, a city populated by shadows and ghosts. A few lights glowed in the frost-etched windows. Locals slogged over wooden walkways slippery with packed snow and crenellations of ice. Walking upright in their bundles of fur and padding, they resembled well-fed bears lumbering along on some private errand, a stark contrast to the sleekly outfitted Company men in their expensive long-coats and insulated blue thermosuits. The sub shuddered, engines throbbing as it inched into port. Icy seawater foamed and crackled around the ship and Sorykah's anticipation peaked. She could taste freedom, hers to savor if just for a few hours.

She didn't want to leave the children for so long at this early age, but Sorykah had to accept this assignment if she meant to keep her job. The Company was ruthless in its firing tactics; it was all policies, percentages, and rules with no deviation from the hard line; productivity and profit was its sole concern. Mining was all she had. Sealing herself in a floating metal coffin with a load of gruff, self-absorbed laborers was flimsy insurance against discovery. It was a matter of containing the danger of exposure. Controlling the circle around her minimized the chance of a surprise encounter with some psychotic hunter or Trader fetishist. She'd repelled plenty of their advances over the years, learning how to protect and cloak herself from those with eyes trained to see the little details that distinguished her kind. Working with the same crew for months on the sub, she learned who to trust and who to avoid; keeping her secret meant keeping away from those who might reveal her. She was always careful, yet a steady undercurrent of fear pulsed behind everything she did; a cool and constant stream of caution tempered her every word and deed, leaving her numbed and exhausted.

Cold stabbed her sinuses and she pulled her scarf up over her nose and mouth. Her heart was as light as a little bird, restless inside the cage of her ribs. Somewhere on shore, her two babies waited. They wouldn't have forgotten their mother after a single month's absence from their lives, would they?

Her babies. A girl and boy when last she saw them, Ayeda the light and Leander the dark. Her coin, her treasure. Ayeda got her coloring from her father; rich olive skin, wispy honey-colored hair and eyes like polished nickels or threatening rain clouds. Leander took after somber Sorykah, seal dark and slender with eyes like inky black wells. Two average Trader babies, one of each and each in one, it was said. So it was with her twins, little shifters they were, inconstant and fluid, taking the change with an astonishing ease that impressed her. She couldn't remember ever having been that way. For her the change was always slow and arduous, an intensely painful and deliberate event that left her breathless upon awakening. Sometimes she envied them; if she could have weathered her own change with more ease, she might not have had such knotted feelings about being a Trader, might even take pride and pleasure in her ability the way some did. A few brave (or foolish) Traders made their living with their bodies, charging by the poke, but it was a perilous road to walk. Sorykah shunned admiration, preferring instead to curl head-down in dark corners. Safe, she hoped—unseen and unnoticed.

The *Nimbus* eased itself into a deep slip ringed with waiting Company men, stamping their boots against the ice and puffing great frozen blasts of impatience into the air. Sorykah stood alone, clutching her duffel bag. None of the other miners was eager or foolhardy enough to brave the slippery deck. They sensibly waited below, playing a final round of cards to earn a little more drinking money before storming Ostara's bars. As soon as a red-nosed docker extended the gangway, she was off the sub, her boots soon thumping solid ground. She was glad she had covered her face. Between her black wool hat, the thick scarf over her mouth, and the bulky black long-coat, thermosuit and magnet boots she wore, she was almost indistinguishable from the tide of miners that would soon surge from the ship, similarly dressed in regulation gear. Few would pay much attention to her. Pushing through crowds of Company men, she kept her head down as if watching her footing. New people made her antsy; never could tell who was who, who might want what. Better to mind her own. Miners' rusty but cheerful voices began to fill the air behind her as the sub disgorged its crew.

Sorykah walked along Port Street, skirting roguish clumps of uniformed men, fur-swaddled locals with narrowed, crinkle-skinned eyes, and a pair of dirty-faced women in patchwork parkas towing a two-handled sledge over the ice. Frozen ropes clattered against their flapping tarp and seeping, red-splattered slabs of thick white animal fat dripped as the women dragged the sledge away. Flickering streetlights cast tepid blotches of waxy yellow light on the wooden walkway, lonely pools of optimism that bobbed over the hard ground in a fruitless attempt to drive away the cold and gloom.

The train station was a half mile from the end of Port, a lonesome walk across tamped-down snow. A battered Quonset crouched beside frost-laced tracks, outlined in gathering flurries. A few caged bulbs dangled from wooden poles and capered wildly overhead, pinning white shards of snow in their glare. The tracks ran parallel to Sorykah's path. Then, steaming up out of the grayness in a cloud of charcoal exhaust, came the train. Hissing and squealing, its brakes bore down with the ear splitting shriek of metal on metal and Sorykah began to run, crunching over the snow, subarctic air stinging her eyes as the train, at last, arrived.

"Hey-oooooh!" called the conductor, leaning from the open door as the train slowed alongside the platform. Sorykah urged herself forward over the packed snow. A few motley passengers disembarked clutching bags and parcels, shoving one another in their rush to obtain the station's scant warmth. The train's open belly spilled swollen canvas mailbags, metal traveling trunks, and wooden crates filled with upland supplies for the few general stores and diners that served Ostara's transient population of ice miners and land workers.

Sorykah searched the crowd for Nels and the children. Nearing the train, she was filled with a growing sense of urgency and disquiet. She pushed past three smartly dressed Company men carrying medical cases. They eyed her as she passed and one pursed his lips as if he were trying to recall some elusive detail before the crowd and the blowing snow swallowed her up. The other two conferred and tugged their companion away. He shook his head and wiped melting flurries from his face, leaving Sorykah behind. Had she noticed the quick exchange, felt the intensity of the man's gaze upon her retreating back, she would have vanished into the crowd or ducked between train compartments, willing herself to invisibility. She was wary not so much of being watched in the casual way that people in a crowd eyed those around them, but being seen by those who might be sharp enough to decipher her careful camouflage and mark her as a Trader, a freak. Rare were the moments when she could elude the dogged sensation of being someone's prey and the desperate need to avoid capture and sexual slavery.

Swirling eddies of snow cluttered the air, making it hard to see. The passengers were misshapen and lumpy beneath heavy clothing; eyes were narrowed against the cold; red noses caked with frozen snot and swatches of mottled skin peeked between hats and scarves. It was hard to recognize anyone. Sorykah tried without success to quell her mounting anxiety. Emptied of its load, the train sat idle for a few minutes as the conductor checked the tickets of a few outbound passengers and ushered them aboard.

Sorykah accosted him just as he swung up into the train and prepared to close the door.

"Wait! Please!" Her voice wavered and she willed her nerves to steady. Grasping the railing beside the door, Sorykah mounted the step and reached through the open window to tug the conductor's sleeve.

"What do you want?" His weary voice was rough, grown tired from use.

"I'm looking for my family. They were supposed to arrive on this train, a woman with two children. Have you seen them?" She could feel the desperation radiating from her eyes, her skin. A simple mistake, that's all. There would be an explanation, a solution.

"Yes, I remember them. Two boys, with their mother."

"Two boys?" It was possible. Ayeda could have changed but it was always hard to tell with babies anyway. A rush of absurd gratitude filled her stomach. "Where are they?"

"Got off in Colchester, stop before this one. The boys had a dogsled waiting. Mum dropped them off. She's still aboard, going all the way to Finn Town." He tapped his gloved hand against the scratched glass, eager to close the window and be on his way.

Why would Nels leave the children? Sorykah choked back panic and scanned the conductor's face, hoping that he'd made some sort of mistake.

"She left the boys alone? That can't be right."

"Them was big strapping lads. I'm sure they can handle themselves." He tapped the glass again. "Boarding?"

"No, I suppose not." Sorykah slid down, releasing her hold on the train. Steam and smoke plumed from the engine car; dirty orange sparks exploded into the air as the coal handler stoked the train's fiery heart. The whistle blew, reverberating in Sorykah's ears. Sorykah watched the train pull away as if in a dream, silent and ethereal as it glided away into another dimension.

She fought her tears, a swelling, anguished tide that threatened to sweep her away. *Calm yourself, breathe, breathe,* she intoned, but paranoia took hold, whipping her thoughts into a maelstrom of suspicion. There was no organized police force in Ostara. Colchester, a hundred miles northeast, had an all-purpose officiate who oversaw municipal matters in the Sigue capital and handled the occasional complaint from the outlying districts, of which Ostara was one. This was a Company town, run with the express purpose of housing core miners on furlough and by proxy supplementing the meager living earned by the scruffy locals. A tribal leader mediated the occasional disagreement but he held no sway with the Company. Unrecognized by the Sigue government, his authority was minimal, and lacking financial resources, he would be unable to help her locate her children.

Sorykah realized that she was shaking. She looked down at her gloved hands, watching them tremble against a grainy white backdrop of blowing snow. The few passengers had departed the station and thickening snowfall had swallowed up the train. She was alone. Although Sigue sunsets lasted hours instead of the usual northern minutes, darkness was fast descending, reducing visibility and stealing the last faint lavender threads of light from the sky. Fat clumps of wet snow beat against the shell of her longcoat. The temperature fell at a rate of one degree every three minutes. Even her thermosuit wouldn't protect her against the night air; she'd freeze to death in a matter of minutes once the sun went down. There would be no train until the following day. She must wait out the night and hope to find them before the submarine left port and she would be at sea for a fortnight with no means of tracking them.

Nels was imminently trustworthy. This was nothing more than a missed connection; she oughtn't jump to any rash conclusions. She began the long slog back to town. The walk seemed to take forever. Her feet were heavy, her soul, just moments before light and winged, had grown leaden with fear that left a taste of metal in her mouth. Her knees knocked together, from effort or cold she couldn't tell. Sorykah dragged her duffel bag, not caring that her possessions might freeze solid. She plodded along, fixated on finding some solace in a hot meal, a night of rest in a proper bed, the quiet of her own home before she awoke to aching emptiness and the long hours of waiting.

The new house, a small Quonset with a main room, kitchen, bath, and upper half story divided into three cramped bedrooms, was in the second outer tier. She'd ordered the oil tanks filled but there would be no food there, no warmth to welcome her. As she neared the fringes of town, Sorykah decided to spend the night at an inn rather than struggle through the dark streets to the new house. Ostara had emptied with the coming of night. Waves of slurry laughter and raucous, good-natured arguments rolled from the bawdy houses along hotel row.

Sorykah selected a weathered wooden building where a strip of red light gleamed in the window through a split in the faded, ancient drapery. A metal sign riddled with bullet nicks swung above the closed door, announcing in the indigenous language the presence of what she could only surmise to be the "Stuck Tongue," judging from the crude painting of a disembodied tongue frozen to a pole. This was a bar for Siguelanders and somatics, a place for the wayward, cast-out, and marginalized. She might be safe here; miners and Company men would avoid it out of fear, ignorance, or some misguided sense of xenophobia.

Somatics were human hybrids with scrambled genetics and bizarre deformities. Fodder for urban legends, they were a secret sect of throwaways, and Ostara was their quiet, underground haven. The heavy clothing required for warmth efficiently hid almost every body part but the eyes; one might never see another person unclothed except in the safety of a private home.

During Sorykah's childhood, her imagination had steeped in the sad and lurid tales of the Great Change, a mythical event heralding the beginning of the Split, the first identifiable mutation that manifested when people began to revert to animals and the long, linear branch of human DNA forked in two, twelve, and twenty. Oman was first. Oman-Noman, the Lost Man. He had led a charmed life, blessed in the cradle they said, and his world was rosy and perfect until he changed.

One morning, Oman awoke with stiff spines protruding from his shoulders, the tops of his arms, and his blackened fingertips. The spines twisted free of his skin, revealing themselves to be rigid-quilled feathers as black and shiny as an oil slick upon the tarmac. He developed a full set of wings, useless because he didn't have the proper bone structure and musculature necessary for flight, but still, it was a gorgeous, rustling pair of feathered ebony veils that whispered as he walked. Oman the Terrified. When he could no longer wear clothes to disguise his deformity, he quit going into the office. His wife left him. His mistress left him. Not because of his wings (the feathers that draped his hands making it impossible to caress a woman, hold a fork or pen, button a suit coat) but because of the hysterical fear that seemed to ooze from him and the helpless apathy with which he succumbed to his fate.

The change reduced Oman to a shuffling apparition of his former self. A gang of unscrupulous geneticists captured him and subjected him to horrible tests, plucking out his feathers in the most excruciating manner possible to see if pain would affect their rate of regrowth. After enduring several years of torture, Oman battered his doctor to death, liberated himself from the institute that housed his pain, and escaped on the back of a wild horse (whose only odd feature was human dentition) to vanish forever into the forgotten wilds of the Erun Forest.

Like any rational city dweller, Sorykah put little stock in the sad story of Oman and his man-molared wild horse. It was a magician's tale—a metaphor for the human condition. She considered it nothing more than an entertaining fiction until it happened to her. The change was the shattering quake that splintered solid ground and opened a gaping, fathomless chasm beneath her feet, tumbling her headlong into its unappeasable throat. Sorykah disappeared. Rather, the simple solidity of her unchanging form disappeared. What remained was something terrifying and surreal that stripped her of the safety and anonymity guaranteed by her old physiology. She now viewed that period of her life as though from a great distance.

The Sigue was a pole, and thus a magnet for the mainland's ostracized somatics who sought refuge in a severe and frigid environment that treated them less harshly than did the humans to the north. A change meant inclusion in a cloistered society so clandestine that its own members avoided contact. Conducted in silence and secrecy, the outcasts traded in the currency of the alienated.

Although the other miners had yet to meet a somatic, fear and suspicion spread like a miasma, leaking into closed spaces and closed minds, fouling the atmosphere aboard the Nimbus. As they neared port, casual speculation blossomed into wild fantasizing about the terrifying, deformed monsters awaiting them. They feared an encounter with one of the sea creatures that worked the ports, crawling out of the vast, black water, its mouth and tentacles hung with bladder wrack and awash in strings of golden morab beads plucked from the slender green necks of mermaids. Sorykah wasn't afraid. She rather liked to think that she might have something in common with these somatics—children with cat's tails, babies that grew in a human woman's pouch instead of her womb, five-fingered card-playing dogs, and human divers with webbed feet. Sorykah didn't think she'd mind them; she might like their quiet ways, the sibilant voices she imagined would burble like rock-ringed springs.

Distant planks of song ice heaved and sobbed while a chorus of leopard seals barked a gruff warning. Turning into the Stuck Tongue, she hoped to find a place to escape the noise, a sound reminiscent of an unhappy woman crying from a far shore. Sorykah tugged open the corrugated tin door, entering a narrow room of hazy crimson darkness. Dull red globes glimmered above the hammered metal bar and the air was thick with smells of burnt sugar and the tarry black tobacco smoke curling from the bartender's ivory pipe. Sorykah maneuvered between rickety chairs toward the bar, leaving a trail of melting slush in her wake. Except for the faint outline of a figure in the farthest corner and the squat, snowy-haired bartender, the room was empty.

Sorykah approached the bar and pulled off her gloves and scarf, kneading frozen fingers as she watched the bartender tamp down his pipe and set it aside to await his return. He mustered an air of careful detachment as he approached, taking in her fancy Company-issued digs, the black hair pasted to her forehead in wet spikes, the worried dark eyes and thin, grim lips set in the weariness of her cold-flushed face.

"Help you," he grumbled, searching the woman for something that would tell him not to be afraid. Finding nothing, he busied himself with a stack of glasses, wiping away faint smears.

"Coffee?" Sorykah queried. A coffee with a shot of whiskey would do her nicely. Put the blood back in her limbs, ignite the embers in her belly. She forced a pleading smile.

"No coffee. Supply train's run late this month. Try again next week." He harrumphed to himself, dwelling on the unreliability of overland shipping.

"Any food? Anything hot?" This too was a stab in the dark; she smelled nothing that suggested anything more edible than mold. A place like this probably had mushrooms growing beneath the floorboards and lemmings nesting in the rafters.

"Nothing to drink but moonshine and tea. Hot tea'll warm you but the 'shine will put a smile on that sad face. If you're hungry, there's the pipe, in the corner." He jerked his head toward the lone customer, unmoving amid concentric smoke rings drifting in lazy spirals toward the ceiling.

"Tea then." Sorykah watched the bartender tip spoonfuls of a gray-green herb into a glass mug with an inch of sticky, honey brown granules in the bottom. Lifting the steaming kettle from a hot plate, he filled the mug, nodding as the granules melted and color rose in amber swirls.

"Stir it up before you drink. Don't leave anything in the glass; it's bad luck." He winked and retreated to his pipe.

Sorykah was surprised to discover that she was hungry. She'd been so preoccupied by worries about her missing children that for once she was able to stop thinking about her stomach. The walk to and from the train station had burned up her reserves. Fishing in her pocket for the half-eaten butter bar—an abysmal fatty concoction of seal meat, bone meal, pulverized nuts, and dried berries in sweetened butter—that she'd stashed there, she took her tea glass and spoon and headed toward the back, where a woman curled beneath a fur rug. Tubing streamed from an enormous hookah and wound about her like a serpent goddess's deadly arms. She did not stir when Sorykah took the seat across from her and peeled off her heavy coat, nor when she sampled the pipe and coughed in surprise, finding that it contained opium, not tobacco. Sorykah sucked sticky butter from her teeth as she held the smoke in her lungs, waiting to see what would happen.

Sorykah inhaled again, uncaring. Weren't the other miners indulging themselves tonight with drink and sex? Would it matter if she sat with the white dragon and let it deaden her apprehension for a while? She needed something to quell her nervousness, to extinguish the flames of her barely controlled panic. Anxiety would prey on her mind throughout the night, tormenting her with visions of catastrophic train wrecks and fanatical nannies who feigned normalcy in order to steal children to populate their religious cults.

Soft, sweet fumes condensed in her head, leaving an ochre tinge of caramelized sugar on the back of her tongue. She drank more of the bitter, warming tea and smoked, rolling the vapors against her palate, sifting them through her sinuses. Openly intrigued, she studied the hookah, following the twisting hose from the intricate, painted glass bowl to the metal mouthpiece clasped between the stranger's fingers. Enraptured by a private dream, the blanketed woman rocked herself, the faintest wisp of a smile playing over the corners of her mouth.

Sorykah inhaled and noticed that the woman mimicked her, and when she let the breath swish out of her, the other's nostrils flared with rising smoke. They were companionable for a long time, finding their rhythm, the woman's outgoing breath tailing Sorykah's ingoing one. Sorykah watched the other woman's eyes, shifting beneath closed lids, and took the opportunity to study her. With its domed forehead and delicate, pointed chin, her face resembled an upside-down teardrop. Her eyes cracked open and closed again, fiery amber drops beneath sleepy lids. She wore a heavy, embroidered tunic trimmed in luxurious fur, and her lank, russet hair slithered over her shoulders with each subtle movement. The hookah's mouthpiece trembled between pointed, mauve-tinged fingertips at the ends of skinny arms. A fur blanketed her lower half, obscuring her legs and feet. She reclined against the cushions; the occasional flash of light beneath her lowered lids betrayed her watchfulness.

Outside, the ice fractured with a sound of shipwrecks and broken teeth gnashing. Sorykah inhaled water vapor; their pipe was dry. The woman shrugged her shoulders, abandoning mouthpiece and tubing on the pillows. Sorykah sighed and wrapped her scarf around her neck and shoulder in preparation for the oncoming night, trying to hold the memory of the smoke inside her like a flame. She took a finishing swig of tepid, grassy tea, realizing that her anxiety, like her appetite, had fled.

There was a commotion at the door. Four men flooded the bar, their low, harsh voices revealing a dangerous undertone of suppressed violence. The peaceful little bartender feigned confidence, but Sorykah saw that he would be easily overpowered. She first thought that they were belligerent drunks hassling for liquor, women, or food, but the arrogant quality of their brutal speech implied a darker design. A starburst of ugly realization dispelled Sorykah's pleasant, pink fog. She was in a somatic bar and these men were trophy seekers. Suddenly queasy, Sorykah recalled the thick, white hair (*fur*, she realized with dread) peeking out around the edges of the bartender's sweater, a glossy, three-inch long pelt sprouting around his collar and creeping from beneath his cuffs.

The bartender shook his head resolutely as one of the men tried to bully him out from behind the bar. The men swarmed the room like flies drawn to the odor of carrion. Sorykah's companion roused herself with ill-concealed terror. There was a flurry of movement beneath the skin rug, an odd rippling of frantic snakes trapped amidst the white heat of the furs, her gown wide with the sensual rustle of . . . legs? But too many of them and no shoes, no *feet*, just the hint of something alive beneath her skirt.

With surprising speed, the woman unfolded a wheelchair collapsed against the wall behind her and threw back the skin rug, dragging herself up into the chair. Shaking with effort, she snatched the fur and furiously tucked it around her legs (or whatever they were, Sorykah grimaced). Once in the chair, she was agile, overcoming her gracelessness as she pushed past Sorykah to the door and the loud, boisterous men—headhunters of the dark Sigue sea. There was a fracas; the men wouldn't let her pass. Sorykah watched her arms strike out, saw an angry flash of skin and something long and fluid uncoil and retreat, a whiplash of white-suckered vermilion flesh that struck one of the men against the side of his face, knocking him off balance. The struck man clapped his face in surprise, rubbing the welt that bloomed across his cheekbone and eye. Shouting in a garbled mishmash that Sorykah couldn't understand, two of the four argued with each other, gesturing at the woman in their midst. The injured man pulled a spear gun from inside his coat and aimed for the woman's head as the fourth man reclined against the bar, shooting a salacious grin at the anxious bartender.

Sorykah shot through the bar like a sprung arrow. Knife in hand she charged, her curved Magar blade gleaming silver and true. The men fell back distracted and the red-haired woman used the opportunity to wheel herself onto the street.

One of the men lunged, grabbing Sorykah's free hand and reaching for the knife in the other. She slashed his forearm and he yelped in pain. The grinning man snatched the spear gun from his friend and fired. A projectile whizzed past Sorykah's ear, slicing away a chunk of hair and a scrap of flesh, and imbedding them in the wooden post beside her. Fighting with a cornered animal's wild and heedless ferocity, Sorykah cut him across the shoulder, his coat splitting beneath the blade to reveal layers of severed clothing and a shallow red wound. The men pinned Sorykah's arms as they attempted to wrestle the knife from her grasp.

Fear soured her mouth and hijacked each of her senses. Every cell and emotional impulse perfectly aligned into a single, vibrating wave of naked horror. Even the change couldn't help her now. She thought of her children and hoped they would never discover how weak she had been in the last few minutes of her life.

2

TO LIFT THE VEIL BETWEEN WORLDS

SORYKAH MET THE BARTENDER'S EYES and mutely begged for aid. He responded with a look of defiant sorrow—an apology perhaps or a plea for forgiveness. His eyes slid to the right, focusing on something behind her.

Two massive creatures filled the doorway, their silhouettes blocking out the fading sunlight. They lurched into the bar, chests heaving with exertion and rage as they reached for the men, their huge, clumsy hands closing around any available limb. Sorykah dropped to the ground as the creatures bellowed, knocking the men's heads together like rag dolls. Sounds of cracking bone filled the bar and the grinning man smiled no more.

Sorykah cowered on the dirty floor beside a fallen body. Blood seeped from the man's ear, dampening his wool collar. The creatures' creased, brown skin had the texture of rough sandpaper and their watery black eyes were dull and red-rimmed. Obscenely long, thick noses dangled in fleshy clumps over their broad upper lips, half-formed organs that seemed to have frozen in the act of melting off their skulls. With cheeks pierced by sparse, spiny bristles and tiny flaplike ears, their faces resembled waxen masks left out too long in the sun.

Sorykah swallowed her revulsion at the malformed men and snatched her knife from the floor where it had fallen and sheathed it at her side. With a last, desperate glance at the bartender's frightened face, she darted out the door into the lavender twilight.

She ran over frozen walkways and packed snow, her boots crunching loose gravel. She didn't know where she was going. She wanted only to escape the hunters and those awful, fearsome beasts. Ducking into a doorway, Sorykah tried to gather her wits and assess her next move. The frigid air paralyzed her lungs; gasping, Sorykah scanned the area, wondering what had become of her smoking companion.

Ostara was a ghost town. Ice broke, ripped, and sang. Night emerged from its primordial lair, creeping spiderlike and silent, a greedy darkness with an appetite to gobble her up. Sorykah heard distant wheels rattling against gravel, heading away from the quay's sloshing seawater. Sorykah sensed that the woman could take care of herself, but she seemed infinitely vulnerable, arduously wheeling her chair across slippery uneven ice, sliding a bit, jerking her wheels free of the occasional snowdrift and pushing ahead. The wharf was dangerous for somatics even during daylight hours; alone at night, unprotected by the simple presence of other bodies on the street, the woman would be a prime target for sport hunters. Sorykah didn't want to help her. She wanted to find a warm, safe place to be alone with her private miseries, but she couldn't just abandon her to some terrible fate at the licentious hands of men like those in the bar.

"Wait, please!" Sorykah closed in on the wheelchair and the woman whose bare head glistened with frost. Condensed moisture had frozen the tendrils of her long hair into stiff, dark spirals. Purple fingers gripped frosty metal wheels, forcing the chair along the path. Sorykah wondered how long the woman would be able to survive in her quilted tunic without benefit of hat or gloves. Panting, she slowed alongside the wheelchair to keep pace.

"What happened back there? What were those . . . ?" She bit off the word *things* before it could escape her mouth.

"Those *things*? Those monsters, is what you mean to say," the woman hissed, forcing her chair over a hillock of ice buckling the boardwalk and skidding sideways into a dirty gray snowdrift.

"No! Of course not," Sorykah demurred, not wanting to provoke the ire of a stranger of whom she had already grown protective.

"They are people, believe it or not. People like you . . . or me. Pavel called them when the men came into the bar. There is an alarm under the counter."

"Pavel? You mean the bartender. But they arrived so soon, how is that possible?"

She screwed up her rubbery face in annoyance. "The alarm works by radio frequency. Each location emits a different signal to alert the sentries. It's their job to patrol the wharf when ships come in, to prepare for the worst. Without them, we are vulnerable."

"As you are now," Sorykah pointed out.

The woman ignored the comment, coughing against the cold.

"It's become quite dark. I should see you home."

"No need," the stranger replied, wheeling faster into the night.

"I don't mean to be pushy," Sorykah said.

"Yet you do it so well," the woman retorted, "one would think you paid to intrude in the business of others. Is that your job, Company lackey, or is this your daily deed of charity?"

"It will get worse for you if you stay out here tonight." Sorykah looked out to sea where a rusted oil tanker sat blinking in the distance. It was coming into port for supplies and refueling before heading north, and its crew would swarm Ostara, intent on satisfying their baser appetites. The Company held its employees to a strict code of conduct. As its representatives abroad, they were charged with maintaining ambassadorial goodwill among the people whose ancestral home they ravaged. The Company was unique in its principles; others were not so conscientious.

"Am I to believe that you are simply a philanthropist fulfilling your quota of beneficent deeds? Not bloody likely," the woman said with disgust, cranking her wheels. Sorykah could hear the stranger's teeth rattling in her head, a cup of ivory dice shaken by a careless hand, and she belatedly discovered herself still opium-befuddled. She'd mistakenly believed the adrenaline charging through her veins at the bar had cleared her head and that the frosty air had sobered her, but now the streetlamps had a pink halo and glowed like neon cherries against the night. It was only the drug that had initiated her uncharacteristic show of bravery at the bar, nothing more.

They reached the end of the wharf. As the first tier of buildings dwindled to a few far-flung homes, the second tier emerged, clusters of dingy, scratched Quonsets. Muffled laughter met them as they neared a tiny, lopsided 'shine shack, where locals sold home brew to sailors and miners.

Six drunken sailors tumbled out of a doorway, spilling across the snow as if poured from a pitcher of creamy gold lamplight. Rowdily clipping one another's shoulders, careening over the icy boards, they seemed harmless enough, but as they parted to allow the women passage, Sorykah saw something that curdled her blood. A wave of deep orange flesh rolled free as a limb uncurled itself from beneath the folds of the woman's fur rugs, exposing its cartilaginous length and pointed, mauve tip. The sailors' smiles alternately faded or spread into wide, foxy grins as they watched her wheel herself ahead; a tentacle dangled down and she narrowly missed crushing it beneath her wheels. Just as abruptly, the tentacle retracted, curled itself back up beneath the fur, and disappeared. The entire incident seemed to take place outside of time, and then the moment passed and the men were behind them, whistling and joking, good-natured in their inebriation and not the least disconcerted.

"None too soon! Hurry now, come on!" The woman stopped in front of a large metal building, its walls and roof coated with a cloudy layer of ice several inches thick. Rust stains seeped from the door's iron hinges and bled onto the ice that swelled around the opening. With reddened, winter-chapped cheeks and drawn, blue lips, the woman's exotic face was neutral as she wheeled herself into the dim doorway.

"You might as well come in. There's a chill brewing; it's too cold to stay out any longer without risking your life. You'll be safe here for now." She vanished inside, leaving Sorykah behind to close and bar the door against the night.

3

NETTED BIRDS

"WHO ARE THEY?" Carac growled, thick hairs rising along his neck.

"I don't know, but if they've been captured they must be valuable. He takes rare treasures now, his tastes become more refined with every acquisition." Queen Sidra's words seemed to hang suspended in the mist.

Crouching at the Erun Forest's inner rim, the couple peered through winter-bare trees. A burly figure trudged across the sloping field, his back burdened by an unwieldy sack containing the wiggling bodies of two babies. Beyond him, a stark, white marble manor crouched before jagged mountains of slate that speared the weak winter sunshine and cast thready shadows across the plain. Five pointed towers spiraled upward, as grim and narrow as the picked-clean bones littering the forest floor. In summer, the meadow transformed into an endless satiny sea of waving grass but now it was a rustling yellow spill, pooling around the peaks that barricaded the white mansion from the world.

The pair had trailed their target since informers first noticed his steady progress through the industrial centers in the Northern Province, doling out bribes and making indiscreet inquiries about a Trader woman rumored to have borne twins. Most Traders were as sterile as mules; a fertile one would generate talk, no matter how she tried to disguise her pregnancy. Discovery would expose her to much unsavory attention and anyone privy to such tantalizing morsels of gossip would sell that information to the highest bidder, unmoved by the etiquette of privacy.

Sidra crept around a bramble hedge wild with looping knots of thorn. Her companion padded along behind, staying within her tracks, his lupine toes marking the damp grass around the edges of her footprints.

Tongue extended over his lower lip, a rime of frozen saliva frosting the rippled edges of his gums, Carac sniffed the air, teasing odors from the mist. He tasted new flesh, fatty and succulent. Urine-soaked cotton, tangy and sharp. The heavy musky sweat of exertion and the lighter, apple blossom smells of sleep and fair dreams, all ringed by the suppressed misery of creatures far from home. Rolling them over his tongue, crushing each fragrance molecule against his palate, the par-wolf was able to trace their targets' trail, though they had abandoned the safety of the thickets and crossed the yellow plain hours before.

The figure neared the manor and was swallowed by its looming and oppressive darkness.

"We'll have to find another way. They belong to the Collector now." The watching woman sighed in dismay. Faithful Carac hovered at her back, and she sensed his hunger to bring down their quarry.

"We will catch him," he asserted.

"Yet each time the noose tightens and threatens to close, he eludes us. He guards his weaknesses well," Sidra countered.

"No man is invincible, my queen. No beast without its predator. Even one as slippery as the Collector can be netted and destroyed," Carac panted, growing restless, eager for the chase and ensuing kill.

"You would seek his destruction, while I am content to see his captives freed," the queen chided.

"That's the difference between us, Sidra. Your totem is a plant eater and yours the doe's gentle heart. You are unused to the taste of blood." He smiled wickedly, or so it seemed, for the grins of wolves always appear wicked, even when innocently offered.

"And you, Carac, would relish the taste of his warm liver on your tongue. Soon wolf and deer will each sate their appetites," Sidra pledged.

Carac cast appraising eyes toward his queen. Sidra the Lovely was a half-wild creature, a keeper of secrets and promises. Her ingenuous face was deceiving in its sweetness, but to the owner of the marble mansion she was a formidable enemy.

Sidra gathered her spotted fawn cloak and tossed it over her shoulder. Gazing through the naked, clattering treetops to the smudged pewter clouds coalescing overhead, she grew skittish, scenting the air. "A storm is brewing. Come. We have much to do."

Carac growled, a sound of both pleasure and regret, and shook his grizzled mane of black hair coarsened by gray. Tiny follicular muscles caused each hair to stand in salute, then fall at ease. Rubbing a careless hand over his tufted ears, he pocketed his dangling tongue between his cheek and gum and wiped the saliva from his chin. Now that they were venturing into the cities, it was time to become a man again. Time to tuck tail, don clothes, and sheathe claws. He didn't care for the deception but it was a small sacrifice, the bit of bait necessary to lure a dangerous fish. Turning their backs on the skeletal manor and its dungeons rife with howling captives, they retreated between the trees and vanished into the forest.

4

WORK OR DIE

"THEY'RE PERFECT. Congratulations, Meertham. You've found yet another set of treasures for my collection."

Meertham, a hulking giant with arms like beer barrels and a torso as broad as a wine vat, suppressed an inward creeping shudder as his employer stretched forward gnarled, bony fingers to caress the plump cheek of one of the children in his grasp. The child, a sullen boy with glossy black cowlicks, squirmed in Meertham's embrace and stared daggers at the offending hand, defiance glittering in his jet eyes. His twin, a dusky girl with pale feathers of hair curling over her opaque gray eyes, smacked four teeth together and arched away from the man's touch.

"She bites, this one." A raw laugh grated through a mouth unused to such things. He pinched the baby girl's leg with enough force to leave a flush red moon beneath his thumb. She screamed with outrage and began to wail. Meertham held the stiff body as if suppressing a deviant mental patient, the whiskers on the fleshy pads of his broad upper lip twitching. Both babies kicked and struggled in Meertham's arms.

Charged with the capture and care of the twins, resolute in the completion of his duty and eager to be rid of his squalling burdens, Meertham could not entirely suppress the vague unease spreading through his bones. Something about this whole situation unnerved him. Not the theft of innocents, for he'd done plenty of that in his time, or the knowledge that he was delivering someone else's dear children to uncertain ends at the hands of an egomaniacal sadist. Rather, a looming sense of disaster clung to the edges of his conscience, casting a pall over the normally guilt-resistant somatic. Meertham had always supposed it was the walrus in him that left him indifferent to the plight of his captives. He wanted to believe that the faint streak of humanity left behind after all the transformations he'd suffered was responsible for this rare compassion, an unfamiliar emotion that threatened to divert him from the satisfactory completion of his job. Whatever its source, he wished it away. The naked greed on his employer's face inspired an unpleasant twinge of culpability that Meertham silenced: *Leave me be. Even if he roasts them both for dinner, I've received my pay. What's done is done and what I do is my job. Their fate is not my concern.*

"They look like ordinary brats. What's their talent?"

Meertham did something he'd never done before. He lied. "Not sure, Master. Heard they was shapeshifters. Their mum had a tail, so I thought . . ."

"We'll have the pleasure of seeing what develops, then. And if they are entirely human, you owe me three babies, to make up for your mistake." Sniffing, the little man covered his nose with a gloved hand and waved them away. "Now get them away from me. They stink of piss and spoilt milk. Give them to Dunya. She'll be glad of a new brood to nurse now that her pups are gone."

Dunya's pups had been taken to the stables to pull the sleds and run over the ice in torn and bloody boots, their furless fingers curled and blackened by the unrelenting frost.

Meertham backed from the chamber, the children's soft bodies draped over his muscle-corded arms. The girl ceased crying and fell against her brother as if resigned to impending doom. They did stink but Meertham hadn't noticed the stench until the Master pointed it out to him. He found the mild scent of urine comforting. It reminded him of freedom and the rare pleasure savored by shedding his human trappings: the clothes, speech, and faint netting of social etiquette that allowed his passage through urban realms.

He made his way through the manor's twisting corridors of white marble, where swirling gray veins lay trapped like smoke in the panels, through vast, windowless corridors into the icy kitchen. Water continually leached through the marble walls, beading, swelling, and running down like tears. The floors were always wet and when the fire was low, they were icy. This was poor Dunya's world. A long wooden butcher's block occupied the center of the room, a grotesque companion to the gaping stone sinks (deep for a proper bleed-out) and an enormous, smoke-blackened fire pit carved into the wall like a put-out eye. Dunya's bed of yellow grass was heaped in a corner beneath the pantry shelves. She kept her few personal items—a hairbrush, trinkets from some half-remembered life, and a stack of folded clothes, much repaired—on a single shelf surrounded by beweeviled sacks of mealie, rice, and flour.

Dunya sat at the table, sorting through a pile of mending. She looked up at Meertham's approach, her ready half smile vanishing at the sight of the babies.

"Oh! 'E 'asn't . . ." she clapped a hand to her muzzle, shaking her head.

Meertham nodded and the tips of his thick tusks brushed his massive chest. The babies flopped over his arms, resigned to their immobility but staring at Dunya with fascination. Setting aside her mending, Dunya rose, wringing the edge of her apron in nervous hands. She approached Meertham with caution, her large, sad eyes fixed on the twins.

"More stolen children. 'Ow could 'e?" For a brief moment, she felt herself falling backward into a past whose terrible pains and burdens she had worked so hard to escape. She heard her children's cries, howling with rage and confusion as her master hitched up the sleds, whipped them, and ordered them to pull, pull over the ice. Arms pinioned behind her back and forced to watch, Dunya howled and begged for their release, through liberation or death, whichever came first. Her darling pups, lost to her now.

"Give 'em 'ere, they look a sight! 'Ave ye not bathed these children? Tsk!" Dunya shook her head in dismay, her silky ears flapping against the ruffled edges of her housekeeper's cap. "Come on me doves," she cooed, holding out her arms. "Nothing to fear now, Dunya 'as ye."

The twins had grown used to Meertham's impartial, utilitarian handling and Ayeda was reluctant to leave him. Leander, however, was instantly drawn to Dunya with her drooping, sorrowful eyes and brown, lightly furred face. Openmouthed, he strained forward, his dimpled hands outstretched and grasping in his eagerness to bundle a floppy ear into his slobbering mouth. Nothing he could have done would have affected her more than the simple act of his reaching for her. Her bruised and battered heart gave a weak, exploratory thud. Leander twisted in Meertham's arms, sliding down so that his chin caught on Meertham's forearm, his body dangling precariously over the stone floor. Dunya bounded forward to extract Leander from Meertham's grip.

He grunted with relief, taking Ayeda by the back of her sack gown and holding her out to Dunya like a pound of potatoes in a burlap bag.

"Here, take it! Be glad to get rid of 'em." He shook Ayeda as if trying to loosen a burr well-embedded in his knit vest. Swinging at the end of his meaty arm, she wrapped her body around his enormous fist and mewed like a kitten.

"Silly thing, always pawing at me," Meertham admonished, unable to conceal the surprising tenderness that swept up and caught him off guard. He peeled the baby from his arm and deposited her in the sewing basket after halfheartedly rifling through the mending to check for pins or needles.

Stroking Leander's black hair, Dunya said, "So, ye 'ave feelings after all! I knew ye weren't dead inside like the Master."

She sensed the baby draw inward, contracted in self-protection. His blood smelled thin and watery. She must feed him, fatten him.

"Ye cared for them all by yerself then?" Dunya asked, not meeting Meertham's eyes.

"'Course I did," he groused. "Nasty business it was. Little buggers shat all over me. I had to steal a ewe and keep the damned dozy thing tethered to me belt just to feed these two." He grimaced at the memory, grappling with the nursing ewe, warm froth spraying every which way as he attempted to milk her for the first time.

"A ewe! Lovely! We'll 'ave fresh milk. 'ow's that sound lambkins?" Dunya stroked Leander's back, unable to resist poking her muzzle inside his collar for another luscious whiff of baby-stink.

"Not possible, miss. Gave her to the Wood Beast as a peace offering. Bit of security. I can handle it but these two would make tasty popovers and I wouldn't be lucky enough to ever find another pair as fine as them."

"What can we feed ye then?" Dunya chucked Ayeda beneath the chin. The baby frowned, noisily sucking her fist. Ayeda was less gullible than her brother and less impressed by the novelty of a dog-faced woman and a talking walrus. Dunya would win her over later when she produced sweet porridge and offered the infant a salty rind of bacon, fresh from the pan and dripping with grease.

Wrapping his cloak over his enormous, bowed shoulders, Meertham left the kitchen without looking at the children. He'd spent so much of his life in the service of his master, he rarely considered how his life might have been different had he been left to live as a free man. When he was five, Meertham's parents sold him to one of the Master's traveling procurers. They were repulsed by Meertham's changing form as their once sweet and docile little boy tested them with mounting aggression. His small frame (the secret joy of his mother, who'd relished her role as caretaker to a fragile and angelic soul) erupted with subcutaneous pads of what she could only describe as *blubber.* Meertham's canines muscled aside his baby teeth as they swelled to the size of carrots, pressing down on his lower lip. Stout whiskers sprouted on his fleshy upper lip and he developed the astonishing habit of braying, barking, and bellowing at wall-flattening decibels.

Meertham's parents could not resist punishing him for this unfortunate and unwanted transgression. Had he become something cute and furry, a Pomeranian or a spider monkey perhaps, they would have adored his novelty, but it was horrifyingly apparent, despite all assurances to the contrary by well-meaning friends and doctors, that their frail angel was becoming a foully stinking, brutish walrus.

When the procurer approached them, it was with a suitcase of cash in hand and the promise of a quick and tidy abduction. Meertham would be spirited away to live with others like himself and spend his childhood away from hard stares and gossip. Meertham's parents could sleep at night knowing their child would suffer no rebuke while making his contribution to science. It was the sort of assurance a butcher makes to a farmer as he leads away his beautiful prize-winning pig; when the butcher says "well dressed," he means for the pot.

Raised in Matuk's dungeons, Meertham eventually earned enough liberty to serve the Master doing small errands and brute work. Once he'd proved that he could take direction and wouldn't attempt escape, Meertham had been made Matuk's personal henchman. At ten years of age, the boy was already six feet tall and weighed close to three hundred pounds, a solid, unyielding slab of meat and muscle with the gruff features of a walrus superimposed over his human face.

Made callous by his parents' betrayal and the unflinching eye he trained on his victims as he committed the most barbaric of fleshly and moral crimes, Meertham's heart hardened. His human conscience was smothered somewhere deep beneath those rich, red layers of savage brawn—small, inconsequential, and forgotten.

Odd that Dunya adored him as she did. Dunya the dog-faced girl was another captive servant whose loyalty proved both her redemption and her downfall. TRAVAILLEZ OU MOUREZ—WORK OR DIE—was the motto emblazoned over the manor's many mantels and doors. Few voluntarily chose death (though ashes blanketed the crematory floor and choked the fire pit many feet deep), and so they worked. Everyone in the Collector's employ had been well aware of the agreement's limitations, for freedom was a precious commodity in his zoo.

Meertham lumbered through the dim servants' corridor into the great hall of the main house. Plaster grapevines festooned the high ceiling and cherubs hovered on arching ribs of marble popping from leathery, skin-papered walls, giving the morbid impression of malignant calcifications thrusting from bones. Belly o' the beast, Meertham called this room. Meertham considered himself but a crumb swallowed up by the maw of some hideous monster. The silence was reminiscent of a catacomb he'd once stormed, taking by surprise a feeble, spider-legged man, an emaciated creature with cracked, peeling black hooks thrusting from spindly, knobby wrists. Spider thing with its limbs overlong and double-jointed, blind eyes and slack, toothless mouth hanging open to catch the flies swarming round the sores on its distended belly.

Meertham stuffed it, deranged and snarling, into his sack but the horrid old man had cut himself free with his hooks, still sharp after years of disuse, dropped into the slime lining his nest, and promptly broke an arm in his rough landing. Meertham bound the arm while the old man howled through withered lips, bucking and kicking skinny legs that were deceptively strong and bristled with coarse black hairs.

Meertham settled the creature by tying a cloth over his eyes and swaddling him with a length of dirty fabric pulled up from the wadded clumps lining the spider's nest, securing his arms and legs tight against his body. Into the sack went the spider, bound like a papoose on Meertham's back as he retraced his steps out of the catacomb and into the light, where the freshness of the salt air cleared the clinging odor of carrion from the lair.

Meertham had followed the shoreline home, pleasing his eyes with the sight of the silver-gray winter ocean rearing on its hinds and bellowing onto the beach, white-capped and frothing. Something about the pathetic creature made his gut tighten with the unfamiliar sensation of fright and unease, as though Meertham was the vector for some loathsome affliction, a plague bearer spreading ill will across a country weakened by starvation and proving a comfortable home for invading viral hosts.

A successful capture generated a strange brew as conflicting feelings fought for dominance. His concern was remedial and haphazard, mere background noise compared to the panicked thrashings of his prey, wrestling for release from Meertham's almighty stuff-sack. He needed to keep his catch alive until he relinquished it to the Master, collected his pay, and went off in search of the next trophy, blind to his own culpability. He'd not concern himself with pity. It was messy and dangerous, a waste of time and thought. He could spare no goodwill for the sad-eyed housekeeper who cowered alone in the dungeonous kitchen, her furred face sooty from the baking fire, smoky from damp, green logs snatched from the forest while the Wood Beast feasted on throwaway bones and marrow. No care at all spent on the beautiful plump babies he'd stolen and let grow thin and streaked with their own filth, twin stars snared from the haven of their mother's arms and deposited in the lap of a sinister man who destroyed children's lives just as spring rains drowned early seedlings that dared to seek the sun.

He continued on to the armory, and the ancient door that protected the manor's secrets with a keyless, unpickable lock. *Not truly keyless,* he mused, pulling from his pocket a slender picket of bone. *This key ain't metal, but she turns the lock nonetheless.* Gripping his hunting knife in hand, he stabbed at his forearm. The skin was denser there, less likely to ache and seep than the softer flesh of his fingers. Blood ran warm and thick. Meertham coated the bone with blood, turning white to red, lifted the little latch, and inserted the key. The door clicked open. He wiped the bone on his trousers, noting that the thirsting lock had absorbed every droplet, and crossed the frost-laced courtyard. The manor was dark and silent except for a lamplit window high in the central tower casting a single ivory ray upon the stones.

Ahead lay the gatehouse and the tunnel before it, through which he passed quickly, disliking the close, curving walls and low ceiling filled with treacherous murder holes designed after some distant and forgotten king. Remnants of these attempts poked from the walls, practice arrows loosed to make a futile marriage with the mortar and wooden posts, dull, lead points that struck home, infesting the unlucky living target with toxemia and slow death.

Reaching the outermost gate, Meertham took up the mallet by the sentinel's post and hammered a large metal disc. The gong shivered loudly and its alarm rippled through the night air. Something stirred and sighed, huffing and muttering as it came to the gate, heavy footsteps thudding on the uneven stones.

"Coming, coming," the creature wheezed. It listed to the side and had to keep righting itself as it walked. Raw pink flesh hung from its giant, misshapen bones. The open mouth revealed tiny stumps of broken teeth between drawn, puckered lips; rheumy eyes peered from beneath drooping, sparsely lashed lids while the knobby head bobbed to an unheard rhythm as it crossed the cobbles.

"Bit of a cold night for thee, lad. Come and keep us company. I've a touch of whiskey I've been saving." He forced a smile through his mangled mouth.

"Not much of a drinker, me. Brings me to sleep or temper and I never know which one so I have to say no." Meertham glanced into the Gatekeeper's milky irises and then away, stroking his long tusks. He would have liked to accompany the creature back to his rooms, warm himself by the fire, enjoy a tumbler of spirits, and make idle talk. The old monster was isolated here; glad of an audience, he'd do most of the talking. Meertham could drift for a moment or two, and dream.

"So he braves the beast again! Twice in one day, that's a record even for you. Urgent business commands him away. Always toiling for the Master. No, he never takes a break, this one." Gatekeeper spoke to some unseen companion. "Toil, toil, he's a regular workhorse, that one. Must please the Master. Oh Master, look at the little lovely I've brought for ye, all pink and plump and juicy." He giggled, a hideous gurgling sound of drowning and phlegmatic lungs. In younger days, there might have been a femur or two from a human specimen among the scraped bones heaped on the Gatekeeper's fire. His was not a discerning palate and whatever creature had influenced his DNA, it was definitely carnivorous. Gatekeeper was a scavenger, as his foul breath and bilious rumbling gut attested. Maggots on rotting flesh were a treat, a little something extra to crunch between his sparse teeth. Doubt flickered in the back of Meertham's mind, loathsome and terrible, danced there for a millisecond and slid away—the sounds of jaws feasting on tender new flesh, soft enough for one used to dining on death. Gatekeeper could not be trusted with those bonny children. Dunya would be wise to be wary.

Loosening the chain, the Gatekeeper winched open the gate,

allowing counterweights to do the heavy work while he sang, knobby head swaying, "Crick crack go the bones, pretty bones!"

"Whose bones, old man?" Meertham humored him, routing him back to some semblance of reality.

"Your bones, boy, when she gets hold of you. Wood Beast likes supper by starlight. Your blood will be her sauce for dipping. Too bad all that fat will go to waste. I could use some new candles." He laughed again.

Meertham laughed, too, a guttural bark devoid of humor. If he was going to die tonight, he'd rather offer himself to the Gatekeeper, nourish an ailing old soul rather than lie half-eaten and wasting on the forest floor, food for ants and beetles, all his fine tallow going rancid.

Beyond the gates, the forest stretched black and impenetrable. Sharp trees scratched at the dark, glassy sky, their restless sighs filling the air.

The world seemed desolate and vast indeed. Not for the first time in recent weeks, he wished he had a home of his own to retire to, secluded and sacred, with a solid door to close against intrusion.

"She'll leave me be. I'm not to her liking. Too tough." Meertham squeezed a meaty bicep and imitated a hungry creature tearing at unyielding muscle.

"Aye, you've a thick and gnarly hide, it's true. Off with you then. I've whiskey waiting for me, I do. Off, off!" The Gatekeeper shooed Meertham through the portal, waving his misshapen arms. A simple melody floated behind him, a jolly if macabre tune picked out in a warbling and ancient voice. "Snack and crack, she'll break your back and suck out all the marrow!"

The creaking gate closed with a rattling of chains and an ominous, final clang. Not that the Master needed protection. No one dared to venture near the manor, for the Wood Beast, the Erun Forest's legendary guardian, mercilessly dispatched those who did. He'd camp at the forest's edge and push through by daylight when she caught her few snippets of sleep. Agile and mouse-quiet, Meertham would traverse the wood armed with nothing more than his brawn and his intention to make it through to the other side. He'd made a couple dozen trips so far during his career and each was like the first time, a virgin foray into the heart of doom. He could never grow careless, let his successes lull him into complacent overconfidence; a moment's laxity would be his death knell and she would come for him without hesitation. Yet for reasons he could never fathom, it almost seemed as though she knew him and let him pass unharmed by mutual agreement. He didn't care as long as the truce held and he could do his job without interference. He hoped she'd enjoyed the ewe.

5

RAVA

"DON'T JUST STAND THERE GAWPING. Get in and shake the snow off." The octameroon wheeled herself down a low tunnel where corrugated tin walls vibrated with cold. Slabs of cracked concrete dotted a floor layered with buckled sheets of remnant linoleum and occasional ice slicks. Sorykah's heel hit one and she skidded forward, catching herself on the uneven wall and recoiling at the feel of it. Vapor swirled as they pressed deeper into the earth and milky arms of sea ice stretched upward from the tunnel's bowel, beckoning them to its secret recesses.

Sorykah shivered violently, more from fear than cold. She had no choice but to spend the night indoors; the setting sun had squashed any thoughts of finding her way to her own Quonset in the outer tier. Sigue nights were reliably fatal; she could not leave until sunrise.

There was little difference between this subterranean lair and the hostile environment outside. Damp air seeped into Sorykah's thermosuit. The effects of the opium had worn off, and with it her calm. She recalled the look on the conductor's face as he tried to shut the window on her, impatient to be off and escape her tiresome questions.

Simple miscommunication, that was all. She must've misunderstood the arrival date, though she'd checked and rechecked a hundred times. Nels and the babies would arrive on tomorrow's train and Sorykah would tuck away her foolish worries, heaping them in the closet like so much dirty laundry. The nauseating sensation of something having gone terribly wrong resulted from her own crushed hopes, the happiness delayed another day, and was not a prophetic harbinger of gut-wrenching disaster. Sorykah stumbled over a rocky ridge on the floor and sagged against the wall, fighting the panic that swelled and peaked inside her. Adrenaline flooded her chest like a bottle of icy vodka overturned inside her, and set her heart racing. She was desperate to snatch a breath of fresh air, however deadly. A minute ago she'd been freezing, but as her blood pressure spiked, hot red poppies blossomed on her cheeks. Heat ran pink and inflamed her ears. Tugging the scarf from her neck, she gasped for oxygen.

Alerted by the noise, the woman in the wheelchair jerked back, little disguising her reluctance.

"Problem?" she asked.

"I'm fine," Sorykah lied. "How much farther is it?"

"Almost there. See the turn up ahead?"

Sorykah nodded, gazing toward a sharp right angle and the faint green light that spilled around the corner.

"You can warm up there. Get comfortable. It will be a long night." Cranking her wheel, she pushed ahead toward the phosphorescent glow.

Sorykah struggled to summon some slight measure of calm. She focused on her breathing, imagined the air rolling in like a tide and washing through her body, filling her lungs, limbs, and belly. She willed her fear to evaporate, to diminish and rise up from her chest and shoulders in lazy plumes of pale lemon steam.

Alone in the tunnel with the soft plish-plash of dripping liquid and heartened by the promise of fresh water after weeks spent drinking the *Nimbus*'s alkaline recycled waste, Sorykah sprinted into the light. The room swelled out to meet her, an enormous underground vault blasted from the permafrost; its walls still scorched from the explosion. Sorykah recognized it as a borehole in the bedrock that had filled with slush over the centuries and solidified into a ball of ice, forcing itself into the earth like a worm chewing into soft fruit. It would have taken only a few sticks of dynamite to crumble the ice and eroded slag, leaving behind this sizable chamber.

"Did you make this? Do the blasting yourself, I mean?" Sorykah ran an appreciative hand along a cool gray ridge, where flecks of raw quartz gleamed in the rock.

No answer. Rava nodded in her wheelchair beside a massive metal tank.

"Are you all right?" Sorykah lay tentative hands on narrow shoulders, thin and tensile beneath heavy furs. Rava's slick, smooth skin stretched to a hairline sprinkled with flat, mauve blisters that vanished into plum-red hair. Translucent papery tissue sagged beneath her jaw and ebbed onto her throat, spiderwebbed with faint wrinkles and florid freckles, a disarming combination of youth and age. White sucker-discs were visible on the upturned palm in her lap, flexing in the cold.

Sorykah rose, frowning. Octopus? The physical laws that governed the body and the division between species blurred and became irrelevant.

What of you? You follow no rules. You carried, birthed, and nursed children who, like you, are of inconstant gender. Are you a woman, or are you a man?

I am a woman because I choose to be. It's who I am, all of me, she countered to herself.

She often wondered if her children would recognize her after a change. Would they wake screaming to discover themselves in a strange man's arms? They had changed numerous times and she never doubted them. Even in a nursery full of identical cots, with matching rows of rosy-cheeked bundles, she would know them. Finding them would be like locating her other hand in the darkness, an effortless convergence of a single being's two limbs. Certainly they, among all others, would trust their instincts and find their way to the unchanging core that was the very essence of the person they knew as Sorykah, as Mother. They would trust that man, when and if he ever showed himself, wouldn't they?

Moaning roused Sorykah from her reverie. She crouched beside the wheelchair, startled by the spreading lavender stain that intensified into a vivid, gentian mask around the woman's eyes and nose. Dozy Rava struggled out of her coat. Clad in a simple silk gown, her deformity revealed itself. Eight muscular arms (*tentacles*, Sorykah realized, nausea boiling in her stomach) twitched beneath the silk, their livid, crimson-tipped points flexing and curling.

Sorykah was reluctant to touch her, afraid to catch the odious disease that had transformed a normal human into this seething ball of snakes. Multiple suction cups on the flailing limbs puckered up with a horrid wet noise, as if kissing the air. Sorykah turned away, covering her mouth.

Within the deep purple flush, Rava's eyes held a sleepy reptilian glint as she pulled herself onto a metal platform, tentacles flailing, hit a switch, and began to rise. With a rustle of silk silenced by water and a flash of vermilion tentacles, she dropped into the tank and disappeared.

Sorykah hovered for a moment, pondering her next move. There was a weathered horsehair sofa, a precarious table, a metal clothing rack hung with a few embroidered tunics, and a black greatcoat. Light emanated from a green glass globe atop a spindled lamppost. An ancient, rust-corroded icebox squatted in a corner, a thin promise of food. Sorykah's stomach rumbled, impatient for dinner.

She rummaged through her duffel bag, finding a few butter bars, a tin of cheap roe, and a packet of dried fruit. Sorykah crossed the threadbare rug to tug open the reluctant icebox. Whole fish and squid carcasses gaped with clouded eyes. Sorykah picked through the few open bottles and discarded tins atop the icebox. Nothing. No food, no fresh water. Not even a clean cup to catch her milk.

She had to eat. She'd taken to snacking on the foully flavored, high-calorie butter bars simply to keep up her milk. Miner's rations were good but served according to an individual's body weight. Being one of the lightest people aboard the *Nimbus*, Sorykah received the smallest portion. It was enough to sustain her but she still had to ingest an additional 1,500 calories a day to maintain her meager milk supply, enough to nurse twins and support the metabolic process of lactation in a harsh climate that burned the body's fuels at double the normal rate. Most of the miners brought treats with them—hard candy, chewing tobacco, canned soda, or chocolate—but Sorykah brought so much extra food she'd had to lie and say the cases of butter bars were menstrual pads in order to get them on the sub. None of the Company overseers was willing to challenge the sole female crewmember by demanding to see the contents of her boxes.

Aboard the *Nimbus*, Sorykah routinely slipped a dish of breast milk to the sub's resident cats, Pip and Squeak, two muscular, heavy-bodied mousers. Their indiscriminate palates were happy for something sweet and bland to round out their diet of rats, mice, and bedbugs. In exchange, they allowed her to pet them and scratch beneath their furry chins, a privilege rarely accorded people. With her cases of pads and eerie feline rapport, Sorykah was but a wart and a chin hair away from declaring herself a witch, an appellation that would not smooth her career path to the *Nimbus*'s engineering room.

Lifting her shirt, she exposed her breast to the chill air. She'd left her pump on the sub, expecting to nurse the children. She'd have to express by hand, a tedious and time-consuming prospect. Sorykah supported her nipple on her index finger and rolled her thumb forward to compress it. After a couple of squeezes and some watery droplets, a steady jet of milk hissed into the empty roe tin. Once it turned creamy and began to cling to the sides of the tin, Sorykah expressed the last of the fatty hind-milk. Faintly blue and sheened with oil, six ounces of roe-dotted breast milk flowed into her mouth and was gone in two swallows. She was very conscious of having ingested a raw food product, alive with nutrients and immunity-provoking agents. No wonder the cats were so healthy.

She spread the woman's fur rug (scented with a familiar yet indistinct perfume Sorykah would later recognize as opium) on the horsehair sofa and lay down, draping her coat over her body. Her eyes blurred with fatigue. The day unfurled against her closed eyelids, a series of disconnected images that grew more chaotic as she slipped from wakefulness into an uneasy dream state. Her last thought before surrendering to a fretful, bleak oblivion was an insistent *Must remember to tell Nels that I am not their father.*

Chink chink. Sorykah cracked open one eye. Something unpleasant rustled out of sight and was absorbed by the shadows. Instantly alert, Sorykah jerked upright, searching the recesses of the cave. "Hello?"

Groggy from her night of heavy, restless sleep, the floor seemed to sway beneath her feet. She'd dreamt of trains steaming into the night as she ran beside them.

Chink chink chink. That noise again. A flash of movement in the darkness.

"Are you here?" Sorykah's voice betrayed an unwelcome edge of worry.

She materialized beside the sofa, clear-eyed and bright, a pale, silk-sheathed female beneath a cloud of spun copper hair, an ice pick clutched in the fist hidden by the folds of her gown. Below the swollen bell of silk, a seething mass of red-orange tentacles, white-suckered and grasping, thumped lazily against the floor. She could walk, after all.

Sorykah jumped, unnerved by her sudden proximity to the pick-wielding stranger.

"What are you doing?" Her voice faltered despite her attempted nonchalance.

"Making tea. Have to chop ice for water. See?" She lifted the pick and demonstrated hacking at the air.

One of eight arms slithered forward and curled itself around Sorykah's empty boot. Sorykah cringed and shifted away from the inquisitive limb.

"I see! Just put that thing down." She was unsure, as she said it, whether the comment was directed toward the ice pick or the tentacle.

The woman shrugged, dropping the pick into a bucket of cloudy, green ice. She stared at Sorykah with naked curiosity, as if she'd never seen her before.

"What is it?"

The woman tilted her head, her bright amber eyes gleaming. "There is something beneath your surface that hides itself." The waterfall of musculature beneath her draping gown flowed without effort, bearing her human head and torso around the room as if she were guiding a canoe across a calm lake surface.

"I hide nothing," Sorykah said. *Have I grown a beard overnight?*

The woman shrugged delicate, child-sized shoulders. "Your secrets are your own." Gathering up the ice bucket, she slithered across the rough floor and parceled the ice into a metal kettle.

Sorykah hadn't noticed the woman's odd, abbreviated manner of speaking last night, nor had she noticed the unfamiliar accent that boxed up her words, keeping them curt and trim, but then she also failed to realize that her smoking partner was a horrible sea monster, some rare and fantastic beast transported from antiquity, a living, breathing myth.

"Thank you. Any chance of food? A cup of tea?"

"Naturally." The woman rustled over to the icebox and extracted a whole, frozen herring. "Fish?" she offered.

Sorykah shook her head, affronted. Was she doomed to starve to death?

"I can prepare for you," the woman offered. Her pencil-thin fingers closed over the fish's head. "Cut this part off, make soup. Would you like that?"

"Will you eat, too?"

"I cook for you, not me. Consider it my thanks, for last night. I was not well." The woman's lambent eyes flickered with shame. She flowed over to the table, placed the herring in a large dish, lifted the steaming kettle, and doused it with hot water.

A lump swelled in Sorykah's throat. "I need to get back to town, to the train station."

"Train? No train today. Sunday."

"Sunday? But it's Saturday! My furlough began on a Friday. That was yesterday. Wasn't it?" Sorykah's breathing grew ragged. The cave began to spin around her head. Groaning, she bowed her head between her knees insisting, "Saturday, today is Saturday."

"Sunday. No trains. Your bars are closed." Grasping the half-thawed fish by the tail, the woman hacked off its head and inserted a knife with a blade as thin as a stalk of grass under the fish's silver scales. She ran it between the skin and muscle, severing membranes and snipping through the fins, then, in one deft movement, she peeled back the entire skin, stretching it over the tail like an empty sack. The raw, pink muscle of the herring's denuded body lay gleaming in the dish.

"Cream?" she queried, cranking open a tin of evaporated milk.

Sorykah averted her eyes, her head filled with fantasies of ambushing the woman and chugging the milk, sucking every last drop from the dented, questionable can and licking her lips with feline satisfaction.

She had an urgent need to be alone. Living with sailors and miners had done little to ease her modesty about bodily processes. “Where can I . . . ?” She fluttered a hand.

Waving toward the recesses of the cave, the woman busied herself with the food, affording Sorykah some faint vestige of privacy.

The toilet was a sordid affair but hot water trickled from a pipe and Sorykah was able to scrub away some of the *Nimbus*'s clinging grime. She pored over recent weeks, searching for the missing hours. Ah yes, there was the half-day delay when one of the ballast tanks required repair, and then the lengthy detour taken around a precipitous drop from the Sigue land shelf. She hadn't kept track, too overworked to mark the calendar. That meant Nels and the children had arrived the previous day and were safe at their new home, awaiting Sorykah's arrival, instead of the other way round. A giddy little bubble of joy rose up in her chest and burst, a brief endorphin flare to ward away all doubt.

Sorykah returned to the table and sat in a rickety chair, rolling a glass of tea between her palms to warm them. Fragrant ribbons of steam danced from the soup pot and a rich, earthy aroma seasoned the air.

“We haven't been properly introduced yet. I'm Sorykah.” She was compelled to offer the stranger her hand, yet withheld it for fear of having to shake one of the flopping tentacles.

“Sorykah?” *Sor-i-kah,* she mouthed, testing the name against her tongue. “You can call me Rava.” A muscle twitched at the corner of her pert mouth; the glimmer of a smile.

Sorykah accepted the proffered bowl of soup and dunked a finger into its oily ring, sucking the fat off her knuckle, wishing for bread to go with it.

“You eat like a man,” Rava smiled. “Always hungry. Always without patience.”

“I'm eating for three.”

“For three? What do you mean?”

"I'm nursing two children. You know, nursing?" Sorykah jiggled her full breasts and grinned. She pantomimed rocking a baby, then two. "You see? One on each side."

Rava smiled politely, perplexed by the demonstration. "Ah, that is why . . . the train."

"My family must wonder what's become of me. It is morning, isn't it?" Sorykah used the eating sticks Rava offered to spear a chunk of fish and something that felt like reconstituted potato, chewing and washing it down with a swallow of creamy broth. An odd aftertaste lingered in her mouth, a briny, herbaceous tang that floated on the back of her tongue—a lick of sea floor and metal.

"Do you want to see the sun? I have a window." Rava pointed toward the business end of a battered periscope mounted on the wall and what looked like miles of old spot-welded pipe ascending through a gap in the rock.

Putting her eye to the scope, Sorykah cast about until she settled on an identifiable shape, the looming gray silhouette of the Devil's Playground, a volcano smoking on the distant horizon line.

Rava's tentacles beat time against the cold rock to the rhythm of her breathing. "Why did you come to Pavel's bar last night?"

What could Sorykah say of her choice to enter the Stuck Tongue? Afraid of everyone and everything, no one place seemed worse than any other. In search of oblivion, she chose the least appealing public house, a damp and dirty fringe bar where she was sure to be ignored. Sorykah shrugged and peered through the periscope. Sunlight careened off the surface ice, smarting her eyes with reflected rainbow displays. She scanned the street, watching a local family waddle about in their furs, fussing over their sled dogs and bickering with broad sweeps of their hands.

"It's not safe for you. Hunters collect trophies when the guards are sleeping. You shouldn't go there." Rava's front arms flickered in vehement agreement, displaying rows of needle-sharp hooks.

"Hunters collect trophies when the guards are awake," Sorykah muttered. Then, her tense, raised voice carrying across the echoing cave, she added, "Hunters work around the clock; your guards don't." Meaning that like Rava, she could never rest. Never sink into complete abandonment, for she slept the restless one-eyed sleep of prey.

"That is a place for locals. Not Company," Rava hissed, her face darkening with angry heat.

"Why? No one bars me from the door. You say Company as if it was a bad thing, as if we're dirt."

"Dirt, yes, that's right. How much do they pay you for what you do?"

"For what I do? Mining? For working in that filthy submarine, running an ice corer like a mindless drone when I should be leading the expeditions?" High emotion sent Sorykah's adrenals into overdrive. Her voice dropped an octave and a male snarl cut through Rava's agitation, silencing her. Sorykah bit it back, stuffed her bared and fleeting masculinity down her throat, and took a deep breath before concluding, "Not enough. That's what they pay." Sorykah finally voiced the anger and frustration that had percolated within her since she first boarded the submarine and found herself demoted from the engine room to the core room.

"It's water, that's all. There's nothing criminal about their business, from their perspective at least. Encouraging people to get high off the necrotic gases of prehistoric bacteria, turning those gorgeous bergs into lumps of Swiss cheese. Still. It's a living. I don't enjoy the luxury of selectivity."

"Few of us do. You haven't answered my question, Sorykah. Why Pavel's?"

"It seemed safe. I was wrong."

"Yes, you were." Rava smiled in that tight, fishy way of hers, all unblinking eyes and cold, bared teeth.

"Now I'm here. I must thank you for your hospitality and be on my way. Must make the most of the sun while it shines."

The perpetual motion of her undulating tentacles sustained the illusion that Rava was underwater. She nodded, a model of decorum.

"I'd like to offer you something as payment, but I'm afraid I don't have much with me. What can I give you?" Sorykah crossed to the old sofa and began packing her duffel, anxious to be on the road and en route to her babies.

"I require no payment but . . ." and Rava licked thin, dry lips, the puckering discs on her tentacles popping softly to themselves.

As if casting her thoughts on the wind, dreamy particles of Rava's desire curled round Sorykah's ears, tentative and wispy as smoke. Smoke. Of course. The hookah. Rava's eyes burned with an inner fire; she yearned to dance with the white dragon again. Daylight was scant protection for someone like her, alone on the surface, wheeling her octamerous, fur-wrapped secret across the icy streets. She would have no panic button accessible beneath the bar, no monstrous, waxen-faced protectors bashing heads on her account, saving her from dire ruin at hunters' hands. She had been kind, after all.

Sorykah recalled an event weeks earlier while drilling a berg that had drifted north into the wake of the equatorial current. Warmer water had eroded the berg's undersea surface, carving smooth pockets in the ice. An octopus had taken up residence in one of the holes, compacting its long quivering arms around its head, its wary gold eye trained on the core team decimating its home. Sorykah floated in her pressurized-diving suit near its hiding place, shining her light along the berg looking for the telltale dark streaks that indicated a rich vein of frozen fossil life. Her beam illuminated folds of loose, rough flesh packed into a tiny space. The startled creature had tightened its grip, as if willing itself to condense to a speck of matter, a pop and fizz away from nonexistence. They locked eyes for a brief second, the octopus's gaze focused on its destroyer and staring death in the eye.

Vibrations from the drill traveled through the berg, making the ice crack and dance apart. Churning blades would soon chew through the ice, shredding the fragile creature to calamari bits. That shy and gentle animal would vanish in a violent red wash of blood and tissue. Sorykah glanced over at the core team, engrossed in burying the drill to its hilt in ice. She thrust her hand into the cave, her fingers closed around a wad of rubbery muscle as she yanked the octopus free. Eight legs unfurled like pennants in a breeze, bearing it into the darkness beyond Sorykah's beam.

Lying awake in her bunk that night, she recalled the stubborn helplessness of a trapped octopus that would rather die than surrender its illusory sense of safety.

That was Rava. Should any hunters follow and find her, they'd capture her as easily as a lame deer in an open field. High on opium she could grow careless, thoughts turned inward, the world rosy and blurred. She might not even resist seizure until it was too late and she floated in some other tank, a fisherman's trophy.

"I'll take you as far as the bar, and then I'm off home. I've got babies to feed," Sorykah smiled, anticipating the feel of their warm little mouths, their soft, padded bodies relaxed in her arms as inquisitive hands stroked her face and fiddled with her shirt buttons. "Are you ready?"

Rava nodded and wormed her way over to the rack to choose one of her exotic gowns. Though growing used to the way Rava moved—her eight legs reaching forward and curling back in waves, the suckers popping free as they were peeled back and the next set applied to the floor—Sorykah was still horrified and fascinated by it. That Rava could walk, in a fashion, defied all kinetic laws and kept Sorykah teetering on the edge of insistent disbelief. Rava's very existence toyed with the boundaries of Sorykah's reality and made her feel as though she verged on a rapid and nasty slide into insanity. She would be glad to deposit her at the bar and be free of her.

Rava settled herself in her wheelchair. "You push," she ordered.

Sorykah felt her eyebrows creep up with suppressed irritation but she said nothing. Though Rava seemed peaceful, her tentacles looked strong. Sorykah had little doubt that if she chose to, Rava could strangle her with those writhing legs, pin her down and use some hideous, hidden nether mouth to suck the life out of her. Sorykah shuddered, turning away to don her coat and seal the open neck of her thermosuit. Slinging her duffel on her back, she gripped the wheelchair handles and said, "Let's go."

The gentle incline that seemed so cautious the night before had transformed itself into a stark, backbreaking mountain as Sorykah labored to push Rava through the tunnel. Beads of sweat erupted at her hairline. She grew warm all over and yearned to rest, but the allure of fresh air and sunlight drove her forward.

Sorykah stood on the broken linoleum, hands on her knees, heart pounding with exertion. Rava lifted the bar from the door and cold air swirled around their exposed heads like a flurry of gulls. Ice crystals danced in the sunbeams like daytime stars, and as they entered the outside world and left the cave behind, the glorious, white morning exploded around them.

Sorykah's eyes throbbed in the brightness. The street swarmed with energetic activity as sledges were hitched and cargoes lashed down, playful sled dogs growled and yipped, and a couple of sailors staggered groaning from a doorway, still drunk from the previous night's excess. There were the distant sounds of creaking crates and pulleys, clanking metal and the occasional shout as ships in port were outfitted and repaired, a snowmobile roaring down a vacant side street and, playing accompaniment to the human hubbub, and the ethereal Sigue ice song keening at sea.

They made it to the Stuck Tongue without incident but as they approached, a tall, bent figure clad in black slipped into the bar ahead of them.

Sorykah paused, reluctant to repeat the previous night's events. "What shall we do?"

Fixated on narcotic satiety, Rava shrugged.

Sorykah grimaced and pushed Rava through the door and into the ringing din. As many as twenty-five bodies crowded the small space, their raised voices sparring for dominance. Sorykah couldn't decipher the gist of the discussion conducted in an exotic blend of accents and local dialects, but Rava could. Her eyes narrowed in her tight, drawn face and her tentacles thrashed in anger.

Rava wheeled herself toward the bar and elbowed her way through the crowd. "Pavel, is this true?"

Pavel nodded. He looked as if he hadn't slept, hurriedly pulling pints to serve the odd assortment of folks loitering at the bar. "Sidra herself has confirmed it. Word came with the tanker this morning. It was unloading at the processing station in Blundt when Carac approached our representative and gave him the report. We're meeting here this morning to decide what it means."

"What it means? It means nothing to us. This is something for the city folk to handle."

"Sidra's orders. If he hunts among his own, it means no one is safe. Rava, this must end."

Sorykah assumed this was fallout from the previous night's terrible encounter with the hunters, but soon she became conscious of a growing hush and the pairs of eyes trained on her as she stood alone, conspicuous among the locals in her neat Company-issued thermosuit and magnet boots. Nervous, she edged through the throng, reaching for Rava's wheelchair.

"What's going on?" she whispered. Beside her, a gaunt, beaky-nosed man with a long neck and sorrowful, hooded eyes gazed at Sorykah with obvious pity.

Rava pinned her with a level, neutral stare. The bar grew quiet as Rava's low voice broke the unpleasant silence. "Official notice comes from the queen. Human children have been taken."

6

DUNYA THE DOG-FACED GIRL

"COME ALONG ME BIRD, EAT! Ye must eat something." Dunya's speech disintegrated into a pleading, mournful whine as she pushed a spoonful of porridge against Leander's closed and resolute mouth. The baby whined, shaking his head from side to side to avoid the spoon, laden and dripping with creamy mealie. Dunya looked at Ayeda, rolling her own porridge over her tongue, spitting it into her palm and licking it off again, her happy little squeals a pleasant background to Leander's annoyed thrashings.

"Look at yer sister, child. See 'ow she likes it? Why can't ye do the same?"

Dunya grunted in frustration. The boy had not eaten well since his arrival, only choking back a few bits of food when his hunger grew too great to bear. Dunya sensed that he might be holding out for his mother and she admired his loyalty. However, it was her duty to keep these two healthy. It would be her head should they sicken or die. Her head, mounted on one of the blackened pikes adorning the outer gate, shrinking and shriveling in the wind and sun, bitten by hoarfrost, turned to leather and crow feed.

She needed milk. These two were still young, six or seven months old perhaps, and just able to drag themselves round the floor. At this age, Dunya's pups had already been weaned to the bowl and bone. She regretted the lost ewe sacrificed to the Wood Beast and made note to ask Meertham for another when he next came round. None of the captive subjects had milk. Except for two shy sisters who whistled and cooed like doves, the zoo's inhabitants were a motley hodgepodge: a tired old crone with a glass eye and the chameleon's two-fingered hands, a gator-skinned girl with tiny pointed teeth and a nasty disposition. There was a merwoman born with legs fused from hip to ankle, a boy with the pelt and appetite of a black bear, the winged girl—a mute with a furred, tubular tongue; the loathsome old spider-legged man; and Gatekeeper. Captivity had warped their minds, making them furtive and paranoid. They revealed themselves through rare glimpses of ringed, lambent eyes glowing in the cobwebbed corners as Dunya made her rounds, exchanging emptied, crusted-over dishes for ones fresh with cabbage and dandelion, offal or lard and mealie. Sometimes the dishes would sit until the greens liquefied, the mealie moldered, and the fat grew rank and maggoty; then, and only then, would it be consumed.

"Never ye mind, love. We'll find something to yer liking." Dunya cupped Leander's silky head in hand and stroked thin shoulders where scapula flared like fragile butterfly's wings. His chubby cheeks had deflated, giving him a distressingly adult look.

Bending close, Dunya's nostrils flared as she nosed the folds of his neck and behind his ears. He smelled sour and dusty, a stark contrast to his sister's robust aroma of sweat (mild and sweet), graham flour, curd, and something oily and rich, like the taste of sesame. He flopped against her muzzle as if he was simply too tired to resist. The baby boy moaned, folding Dunya's fuzzy ear in his fist, his mouth working on the soft tip, nursing any warm scrap of flesh he could maneuver into a makeshift nipple.

He fell into a sudden and deep sleep. Dunya carried him past gleeful Ayeda, preoccupied with a lump of regurgitated cheese and a wooden spoon, to settle him in the sewing basket. Dunya turned her attention to the girl. *Bright* and *sensible* were the two words that sprang to mind when Dunya regarded the child with the calm gray eyes and inquisitive brows. Adaptive and keen, she seemed to realize that her fate was in transition and that she ought to keep current with events as best she could. She went about her business and demanded little of Dunya's attention, only growing fretful when she was hungry. Sucking gruel from her fist, the baby followed Dunya's movements, tracking her around the kitchen as her caretaker began the work of preparing the Collector's captives their one daily meal.

Meat was in short supply. The side of venison hanging in the meat locker was pared to the bone; tatty tissue clung to the ribs between white score marks where Dunya had slashed it free. Beside it, the frozen corpses of small birds lay scattered across the shelves, their feathers crisp with frost.

Surrounded on three sides by the Erun Forest, a dense and foreboding thicket haunted by a single-minded slavering beast and backed by the Glass Mountains' sharp peaks, the manse was cut off from the sea, yellow plains and flower fields beyond its cloistered domain, each one a rich source of food. Dunya relied on Meertham's donations and trapping the occasional foraging grubbit, a rodenty, round ball of grease and fur that burrowed among the tree roots. Traps lay in wait but sat empty for weeks as Dunya made her rounds in vain, hoping for a scrap of fresh meat, not just for herself but for the poor creatures lowing in the dungeons. None of them was healthy, she knew. None of them adequately fed, groomed, or tended to when ill. Though they shared normal human features, the little quirks distinguishing them from people made them nothing more than animals in the

Collector's eyes, beasts who bore the burden of their captor's mania.

Dunya eyed the baby boy nestled in the sewing basket. Wisps of black hair veiled his forehead, casting a faint shadow upon his brow. She was certain that if she did not find a way to make him eat he would vanish before her eyes, wither and curl into a fetal ball and cease to live.

She'd fought hard to protect her pups, to keep them hidden, silent, and protected but all the caution in the world hadn't saved them. Here was an opportunity for redemption. No one had offered or was able to help when she'd most needed it. Dunya's children suffered for their mother's unanswered prayers. She had suffered as well, choking back tears of humiliated rage as she served the man responsible for all her woes, cooking his meals, butchering his meat, caring for the tenants of his absurd and terrifying zoo. Why had she never left? Certainly, Meertham could be convinced through bribery or pity to cross the wood with her. However, freedom from the Collector meant the loss of a certain protection and exposure to the wider world's predatory whims. Dunya had been at the manor so long she doubted her ability to survive on her own. There were many things more terrifying than mistreatment, servitude, and the Wood Beast; jeers and stares and sharp tongues cut more deeply than the Master's whip and so she stayed.

What of these two bonny babes? Where had they come from and why did the Master want them? Dunya had inspected them upon arrival, examining the curve of their ears, noses, and gums. She had sniffed them and licked their hands and faces, yet her sensitive olfactory glands hadn't smelled anything foreign or damning. Ordinary body hair grew where it should: fine, fuzzy sideburns and a spray of downy, almost invisible hair sprouted on the boy's shoulders, but it wasn't fur. Five fingers on each hand, nails—not claws, no hooves, horns, or curling tails. In other words, the children appeared normal, striking, intelligent, and wholly human.

The long years brought a steady trickle of new inmates whose unusual attributes revealed themselves under duress. Exhaustion, starvation, emotional manipulation, and sensory deprivation ignited a fury of changes, as repressed sensitivities were aggravated and revealed, sometimes in terrible ways.

There had been a young boy—a gangly adolescent with huge, exhaustion-ringed eyes—who seemed quite harmless at first. His palpable sorrow seeped into the corners of the cells he crept through. He haunted the shadows, nervous and frantic when confronted by the Master's lone servant. He was not interested in food, comfort, trinkets, or tobacco, and as the days passed, he withered before Dunya's eyes, shedding hair like dandelion fluff upon the dungeon floor. How she struggled to keep him alive when he paled and doubled over, taking no drink, no sustenance, as though willing himself to die. Finally, when Dunya felt she could do no more, she closed his cell door and left him to the darkness he seemed to prefer. She could not play nursemaid as well as jailer and hold his hand while he died. It was asking too much. She would remove the body afterward, load it onto a sledge, and drag it to the charnel house for burial during spring thaws. She would burn the hay, wet with his decomposing body's fluids, and scrub down his cell in preparation for the next tenant, but she would not offer the comfort of her solitary presence during his passing. To court Death like that was to invite the stillness and spider silk down upon her own head. Better she should tarry at the cemetery and dance upon her own grave than shine as its unwelcome angel.

She waited a week before going back.

She walked to his door in the company of Chulthus, one of the Master's great hunting hounds with wiry hair like boar bristles and a terrible slavering jaw that quivered at the scent of fear. Earlier that spring, the bitch had borne a litter of six. Five had grown sleek and densely muscled and prowled the manor, carousing and knocking one another across the great hall as they wrestled and fought, dogs so great their height would be measured in hands, like a horse.

The sixth pup had been a runty female with glossy black fur and a thoughtful face. Rather than abandon it and withhold her milk, Chulthus was tender with the weakling, nudging it toward her nipple and snarling at its greedy, interloping siblings. The tenacious pup clung to the scrap of life offered her and, astonishingly, began to thrive. Small and good-natured, the runt was a companion and not a hunter. She divided her day between the great rooms and the kitchen, snuffling beneath the table as Dunya chopped greens or ground mealie, tucking herself into a corner where she could warm herself against the fireplace stones, earning the name Soot. When away from the kitchen, Soot trailed her fearsome mother as faithfully as a shadow, but that day, she was not to be seen.

"Where's yer child gone, old mother?" Dunya asked the dog, thumping her sides and rubbing the scarred, pointed ears, pricked up to catch her familiar voice. Chulthus whined and circled Dunya's legs, buffeting her mistress, nudging her along the hall.

"What is it, Chulthus? 'Ave ye caught a rabbit for me? Do ye have a prize for Dunya?" Crouching, she wrapped her arms around the big animal's neck and rubbed her furred cheek against Chulthus's muscular snout. Dunya's canine proclivities had been the subject of endless ridicule before the Master took her away. Hirsutism, a prominent misshapen jaw, a muzzle-like nose with supersensitive olfactory chambers, and floppy, pancake-thin ears had made her "Dunya the dog-faced girl." But she wasn't dog, nor wolf nor animal of any kind.

She liked the simplicity of the manor dogs' social order, the liberties they took, walking uninvited into any room, free to come and go as they liked without having to answer to ringing bells or cower beneath a rain of invective. Chulthus and her family received scraps from the Master's table and supped on whole roast fowl (for the Master only deigned to eat the "oysters," two soft scallops of meat atop the birds' backs, before throwing them to the dogs), and slept in the warm, dry, and lavishly adorned tower rooms rather than the damp and chilly underfloors. Had Dunya been a dog, she would have led a better life.

A thick, cloying silence clung to the walls, oozing from behind the dungeon's closed doors and clogging the stone corridor like plaque in an artery. Chulthus's hackles rose and she grew skittish, bounding ahead then leaping close to Dunya's side. Even the hairs on Dunya's spine stood on end as they descended into the lower dungeons. Well familiar with the pervasive odors of fear and exhaustion that permeated the dungeon, she detected something new, a sinister undercurrent of malignant terror, and the pitiful, sick smell of a hasty, unwelcome death. Murder was in the air.

She'd smelled it before. Caged together, two of the Master's acquisitions had killed each other in a brief territorial spat. Slit throats and gutted bellies tainted the dungeon air with their death stink; it had taken weeks for both the smell and the memory to fade.

Chulthus stopped before the thin boy's cell, growling and scratching at the door. Dunya noticed deep claw marks in the wood and realized that Chulthus had been here many times before, begging entry into the cell. The silence was so sharply barbed that it hurt her ears. Taking her ring of keys, she gingerly unlocked the door, steadying herself to meet whatever lay on the other side. Chulthus forced her way through and bounded into the darkness. Dunya heard whining and snarling, a low protracted grinding, the motor of Chulthus's maternal revenge goading itself into action.

Entering the chamber with lamp aloft, Dunya allowed her gaze to circle the room, taking in the bare stone walls, the autumn-pale light sifting down from the ventilation slits, the discarded dishes furred over with a thick growth of mold. She saw the boy, his color renewed and burning high on his cheeks, took in the sight of his bare narrow chest streaked with something dark and viscous that had dripped from his chin and mouth to cake and crumble from the joists of his flesh. Chulthus crouched low, teeth bared but reluctant to advance.

Dunya crept forward, her heart in her throat. There, heaped in the boy's lap, lay a sorry sack of ebony fur, stiff with blood, the days-old carcass gone soft with set-in rot. His fingers played among the dog's curls, smoothing them as if to offer comfort.

The sweet puppy had been easily enticed by his crooning and his pale, waggling fingers flickering through the cell's muted light. She would've peered through the low slot used for sliding in food trays, squirmed and pushed her way into the cell toward her doom. Gentle to the end, the teeth at her neck would have surprised her but doubtless, it would not have occurred to her to resist.

"Oh, me poor innocent!" Dunya gasped, catching the hopeful flicker in the boy's eyes.

Galled to realize he believed her pity meant for him—Dunya recoiled and grabbed at Chulthus's neck, dragging the reluctant dog from the cell.

"Stay there!" Dunya shouted at the boy, fear weakening her legs. "Don't ye move!"

She slammed the cell door and locked it, certain she could hear the thin boy creeping toward them, his huge haunted eyes blinking audibly, the lids clattering in his head. At any moment, a bloodied hand might shoot from the tray slot to clutch her ankle. Dunya staggered back, the oil sloshing in her lamp. Chulthus pawed the door, shoving her great nose into the slot and barking.

"Poor girl," Dunya moaned, the image of Soot's drained and lifeless body fresh before her eyes. "Comin' to such an awful end! What's 'e done, 'orrid boy!"

"Be still now. Shhh, good girl, shhh . . ." Dunya ran her hands over the big animal's body, scratching the grizzled chin and feeling the grief traveling circuit-like through Chulthus's body, where naked sorrow and mindless vengeance ran parallel, forming a single, charged current of despair.

Dunya was relieved when the Master ordered the boy released

onto the grounds. Gladdened, but ashamed of her pleasure in the end he'd earned himself.

His head decorated one of the pikes, a disturbing visage whose sunken eyes and drawn mouth were still stained, after so many years, by the black pup's blood.

Leander sobbed in his sleep, remembering some private sadness. Dunya collected Ayeda, dampened the corner of her apron, and wiped the baby's hands and face.

The little girl gazed at her caretaker with solemn resolution, as if determined not to humiliate herself by crying. Her eyes were as cool and clear as alpine lakes. Dunya hugged the child's small body, wondering again where they had been before Meertham's ruthless abduction. Were they from the grimy northern cities or one of the quaint villages that populated the flower fields beyond the great wood? Were they missed?

"I wish ye could talk, little one," Dunya said, "and tell me yer story. Tell me yer names, at least." She smiled and cupped the child's face in her palm.

"Ye aren't foundlings, 'tis certain. Ye belong to someone, I'm sure, but who? Who is missing ye tonight?"

There was no cause to keep the children alive if no one searched for them. Dunya would sooner dispatch them herself than allow the Master to satisfy his cruel whims with the evils awaiting them.

Blinded by an idiotic burst of hope, Dunya considered the two possible avenues of escape—the charnel house or the wood. Both were terrifying, but she could do it, couldn't she? Save at least two innocent souls. Though this small deed would not tip the scales in her favor, it was at least a hedge against damnation.

Ayeda slumped against Dunya as she relaxed into sleep. Stroking her bowed back, Dunya nestled the limp baby into the sewing basket beside her brother, tucking a blanket around both babies and sighing ruefully.

"Someone misses ye, sweet angels. Someone will come. We must believe it."

7

ENTER THE STUCK TONGUE

"TAKEN? WHAT DO YOU MEAN *taken*?" Sorykah said, the breath constrained in her throat. The coincidence was too terrible, too convenient. Rava reached for Sorykah, taking the sleeve of her thermosuit in a lavender-fingered hand. She waved away a squat, rotund woman with an explosive mane of clown-red ringlets who loitered near Sorykah, eager to sop up a few scraps of pity for herself.

"We must talk more. It is not for you to worry about yet." Rava patted Sorykah with caution, as if unused to gestures of love or concern. She turned to Pavel, speaking in a loud voice for the benefit of the Stuck Tongue's other patrons. "We have no details about these children—"

"Babies!" injected a shrill voice from the back. "Not just children. Babies!"

"Boy and girl, right Jodhi?" inquired a husky man with a pimpled nose and frothy yellow eyebrows, jostling for space at the bar.

His companion, a sun-ravaged older woman with unkempt salt-and-pepper hair, nodded with vigor, rubbing together hands curled like claws.

"It could be anybody," Rava added, her rubbery forehead wrinkling in a distinctly human expression of dismay.

"Something unusual about them two," continued Pimples. "Weren't just any nabbing. It was that walrus, the Collector's man. Right Jodhi? That's what we heard."

A collective shudder rippled through the room at the mention of the Collector's despised henchman.

Sorykah found her tongue. "What walrus? Who is the Collector?"

Pimples looked from Jodhi to Rava, licking weather-creased lips with nervous anticipation. Stoicism occluded Rava's expression; it was impossible to gauge her thoughts. Sorykah searched the faces around her, desperate for some indication that things were not as bad as she feared but finding little reassurance to the contrary.

"Someone tell me what this means! These are my children, aren't they? It's why you're all here, isn't it?" Her cry cut above the steady murmured undercurrent. For the second time in as many days, her voice pitched and dropped awkwardly, betraying her secret.

Heads turned, ears pricked up, and eyes narrowed with sudden knowledge. Sorykah could not hide among fantastic hybrids like these, strange amalgams of humanity and the animal kingdom skilled in both revealing and concealing their differences.

Pavel swabbed the bare bar and cleared his throat, an empty gesture made to fill the awkward silence.

Sorykah's knees buckled and she collapsed against the tall gaunt man with the beaked nose who'd entered the bar before them. He led her to a stool and deposited her at the bar, where she hunched trembling, head in hands.

She thought she might faint, vomit, scream, or die.

"I can't breathe! Oh, I can't breathe!" Sorykah fumbled with the neck of her zippered thermosuit.

"It's just a bit o' whimsy passing by, nothing to make note of," he consoled, a comforting hand on her shoulder.

His stringy hair leaching oil into the upturned collar of a sweeping black coat dusty with age and wear, Sorykah's benefactor appeared more Grim Reaper than guardian angel. Although his expression was kind, the man's face, with its stark angles, deep creases, and hooded, red-brown eyes, was off-putting.

He sidled closer, taking Sorykah's hand in his own. "You asked about the walrus, the Collector." A rumble of resistance surged from the crowd. Secrets were poised to spill and the somatics did not care to break their covenant, no matter the cause. The crowman raised a hand to silence any forthcoming objections. "Matuk the Collector and Meertham, his henchman. Each one is very dangerous for they are equally formidable and equally feared by those in our circles. As diverse and scattered as we are, the Family has always been easy prey, but it's worse when one of our own hunts us, for he knows our methods of camouflage. Meertham can detect the faintest streak of animalia. We cannot defend ourselves when he comes. His master is a warped and nasty little man without respect for life, or our diverse gifts."

Sorykah glanced at Rava for confirmation. She hunched in her wheelchair, rusty locks of hair shielding her face from the crowd. Sorykah would have believed her asleep but for the delicate hands gripping the chair's arms, rigid with suppressed emotion.

The man grimaced, his sallow face growing even more severe. "He takes us to suit nothing more than his own pleasure. We disappear when the walrus comes to call. He drags us off in his stuffsack and we are never seen again."

"But what does he collect?" Sorykah insisted. "People? Somatics?"

"None of us has ever returned from the manor so we cannot be sure. They say he keeps us posed in rigor and rot, our heads on pikes, row after row of innocents skewered and left to the elements."

The blood drained from Sorykah's face, leaving it chalky and drawn. Speech eluded her. She felt her jaw working soundlessly as she struggled to retain the last of her composure.

"Your babies are there," offered an arthritic crook-backed woman with flaking, scaly skin. She scratched her neck, reaching up with much difficulty as she inched through the crowd. Grunting with effort, the old woman was stiff and moved with obvious pain.

"He'll have them awhile yet," added the woman. "Not much sport in hunting such easy prey."

Crow-man frowned and waved the old woman away, her wrinkled face as brown as a nutshell.

"We don't know why he's taken them. Children yes, but seven, eight years old at the youngest. Never a baby, much less two. There must be something unique about your children, something that might appear with time and age, perhaps. He'll wait until they reveal themselves before taking the next step."

"The next step?" Sorykah whispered, clutching her throat.

Catching her horrified gaze, the crow-man squeezed her shoulder. "As long as they don't change, they're safe. There's still time."

Memory flooded Sorykah's senses—a chilly morning months ago, the babies weak and completely dependent, their squishy limbs still cartilage soft. Ayeda'd had a scare, tumbling off the edge of the low mattress in her sleep, waking her mother and brother with the nauseating thwack of her unprotected head on the wooden floor. The fall wasn't severe, a two-foot drop, but she'd hit the floor like a dead weight and had the wind knocked out of her. Once Ayeda recovered from her fright, she'd slipped into a deep sleep. Exhausted from her first week on the *Nimbus*, Sorykah had been unable to stay awake to watch the baby. She slept with the children moored against the comforting island of her body until Leander's anxious rooting at her breast woke her. Groggy with lingering dreams, she'd nursed him while his sister slept, changed his diaper, and tucked him into a nest of flat pillows. She rose and attended to her morning ablutions, savored a half hour of calm and a fresh cup of tea. Odd how such a meaningless moment had burned itself into her memory. Clear as the long icicle teeth bared beneath the Stuck Tongue's eaves, she recalled every detail of that otherwise ordinary day. She remembered the gleaming white snow dancing lazy pirouettes beyond the window, a seeping diffusion of sporadic sunshine, radio static fragmenting the daily world news report, rising ringlets of steam hovering above her teacup.

Leander had awakened and fed; afterward he lay on the rug, playing with a string of plastic bells, making joyful, discordant music. The morning slid by, a silent whirl of winter white, Sorykah and her children insulated from the unseasonable cold. Ayeda slept on. Sorykah crept over to listen to her breathing. She pressed a hand to the baby's heart, measuring its rhythm and lifting her eyelids to check her pupils for symmetry. Mild unease turned to active worry as the hours vanished. Sorykah was on the verge of calling for an ambulance when Ayeda finally stirred, croaked, and opened her eyes. Relieved, Sorykah had swept her up, doused her with kisses, and changed her sodden diaper. Then she saw it. Her little girl had a fully formed penis and testicles. Sorykah screamed, startling both babies into fits of hysterical tears. The trauma of her fall had triggered an emotional response intense enough to cause a change. Ayeda was a Trader.

Sorykah's daughter reverted to her feminine gender within a day, but it was the first of a series of repeated alterations as the twins explored their newfound ability. They were mischievous and playful, shifting through the change with ease, as if it were merely another developmental task to master, like learning to crawl, eat with a spoon, or speak.

The man's brow crinkled with worry as he watched Sorykah working loose the problem's stubborn knots. Resolution set her jaw. It was too late then for ignorance to save them. She would have to follow and save them herself.

"How can I get there?" Sorykah demanded amid a flurry of clucking tongues and shaking heads.

"It's a journey far too perilous for one woman to undertake alone. How would you reclaim your children? His mansion is carved from white marble. The keeper of gate and key? A cannibal. A dense forest circles the manor and the dread beastie inhabits the wood, she with the endless hunger, a gullet that cannot be stoppered or quieted by blood or gristle or bone." A dour scarecrow, the man hovered over her, his mouth downturned in a grim line.

Sorykah gaped at the man, her eyes wide with naked panic. She clutched her duffel with white-knuckled hands as she envisioned the Sigue's barren white expanse stretched brilliant and naked beneath the glaring subarctic sun, the Southern Sea riled by crosscurrents, the northern mainland with its grimy cities, depleted forests and fallow, wasted plains divided by a shark-toothed mountain ridge, zippering the planet's breast like a lumpy surgical scar. Centered in this ever-expanding universe, a tiny black dot no bigger then a pepper speck, sat Sorykah herself.

The distance between mother and children grew greater by the hour. Soon their tracks would vanish, along with any hope of finding them. Paralyzed by fear, her thinking muddled and erratic, Sorykah teetered, broken and staring, too stunned to cry.

Pavel poured a finger of whiskey from his emergency supply and pushed the glass across the bar. Sorykah gazed at it blankly; in her stupor, she had forgotten what to do.

Pavel nudged her arm. When she didn't respond, he forced open her hand and inserted the whiskey glass. Sorykah automatically raised the glass to her lips and drank. A river of liquid smoke seared her gullet and she coughed, tears springing to her eyes.

"Good stuff, innit?" Pavel beamed. Sorykah spluttered in return as the elderly bartender patted her arm.

"There, there, missus. Have you the will, your will makes your way." He paused and studied her, the ruffled ivory fur on his exposed forearms shifting as if in a breeze. His wild eyebrows knitted themselves together, obscuring the bridge of his nose.

"Hang on," he urged, his voice grating and low. "Not much passes on this island that I don't catch wind of at some point along the transmission lines. There's one who knows the way . . ." he trailed, lost in his own thoughts.

Enlivened by the whiskey, Sorykah followed Pavel's sight line. She expected to see the crow that had been so helpful, but like most of the others, he too had vanished. Only the decrepit crone and the withered old couple, Jodhi and Pimples, her beanbag of a husband, loitered near the hookah, watching Rava smoke. Sorykah surmised that they were scavenger addicts, too poor to front their own habits and waiting for the dirty dregs of someone else's pipe.

Did Pavel expect her to accept help from one of those scoundrels?

Shaking his head, Pavel clucked his tongue and sighed.

"She'll die this way, you know. The dragon's got her in his fist and he'll not let go," he murmured. "Her kind aren't meant to take in all this air. I know she does it to ease her way but it's the wrong path. You see her?" Pavel thrust his chin toward the rear of the room. "A true beauty, just like the poppy she so loves. She'll die if something isn't done soon."

Sorykah stared at Pavel, stunned that he would plead the case of some hopeless junkie at a time like this, trump her own cause in favor of dreamy ruminations about some airsick octopus. She drank her whiskey, picking over the few remembered shards of conversation. She couldn't remember what she was supposed to do. Take the train to Colchester and make a report to the magistrate? Go back to the submarine and radio for help? The Company would extend her furlough by a day or so but they expected her to rejoin the crew when the sub left port or forfeit her job.

The other option was to embark on some wild goose chase, following a scanty trail of clues in the hope of finding them. What of Nels, charged with the children's safekeeping? Was she culpable? Had she played a role in their theft, or was she, too, a victim of the Collector's mania for novelty? Confronted with so many obstacles, she needed someone to point her in the right direction, set her feet on the road to her children's salvation, and order her to march. If she worshipped the Holy Mother Jerusha like her missing nanny Nels, she could rely on simple faith to orient her, but without it, she spun in confusion, a twisted compass needle.

"There is one who can help both of you," Pavel urged, his hairy face inches from Sorykah's. She startled, taken aback by his sudden proximity. "She will know where you need to go, and she can prepare you for the undertaking. But first you must agree to take Rava, if I am to tell you."

She nodded. What choice did she have? He was blackmailing her, bargaining that morose addict's life for her two innocents as if they were equal. Still, it was a direction to follow.

"Matuk's sister, Shanxi, lives at the edge of the waste, within the green ring around the Devil's Playground. Dogs'll get you there in a day. On foot it can be managed in two, that is, if you outlast the Sigue night."

"What am I supposed to do with Rava? I can't force her to accompany me."

"Get yourself ready and come back for her. She'll be limp as an earthworm and just as quiet." Pavel winked in a way that sent shivers cascading down Sorykah's spine. Who was he to make such rash promises? She must trust that he held Rava's best interests at heart, that he wouldn't send Sorykah on an insane errand to suit some peculiar fancy.

"Get gone and don't dally, gal. Time's on fire today." Pavel lifted the glass from her hand and placed it in the sink.

"Well? Tick-tock!" He shooed her away.

Sorykah chucked her duffel behind the bar and headed for the door. For a moment, she considered returning to the *Nimbus.*

She'd walk away, leaving everything and everyone behind, but of course, that was not an option. Wrapping her scarf over her mouth and tucking hands into pockets, she scanned the street, assessing the assorted shop signs crudely painted in the local dialect and attempting to suss out which door would lead to a sled and a hardy dog team.

8

PAVEL'S BARGAIN

WITHIN THE HOUR Sorykah secured an eight-dog team and a sled stocked with three days' supplies: water in fur-covered canteens to prevent its freezing, elk jerky, fruit leather, tinned beans and roe, wax-paper-wrapped rolls of flat bread, and a jar of salted, seasoned seal fat, plus a hefty bag of ground meat and meal for the dogs. She'd located a musher willing to give her a crash course in sled driving and dog handling, along with a cheat sheet of commands in exchange for a month's salary and a coveted bottle of fossil water.

Her insulated Company thermosuit and waterproof long-coat were designed to withstand extreme temperatures, but aside from the few clothes she carried in her bag, Sorykah had little protection from the elements. Seeing how poorly prepared she was to journey into the interior, the musher had included a nylon tent, padded musher's mitts and samilkâ, a fur-lined sealskin pullover favored by the locals. He handed her a massive, shaggy bear pelt and demonstrated how to rig the dogs' lines and pitch the tent, hooking one side to her sled and staking the opposite end in ice, driving in thick prongs with an umalå, a compact, triangular hammer with a pointed claw.

She had no map, compass, or radio. She had a flint fire starter but there was no wood to burn on the Sigue. Inside the tent, bundled up in the bear pelt and snug beneath a puppy pile of sleeping dogs, she might survive the night but once her supplies were gone, she would be in danger of starving to death within a matter of hours. Her body's hypermetabolism would burn its own fat for fuel before turning to her internal organs.

The morning's diamond-cut sunshine surrendered to encroaching cloud cover as flurries gathered on the horizon. Sorykah accompanied the dogs through the second tier, her hand awkward on the driving bow, aware of the curious stares trailing her.

"Easy," she commanded, her flimsy voice losing itself to the wind. The dogs slowed before regaining a fast trot. She sensed the locals giggling behind parted curtains, amused by her clumsy mushing attempts.

"Easy! Halt!" Sorykah hissed as the dogs cantered past the Stuck Tongue. Scanning her cheat sheet, Sorykah mustered every ounce of authority and bellowed "Whoa," pleased to see the dogs skid to a stop. Trying to maintain her fledgling influence over the team, she pointed at the snow while staring the team leader in the eye. "Stay! Sit!"

Well trained and agreeable, the dog lowered her haunches and the others followed suit, gazing expectantly at Sorykah.

"That wasn't so hard now, was it," she asked the lead, a russet-and-cream-furred dog with icy green eyes. Perhaps this was a good omen. She imagined herself out on the waste, masterfully driving the dogs, which moved as one sleek body, towing the sled over fresh powder. Together they would shush over the icy sub-arctic desert, deposit the dozy Rava on Shanxi's doorstep, and vanish into the sunset like an Eskimo cowgirl with her trusty canine steeds. Her breast full of fire, a steely glint in her eye, the vengeful and dangerous Sorykah would home in on the thief, brandish her Magar blade, and reclaim what was hers with nary a drop of blood needlessly shed.

Her hand trembled as she reached for the door handle. Within her fantasy, she was glorious and triumphant, a maternal goddess who held the power of the seasons in her hand. Reality spoke differently. An ever-tightening knot cinched her belly, all her nerves in a bundle. She felt queasy. Perhaps she didn't have the strength for this after all. She was a wallflower, a coward, and an apprehensive little mouse.

She took a deep, calming breath and entered the bar.

Pavel stood guard over Rava, who had passed out midtoke and lay in an awkward heap in her wheelchair, her skirt twisted around her torso, limp tentacles poking out beneath her skirt hem. Three scavengers bickered over Rava's leftovers, scrabbling for temporary ownership of the pipe.

"She's ready for you." Pavel swung a sausagey hand toward the stoned octo-girl.

He scooped Rava up with short, powerful arms. Grunting with effort, he hoisted her over his shoulder. Rava's tentacles dangled like useless rubber hoses. Her dirty garments bunched and snagged, and her head swung from her neck, bouncing against Pavel's back as he carried her out of the bar.

Sorykah followed them into the graying morning. Pavel stood by the sled Sorykah had parked in front, his mustache twitching with impatience.

"This is it?"

"Yes. Is something wrong?" Sorykah cast a dubious eye over the sled. The pride she'd relished over her bargain and mushing accomplishments dwindled beneath Pavel's harsh gaze.

"I suppose you could do worse," he grumbled, shifting Rava's body. "Well? Are you ready? She may look light but I'm an old man and these legs of hers weigh like anchors after a while."

Sorykah jumped forward, pulling open the gear straps to expose the sled's empty bed.

Pavel huffed and shook himself, ruffling the white fur that escaped his clothes. "You've got to wrap her up or the snow will wet her when it sprays up from the runners. What have you got?" Sorykah carried a quilted insulate blanket made of metallic thread inside her duffel in case of emergency. Lightweight and waterproof, it would protect Rava from snow while maintaining her core temperature. Pavel grumbled under his breath and laid Rava down without ceremony, unloading her like a bag of flour.

"Go ahead, wrap her tight. She won't wake."

Sorykah tucked the blanket beneath Rava's body, trying not to mind the slippery, gelatinous feel of her tentacles. Wrapping each side in turn, she felt as though she was swaddling a baby, or worse, a mummy. Next she took the sturdy bear pelt and cocooned Rava within a furry papoose, crisscrossing the binding straps and buckling everything into place. Rava's bare head looked terribly exposed, so Sorykah removed her own hat, pulling the still warm fibers over her ears and then tying her scarf around Rava's mouth and neck, leaving the tip of her nose exposed.

"That wee nub of flesh will freeze right up and snap off if she sneezes. Best to cover everything," Pavel instructed.

Sorykah rewrapped the scarf, this time covering Rava's entire face.

"Better," Pavel admitted. He lifted the dowsing rod from the sled and used it to draw a crude map in the snow. A long line connected two rectangles across an empty field. Pavel drew a double ring around one of the rectangles.

"This is the volcano and around it a ring of green. The heat has warmed the soil and thawed the permafrost; it's the only region on the Sigue where plants grow. Look for the green and she won't be far away."

"That's it? Look for the green? It could be miles around the volcano. How am I to know what I'm looking for?"

"You'll know without my telling you." Pavel raised a meaty arm to point away from Ostara into the haze. "That way lies the Devil's Playground. You can see it from here, just drive in a straight line. Follow the smoke and try to get there by nightfall. If you push your team hard today, you might make it."

"What shall I do with her?" Sorykah pointed at the cocooned body on the sled.

"Turn her over to Shanxi. She'll be treated and you'll be rid of her. Then you're on your own."

Sorykah grimaced, observing the rickety sled, the scruffy dogs, and Pavel's furrowed face, his bristling white brows fluttering on the sea breeze. Every impulse urged her to back out of this ridiculous charade, abandon her hopes of rescue, and admit defeat, but her cowardice would burn forever in her heart. Shame would move her, if not bravery. She'd once seen a reptilian mating ball, scads of male snakes entwined and pulsating as they wove themselves around a female buried deep within the knot, and this is what seethed in her gut as she gazed between the untidy houses to the blowing waste beyond.

Mounting the runners, her legs like overcooked noodles, Sorykah gripped the driving bow. "Well, then. We're off." Her false cheer rang hollow; worry was evident in her voice.

"I don't follow Jerusha but I hope that the old gods have an eye trained on you." Pavel released the bow strut. "Keep her well."

Pavel turned back to the bar as if their leaving was of little consequence. She watched him enter and disappear, and then turned to stare through veiling flurries to the ominous, smoking mountain on the far horizon. Keeling her dogs toward the volcano, she steeled herself for the coming journey and yelled "Hike!"

Hours passed before Sorykah dared to stop. The dogs were wearying and her legs were numb. Her hands gripped the aluminum driving bow in a frozen rictus, frosted white with sleet. She commanded the team to slow and it did, with obvious gratitude. Sorykah opened the face flap on the samilkâ, relieved to be free of the poorly tanned hide's gamy odors of rancid fat and spoiled meat. The air was so dry and frigid that her sinuses froze in a single, crackling inhalation. Snow met sky, dissolving in a monotonous wash of gray-and-lime-tinged streaks. The color unnerved her; she spent weeks at a time below sea but understood that when the sky grew pregnant with storm it turned green, like a morning-sick mother. Gunmetal gray clouds swelled, pushing aside the white wisps that had strayed across the sky all day, and soon the light disappeared. Snowflakes began to swirl as the temperature dropped. A rabid wind howled and bore down from the northeast, whipping at her clothes as if to lash them from her body.

Blinded by sleet and snow, Sorykah lurched forward, grabbing the dogs' lines, and pulling them close. She was afraid to move in case she became separated from the team and hopelessly lost. Snow beat down and smothered her beneath a blanket of ice. Clutching the dogs to her as she watched Rava vanish beneath a layer of white, Sorykah wondered how she was to save them all.

9

LA BELLE DAME SANS MERCI

SORYKAH SQUATTED OVER Rava's filthy toilet, a gaseous hole in the ground beneath a wooden chimney-seat. Thick runnels of ice spilled down the cave walls; water trickled and ran as a bubbling belch rumbled up from the toilet's dark recesses. Rava swam into the room, her livid, hard-pointed tentacles erect and stabbing, her yellow eyes swimming in their sockets. A large, central tentacle rose, searching out a target, its single, curved claw striking with precise aim and skewering Sorykah's soft belly, piercing her bladder, threading its way between close-packed intestines to lodge against her spine. She felt the scrape of the claw grinding and shearing against her spinal nerve while Rava twitched and shook, blowing out rings of filmy white opium smoke with every exhalation.

Sorykah awoke, keenly aware of the pressure from her overfull bladder and one of the sled dog's sharp-nailed paws digging into her backside. The dream subsided, leaving a nasty taste in Sorykah's mouth. She struggled to emerge from beneath a heap of furs and sleeping dogs who whuffed and whined as Sorykah extricated herself from the warm pile. Rava lay on the sled, wrapped in furs and secured with tight seal-gut lines to prevent her escape, Sorykah being strongly disinclined to chase after some jonesing poppy fiend in the middle of the night. Giddy with fatigue and burgeoning snow blindness, she was just able to pop the tent and usher the dogs inside before the worst of the storm hit, burying them in a hail of stinging ice shards and bombardier snowflakes.

A diffuse glow of sunlight warmed the tent's ceiling, but the lower half was encased in snowdrifts. She would have to dig their way out. First things first, however. She needed to pee.

Sorykah donned the stinking samilkâ and unzipped the tent flap. The sticky snow held its form, even down to the imprint of the zipper on its face. Sorykah rummaged in the sled's tool bag for the vllå, a broad, spatulate scoop used for snow digging, and began carving out an exit path. After many long minutes, whose silence was broken only by the rasp of the vllå against packed snow, she staggered through fresh powder before tearing open the waste flap on her thermosuit, grateful to relieve herself. For once she wished she was male so she wouldn't have to squat above the snow, frigid air making her exposed bum feel like an ice block. So much easier to poke her pecker through a buttonhole!

Much improved after the night's constant bellyache, she scanned the horizon to assess the storm's damage. The tent was a mere hillock, a mole marring a pristine landscape that stretched away in all directions, an unending sea of white. Unease rattled in her gut as she searched for landmarks. "Shit, shit, shit," she murmured, turning a slow circle to survey the skyline. Blowing snow and vapor turned everything the same anonymous shade of gray.

There! A smudge upon the gray horizon: the Devil's Playground. Sorykah had driven the whole day with it in sight. Now she needed to rouse the dogs and set out again before the clouds released their burden, forcing them all to spend another night alone on the waste.

Boots crunching through starchy snow, Sorykah ran back to the tent. Hunger was foremost in her mind as she ducked inside, rousing the dogs with brisk claps and rump taps. Sorykah had never had any pets as a child and limited contact with animals during her adulthood. At first, she had believed the dogs were mindless robots operated by her commands, but her opinion changed as she observed their different personalities. Intelligence shone in their eyes, and she knew that they understood her. Growing familiar with the idea of herself as a dog handler, the team had responded by relaxing its vigilance, allowing her to earn a small measure of their loyalty. Sorykah's stomach growled as she hitched the dogs to their lines and checked the fastenings on the padded leather booties that protected the dogs' paws from the subzero weather. They responded much better if she called them by name, and she had worked to memorize the musher's list, complete with a diagram of each dog's position, markings, and preferences.

Bundling tent and stakes into a careless wad of fabric and ropes, Sorykah lashed the whole mess to the sled. She poked a finger into Rava's wrappings and discerned a bit of body heat. Good enough.

"Hike!" The dogs jumped at her command, eager to flex and stretch their bodies. Sorykah grabbed the sled's handlebar and mounted the runners with an exhilarated cry as the dogs shot into the white, savoring their freedom and the sensation of blood thrumming through warming muscles. Sorykah's occasional footprint broke the dog's rhythm as she pushed off, urging the team forward, harder and faster.

Fresh snowfall softened the otherwise ugly landscape, burying the shallow, marshy bogs that pitted the empty fields and filled the brief summer months with a cloying stink of rotting vegetation and the ceaseless drone of black flies, who circled over maggoty fish corpses abandoned by migrating seabirds. Keeping the volcano ahead of her, she drove farther into the waste, a desolate stretch of permafrost stringing together frigid, irritable seas.

Pavel had been vague in his directive; as a result, she raced to find a stranger's house somewhere on the earth's unmapped backside before the sun descended, the dogs tired, and the permafrost claimed them all.

Sorykah drove the dogs for an eternity, circling the same patch of ground as earth and sky wrapped them in its seamless, winter-wrought skein. The volcano remained elusive, hovering just within sight yet never nearing, and as she passed by yet another featureless snowy blob, panic rose and crept through her chest. The landscape blurred; the shushing noise of sled runners and panting dogs amplified until her ears rang with sound. Stars of light blossomed and burst before her eyes and she found herself sobbing as they pushed deeper into the brutal wilderness.

Her wailing startled the dogs, who ran even faster to escape it. Her knees buckled and her grip on the driving bow loosened as her cramped fingers cracked free. Sorykah plummeted into the snow, tumbling over the hardened earth, coming to rest with frozen tears clamping her eyelids shut. She scraped the ice from her face and scanned the surface for the sled, her breath exploding in harsh gasps. Wearied and a little frightened by her outburst, the dogs had meandered to a stop some yards away where they stood with drooping tails and downcast eyes, their snow-frosted sides heaving with effort.

Sorykah stumbled toward the sled, ignorant to everything but her own grief. She would soon lose her mind if she couldn't rest her eyes on anything but snowy vistas and distant, soot-stained hills.

"This is it!" she cried. "I'm going to die in the middle of nowhere with a bunch of scrawny dogs and some comatose junkie strapped to a toboggan. My children will forget me and the world will go on, while I haunt this godforsaken wasteland." Loud and shrill, her voice hovered across the snow-packed plain, tainting the air with hysteria.

"I'll die but the stench of this bloody samilkâ will linger on, fouler than the devil's breath on a hot day!" Sorykah pointlessly punched a snowdrift and tripped over one of the sled runners, landing facedown beside Rava's bundled body. She lay there until she couldn't feel her fingers, until her exposed cheeks had gone numb and the dogs came over to nose at her body, presumably to determine whether her corpse was ready for eating.

"Go ahead," she moaned to the lead dog, Kika, who was chewing a loose seal-gut string dangling from the samilkâ's sleeve. "Eat me raw. If there was a fire going I'd roast and eat me, too."

She sniffed dramatically to make her point, and then sniffed again. "I smell smoke!"

It filled the air, tangy and glorious. Squinting at the black, magma-streaked volcano, she saw a misshapen lump of gray and brown huddled against its dark backdrop. She stood and tugged seal gut from Kika's reluctant jaws.

Sorykah dragged Kika back and mounted the sled, cracking her whip, surging into motion. The snow thinned and soon the dogs cantered over brittle slag that gleamed in the waning sunlight. Tufts of pale grass sprouted underfoot and orange lichens flowered on the rocks. Tiny leaves twisting in the harsh air, alpine plants flashed tender undersides as the distant volcano gasped and coughed up a plume of sparks and ash. The dogs danced over the warming rock, their paws hot against the steaming, black crusted ground. Sulfurous clouds drifted from the volcano's open mouth, choking Sorykah and the dogs, who shook dusty heads and pawed stinging eyes. They would soon asphyxiate if the cold didn't do them in.

Shanxi's house was a low-slung amalgamation of small, mossy boulders and glossy black slag. Luminous blue smoke puffed from the chimney and the soft muttering of some animal sounded as it rooted deep within a sprawling stone barn.

Sorykah approached the crumbling little rock pile with her heart in her mouth. From the corner of her eye, she saw a figure emerge from the shadowed interior, tall and thin, dressed in a trailing crimson robe. Sorykah bent to release the dogs from their lines, keeping her gaze averted from the door creaking open behind her as if to delay the revealing moment.

"Too afraid to look my way?" The woman's amused voice was kind.

Sorykah and Kika sought reassurance in each other's eyes. Ruffling the dog's silky, tufted ears, she straightened and turned, meeting Shanxi for the first time.

Her beauty was the sort that pierced hearts like poisoned arrows, one whose leaving would crack a soul in two and whose shoulder, when turned in anger or disinterest, would curdle a lover's blood. With unlined skin the color of a toasted almond and a shorn, elegant head atop a regal neck, Shanxi stood in the doorway, resplendent in a fur-lined robe, its beads and spangles twinkling like dying stars. Shanxi ducked beneath the lintel. "Everyone inside now, sled, dogs and all. We must close the door to preserve our air."

The dogs bounded indoors as Sorykah broke a sweat dragging the heavy sled over lumps of volcanic slag and wrestling it through the doorway. Shanxi barred the door and squatted beside the sled, peering at the mummy. Rava, a sickly creature the color of old cheese, lay snoring on the sled. Her freckles stood out in stark relief against her clammy skin and her plastic baby face lay submerged in a nest of loose skin and matted red hair.

"What have we here? If you're bringing her to me, you must be desperate. No one travels the waste unless they don't mind dying on the journey." Shanxi peeled back her layers as if unswaddling a fragile newborn. The familiar violet stain had begun to congeal around Rava's eyes, making them appear sunken and hollow.

"Unbind these ropes, while I prepare the treatment." Shanxi vanished behind a curtain of milky plastic strips that concealed an ocean of green. The foggy outlines of nosy dogs blundered through the next room as they investigated the contents of Shanxi's cabinets. She returned with an upright needle in one hand, coiled tubing and a bottle of murky green fluid in the other. Shanxi lit an oil lamp beneath the metal tripod and warming pan that held the IV bottle. She opened Rava's greatcoat, retrieving a slack human arm and rolling up the sleeve to locate a suitable vein. Sorykah turned her face away as Shanxi cleaned Rava's splotchy arm with iodine, maneuvering between the puckered edges of the dry suckers decorating her limbs. Staring at the mossy interior wall, Sorykah was certain that as the needle punctured Rava's skin, she heard a rubbery sort of pop that made her knees tremble. Sorykah scanned the dim, close room for a safe place to rest her eyes; between the bizarre sight of Rava on an IV and dazzling Shanxi, there wasn't much to look at that wouldn't cause an anxious sort of hum in her belly. She felt compelled to make idle chatter to cut the tension.

"What is that you're giving her?"

"Oh, rock of ages, blood of life, with a splash of bat's bile and a wee sprinkle of toad tongue." Shanxi burst into laughter at the sight of Sorykah's dropped jaw. "It's recombinant oenathe sap and fossil water. The oenathe possess amazing regenerative abilities. Like a salamander regrowing its own severed tail, or the earthworm that gains a new head if cut in two."

Shanxi lifted the collar of Rava's gown and ran a finger along a series of flat, closed slits along her collarbone. "Here." She indicated a throbbing pane of thin, crêpey skin at Rava's throat, sliding a fingernail into a faint crevice and raising a purpled flap. "Sensory organs that detect chemical signals and filter nutrients from seawater." Shanxi licked a finger and pressed it into one of the wrinkled suckers on Rava's forearm, which responded by drawing itself around her finger in a horrible embrace as if milking a dry teat for a final drop. Shanxi peeled Rava's thirsting sucker from her finger and massaged the arm, moving away from the IV site to her hand, kneading warm fossil water into Rava's slack muscles.

Shanxi hummed as she worked. A radiant intensity flowed

from her fingertips; tranquility seemed to emanate from her and impart a supernatural glow. Here, perhaps, lay the root of all those pernicious rumors of witchery.

Sorykah felt that she was intruding on a private moment, as if she had pulled back a hospital curtain, interrupting an ill-timed sponge bath in progress. She longed to enter the green room where the dogs frolicked but it would be rude to abandon her charge to this stranger, however capable she might be.

Lifting the muddy hem of Rava's heavy quilted gown, Shanxi warned, "Brace yourself for the grand unveiling. If you haven't a strong stomach, you'd best turn your head."

Sorykah steeled her nerves as Shanxi revealed a rather artificial-looking heap of cold calamari—Rava's eight legs—each the size of Sorykah's own slender thigh, speckled and splattered with fading maroon and spots the color of old blood. Six feet long and strewn with wrinkled white suckers ranging in diameter from craters the size of Sorykah's palm to shallow depressions smaller than a dime, their tips were curled and callused by heavy use.

Sorykah was aware of the extraordinary differences between Rava's physique and a normal human's, but to see her laid out so exposed was a newer sort of horror. The ordinary and the fantastic collided in her brain with sickening force. The room began to reel about her head and Sorykah wondered if she was dreaming.

"The first time is always the worst," Shanxi said mildly. "Once you accept that beings like this exist all around us then you can learn to appreciate what astonishing and wonderful creatures they are."

Something plopped onto Shanxi's foot and she looked down. Wetting the back of the woman's gown was a spill of something black, but neither blood nor bile. Shanxi bent close and sniffed.

"Ink?" She wrinkled her nose and rubbed a bit of it between thumb and forefinger.

"Well, she *is* an octopus," Sorykah said.

"That's a mystery to be solved later." Shanxi covered Rava and turned to Sorykah. "I expect you're rather worn from your journey. Perhaps a hot meal and some oenathe exhalations will refresh you before you tell me why you've come."

Sorykah nodded, afraid to open her mouth lest she scream. She forced herself to slip between the plastic strips into the green room where life throbbed from every surface. Hundreds of plants littered the room, stacked on shelves, hung from beams or crowded onto tables and cabinets, each one dewy and vibrant with large ovoid leaves that glistened as if perspiring. Vines climbed from floor to ceiling, inserting sticky tendrils into grooves and cracks along the rock face and generally running riot. With every movement Sorykah and the dogs made, the glossy runners trembled, reacting to minute variations in the air current and electrical force. Shanxi's proximity aroused the plants to flutter and turn their leaves toward her, moving with the rhythm of Shanxi's breathing as though she and the plants were one.

A vast array of glass containers crowded shelves beside tattered, dog-eared notebooks with tortured spiral bindings, and a table cluttered with sharp blades and liquid-filled jars bearing flimsy, straw-colored seedlings. Its potbelly open and smoking, a small cast iron stove taunted the room with a vague insinuation of heat.

"It's been five years or more since my last guest. It's not my goal to treat the wounded and heal the sick, however often they turn up at my door. One success fosters a legacy, I suppose," Shanxi said. "Three men who came from Bokhara in the northern country, searching for their sister. Matuk's henchman abducted her from a café in Dirinda because she was a nightingale. Not so much an actual bird, but a feathered woman with a beautiful song, prize enough for one such as my brother."

"Matuk! He's the reason I'm here." Mention of her enemy's name stoked the flame of Sorykah's vengeance to leap and burn.

"Ahh." Shanxi rubbed her eyes, suddenly tired and showing her age. "So it continues. We've already determined that you are a woman of unusual character to have braved the waste. Whatever drives you, it is neither lust nor greed. I venture that yours is the quest of ancients. Noble heart, noble steed." The corner of Shanxi's mouth quirked up as she looked at the snoring dogs. "A damsel in distress and no doubt, a rather nasty dragon to slay. Have I got it?"

Shanxi's kindness eroded Sorykah's carefully maintained façade of bravado. Suffused by an intense body-memory of her babes, warm and chubby in her arms, Sorykah bit back her tears.

Shanxi listened with evident horror as Sorykah described the arriving train, empty of her babies, meeting Rava at the Stuck Tongue, and the discovery of her children's abduction and the somatics' meeting. She confessed Pavel's blackmail and her promise to bring Rava to Shanxi in exchange for some hopeful glimmer that the hermit could aid her search for Ayeda and Leander.

"So here I am," she concluded, blowing her nose into the hanky Shanxi handily produced, "at your door and still miles and days away from finding my twins."

The oenathe plants shivered in a flurry of movement, as if shaking their leafy green heads at Sorykah's predicament.

Rising from her seat beside Sorykah, Shanxi frowned at the plants as if to shush them. "Tell me again of the man who stole your children."

"He is some sort of monster. A somatic, but not like the others, he preys on them instead. His own kind! I'm told"—Sorykah choked on the words—"that he hunts down his prizes and takes their heads. Their heads! And my two, led like lambs to slaughter!"

"Meertham!" Shanxi snapped. "He was once a friend, but that child is long gone."

Sorykah's stomach contracted into a tight ball. "Your brother." She covered her mouth with her hand, stuffing back her sobs.

The oenathe shuddered and drew back, lazy tendrils furling into tight, angry fists.

Shanxi turned to Sorykah, her face mottled by furious storm clouds. "Do you know what you ask? Do you understand what you must undertake in order to subdue him and reclaim what's been lost?"

Sorykah, who had a vague idea of the horrors that lay ahead, nodded.

"No," Shanxi said, "I don't think you do." She paced the room, brows knit and muttering.

A rustling from the entryway broke the tension. Both women turned toward the sound, their breath held as they waited, ears straining in the sudden silence.

"The hours will pass quickly now. She will wake before long, and wonder." Meeting Sorykah's gaze, Shanxi paused, one tapered finger tapping her jaw. "Are you familiar with the tale of the Seven Ravens?"

Sorykah was confined in Shanxi's cabin until Shanxi agreed to help her. Impatiently, she shook her head.

"Then it falls upon me to enlighten you. After all, to a starving woman a good story is better than bread and butter." Shanxi rummaged through her cupboards, assembling items on the table as she talked.

"A king and queen had seven sons but they yearned for a daughter. She was born early, and was small and frail, and so the friar urged the king to baptize the baby, should she not outlast the night. The king sent his sons to the well but the boys squabbled over who was to draw up the water and in the heat of their quarrel, they broke the queen's prized pitcher. Too ashamed to return with shards and no water, the boys dallied and their father, fearful that his daughter would die unblessed, cursed his sons. "Dreadful children! How I wish they would all turn to ravens and fly away!"

No sooner had the words left his lips than the boys flew from the ground in a maelstrom of coal-black feathers. The king and queen were devastated when their sons never returned, but their daughter survived to become a shrewd and resourceful young girl. One day, the princess wandered into a deserted wing of the castle where she chanced upon a locked door that she had never seen before. She asked to door to open and admit her, and it swung open on its rusted hinges to reveal a deserted playroom, dusty with neglect. There were seven rocking horses, seven toy swords and shields, and portraits on the wall of the seven black-haired boys who had been her brothers.

"When the princess told her parents of the secret room, her mother wept and her father wrung his hands as he spoke of the wish he'd made in anger on her baptismal day. Though her brothers had been lost for many years, the princess felt that it was her duty to find her brothers and bring them home. She claimed a little gold ring of her mother's as a reminder and then she set off on her journey, taking a loaf of bread, in case she grew hungry, a little jug of water, in case she thirsted, and a little chair, so that she might rest when her feet were too weary to carry her forward. And because she was an artist and her hands never tired, she brought a length of embroidery thread, a needle, and a little pair of scissors, so that she might record along her skirt hem the wondrous things she would see."

Shanxi measured something into a large cloth bag brimming with white grains, threaded a large bone needle with red yarn, and sewed the bag closed.

"She journeyed far and wide, over hill and dale, in sunshine and in rain until she came to the house of the moon. The cold, beautiful moon had a terrible reputation for eating children raw and picking her teeth with their bones." Shanxi looked up from her task and winked.

"So the girl did not venture there. She continued to the house of the sun, a fierce and temperamental ruler. Too busy brooding into his mirror of polished bronze to turn away and greet his guest, the sun muttered and moaned, his loud, low voice pealing through the golden halls of his mountaintop tower like a stricken iron bell. Taking a bit of bread and a sip of water, the princess sat upon the ground, resting her little head on the cane seat of her chair. While she slept, the kind stars, who had watched over her throughout her difficult journey, floated down from the sky and lifted her up, carrying her in arms of mist and starlight to the base of the Glass Mountains.

"When the princess opened her eyes, she was delighted to find herself before a sturdy door set in the mossy mountainside. However, the door was shut fast, and all her efforts could not budge it. 'If only there was a keyhole, that I might peep through,' she sighed, 'to see what is on the other side.' She curtsied and inquired 'Little door, won't you let me see in?' The breeze blew and ruffled the vines, parting them to reveal a keyhole. The princess put her eye to the keyhole and saw a long table, spread with a fantastic array of delectables. She pushed her nose against the keyhole and smelled the steaming food, freshly buttered and salted and waiting to be eaten. She stuck her tongue through the keyhole and tasted something like sadness and she said, 'I think men live here, for there is sorrow in the face of bounty.'

"As the princess pressed her ear to the keyhole, she heard the raven's rough song. Now, a lock will not turn without a key and having no key, the princess took her embroidery scissors, cut off her little finger, and used it to pick the lock. When the catch sprang free, she took her thread, sewed her finger back on, and walked into the most splendid hall she had ever seen. The table was laid with seven golden plates and seven goblets brimmed with ruby wine. The vast corridor rustled with the beat of approaching wings, stirring the air and lifting the hair from the princess's neck.

"Faint calls grew louder and raucous caws rang down the corridor, shaking dust from the eaves. The princess's resolute heart grew fearful, and she ducked behind a pillar, but not before slipping her mother's gold ring into the last and littlest goblet. With wings that beat like thunder, seven enormous ravens flew into the hall. One by one, they alighted at the table and as their beaks pecked at the food, their feathers fell and littered the floor, and the birds became men again.

"Delighted to see the brothers she recognized from the portraits, she would have revealed herself, but just as she was about to step forward, something about the tone of her brothers' speech stayed her. Each in turn complained bitterly about his lot and set afresh to cursing the sister whose birth had ruined them. All except the last and smallest, who plucked the feathers from his arms before lifting the goblet to his lips.

"'Dear brothers,' he began, 'we have grown old before our time while trapped in these bodies. It's clear that our human selves diminish at the rate of ravens, and I fear that we are not long for this world.' The brothers grumbled in agreement.

"'Year after year, I have listened to you heap curses upon the head of our sister, while you have pickled yourselves in resentment. Grave dust gathers on our wings! I for one, have no wish to die with a broken heart. If our sister were here now, I would ask her forgiveness, so that my passing would not be tainted by sorrow and anger.' He pulled a golden ring from his mouth, holding it to the light for the others to see.

"'This is a message. Now, meet the messenger.' He beckoned his sister from her hiding place, where her red embroidered hem had given her away. She revealed herself, meeting her brothers for the first time.

"Now," Shanxi said, clipping leaves from her horrified oenathe, "what do you suppose happened? The possible endings to this tale are many and encompass the range of human response. Do the brothers forgive their sister, emerge from the constraining cocoon of their bitterness, and seize their redemption? Do they allow their resentment to fester inside them like a cancer? Are they grateful, impartial, or vengeful?"

Sorykah shrugged; was the question actual or rhetorical? Rhetorical, she decided, as Shanxi continued: "Imagine that the brothers, consumed with vengeance, rise up as one body to strike down their sister. The curse remains and they wither and die with black hearts. Should they choose to do nothing? They can remain as birds, living shadows in their mountain home, or return to their parents and reclaim what is left of their royalty. Perhaps they will come to forgiveness; perhaps the curse will weaken and lose power with time. The last feather will drop. Yet, having not embraced forgiveness"—here Shanxi looked at Sorykah with a single raised eyebrow—"their spirits remain polluted by a corrosive anger. Now," she said, stuffing a small fabric sachet with spoonfuls of dried herbs, "there is a third ending to the story. Can you guess what it is?"

"Complete and immediate forgiveness. The brothers embrace their sister, welcome her, their feathers drop out, the curse is lifted, and the mountain cracks open while rays of sunshine pour down from the heavens, illuminating the happy scene," Sorykah said.

If Shanxi caught her sarcasm, she chose to ignore it. "Yes, but with less drama. All great prophets counsel compassion, the abandonment of vendetta."

Sorykah scowled, perplexed by the story's odd turn. "And you? What would you counsel?"

Shanxi stared at Sorykah with an uncomfortable intensity. "Plunging a sword into your enemy's heart is a sort of suicide. You kill part of yourself when you kill another."

"However, there is also a certain nobility to killing an enemy," Sorykah countered. "Many cultures believe that you absorb your enemy's strength when you kill him, that his powers transfer to you."

It was Shanxi's turn to frown. "A forced and unwelcome death is never justified."

"Unless it has been earned," Sorykah retorted. She sensed coercion into a pact that she was unwilling to make. "Sometimes the crime warrants a death sentence!"

"Such as the theft of innocents? The abduction of your children? Be warned: Matuk will not suffer your trespass."

"Why do you evade me?" Sorykah's voice was so shrill it pained Shanxi's ears.

"Please," she hissed, "lower your voice. You'll frighten the children." The oenathe recoiled from the stranger's anger, a red surge pulsing through the air, singeing their tender leaves. Shanxi busied herself with the task at hand, tucking harvested oenathe leaves between the wooden rollers of a small press and turning the crank to extract their precious sap. A deliberate and lengthy pause allowed the oenathe's soporific fumes to dull and disperse her visitor's venom, leaving her again placid and mild after her brief outburst. Swinging red thread through the lip of a fabric bag and cinching it tight, Shanxi intoned, "This is mealie, a grain that grows wild in the Erun. Well, it was once wild but has been cultivated now and thrives in hidden plots, pocketed within the woods' fringe where the beast is too shy to venture."

Sorykah gaped at her, too astonished by the casual brush-off to respond.

"I've given you twenty pounds. It ought to last for weeks, if you're frugal. The wonderful thing about mealie," Shanxi continued, assembling a glass tumbler and screwing on a metal lid and funnel and setting it aside, "is that you only need a couple spoonfuls and a cup of water to make a meal. No heat required."

Shanxi set out a shallow dish and poured an inch of water from a pitcher. With a flourish, she scooped two teaspoons of mealie from a tin and sprinkled it into the bowl. The grain puffed and swelled, rising up like milk froth, settling into a heaping helping of something that resembled porridge.

"Mealie is manna for us outlaws. Complex sugars, high-quality protein equal to its weight in meat, and enough fat and vitamins to prevent the wasting disease that strikes so many in the Sigue. The taste is a bit like mashed turnips, so I've prepared yours with a pinch of salted herbs. I'm quite sure you'll like it."

"Answer my question," Sorykah pressed, her rage having dwindled under the oenathe's influence.

"I cannot hand him to you, heart in hand and awaiting his death. He's my brother, you must understand." Shanxi tipped her head, a dewy tulip upon its frail stem and just as pretty.

"And he has my children," Sorykah asserted, though she quailed inside.

"Are we to haggle over whose life has the greater worth?" Shanxi asked.

"No need," Sorykah said. "The answer is water-clear. I will find your brother and take my children back, and slice off his foul head, if necessary." Sorykah fondled the Magar sword sheathed in her belt, its beautiful blade thirsting beneath her hand.

As the yolk within the egg, the secret disguised itself within the story of the Seven Ravens. Sorykah did not yet realize that Shanxi had nothing left to give.

"Will you help me, or hinder me?" Sorykah folded her arms over her chest.

"I can tell you the way, but I cannot instruct you in his defeat." Shanxi's words were weary. "My Matuk always was a cunning one. He's managed to live some forty years in secrecy, hidden from the eyes of the world. He'll have disguised himself well. You'll have to work hard to find him. Are you prepared for that?"

"Of course!"

"All right then, darling, I wish you every lucky spell in the book." Shanxi pulled her arms around herself, staring hard at Sorykah. "The journey for you will begin the same as all the others. Head north across the waste to the floe fields. You'll have to jump the floes to reach the mainland on the other side. It won't be easy, with dogs for company." Shanxi looked at the sleeping dogs and licked her lips. "Are you taking them along?" she inquired with forced neutrality.

Sorykah nodded.

"A shame, really," Shanxi said. "They'd make such fine pets." She continued, "If your children survived Meertham's awkward care, misfortunes await them at my brother's manor. I am not persuaded that Matuk tortures or kills his captives, but the evidence seems to convict him of it."

Sorykah sucked in her breath. Blood roared in her ears.

"Matuk is a father himself; perhaps he will have compassion for two helpless babes." Shanxi closed her eyes in a moment of silent prayer, then opened them and smiled at Sorykah. "I'm sure you will find them. When you make the mainland, follow the coast and head east. It's a long way to the Bay of Sorrows but you'll be close when you hit the flower fields that thrive between the Erun and rocky beaches. From there you'll be able to see the Isle of Mourning where Matuk's son Chen resides with his coterie of pleasure seekers. It is there you must first venture. Now, my sweet, there's a long night ahead that wants filling with stories. Let's get you all fed and bedded down. Death may deal its hand in our game and you'll want to be prepared." Shanxi stepped into the gated enclosure behind her house to light the fire pit and prepare a supper for the dogs.

Shanxi would have liked to keep Sorykah's dogs. They'd be delicious breaded and fried with a little salted mealie on the side, but she'd have to do the butchering herself and she wasn't hungry enough for it. They were safe, for the moment.

As she fed the fire, Shanxi recalled another wanderer some twelve years gone. That fellow had been searching for his fiancée—a rarity of gossamer fur who came from the foxes and had a fine white-tipped tail—snatched from the streets of Finn Town in crass daylight, crammed into a stuff-sack, and borne away by a hideous creature whose blunted tusks brushed his massive chest.

Shanxi knew he would never find her, but she gave him mealie and dried, shed oenathe leaves called lost souls to replenish his own and pointed him toward the floe fields and the mainland beyond. She warned him of the dangers and watched him depart on his mission through a chink in the shuttered window. Now it was certain that he lay beneath the snow, long dead and preserved somewhere on the waste, half eaten on the Southern Sea floor or in a pile of gnawed bones deep in the Erun Forest.

Maybe this one would earn a different fate. While destiny was a false idol that pragmatic Shanxi would not court, she did trust the energetic cycle of things and creatures, their impulsive, electrical shift and flow and the existence of something loosely defined as "comeuppance." If she was certain about anything in this life, it was that her brother Matuk had earned a hefty helping of his retaliatory due. Shanxi feared her own imminent day of reckoning; the boundaries of the enchanted circle of safety she and Matuk had magicked around themselves such long years ago were finally losing their power.

She was old. Though the lines on her face whispered few of her years' many secrets, she had lived three lifetimes in the space of one. Was she one hundred and ten? Twenty perhaps?

She remembered Oman, the original Lost Man and the Beginning of the End. Oman's change was the first explosion, the bullet that zinged through the stratosphere and ricocheted round the globe.

Was that when Matuk had cracked? No; he had been quite sane back then. He had a new, young wife and earned a baron's living. The backs of the poor shored up his mighty empire. In itself, that wasn't a crime. Matuk's offenses would eventually be far, far worse.

Matuk was indifferent to the somatics' plight. Desperate to harness his power as a wealthy mogul and mouthpiece, countless organizations approached him, pleading for donations or the use of idle and abandoned buildings to convert into hospitals or safe houses, but her Matuk was no bandwagoneer. Shanxi's brother considered himself above the petty plagues of his inferiors, imagined himself untouchable, safe up there on his cloud of riches.

His first wife, Tirai, was quite sweet. Shy and small, she had tiny, childlike hands, a doll's teeth, and a shining waterfall of glorious auburn hair. Matuk had little impulse toward humanitarianism. He rescued Tirai from poverty because of an unquenchable desire to possess her and keep her from all others. Shanxi suspected Matuk had found Tirai working in a brothel but she'd never had the nerve to ask. Despite her heady intelligence and laissez-faire manner, Shanxi was quite old-fashioned. By the time Tirai came along, Shanxi was already nearing sixty, prim and virginal, with the unbroken seal and high breasts of a young girl.

Tirai. Time's tides had not washed away Shanxi's sorrow or dulled the sting of the Little One's death. She could cast her eyes from pain, in fact had done so many times, numbing herself to the searing scrutiny she suffered as Matuk's sister, guardian, and champion. They were blood. She'd indulged his terrible whims like any cosseting nanny with a beloved, spoiled, only child. In the end, Matuk was only her half brother and Chen the son of Matuk's third wife. Their family ties were fragile.

No one loved Tirai more than she, and none had missed her more. Tirai's lips . . . Tirai's touch upon the pristine sanctuary of Shanxi's hallowed skin. Her heart bled afresh for her loss.

Matuk had burned down her house as punishment for her transgression. Had held a lit candle to the curtains, watched with terrible calm as the fire took hold and ate its way through the antique lace handmade by their shared grandmother. Her oenathe were mere seedlings then. The first family of sentient plants had been burned alive, leaves twisting in shock and crisping into flames. Shanxi had grabbed a beaker of grafted stems, her notebooks, and her pollination tray and run for the door, leaving Matuk behind, uncaring whether he lived or died.

However, Matuk had grand plans and would not let himself perish so quickly and so foolishly. Shanxi did not witness her brother's long-simmering wrath spill out to consume everything it touched, as cleansing and obliterating as the fire that destroyed Shanxi's home. Tirai was not seen again after that day.

Meertham found her crumpled carcass dismembered and stuffed into a refuse barrel on the construction site of Matuk's unfinished Quartz Tower, a pillar of luxe office and residential suites in Neubonne. It was Meertham who tracked down Shanxi, who had fled to the waste and set up housekeeping within the green ring. She'd selected the safest location to raise her plants, some inhuman terrain where no one would harm them.

Matuk could be lazy; Shanxi knew he wouldn't bother to chase after her, though his tusked spy knew everything. He appeared at her door weeks after the fire to unload fabric bolts and a sewing kit with red embroidery thread and solid gold needles—Matuk's apology.

After that first visit, he materialized every few months with his treasure-laden sleigh to buy her silence and lull her into complacency. Having abandoned Tirai and living in self-imposed isolation, Shanxi wallowed in guilt, thinking her suffering just penance for having angered her brother. Once, Shanxi made the mistake of asking after her lost love. Meertham had just unloaded his sledge and was preparing to leave. Unease and lingering worry left Shanxi desperate for news of her girl. Yanking Meertham's sleeve, a little appalled by the sheer size of him, filling up the doorway as he forced himself beneath the low lintel, she asked, "What of Tirai? Is she well?"

Meertham spoke with difficulty, the words fighting themselves in an effort to escape his clumsy, whiskered lips. "Forget Tirai."

Something in his tortured stare turned Shanxi's blood to ice water and put out all her fires. She sank to her knees and watched him trudge over the rocks and snow until she could see him no longer.

In her grief, she had closed her ears to the venomous rumors and escalating accounts of disappearances, torture, and body parts discovered by hunters in the Erun Forest. The pilgrims who arrived seeking news of missing loved ones brought stories of a new menace in the Great Wood, a beast so cunning and bloodthirsty that the forest itself had emptied, all the birds and mini-beasties having run away. The rumors were true then; Tirai's daughter had suffered the Change. Father and daughter were both crazed with lusts for flesh, stripped like soft meat from soup bones, and power, wielded like a sword, terrorizing the innocents in their path.

Still she did nothing. Drowned herself in research. Tinkered with genomes and DNA, spliced, grafted, and crossbred to her heart's content, burying her guilt beneath weighty stacks of bound paper, cluttered with her meticulous handwritten notes. She helped no one but herself and she was a coward, in the end.

The past fell away, discarded like a favored lover grown tiresome.

Judgment knocked; it was time to atone for her sins. Shanxi had ladled out so much forgiveness over the years—she now found that she had not a drop of it left. Matuk would have to suffer as she had done. She would protect him no longer.

10

MEANWHILE, BACK AT THE MANSE . . .

THERE WAS SOMETHING about this new woman in the Master's chamber that Dunya couldn't pin down and it bothered her. Lost in her thoughts, she neglected to skip the fourteenth step on the tower stairs, the one with the inward-sloping marble slab, and she stumbled, nearly dropping the tea tray. Righting a tipped china sugar bowl, Dunya blew away the few loose grains of sugar. A dirty tea service fouled by splashes and stray crumbs would earn her a sound cuff on her floppy brown ears. For all his love of blood sports and splatter, the Master was an exacting, tidy man.

Melancholy notes drifted down from the Master's library and filled the spiraling stairwell. The woman would be at the piano then, playing for the Master until he commanded her to cease. It could drag on for hours. Even with her limited repertoire, he would force her to play until he wearied and banished her or slumped sleeping in his wingback before the fire, his small feet pointed toward the grate to soak up the hearthstones' radiant warmth.

Dunya loped past the armory with its racks of antique gunnery, the executioner's double-edged axe, and waiting stakes, sharpened pikes cured by the Gatekeeper, their high points blackened by smoke. She habitually averted her eyes from the path (the tread-worn groove like a river set in stone) that traced the Master's midnight walk from the high tower chamber to the armory and then, weapon-weighted, his determined parade toward the dungeons and some pathetic captive's doom. Plodding upstairs, Dunya passed the wives' chamber, an opulent prison of sky blue brocade and gaudy gilt furnishings where shelves of dusty, dog-eared romance novels lined the marble walls—a lady bird's coldly beautiful cage. Uppermost in the tower was the Master's suite, where the Collector formulated his lofty ideas and their manifold, terrible executions. Years' worth of collected medical journals and news clippings crowded the cobwebbed library. Tall, narrow windows that offered slivered glimpses of the starkly pitched Glass Mountains and quivering Erun treetops ringed the old man's sitting room and personal chamber—a dim and dreary place, its walls and windows black-draped to repel the light and counter his plaguing insomnia.

She hurried, not wishing to leave the babes too long. The kitchen door was locked fast, the sturdy iron key hung heavy on its ribbon between her breasts, and the twins slept snug in the sewing basket. Still, no telling when they might wake and set to squalling.

She ticked off her checklist—dungeons in lockdown, fire banked behind the grate, kettle set back on the stove, and the windows barred against Gatekeeper. He wouldn't venture into the manor but what prevented his breaking a window and nicking a handy human snack from an unattended kitchen?

Pray the Master didn't keep her. Now that he had a captive audience in the piano player, he was less inclined to burden Dunya with his ramblings. She paused at the top of the stairs, enjoying the rarity of music, even if flowing like a sluggish stream. Dunya smoothed her apron and cap, brushing a hand across her fuzzy face to calm any rogue hairs. Adopting a careful mask of calm, Dunya knocked once to announce herself, then pushed through the door.

The music faltered as the pianist swiveled to stare at Dunya, beseeching plain in her pale, terrified eyes.

"Master." Dunya addressed the shadowed figure in the wing-back chair.

A small hand, gone bony and liver-spotted, gestured her toward windows filled with waning lilac light. She set her tray on the table, conscious of the pianist's eyes on the sweet biscuits and hot tea. Dunya's hackles prickled as she poured a single cup of tea, balanced two biscuits on the saucer, and carried it to the Master. The pianist swallowed; Dunya could hear that her throat was dry. How long had she been playing?

The strong, smoky fragrance of black tea filled the air. Dunya waited as her employer crunched his way through the biscuits, dunking them in his tea and slurping at the crumbling treats. Matuk grunted with sharp irritation and the reluctant pianist turned toward her instrument, fumbling for her place in the interrupted song, then finding it and staggering ahead.

Matuk extended the emptied teacup and Dunya refilled it, hoping he would not demolish the entire pot so she could leave a bit of something for the woman on her way back to the kitchen. The poor thing was at his mercy and dependent on Dunya's charity for her sustenance. Dunya wished she could signal her somehow, reassure her that she would sneak the leftovers to her, but alas, she could do no such thing. It was Dunya's duty to remain stone-faced and impartial, to harbor silence like a vast and empty ship anchored amidst still waters. She could not risk any allegiances lest she imperil herself and the children by provoking the Master's capricious temper.

Matuk's eyes closed. The cup slipped from his hand and bounced against the rug. Dunya retrieved it and backed from the room to the diminishing strains of piano song. There were two more biscuits and a third of a pot of cold tea for the pianist, which

Dunya left in her room. There wasn't any need to worry now; the Master would never eat leftovers or dine from the same dishes in a single day, so he wouldn't notice what was missing. After Dunya fed the dungeon dwellers, she could sneak the woman food wrapped in wild cabbage or dandelion leaves to disguise any evidence of their treachery.

People, somatics . . . *bodies* came and went, arriving in Meertham's stuff-sack and exiting by the charnel house doors. The appearance of another stranger wasn't unusual. The Master had made efforts to replace his first wife, Tirai, for years, installing women one after another in the powder blue chamber. One by one they disappeared, nameless and faceless, Bluebeard's silent succession of false wives.

Back at the kitchens, Dunya freed the lock and went to the sewing basket where the twins had just begun to stir and fuss.

"Now, now, wee ones, what's all the ruckus?" A leaking diaper had saturated the blanket beneath the boy and she lifted him out, spreading a clean tea towel on the table before laying him down.

"Let's get ye out of these wet clothes, then." Dunya chucked the baby's chin and he rewarded her with a sleepy smile. His progress pleased her. After several frightening days of struggle as she searched for something that he would eat, Meertham had saved the day, returning to the manor carrying a fat, short-legged nanny goat, her overfull udder painfully distended. Dunya had been giddy with relief, confident, as she boiled and strained the goat's milk, that her feeding problems were solved. The girl had taken the milk without hesitation, drinking from a cup Dunya held to her lips and smacking with satisfaction. The boy had drunk, too, but his pleasure was broken by the sudden blisters that welled on his tongue and arms.

Wisely, Dunya had withheld any further milk, feeding him a combination of mealie, water, and animal fat stewed into a loose gruel. It wasn't the most appetizing meal, but he ate it and thrived. Now he and his sister were both round and sparkle-eyed.

The manor's unforgiving atmosphere hadn't yet quashed their spirits.

Preoccupied with his pianist and his "work," the Master hadn't summoned the children or inquired about them after his initial assessment. Dunya prayed that he would forget them. Nothing had yet marked them as "other" and as long as they remained ordinary, uninteresting babies, they might have a slim chance of being rejected as unfit for experimentation and released from their obligation as test subjects.

Dunya grinned as she undressed the baby boy, patting his downy, padded shoulders and the belly that sagged over his cloth diaper.

"That's right, me bird. There's nothing special about ye at all. Ye're just a regular little boy." He gazed at her through long black lashes as she unpinned his diaper and laid him bare.

"Oh dear," Dunya breathed, collapsing against the table. "Ye've gone and done it now," she whispered to the child.

Blessed Jerusha, protect me! Just a bit quieter now, soft . . . soft . . . ease off, that's it. Holy Mother, I've done it. My fingers are killing me! Listen to them crack!

The pianist lifted her hands from the yellowed ivory keys, not daring to breathe as she slid from the bench amidst the nerve-racking fury of rustling, antique skirts the Collector had forced upon her. Taffeta and net crinolines crinkled and crackled, her movements loud enough to wake the dead, never mind the slight, rather diminished man keeping her captive. She paused, the breath penned in her throat, her heart leaping as she measured the careful rhythm of the sleeping man's snores. She'd played for hours, sitting on the hard bench with an aching back and empty gut, desperate for relief. The furry housekeeper (yet another nightmare in a growing litany of horrors) with her long, protracted jaw and gleaming canines brought biscuits and tea (sedative-laced, she hoped) and at last, her watchful guardian slept.

Creeping to the door, she sensed freedom within her grasp. The tower itself was locked, its narrow windows barred. Beyond them stretched a wide, empty meadow. If she managed to escape, her fleeing figure would contrast against the yellow grass, a flaming beacon, a soft and screaming target. If she made it to the woods, she would have to contend with another sort of terror before finding her way home.

How many nights had she been awakened by the tortured, ruinous bellows echoing in the wood? That ringing, knife-sharp scream sliced her open and laid bare the worst sort of terror—fear of the unknown.

Nels crept down the tower's slippery stairs to the wives' chamber with its overwrought gilded cupids and rigor-glazed flowers, stiff with gold leafing and frosted with dust. Nels still fought in vain to escape the dreadful manor. She prowled through her waking moments searching for some hidden trapdoor in the floor, a forgotten knife, a loose brick, or crumbling, rusted lock. She'd crept the perimeter of the room, worming her fingers into all the cracks, seeking to pry free a stone or plank of wood and take her chances in the wild, but the tightly sealed tower was impermeable both inside and out.

The tea tray awaited her attentions. Giddy with hunger and delight, Nels drank straight from the spout. Sedative or no, the cold and bitter tea was delicious in her dry mouth. Perched on the edge of the tented bed with its faded linens and creaking springs, Nels devoured the biscuits, which pinged in her empty stomach as if she had thrown two pebbles down an empty well. She ran her hands over her ribs, prominent now beneath her once-plump skin, and wondered how much longer she had to live.

Her dreams used to be prayers to the beloved goddess Jerusha. Now her dreamtime visions were torments of red berries and cream, honeyed baby carrots, and steaming bread loaves dripping with salted butter. The trauma of her abduction had capsized her buoyant optimism. Though she'd managed to push the memories away during her waking hours, restless ghosts rose from their graveyard to haunt Nels's dreams. The memories became confused, clashed with one another, melded with motion picture images and fairy tale snippets to form a single, seamless reel, her nightmare unfolding and replaying throughout the hours of her tortured sleep.

It had happened on a bright afternoon when the air was alive with winter smells of crisp fallen leaves and snowmelt. A hideous creature (she couldn't think of it as a man) with enormous tusks and thickened, gritty skin materialized in the street beside her in an open manhole, his sandpapery hands clasping her calves and pulling her down against his rock-hard muscled bulk, smothering her mouth, bittersweet fumes stealing her wakefulness.

Her last memory before coming to in the blue tower room was of the creature's tiny, dark, impassive eyes, and the fleeting predatory glint revealed as he glanced up at the baby carriage visible just beyond the pit's edge. Flung from the light into a shadowy corner, fighting against the effects of the drug he'd subdued her with, she saw the creature reach for the carriage, a large, filthy bag clenched in his massive hand. Enormous rough fingers closed around the pram's frame, just as the darkness closed in over Nels's head and then a gap in time, the blue room, and Him.

What had become of gentle Sorykah's charming twins? Nels presumed the very worst. In the most trying circumstances, she would have remained cheerful despite her dread, but the things she'd witnessed in this horrible place soon dampened any fledgling flicker of hope. Nels shook her corn silk head in despair, fishing for the rosary she wore beneath the ancient dress. Counting her beads as she prayed, she searched her soul to find Jerusha, the Blessed Virgin, and once again request her help.

11

BRAVING THE WASTE

SHANXI'S WORDS ECHOED in Sorykah's head: "The way is hard and the mountain steep for she who dies in her sleep." Was it intended to serve as a warning or was it mere conjecture? Sorykah left the green ring to face a broad ridge of imposing hills, the volcano's diminishing spine. Brittle black magma crumbled and peeled beneath her boots.

Honeycomb snow burst beneath her cleats. A series of miniature explosions loosed upon the subarctic terrain and deafening in their intensity, they made an arduous journey even more difficult. Focused on keeping her pace and balance on the uneven ground, she began to lose track of time. Sorykah found herself slipping into daydreams so realistic and intense that when she stumbled into an air pocket and sank knee deep in the snow, she was astonished to discover herself on the waste and not aboard the *Nimbus,* strapped to her bunk and sleeping.

Sorykah rubbed strained eyes and blinked against the glare.

Glittering light haloed tall snow formations cresting a distant ridge. The sun parted thick, opaque clouds and burned its mark upon the ground before retreating. White plains rolled by and vanished in the distance. It seemed that she had stumbled over the same snowy clump, passed beneath the same shapeless cloud yet again. Little points of light advanced and receded, and it appeared that the earth itself was racing away from her even when she stood still. The sky became snowy ground; the world inverted and went topsy-turvy. The Company called it a whiteout, a perceptive condition that happened when the senses failed to communicate with one another, as the brain refused the eye's messages of endless sameness. People had wandered into the waste and died this way, becoming ghosts in a purgatory of clouds.

Shanxi advised keeping the volcano behind her but Sorykah could venture off course and still feel that old Devil breathing down her neck. Better to rely on technology than fancy at a time like this.

Sorykah halted the team, who sat panting, frozen saliva lining their jaws like jingle bells. She had to remove the musher's fur mitten to get her gloved hand inside the kit bag and fish out her compass. The cold made her hands burn with impending frostbite. Nothing would have felt better than to pitch her tent, crawl inside with the dogs, and curl up in a ball. She would leave the outside world behind, forget the urgency of her mission, and let her mind float free in a silver fog, all cares abandoned.

Ayeda's face swam into view, her clear gray gaze crinkling in laughter. Sorykah closed her eyes and could smell the fresh strawberry scent of Leander's downy head, the lanugo tickling her lips as she kissed his furry forehead. "Baby monkey," she whispered as tepid tears stung her eyes.

Sagging against the sled, she gave in to emotion and sobbed briefly, letting the grief swell to its full fury before it ebbed away. Wiping her face, she raised Shanxi's compass, finding true north.

Somewhere ahead, the Sigue Sea and mainland waited beyond the veiled horizon.

Shanxi had assured her that it was a two-day journey to the ice shelf edging the floe fields on the Sigue's north shore, and she was hopeful that she'd ventured at least a third of the distance by the time the weak sun began to pale. Twilight stole down from the sky, smothering her with milky blue kisses. She had driven herself past the point of exhaustion and was now running on pure adrenaline. She would burn out if she didn't recharge.

The tent setup went a bit more smoothly now that she was familiar with the equipment and soon both she and the dogs were tucked inside, eating a crude supper. The pungent odor of horse meat mixed with butter bars and wet-furred, hardworking dog bodies was overpowering, but it was far too dangerous for Sorykah to open the tent flap for fresh air. She wasn't going to be cocky and foolish now, just when she was starting to get the hang of things. She removed the samilkâ and tucked it beneath the fur where it would be out of the dogs' sight. They had a fondness for the stinky thing and she'd had to beat them back once or twice, jerking dangling seal-gut ties from their jaws.

Night closed in, black and oppressive. If not for the darkness pressing down on her, she might evaporate and be tossed away like the blowing snow that skittered across the ice. She felt weightless without her children, as though she had lost mass and could now defy gravity. Reclining on the fur with the dogs clustered around her, Sorykah recalled the heavy solidity of her belly when the twins somersaulted in her womb, pushing off from her sides and stretching out short limbs. Her thoughts tumbled free but not before her baby memories triggered her milk reflex. Her breasts swelled and tingled and she sighed to think of the wasted milk leaking inside her thermosuit.

It was hard not to anticipate the worst—that she would arrive too late or fail altogether. She would not dwell on cruelly tantalizing what-ifs as long as there were sunnier possibilities. Sleep was a better companion than the malingering death waiting to ambush her round every corner, and so she surrendered to its charms.

Kika leapt to her feet growling, roused from slumber by the strong and distinctive odor of bear. There were no viewing panes in the tent, but she smelled its ursine musk as it prowled the perimeter of the tent, investigating the strange amber-colored bubble. Trained from birth to serve and protect her driver, Kika's first instinct was to raise the alarm and marshal the rest of her team against the interloper. She barked, alerting the other dogs as her teeth strained for a bite of that good meat just beyond her reach. The team scrambled up from its cozy pile as one body, hackles raised and barking like mad. Sorykah jumped up amidst a panicked mêlée, smashing into the tent roof and rubbing bleary eyes. The dogs clustered near the flap, pawing at the zipper in their eagerness to get outside.

"Okay! All right! You can go!" She lurched forward, tripped by a capering wheel dog, and fell against the tent, going down in a sea of flying dog fur.

"Get off, beasts," she snarled, desiring nothing more than a few more minutes of warmth before she had to face the day. As soon as the flap was half drawn, the dogs forced their way through the opening, dragging their bodies out onto the snow and clogging the zipper's teeth with their long hair. Dogs barked and growled, a sound like motorcycle engines revving in concert, punctuated by a fierce rumbling roar that rolled out and shook the very ground, igniting raw fear in Sorykah's heart and turning her bowels to jelly. A furry body crashed into the tent, capsizing its poles. Sorykah groped beneath the fabric heaped around her head, searching for the flap. She found an opening and thrust her head into the stunning cold. A bear's black-rimmed maw gaped three feet from her face, radiating hot, foul breath and shaking its massive head. Sticky saliva threads frothed over its teeth. His small black eyes dulled by exhaustion and starvation, the bear lunged toward the nearest dog, swiping a snow-clotted paw at its head and scratching it across the muzzle. The injured dog yelped and danced away while the others careened in mounting frenzy, snapping and growling, leaping at the bear to drive it back from the tent.

Crazed by the smell of blood and maddened by hunger, the bear lurched forward, ignoring the dogs snapping at its flanks as it closed in on its chosen prey. Blood dripped from the wheel dog's slashed nose and froze upon the snow. Sorykah watched in horror as the animal lunged with fatal purpose, striking the injured dog and knocking it to the ground. The bear attacked, tearing open the wheel dog's throat, jamming its muzzle into the warm cavity and lapping at the blood.

Sorykah stood fear-frozen, her fingers knotted in the sled lacings, watching a bear eat her dog. There were no large animals of any kind on the Sigue. Sorykah surmised that it had wandered over from the mainland, perhaps chasing a seal, become trapped on a piece of ice in the floe fields, and traveled on the current to the Sigue, where it had wandered for days or weeks, cold and starving.

At the rate it was tearing into the dead dog, there would soon be nothing left but bones. Sorykah could count the ribs lining the bear's shaggy side and she felt a moment's compassion for the poor creature; her dog had staved off its inevitable death for a day or two, but still, the end would come, slow and painful.

She gawked at the gut pile steaming on the snow and the emaciated bear gnawing muscle and tendon free and knew she would lose her whole team to this glutton.

Sorykah ducked into the tent, snatched on the overripe samilkâ, and ripped up the tent stakes, her arms strengthened by fear. There was no time to dismantle it. She had to get the dogs on their lines and move, fast.

"Line up!" she hissed, trying to bundle the tent and secure it with rope while wrangling the nearest dog into its harness.

One of the dogs lunged at the bear, chomping into its side and coming up with nothing but a mouthful of fur.

"Dammit, get over here!" Sorykah would leave him behind if he didn't fall into line. With trembling fingers, she latched the dogs into position accompanied by a sound of cracking bones and a very hungry bear enjoying its meal.

Her cold fingers could barely grip the lines. Her hands shook as she clipped, lashed, and tied as quickly as possible, cringing at every nauseating crunch as the bear polished off its appetizer. There was a hole in the team from the missing wheel dog. No time to try to rearrange them; they would have to work around it.

She slammed her bag onto her back and screamed "Hike!" running behind the sled to give the dogs a better start. Once they were in stride, she jumped the runners, yelling at the dogs to go faster, faster. They needed little encouragement. Spurred by excitement, the team raced over the snow-packed ground, barreling into the white horizon.

Certain she could feel the bear's hot breath on her neck, Sorykah whipped around, her eye drawn to the killer yards behind them. The bear had finished eating and pawed the carcass, howling with grief, his hunger unsatisfied.

He raised his head and scanned the area, searching for the second course now beating a hasty retreat. Putting power into his stride, the animal shook its blood-soaked muzzle, spraying droplets of rosy saliva in an arc over the snow as he charged them.

"Hike! Hike!" Sorykah screamed, clinging to the precarious sled as it skated over the snow.

Determined to survive, the dogs raced away from their enemy. Their best hope was their solid lead and the possibility of outrunning the bear lumbering after them. Soon the dogs would tire; she had pushed them too hard on empty bellies. Even her own legs were quivering, her grip on the driving bow weakening.

The bear slowed and released his quarry, lurching as if drunk and bellowing woefully before tipping over into the snow, exhausted, engorged, or dead. Sorykah sagged with relief, her shoulders drooping as she prepared to slow the team. Suddenly, she flew through the air, landing with a whump and a crunch in an ice-encrusted shallow. She tumbled over, wiping snow from her face and trying to catch her breath. The overturned sled lay fifteen feet away, the team tangled in their lines and struggling to free themselves from their strangling grip. Panting and restless, the dogs whined and clawed the ice in a desperate instinctual urge to escape the spreading red pool beneath the sled.

Sorykah struggled across the choppy plain, tripping over chunks of rock-hard ice and cracks deep enough to swallow a leg. Panic surged through her at the sight of blood, stark against the white. She reached the sled and heaved, tugging it upright, her muscles screaming protest.

Her right swing dog, Kite, Kika's sturdy second-in-command, lay twitching in the snow, his luxurious fur matted with guck.

Sorykah dropped to her knees, sobbing. "What happened to you? Where are you hurt?" She pulled off her gloves with her teeth and ran her hands over his sides, searching for the source of the bleeding.

His ribs were cracked and spongy beneath her hand. Perhaps the weight of the falling sled had broken them and punctured a lung. She slid her fingers through his fur, keeping her shock at bay with a calculated analysis of his wounds. "Easy now," she murmured. "Hey boy, hey Kite, take it easy. I'm going to slide my hands beneath you and see if we can find what's hurting you." Kite's glassy eyes rolled back in his head. He was dying and she could do nothing.

His warm blood melted the snow, soaking her cuffs with pinkening water as she reached beneath him and grasped the stout wooden handle of the umalå buried between his ribs. She recalled tucking the tool between the loose bindings of the sled as they fled the rampaging bear.

"Poor, poor boy," Sorykah murmured, working it free. Fresh blood pulsed from the wound, slowing as his heart weakened. The gore-drenched umalå lay discarded on the snow. As much as she wished to throw away the instrument of Kite's terrible death, she would need it later to hammer in the tent stakes.

Rising, she wiped the tears from her eyes with a bloodstained hand. The rest of the team sat watching, their normally expressive faces inscrutable.

Sorykah stared as if seeing the world anew. Distant explosions popped and fizzed as molten lava from the Devil's Playground spilled from buried lava tubes, dumping rivers of red-hot rock into the sea. Tephra jets of contaminated steam gushed skyward from the far shore, their bitter, acidic taste thick on Sorykah's tongue as the volcano purged itself of plumes of hydrochloric acid, heavy with silica, dust, and fragments of ore and debris.

Coughing, Sorykah dragged her scarf over her nose to filter the air. Her lungs were beginning to burn and she was afraid of choking to death there on the open snow. Panic surged and she stuffed it down.

Grabbing the umalå, Sorykah used the prongs to loosen clots of clean snow that she kicked and packed around the body until he was covered and the red snow had been erased. Kite's partner took a final sniff and nosed the snowy mound until Sorykah forced him away from it and back into his harness. With low spirits, she doled out food and melted snow in Shanxi's metal tumbler, watching as the remaining dogs chewed and swallowed. She forced herself to eat and drink even though she had lost her appetite. Their sorry graveside breakfast concluded, they resumed their trek toward the floe fields.

Sorykah's compass was a feeble wedge between finding the shore and losing herself, but it was all she had. She trudged beside the sled to prevent her weight from tiring the dogs. The wind subsided and the sun burned through the heavy clouds, illuminating a gray line in the distance. At first she thought it was a bald, rocky ridge poking up through the snow but as the hours wore on and she drew nearer, she realized that she was looking at the Southern Channel, flowing between the mainland and the Sigue.

Relief coursed through her body in waves and she slowed the dogs, dropping to her knees in gratitude. Clouds swarmed overhead but the sun was a bright beacon guiding her forward. The dogs bowed their heads and charged the light, their paws churning up snow that snapped crisply beneath the sled's runners.

A constant low-level whine hovered at the edge of her awareness. For a while she'd been able to ignore it, but as she drew nearer to the floe fields, it grew louder and more insistent, transforming itself from a moan into a crashing cacophony, drums and cymbals in loud accord.

The Sigue. Ostara's siren song had become this bleak, mournful wail, where chain-rattling ghouls haunted the lonely seaside as bergs and ships met in an agony of death. The dogs howled and whined, butting their heads against the snow, pawing their ears to block out the sound. She yelled encouragements but her voice was lost amid the din. They could not stop, or they would go mad from the racket. Twilight was a dangerous time on the waste. Without landmarks, trees, or variations in the natural features of the terrain, the snow and sky melded into one. Perspective was lost, distances misjudged. She and the dogs could not safely cross the channel if they couldn't see well enough to tell ice shelf from slush, or floe from open water.

The ground faltered and broke. Long, jagged cracks appeared and snaked away. Curious holes peppered the surface, some as small as tennis balls, others larger than Sorykah's head. Kika picked her way across the ice, sometimes stopping to cock her head and prick up her ears as she peered into the holes. Sorykah urged her forward but soon the other dogs began to stare into the seawater that frothed like water boiling in a pot.

Sorykah was nervous. Yes, the Sigue's funerary dirge put her in a miserable mood but there was something else, something worse. She felt *watched.* Spied upon. An impossibility here in this empty vastness. Perhaps the bear had followed them, but it was too hungry and too clumsy to mince about, watching from a distance.

She quickened the pace, snapping at the dogs, jerking them away from another hole, her mind fastened upon the ill-advised logistics of trying to get a sled and six dogs across the floe field, where blocks of ice as big as tractor tires collided with gusto, filling the air with noise.

The dogs were nervous; the ground threatened to break apart underfoot. They whined as their booted paws scrabbled against the slick, wet ice. An island of ice bubbled past and Sorykah drove the dogs hard across the gap.

She had to keep crossing or the current would pull her farther from her goal, the mainland's jutting tail directly north. If she tarried too long, the tide would carry them out to open sea. Another large parcel of ice was coming up, smaller than the first but just big enough to hold them.

"Hike!" she bellowed, cracking a whip overhead as the dogs bolted, barking and snapping. She cracked the whip again, pushing the sled and the terrified animals toward the edge. Something flickered there in the gap. There was something alive within that fast-moving mess of ice and slush.

Sorykah shoved the sled onto the ice floe, her foot knocking into the round, spotted face of an enormous leopard seal. Its large black eyes were neither kind nor curious, just flat and inert. Just as abruptly as it had appeared, it vanished again.

Panting, she urged the dogs onto another floe. The seal was there again, too, its head popping up and descending. Sorykah maneuvered the sled and dogs across the gap and onto another ice block. Floes collided and shook, as if ridding themselves of clinging pests. Another leap—the sled like an anchor towing them all to their deaths. She hesitated, desperate to rest, afraid to stop. The Sigue's scream pierced her brain, and she snapped her whip, taut and half frozen over the dogs' heads. As one body they surged across the gap and the spotted back of the watchful, diving seal. With silent-movie ferocity, its mouth opened, the fierce bark lost in the noise. The seal was following them. No, Sorykah realized with a shiver of dread, it was *stalking* them.

She felt ill. The mainland shimmered; its icy beaches lay two hundred feet away, perhaps less. Circling the floe, the seal awaited its moment, then dove, and in that thin and precious instant when she had thought them home free, it attacked. Buffeted from below by the seal, the berg almost capsized. Dogs and sled slid toward the sea as Sorykah dug her heels into the ice and pulled until her muscles tore beneath the skin. Teeth bared, mouth yawning wide, the seal leapt.

Sorykah was horrified by the sheer bulk of the creature heaving itself onto the floe; massive, clawed flippers grappling for purchase as it lunged, snapping a dog's leg between its jaws. Blood spurted and the sled dogs went wild. Sorykah screamed and yanked the gang line to wrench the dogs away but the seal's weight was too much and they slid across the ice. She knew she could not save them. Grabbing Shanxi's canvas bag and throwing the strap around her neck, she released the sled. Hoping that the freed dogs would jump onto another floe and save themselves, she unsheathed her Magar blade and slashed the tow lines connecting the team to the main gang line.

The dogs rolled like pebbles across the slippery floe, their booted paws gouging long, agonized troughs in the ice. Two of them skittered into the slush and disappeared. Kite's partner tumbled end over end into the seal's gaping mouth and the beast ripped him apart like a soupy, overcooked chicken.

Sorykah snatched Kika's line and forced her away from the carnage as the two remaining dogs ran frenzied circles around the sled, the red-splashed floe gaining speed as the channel opened and spirited it away.

She would not look back. They ran careless and driven for the shore, stopping when Sorykah realized that the ground was no longer moving beneath their feet. Her guts were full of ice, her heart frozen. How she regretted the loss of those beautiful animals!

Kika nosed her hand, and Sorykah saw that the light in her electric green eyes had died. Kika was her charge now, and keeping her alive, Sorykah's obligation.

"Come on girl, let's find a place to rest our weary bones." The dog's tail thumped once, and lay still. Sorykah used the trailing tow line like a leash and led her inland where the ice gave way to a thin frost and then smooth gray stones, clicking and clacking underfoot, growing in size until they became boulders. Sorykah gathered sticks and driftwood, warmed by the idea of touching something once landlocked and living, until she held a substantial bundle, enough to start a small fire.

There were gaps in the rocks, dark hollows rife with rats or snakes. *Food*, she thought and readied her blade. Peering into the gloom, Sorykah used a stick to dislodge any tenants. Hard to tell over the distant soughing of the Sigue, but it didn't sound like anything had moved. It was as safe as any other place and so she hunkered down to dig through Shanxi's bag for the flint fire starter and light damp wood, tossing it into the rock cave.

She peered in and saw the abandoned nest of some furry creature, inviting and snug with leaves and spiderwebbing, forced Kika through the hole, and crawled in after her. She built up her fire, keeping it small and meting out her precious firewood. She fed the fire a few handfuls broken from the nest, which it devoured before settling into a steady burn. Kika lay down and rested her head on her outstretched paws, gazing at her mistress with obvious sorrow.

"No worries, my love. We've still got each other." It was a poor consolation but it was all they had, themselves and Shanxi's bag of magic. She rummaged through to see what she could find. The tumbler was full of water and Sorykah sat the jar near the fire to warm after adding a handful of mealie from the cloth sack. Soon they had a nice little pot of salted porridge, which Sorykah ate with her fingers and let Kika lick from her hand.

Days of wandering followed, Sorykah keeping to the rocky shoreline as she followed it northeast. The hours fell into a comfortable if exhausting rhythm of mixing mealie, making and breaking camp, and endless silent miles of walking, a stark solitude broken by the occasional circling seabird. Sorykah pushed forward through sparse sunshine and sleety rain, thinking of food, her children, and food again. After the slaughter at the floes, Sorykah wasted an entire day, catatonic with remorse, as she willed herself to move from her scant shelter and continue her trek. The loss of the dogs haunted her. She chastised herself like a religious penitent, self-punishing and morbid until even she grew tired of the flagellation and shook it off, determined to push forward.

Mealie wasn't fit for dogs and Kika had grown bony. A well-trained working dog, she seemed to have no instinct for the hunt and ate what Sorykah offered. Despairing at the thought of losing her companion, Sorykah knew she would have to do something for her soon or risk Kika's slow death from starvation.

The leopard seal attack had her too spooked to venture near the sea again. That left inland. A wide marsh stretched away from the rocky beach toward low, tree-flocked hills. Without any hunting equipment besides her blade and some fishing line, Sorykah would have to settle for small animals. There might be snails, frogs, fish, and birds living in the marsh and rabbits or small rodents in the low hills. All of them gamey and wild, but unafraid of humans and tasting of life. She hoped to catch a rabbit or plump bird, imagined it plucked or skinned and spit-roasted, the vision of hot, dripping fat and roasted flesh making her stomach cramp with want.

Problem was, Sorykah had never hunted, much less butchered her own meat. How was she to rig a trap, slaughter and dress a wild creature? Everything she knew about the world came from books. Before being hired by the Company and going to work aboard the *Nimbus*, Sorykah had lived her entire life in cities. The Sigue was the first wild place she had ever ventured and even there, the Company's umbrella of influence sheltered her.

She would have to rely on paper knowledge and instinct, and hope that she didn't inadvertently kill herself, Kika, or both of them.

"Come on girl, let's go rustle up some grub," she said, her voice bright with false cheer.

Sorykah led Kika toward the marsh, looking for signs of life in the reeds. Water that welled in their footprints now sloshed around their ankles; the reeds grew taller and crowded together, their stout stems creaking in the breeze. The quiet marsh was devoid of life. No birds or frogs croaked out of sight. There was only the rustling of catkins and the empty husks of last autumn's seedpods, vibrating in the wind.

The season did not favor her. It was almost spring but still too soon for the frogs to emerge from hibernation in the marsh mud. The fishers and other birds would remain in their winter hunting grounds until the thaws, when frogs swam free, soaking up the gaining sunshine and looking for mates.

There would be no berries or seeds to eat. If she was lucky, she might stumble on some drowsy creature and capture it and beat it to death with her bare hands. She could chop it up it with her Magar blade and throw Kika the raw carcass, but then what would she eat? Mealie, mealie, always mealie . . . she longed for something sweet or green to break up the monotony.

Sorykah dragged herself through the marsh. The air smelled of rain and cold, and the wind complained. Sorykah saw that the pale lumps stippling the catkins were snails, clustered in groups just above the water line. Determined to nourish Kika, Sorykah bent to examine the snails. Beneath cream-colored shells, their large, soft bodies were an ugly yellow-gray and gripped the reeds with fluted sides. Sorykah swallowed her disgust as she plucked one from a leaf, squirming in irritation. She wanted to hurl the horrible thing away and run screaming but forced herself to pluck several more.

She struggled through thick grass until she reached the muddy marsh edge and sat down with Kika to inspect their find. The listless snails curled in her hand. She would have to kill and cook them, somehow. Lacking an escargot fork, Sorykah settled for a primitive method of extraction. She dug a rock from the mud and balanced a snail on it, then used another rock to bash it and crack open the shell.

Snail guts oozed over fragments of broken shell as the nasty thing squirmed in the midst of its final death throes. Sorykah grimaced and looked at Kika, who stared at her with a dubious expression. She crushed the remaining snails, picked out the shell shards, and made mealie, throwing the slimy bits into the jar and stirring it with her finger. The resulting concoction tasted of snot and dirt. She choked back rising bile.

Kika took one sniff of the revolting mixture and turned away. She'd rather starve than subject herself to raw slime porridge.

"Oh," Sorykah gasped, her eyes watering. "How awful!"

Kika bowed her head and pawed the ground, then looked cockeyed at Sorykah as if to say, "I'm a dog and even I won't eat that mess!"

Even one of the hated butter bars would taste sweet to her now. Sorykah curled up on the spongy ground with her head on the pack and Kika tucked up beside her, and tried to keep her food down. Most of the provisions had been lost on the sled. The dogs' kibble, Sorykah's stash of calories brought from the *Nimbus*, the bear pelt, samilkâ, and tent, all had vanished into the slushy deep. If it weren't for the north shore's warmer climate, she would have died of exposure long along. She was uncomfortable, but at least she wouldn't freeze to death as soon as the sun went down.

At some point she'd have to cross the marsh and return to the shoreline, but for the moment she was content to lay with her dog and her churning belly and watch the clouds shift and roll overhead. Rubbing Kika's fur, Sorykah closed her eyes, listening to the relentless, sighing wind and rattling reeds.

Sorykah could not rest easy, as much as she yearned for sleep. Danger signals prickled inside her skin as the ground began to shake and a dull hum built to a thundering roar. Sorykah opened her eyes and sat up. Kika stood beside her, four legs splayed wide, her terrified eyes scanning the horizon. Marsh water foamed and rose in the gathering current as Sorykah stumbled to her feet, with noise all around and the ground shaking, the ankle-deep water now swirling around her waist. An uprooted sapling swam by, knocking her over and pushing the dog away, caught in its web of branches.

"Kika!" Sorykah yelled, lunging into the marsh. Her fingers closing around a handful of Kika's fur just as a massive wave of icy, debris-choked snowmelt surged down from the far Glass Mountains. Floodwater closed over Sorykah's head as she fought to find the surface. She rose gasping and saw Kika bob along an eddy in the wild current. Sorykah fought her way over to the dog, her fingertips just brushing a paw that swirled by and floated out of reach before the water swelled to part them. Something snagged her coat and sucked her into a bubbling vortex where branches, plants, dead snails, fish, rodents, and assorted other furries tumbled in the churning waters. Sorykah dunked into the silty flow and surfaced spitting dirty water. Kika barked and Sorykah turned just in time to see her swallowed by a greedy floodmouth, sucking her down into a gorging, wet funnel.

Something sharp and hard cascaded down from the mountains and struck Sorykah's head. Silence settled around her as the light inside her dimmed and winked out altogether.

Consciousness bloomed, a pink and muted awareness. Sorykah tasted dirt; grit and mud caked her teeth and plugged one nostril. Her first attempt at movement yielded no response from her frozen body. Broken grass jutted from clumps of upturned soil near her cheek. Beyond that, the jagged outline of a split tree loomed black against a hard, opalescent sky.

Come on, move, she urged, as if willpower alone could defeat her paralysis. Her calf muscles twitched but her legs remained immobile. With a final, desperate lurch, Sorykah wrenched her upper body from the ground, freeing her arms in a crackling shower of ice shards. She twisted around to view her legs, submerged in a deep puddle that had frozen overnight, trapping her feet in the ice. Wiggling her toes, she saw a small bubble rise from the seam of her boot. The puddle hadn't yet solidified although the shallows beneath Sorykah's hips had leached into the fur lining of her coat, holding her fast, a petrified gnat entombed in amber. Again she fought the ice, straining to pull herself free until sweat beaded on her forehead and her arms shook with effort.

Sorykah lay on the wet grass, listening to the sounds of the valley, silent but for the bubbling pop of the earth absorbing floodwater and a murder of crows cawing in a nearby tree. A wolf's howl carried on the wind, moved like a will-o'-the-wisp through the scrubbed air, to ignite her nerves.

With renewed vigor, Sorykah unearthed a jagged rock and hacked at the ice imprisoning her. Focused on her task, she didn't hear the men's voices, loud and self-important, at first, or the recklessness of their heavy boots slogging through the mud.

Sorykah managed to free her left leg, sodden and cold, but still functioning. Something else had a grip on her, though; her right leg was still stuck fast. The men were getting closer and though not yet visible over the muddy rise behind her, they had the advantage. Was it better to play dead or ask for their assistance? She didn't have a chance to decide because the hunters materialized from a copse of trees, long-barreled guns slung over their shoulders, and stood gawking at her.

"What are you doing out here?" asked a stocky bundle of muscle in camouflage fatigues. His gaze skimmed Sorykah's body, taking in her bloodied mouth, muddied face and clothes, and the leg twisted beneath a tree root.

"The flood caught me off guard. I lost everything." She was torn between exaggerating her helplessness to appeal to their sense of chivalry or downplaying her situation.

His companion, a chunkier blond version of his friend, scanned the area, a dark look on his face. "Are you alone?"

Something didn't sit right . . . Perhaps it was the feral glint in his eye, the way he set down his gun out of Sorykah's reach, or the frown that deepened as he eyed her, trapped facedown on the boggy ground.

"No, of course not," she fudged. "I'm with my husband and our dog team."

"Then where are they? Seems he would want to help his wife if she was trapped the way you are," said the blond.

"We were separated by the flood," Sorykah snapped.

"No need to get huffy about it," retorted camo-guy. He shrugged and looked away, nudging his friend. "Come on mate, let's go."

"Wait a minute," answered the blond. His bright orange jumpsuit was an affront to Sorykah's eyes. "What about her?"

"What about her," parroted the other. "Pull her leg out and leave her. We got to keep going or we're gonna lose its trail. I want that wolf."

The blond was reluctant to go. He squatted down and scratched his head.

"We been out here a long time, Neil. Why don't we take her with us? She can cook or something." He licked his lips and lifted the edge of Sorykah's coat, trying to suss out the shape beneath her clothes.

"Your cooking's good enough for me. Anyway, she'll slow us down. Let's go. I'd rather have that wolf's skin than this rough bit of stuff." Neil walked away, cresting the nearest rise to watch the far hills. The wolf howled again, its cry thin.

"Dammit, he's getting away. Come on! If we blow this because of your little detour, you're gonna owe me a lot of money." The wolf howled once more and Neil sprinted toward the sound, his fatigues whuffing.

"I'll catch up." The blond turned to Sorykah. "So you really can't move?"

Sorykah still had the sharp rock clenched in her fist; she tucked her arm under her side, where the man wouldn't see it.

"He's leaving you behind," Sorykah threatened.

"He's old. He don't think about women anymore. Don't get lonesome, the way I do." He lifted her coat, bunching it up around her waist.

"I promise this won't take but a minute. I can be pretty fast when I want to be." The blond hunter laughed, pleased by his little joke.

Sorykah gripped the rock, running her finger along the flinty edge, determining the best place to strike him once he attacked. Sorykah watched him draw his zipper down as if in slow motion. Until that moment, she had hoped that some essential human kindness inherent in all people would serve to protect her honor. This man had no honor; he would not concern himself with spoiling hers.

His grubby hand groped beneath her coat and his face contorted when confronted with the complexity of the thermosuit's invisible hooks and zippers.

"How do you get this thing open?" he complained, as if expecting Sorykah to offer herself to him, trussed on a serving platter with an apple wedged between her teeth.

"Goddamn, I don't have time for this!" The hunter unsheathed a short blade and grabbed a wad of fabric, intent on cutting Sorykah out of her clothes. She thrashed once, tugging her pinned leg in a final desperate attempt to free herself and as the knife pierced her suit and grazed her skin, a shot rang out.

Sorykah jerked with surprise and the hunter paused, Sorykah's thermosuit snagged on his serrated blade. In the stillness, she could hear the threads breaking one by one.

Grunting, he bent back to his task, tearing open a twelve-inch gash and revealing a strip of clammy, winter-pale skin, marked with a line of fresh, beading blood.

Another shot broke the tension, followed by a series of short sharp barks. They both paused midstruggle as they waited for the hunter to take action and finish the job, destroying one of two quarries.

Sharp and sorrowful, a long howl rippled through the valley. A final shot terminated the wolf's cry and the blond hunter sat back on his heels, listening. He gazed at Sorykah with a slack expression before stuffing the knife into its case and pulling up his zipper. He smeared his grubby fingers over her damp and bloodied skin before stumbling to his feet and lumbering over the rise after his partner.

Sorykah listened to the sounds of his retreat, his reunion with his friend and their faint laughter, absorbed by the trees lining the valley. After what seemed like an eternity, she relaxed her grip on the rock that had left a distinct impression in her flesh. Waves of relief washed through her body as Sorykah turned her head aside and vomited into the grass. Biting her lip to suppress her cries, Sorykah shook with fear and insane glee as she lay in the mud. To have come so close and escaped so easily.

It would only be a matter of time before she faced another man interested in his own corporeal satisfaction. She was so used to downplaying her womanliness, to keeping herself hidden, that she forgot, sometimes, that there were other risks to her person than discovery as a Trader. She couldn't afford to be so lax with her safety when she was the children's only chance of rescue. She owed it to them to protect herself.

The rampaging tide had picked her pockets and left them empty. Only a small knife remained strapped to her ankle, its thin, dull blade a hollow travesty of defense. How she longed for her beautiful Magar blade! Her ankle began to throb and the cloying smell of her own sick lingered under her nose. She couldn't afford to spend another night alone beneath the open sky, as tempting to a carnivore's eyes as a snared rabbit.

Sorykah dug away the mud imprisoning her foot. The root was sturdy and gnarled; the heel of her boot had become wedged beneath it and mud had packed itself in the gaps, cementing her foot in a block of natural mortar. The pain in her ankle flared with every twitch and turn, and as the waning light began to soak into the misty mountain ridge, panic made her movements frantic and less assured. The balmy thrity-degree afternoon would soon become a frigid night and Sorykah's wet clothing and torn thermosuit would increase her susceptibility to the windchill. A sad end indeed, to die of exposure in this pretty green valley after having come so far. She refused to let this minor setback deter her. Sorykah finally wormed free and stood on her good leg, gamely testing the sore ankle. It buckled under the pressure of her weight and she almost fell but steadied herself, holding aloft the swollen joint.

Surrounded by mountains whose naked rocky peaks scored the sky, Sorykah gathered that she'd have to wait until morning to get some sense of direction. Without a sun to orient her, she could spend the night wandering back in the direction she had come, toward the screaming Sigue and its nimbus of bobbing ice floes.

A silver half-moon rose above the mountains, icing them with lunar frost. Limping and hopping, Sorykah picked her way among the refuse and edged closer to the tree line. She was undecided about whether to risk venturing into the forest or stay in the open meadow, where she could see anyone approaching but would be visible herself.

The sound of human chatter reached her. Men's mingled voices flowed around her, a deep and steady baritone stream, as if to submerge her in their noise.

The hunters.

Sorykah's gut knotted at the thought of their return and what they might do to her during the long night ahead.

She lurched into the trees, making a terrible racket she was sure would alert everyone to her presence. Branches, twigs, dead leaves, and pinecones cracked and snapped underfoot. Her breath hung in the night air like telltale tracks as she hustled deeper into the forest, looking for a safe place to hide.

She blundered into a clearing and almost had a heart attack. A small campfire burned nearby, its green kindling emitting sparks and sheets of black smoke as the hunters cleaned their guns, polishing the hilt and barrels with a cloth while they chatted.

The seconds seemed to stretch into an eternity—when might the men turn and spy the traveler they had abandoned on the meadow? She stumbled over the uneven ground and crashed into a fallen branch lousy with crisp leaves. The noise was terrific and she crouched, frozen, heart hammering against her ribs.

The men ceased their discussion to listen for further sounds of movement. She heard them whispering as they advanced around the clearing, guns pointed into the shadowed forest.

"My gun's not loaded, what about yours," asked the older man.

"Uh. All my shot's in the box. What do you think it is?"

"Only a bear would be so clumsy and make so much damn noise. Could be a cub . . ."

"Which means the mother isn't far away."

Sorykah held her breath as she searched among the darkened trees for a suitable hiding place. Inch by inch, she crept backward until her hand broke a dried twig in two and the loud snap resounded through the forest.

"Over here!"

She couldn't tell them apart very well but thought that the man in fatigues was advancing her way. Though he didn't seem to have much interest in her, she doubted he would be very vigilant about protecting her from his friend. She had to disappear, and fast.

Moonlight slanted through naked tree boughs and glanced off

a gaping black hollow. Sorykah stretched out her hand, feeling into the darkness. Lightning had struck this large tree and the resulting fire had eaten away its pithy core, leaving a sizable opening. She grappled in the underbrush and found a rock and a few pinecones, which she threw into the trees opposite her.

The distraction worked. The hunters spun toward the sound and move away from her, searching for the elusive cub. Sorykah scrambled toward the tree, scooting in backward and drawing her knees up to her chest, then strewed fallen leaves over her protruding feet. Her face and torso were hidden inside the tree; her lower legs would show if anyone shone a light at them, but otherwise her black coat would shield her.

The hunters returned to the fire and their idle conversation. She leaned her head against the charred heartwood and wiped away the dusty cobwebs that tangled in her eyelashes. A faint smell of burned wood enveloped her, reassuring and warming. Though cramped and pitch-black, the hollow tree protected Sorykah from the wind and night dew. She felt invisible and safe. After all her recent trials, it was a pleasant feeling. Hunger and thirst were foremost in her thoughts, but sleep was more powerful and she allowed it to claim her, dropping through the layers of her memories to a place of silent anonymity, where she remained for many hours.

12

SORYK

MORNING. A RICH AROMA of frying food saturated the air. Wiggling stiff, cold toes, the man stretched out his cramped legs, numbness replaced by the sting of pins and needles as blood rushed into waking limbs. He opened his eyes to darkness, confused by the black hollow surrounding him. Long hours of sleep had disoriented him and as he struggled to gain his feet, he realized that he was wedged into a tight space, his shoulders jammed against something hard that crumbled with his movements, emitting a curious smell of fire. Misty blue light seeped upward from the gap around his legs and he managed to scuttle along his bottom, pulling himself into a monochromatic morning of towering trees woven together with wisps of lingering fog. Black fingers clawed at his boots as wet tree roots erupted through a carpet of pine needles and crisp fallen leaves. Dew dripped from overhanging branches, adding a soothing repetitive "plop" to the muted symphony of sound.

As he stood brushing leaves and cobwebs from his coat, he was struck with the sudden sensation that he shouldn't be doing this, standing here out in the open for all to see. Yet he couldn't recall the reason, and attracted by the lure of a nearby campfire, the man decided to beg, borrow, or steal a bit of food from the chef.

A woman knelt near the fire, preparing something for a pan heating on the hearthstone. She was an astonishing sight, and sported a fantastic costume of layered, chamoislike robes over a gray-green homespun gown that dragged the ground. A wild tumbleweed of hair spilled from beneath a red fur hat crowned by a magnificent set of deer antlers, and flowed to her hips. She crouched beside the open flame, humming as she worked.

Stepping into view, the man coughed to alert her of his presence.

Without raising her eyes, she said, "It's about time. I thought you were going to stay inside that tree until I left."

Taking ingredients from the clutch of small leather pouches bound to her waist and mixing them with wild greens in her frying pan, she continued, "I said to myself, Sidra, my lovely—for that's what they call me, one and all, Sidra the Lovely—a man who sleeps in a tree hides for one of two reasons, fear of being caught or fear of being caught." She looked up at him with a smirk and a twinkle in her eye. "So, which is it?"

He was surprised to find himself at a loss for words. His voice rumbled in his throat as it wakened and stretched after what felt like years of disuse.

"Just as I thought," Sidra said with obvious satisfaction. "There's none here but you and me and the brothers three." She pointed to a trio of glossy ravens lurking in the overhead branches. "So seat yourself and tell me your tale. We won't be interrupted." Squatting to tend her cooking pot, Sidra wrapped her arms around her knees and hunkered down for a satisfying story.

The man rubbed his throat, feeling the knobby Adam's apple protruding there and thinking that he didn't remember it sticking out quite so much. His chin and upper lip were rough with sparse stubble and his hands felt large and clumsy against his face. He was unfamiliar with himself and it was a disorienting, disturbing sensation. Cobwebs muffled his memory. He looked at his clothes, examining his handsome and well-made coat with its embedded steel insignia on the lapel, a small, stylized C. Beneath it, however, his black one-piece bodysuit was tight in all the wrong places and torn on the side, his bare skin flashing the vivid red warning flag of a fresh wound. His boots were good but had seen better days. Running a hand through his shoulder-length black hair, the man caught the tail end of some fleeing image as it dashed through his brain. He groped through his memory box, searching for something familiar, something *known.* Distorted images flared and evaporated; snatches of scent, song, and bits of tactile recall knit themselves together, a crazy quilt of sensation.

He faltered beneath the crush of images and snatches of events, then staggered a bit, clutched his head, and almost toppled into the fire. He would have fallen on the hot stones had Sidra not leapt up to catch him with surprisingly strong arms and helped him to a seat on a felled log. Tagged with burrs and leaves, her shawls rustled against him, smelling of the outdoors.

"Goodness," she exclaimed, kneeling to peer up into his pale face, "it's as bad as all that, is it?"

The man closed his eyes, swept up in a gathering tide of remembrance. His entire life uprooted itself as the days and nights of his existence swam into view and receded with nauseating speed.

"I think you haven't eaten for longer than you'd care to admit." The antler-crowned woman examined him with kind eyes. "Your clothes are damp and you're bleeding. Won't you let me dress that wound while your coat hangs over the fire?"

After a moment's hesitation, the man nodded. He was embarrassed to find himself in such a position of weakness—hungry, injured, and confused. His male pride had suffered enough blows. Or was he wrong in thinking himself male?

Astonished by this, the man frowned. Something important he had to do . . . no, not he, but the woman. A woman he knew well; she'd initiated this quest, she was the lady whose love token he'd accepted; her honor was the scarf he carried into battle, wrapped around the end of his lance.

Crazy thoughts. They didn't make sense. He opened his mouth to speak, startled by the deep voice that seemed to thunder in the clearing, as if hearing a stranger speak for the first time.

"Where am I?"

"You're in the Erun Forest, near a watershed that courses from the Glass Mountains. This valley is flooded every spring by snowmelt running to the Southern Sea. There was a flood here two days ago, in fact. I think that might explain how you arrived here, and why your clothes are wet." She helped him shrug out of his coat, ran a slender tree branch through the sleeves, and hung it to dry downwind of her fire. The tangy smell of wood smoke would saturate the coat, but at least he would be warm again. He sat shivering on the log, eyeing his legs in the tight body suit. The woman seated herself beside him and lifted his arm to examine the cut at his side. She palpated the wound and scratched away some dried blood with dirty fingernails.

"Not so bad after all. It looks worse than it is, I think. But left to fester, it could turn grave for you. Best to help nature work its miracles whenever there's an opportunity to do so." Reaching into yet another leather pouch, she extracted a small, battered tin, popped open the lid, and smeared a familiar, viscous green salve on her forefinger. Her cold fingers warmed upon contact with his skin, assailing him with a flush of emotion, at once repelled and aroused. Coughing to disguise his feelings, he turned away, shamed by the hunger in him, as if he had never been touched before, his body as raw and pristine as the wilderness surrounding them.

Sidra retreated to her cook fire, sagacious and impartial. She tossed a few fiddlehead ferns into the pan and gave them a quick rotation through the oil-soaked greens. Distasteful as it looked, his stomach turned inside out in an effort to leave his body and get itself to the food that much sooner.

A breeze stirred the ashes. Orange sparks danced and another memory slithered through the back of his mind. He remembered a dancing devil and an odor of sulfur and the woman. Which woman? The faces were confused, at once creepy or gorgeous, ruddy or golden. Then there was that woman with the dark hair so like his own, lurking in shadows and skulking through darkened doorways. He sensed that he knew her well, and that her memory would never leave him in peace until he remembered her in full.

Doling steaming food into a stained wooden dish seasoned by much use, Sidra approached, her tilted eyes canny and watchful. He accepted the bowl and the eating sticks she produced from a pocket.

Squatting next to him, her eating sticks clicking a soothing cadence, Sidra twirled a limp fiddlehead into her open mouth. A droplet of dark yellow oil glistened on her chin as she ate with relish, slurping in thoughtful appreciation.

The food wasn't as bad as he'd feared. The flavors were sharp and woodsy, the greens chewy but nourishing, and he enjoyed crunching the salted seedpods that crackled in his mouth.

"Now that your belly is full, I expect you'll be grateful enough for my feeding you to tell me what you're doing in my forest." The wild woman eyed him gravely.

"Your forest?"

"Yes, my forest. This isn't a wild place. It's my realm and I am its guardian."

"Then who do you guard, or what against?"

"Better you should hear from me than a chance and unfortunate encounter with Her."

"Her? Who is she?"

"Why, the Wood Beast, of course. You are a stranger to these parts!" Sidra cocked her head and gazed at him. "Having never heard of the dread beastie he ventured unawares . . ."

They sat without speaking for a moment, each one appraising the other. Upon first meeting her, the man guessed her to be some forest hag, slightly daffy and rejected by society, forced to make her way in this wood because no other would have her. Now it was clear that she was close to his own age, her skin firm and fine except for the laugh lines bracketing her wide, soft mouth. Her humor revealed her to be sane and clever; she was deft with a knife and knew her herbs. A tiny spark flared within him as he gazed into her hazel eyes.

"Where were you going, before the flood carried you away?" Sidra scrubbed her cook pan with a handful of leaves.

The man shrugged. "I don't remember."

"You're no poacher. They sneak into my woods, hunt my kin, and think I will take pity on them when She comes, just because they are human. Bah!" Sidra spat onto the leaves. "You haven't the right gear. And what's with that suit? It ill suits you, that's what!" She cackled, admiring his lean legs and bum through the tight, embarrassing outfit.

The man reddened and folded his arms over his chest, his hand grazing the tear in his clothes. True, he wasn't properly dressed for this wilderness. Had he no bag, no gear? He wouldn't have ventured into this forest unprepared and expected to survive, would he? A growing sense of impatience rocked him. He was wasting time, sitting here, making nice with this stranger when he had something better to do. Must be up and on his way, but to what and for whom? The details eluded his grasp.

"Thank you for the meal," he said. "I have to go." He scanned the treetops, where leaden clouds were gathering.

Sidra sniffed the air and stuck out her tongue, searching the sky. "I think we're done for today. A sprinkle maybe, but we won't be doused. Time enough, then, for a story." She squatted beside him, turning up her cheerful, expectant face.

His story? He racked his brains, searching for clues with which to piece together a narrative. He found scraps of story, his own, he supposed, or remnants of a dream. They would do.

"My parents waited years for a child. At last, my mother found herself pregnant but spoke too soon, announcing her blessing before the twelfth week. That night, she dreamt that a raven had carried away her child and awoke in a pool of blood. After many tears had cleansed her womb, she conceived me. Terrified of another loss, she vowed not to speak a word of her condition until the thirteenth week but her joy was so great and the secret so grand, she felt that her own small body could not contain it. She had to tell another living soul—the rocks and trees were poor companions and though they kept her secrets, they could not congratulate her. And so she whispered it to her pet cat, a tatty, yellow-eyed tom. Because he had half an ear on one side, she felt that she only gave away half of her secret and could not be faulted for breaking any covenants.

"When I arrived, they rejoiced in having a son firstborn, but childlessness was a specter unbanished, and the brothers and sisters who came after me soon went the way of the spirits.

"My mother always felt that a raven hovered too close to the house, swooping through the sky, its enormous black wings beating the air and stirring up the clouds. As my sister approached her twelfth week awomb, my mother grew frightened that the raven would claim yet another of her children. One morning she awoke to find the bird perched on the bedpost and wept to think that he had come to take her baby away again.

"She called for my father, who came with his gun and slew the raven on the bedpost. He threw the carcass in the garden, where it was devoured by the yellow tom, eater of secrets. With the raven vanquished, the sky was empty and the dreams done. That winter, my sister arrived, bringing the first snows. My fearless mother stood by her window, welcoming the season.

"She found her peace, but the raven's wife lingered in her nest upon eggs gone cold, searching the sky, awaiting her slain mate's return. There were no ravens born to the garden the next spring, nor any after that. Raven's wife is long absent but her eggs remain in the abandoned nest, as still as marble, as hard as stone. My mother considers it a fair exchange."

Wind rattled the naked boughs and disturbed the trio of crows above, who squawked in complaint.

Sidra the Lovely smiled. "Perhaps your story offended them."

"A family will always leap to the defense of its black sheep, even if they have already cast him out," the man said, poking at the fire and stirring up the embers. He was chilled and growing surly from the discomfort of it.

Rolling her pots and wooden dishes in a cloth, the woman stashed them in her traveling bag and slung it round her neck. Scattering dirt over the fire pit and tamping down the ashes, the wild woman tucked her shabby wrap over her shoulder and stood, stretching her arms overhead and yawning like a little cat.

"You ought to find a dry place to shelter tonight; you won't want to get soaked again."

"I'll be all right," the man replied, feigning bravado.

Sidra tossed him a woolen shawl. Wordlessly, he caught the blanket and tucked it around his shoulders, grateful for the warmth, if not the smell.

"Have you protection against the Wood Beast?"

He shook his head.

"Well," she said, "stay clear of dark hollows and water. That's where She waits. She can't climb trees, either. The way out is there, if you want the cities." She pointed west. "Blundt is closest, about three weeks walking. Farther north in Neubonne, the Merciful Father's Charity Hospital will keep you till you recover your memory, and forever, if you don't."

She righted her crown, which had snagged a low-hanging branch, and disentangled hair, leaves, and antlers. "My blessings to you and yours. Don't forget your coat."

Turning her back, she slipped between the trees and went on her way.

"Do you have a knife?" the man asked the empty clearing. He was bothered by the C on his lapel and wanted to remove it, hating to have been stamped as if in ownership. Silence answered him and he looked up from the coat bundled in his hands, searching for the wild woman.

Soryk was alone. He cursed and sat on a rock, flicking at a weedy stalk of something while he tried to gather his wits. What had she said? He was half listening. And why all the scare tactics about the "dread beastie"? The forest was imposing but didn't strike him as being particularly dangerous. He shifted, uncomfortable in his clothes. A band of fabric cinched his chest like a harness. He groped inside his coat and sat up to wiggle his torso from the tight thermosuit and yank off the contraption digging into his flesh. He held it high in the wan light, examining the white elastic straps and snap closures on the cups. He recoiled with shame and wadded the brassiere in his pocket, vexed by his finding. Fretting about the vague possibility of Sidra's discovering the bra in his coat pocket, Soryk quickly dug a hole and buried it, sweating with fear. He was steadfast in his refusal to question himself about how he'd come to possess, much less sport, such a garment. Jamming his arms into the thermosuit, Soryk hunkered down to formulate his plan.

Thunder rumbled across the sky and silver droplets splattered the treetops. A distant snarl broke the sounds of gaining rainfall. Sidra's words drifted back: "Stay away from dark hollows and water." How could he avoid water during a thunderstorm? Did she mean standing water, falling water, or just any sort of water?

An anguished cry resounded through the forest, ascending the scale then pitching low, finishing with a protracted, distraught growl. The sound echoed again, nearer this time.

She can't climb trees.

The man scampered up a large, sloping pine, finding a relatively dry, sturdy crook, and propped himself against the tree trunk to await the passing of both rain and beast.

Another howl again, to the north but closing in. The danger of a lightning strike seemed less worrisome than the possibility of being gulleted alive by some ogreish beast. He pulled branches close to disguise himself until he'd had a chance to size up his opponent.

He strained forward, his breath held as he listened for the beast's clumsy and careless approach. Something stomped through the underbrush, crushing saplings and snapping branches as it neared.

Was the woman safe? She certainly seemed to know how to take care of herself, but was a giggling, self-appointed queen of the Erun a fair match against the beast? Moved by an intrinsic sense of chivalry, he considered pursuing her to ensure her safety, but some wiser intuitive sense urged him to remain hidden. At the moment he yielded to his masculine rescuer's impulse, the brush parted and he spied an immense, furred thing, its dangling, serpentine arms corded with jutting tendons and muscle, the burled knuckles and bloody claws dragging the wet ground.

He shrank back, clutching branch in hand. The beast snorted and slammed through a thicket, rain steaming against its diminishing hide as the water-beaded leaves drew closed.

He leaned back and exhaled. His legs were shaking from the pent-up tension of his crouch. All atingle now, he stretched out, careful not to make a sound or loose a single pinecone lest he draw her back. His mouth was dry and sticky; his heart hammered in his ears.

How could such things exist in this otherwise ordinary world of forest and mist-draped hills? *Am I awake?* he wondered. *Am I dreaming or is this real?*

The more he thought about it, the more confused he became, certain that this was not *his* life but some other stranger's misplaced existence and that his actual life throbbed and hummed elsewhere in another inaccessible dimension, far from the illusory presence of queens and monsters.

Closing his eyes, he leaned back in the tree, sifting through a jumble of memories, looking for something to wear, a name that would fit. The last clear memory he could claim was eons old. He saw himself as a gangly teenager, fingering the fuzz that grew in patchy on his cheeks and upper lip, staring at himself in the mirror as if he were a stranger. The door opened. His mother walked in, saw him there in a pink, flower-printed nightgown, and froze, one hand to her mouth as her legs folded beneath her.

He could recall the terrible fight they later had about his continuing in school. (Such strife! So much work demanded when creating an identity from scratch.) Then there was the humiliating and detailed exam suffered at the hands of an unlicensed doctor who worked from his home on a strictly cash basis, an ash trailing, hand-rolled tobacco cigarette dangling from his lip as he poked and prodded, probing, lifting, separating, and inserting his fingers in all the untouched places of that boy's body.

He remembered the ensuing days of restless roaming over city streets—mind, soul, and heart shuttered against intrusion, his jacket pulled tight, hat drawn low over his silky black hair. "Too long, too long," they'd said and forced him, squirming and yelping, under the blade as the locks of his only vanity were unceremoniously shorn. Now as the filmstrip faded, the image of that stark, stick-straight hair lying puddled at his feet resonated within him like a mourner's grief-stricken wail.

He asked the rain-occluded sky "Who am I?" and remembered that his name was Soryk.

13

SIDRA THE LOVELY

SIDRA HEARD THE WOOD BEAST'S tormented roar and froze. With a canny, noiseless ease, she settled on the forest floor, wrapping her shawls over her hair and burying her face in her drawn knees. She concentrated on a little bouncing spot of orange that danced on the inside of her closed lids and waited for the Beast to pass.

The beast was clumsy and near deaf. Her sense of smell had been dulled by malformed nasal lobes, her hearing destroyed by the ringing decibels of her own repeated cries. The Beast was only a threat to those idiotic enough to try to outrun her, to scream or stumble within reach of those ungodly long arms. Judging by the bone piles strewn along the Erun walking trails, many were.

Sidra was determined to make this forest her domain and no threat, human or otherwise, would prevent her from conquering it. Like the other somatics who dwelled in the Erun, Sidra was an exile. Unlike them, she was not content to carve out a solitary little niche, grateful to be left alone. Sidra's politicking heart had convinced her that every step led to the dominion of the forlorn forgotten, to unite and rule them as members of a peaceful and benevolent democracy.

The forest had grown quiet again; even the trees seemed to hold their breath when the Beast was near. Sidra peeped out to scan the surrounding area. The Erun seemed to exhale and shake itself in relief. Blood would not sully the forest floor, at least for the moment.

She rose, watching a large raven hop from branch to branch in a nearby pine, stretching its toes and preening as it cocked its head and eyed the glass beads decorating one of Sidra's packs.

Sidra frowned as she remembered the dark-haired man's tale of slain messengers and thwarted births. Had he taken her advice and managed to evade the beast or did he lie dismembered somewhere, snared in a pool of his own entrails?

Her impulse was to leave him to his own devices and continue her rounds in service of the Erun's somatics, but she could not be so callous. In her former life, Sidra had been a nurse in the neonatal wards of the Merciful Father's Charity Hospital in Neubonne. Lingering remnants of a missionary upbringing left her unable to abandon anyone in need, a character trait that, while admirable, drew her into many a draining and unsavory situation.

Sidra found him dangling high in a tree, one fist tight around a flexible pine bough, his leg slung over a broken branch as he attempted to maneuver his way down from an imposing height. She couldn't help laughing aloud as he slipped and caught himself, legs churning wildly beneath him before he found something solid enough to support his weight.

The man looked down at her, wearing an expression of intense annoyance and masked fear. He reached for a branch but another swung forward and thwacked him full in the face, showering him with pine needles.

"Where'd you learn to climb, city boy? Didn't they have any trees where you grew up?" Standing with her hands on her hips, she giggled up at him as she followed his awkward progress. Sidra's eyes shone with mirth. Against his judgment, Soryk was charmed. He feigned a scowl as he spit out a mouthful of wet pine needles.

"Never you mind, I can handle myself just fine." His coat snagged on a broken branch, yanking him backward as he attempted to leap down. Soryk tumbled forward and swung through empty air before finding his footing.

"Take off your coat," Sidra advised.

"I can handle it," Soryk insisted, losing his grip on both coat and branch and toppling ten feet to the springy, leaf-strewn ground with a painful sounding "Oof!" as the wind left him.

He sat up, rubbing his head.

Sidra composed herself, swallowing her gaiety as she examined him.

"Are you alive?" she asked.

"Just barely," Soryk answered. They smiled at each other and their eyes locked and held.

"You could've cracked your skull, and here I am, sans vinegar and paper," Sidra jested.

"Vinegar?"

"Perhaps you don't know the second verse, most don't." She cleared her throat and recited in a toff accent, "Jack and Jill went up the hill, to fetch a pail of water. Jack fell down and broke his crown, and Jill came tumbling after. Up got Jack and home did trot, as fast as he could caper. Went to bed and bound his head, with vinegar and brown paper. When Jill came in how she did grin, to see Jack's paper plaster. Mother vexed, did whip her next, for causing Jack's disaster." Sidra curtsied with ladylike flourish, one hand capped to her antlers to hold them steady.

"You're due a whipping then," Soryk said, rising to his feet and shaking the leaves from his clothes.

"Would you be the stern gent to administer such a punishment?" Sidra teased.

Soryk raised one eyebrow. "That wouldn't be very gentlemanly of me, now would it? You being the queen I suppose there's a royal guard posted somewhere nearby to haul me away in chains should I dare to try—"

"No royal guard today. He's taking one of his rare but much needed sojourns. Even the queen's favored advisor deserves a break from her now and again. Here, let me help you with that." Sidra pressed a faded handkerchief to the small cut that had opened on Soryk's brow.

She gazed into his long-lashed dark eyes, seeing herself reflected there in the black wells of his pupils. His beard was but a shadow and she had to suppress the urge to stroke the silky hair that strayed along his jawbone. His features were a bit soft and he had fine, smooth skin. Standing so close, she could smell him—a bit smoky and peaty from the fire but otherwise, nothing. She didn't pick up any of the usual male odors of sweat and effort. Granted Carac was a par-wolf, so his scent was stronger than an ordinary human's, but she rather liked his earthy, masculine odors and the way they announced his presence as he moved through the woods around her.

Soryk tested the wound with his fingertips. "It hurts, but I'll live." He smiled as she folded the bloodied handkerchief and tucked it away.

"Yes, I think so, too." Sidra dislodged Soryk's coat from the pine. It dropped down and he snatched it from the ground, eager to cover the ridiculous thermosuit.

"City boy," she laughed.

"Perhaps," he agreed. There was a moment of laden, awkward silence. Soryk wanted to hear her laugh again so he scooped up a pinecone and chucked it at her.

"Oh, it's like that is it," Sidra said. "I wouldn't start something you can't finish. I have a great throwing arm. You'll find yourself outmatched." To prove her point, she took the same pinecone, aimed with comic deliberateness, and fired, knocking down a single leaf that had hung from a high, bare branch.

Soryk clapped. "My hat's off to you, my lady."

Sidra offered her elbow. "Shall we, my lord?"

He was glad she'd come back for him. "Where are we off to now?"

"To find a safe haven for the night. You're welcome to tag along, unless you'd rather return to your lofty aerie," she said, indicating the tall pine that had been his refuge.

"I think I'll stick with you, if you don't mind. I got a glimpse of Her and I'd rather not be caught out again. Safety in numbers, right?"

"Indeed," Sidra smiled, leading Soryk through the wood. "Not to worry. If she comes again, I'll save you."

"I'm counting on it," Soryk laughed. He was astonished to find himself so comfortable in the company of this fantastic stranger. He ought to be more addled, more angry, confused, or paranoid about his strange situation, but he felt as though he was in the best possible place and with the best possible person to retrieve his flown memories. They would come back in their own time, and if they didn't, he had Sidra the Lovely to look after him, if not forever, then at least for a little while.

Sidra turned to Soryk and caught the light in his eyes. She saw in this man a calm, cool reservoir of strength that seemed out of place in the Wood Beast's forest domain of fear, oppression, and seclusion. He was gentle, she was sure, and kind, and capable of great and lasting affection.

He turned to her and smiled. The last rays of sunlight glistened among trees graying in the twilight. She took his warm hand and together they moved deeper into the cool forest.

"Have you remembered who you are yet?"

They had been walking for an hour or more; Sidra stepped

with ease but Soryk picked his way along in the gloom, unable to see much of anything in the oppressive darkness.

"Little things come back here and there, but they're like slippery dream fragments . . . so, the answer is no." He laughed and his teeth gleamed blue in the moonlight.

"At least your sense of humor is intact if nothing else," Sidra said. "That's a good sign, don't you think?"

"Yes, I do." He was growing hungry again, beginning to lose his taste for this adventure and wanting nothing more than a hot meal and a comfortable bed. Perhaps a bit of company as well, Soryk thought, wondering about the body beneath Sidra's layers of clothing. A light flickered in the gloom and winked out.

"Nearly there," Sidra said, quickening her pace.

Soryk stumbled after her, snaking tree roots threatening to trip him at every step. Then Sidra was gone and the ground disappeared as if a sideshow magician had yanked it from beneath his feet. He toppled into a deep hole, clawing at the sides as he fell, landing about fifteen feet below ground in a deep pit. Sidra rose from a crouch, rearranging her crown and wrap, casual about their surprise exit from the surface.

Soryk's ankle ached and he had a vague sense of having agitated an old injury. The waxing moon glimmered through the cavernous treetops swaying overhead, and then the ceiling closed in and plunged them into blackness.

A spear of yellow light cleaved the pitch. Soryk blinked a few times as his eyes adjusted and followed Sidra into a warm, soot-stained, lamplit tunnel. The loose dirt was soft underfoot, the walls scraped clean and bare. Stout branches fanned out, clenching the soil tight.

They passed a sturdy door with an incongruous brass bell tied with a gaudy red bow. Farther down the passage was another door, this one warped and stained as though it had been ripped from a grand old home, mounted with oarlocks and rafted downriver. Sidra led Soryk past several more doors, one that Soryk recognized as the insulated metal lid to a freezer and another that was nothing more than an elaborate, matlike weaving of something that resembled human hair. Soryk shuddered at the hair door as they left it behind, glad he would not have to touch it.

"What is this place?"

"Welcome to the Erun city. The tunnel that we just came through extends most of the way around the perimeter of the forest. Many of our great trees are hollow and serve as dwellings for those of us who can no longer travel through society, because our changes are too pronounced. Most of the refugees here have escaped terrible persecution—ostracism, maiming, and attempted murder by antisomatic extremists who hunt us for sport."

A sudden explosion of voices broke the tunnel's comfortable quiet. Sidra pushed on toward the fray, moving unerringly through the twisting, turning hollows. One person snarled as another yelped in pain.

"Of late there has been discord in the east tunnel," Sidra said. "We have become too dependent on surface-world charity parceled out by petty policy makers and the criminal class. There is to be no caste system here. The Erun city must remain a haven for somatics or else all is lost."

A body capered down the corridor, a rolling bundle of flailing arms and legs. Sidra leapt forward, arms extended to break the creature's fall as it tumbled to a stop at her feet.

"Pieter! What has gotten into you?" She lifted the boy by his lapels and swiped the dirt from his face and clothes. He was young and coltish, no more than twelve years old, thin as an icicle, with a spray of snow-white hair and long translucent whiskers.

Pieter swabbed at creased, sightless pink eyes and his seeking fingers roamed along Sidra's arms as he searched for something recognizable that would pair voice with body.

"Queen Sidra! It's Jodhi and them again. They've brought the city folk underground."

"Here?" Sidra loomed over Pieter's scarecrow-thin frame. "In the city?" She clenched Pieter's lapels as she stared down the tunnel, her eyes narrowed to slits.

"Jodhi's coming this way," he warned.

"Pieter," Sidra released him. "Why don't you head home?"

Needing no further encouragement, Pieter dashed away, his outstretched hands skimming the tunnel walls and guiding him to safety.

Sidra sprinted toward the voices ahead. Soryk ran after her, not wanting to lose his sole ally in the confusing warren of passages that fanned out beneath the forest floor. They soon reached the source of the trouble, and Soryk was impressed when Sidra silenced the bickering group and isolated the troublemakers, an older woman with frizzled, graying hair and a squat, barrel-chested man with a bubbling, pimpled nose and furry yellow brows.

"Jodhi. Monarch." Exuding steely calm, Sidra pushed her way to the center of a gathering of somatics. Recognizing Sidra's authority, everyone except Jodhi and her partner scuttled away, disinclined to defy their protector. They blocked the tunnel, defiance burned across faces pitted and gouged by years of hard living.

"Queen Sidra." They bowed halfheartedly, keeping wary eyes trained on her as if expecting to dodge sudden blows.

"Rumor reaches me that visitors from the surface world breached the city at your invitation. Is there truth in this, Monarch?" asked Sidra.

Singled out and nervous under his wife's murderous glare, the fat little man began to stammer, tugging at his wild brows. "Not really a threat a'tall, my lovely. An animule, not e'en one a' us."

"I'd like to know how an outsider in the city is not considered a threat. Do enlighten me."

"He means it's just a dog. A true dog; not half-bred or changed," Jodhi interjected, her hairy chin thrust forward. "Look at it." She opened a door chipped and scarred by abuse. Monarch reached into the shadows and grasped something reluctant to emerge.

He grinned weakly. “Not wantin’ ta come out,” he remarked to Sidra, who stood tapping her foot with growing impatience. Monarch plunged inside, grappled with a yelping, snarling body and dragged out a terrified rust and cream-furred dog.

Recognition jarred Soryk like a shock to the heart.

Sidra, who missed nothing, asked, “Do you know this animal?”

Longing, sorrow, and joy crashed together and Soryk knelt to rub the dog that nosed him, licking his hand and yipping in delight.

“I must.” He gazed at her with wonder in his eyes. “She certainly seems to know me. Where did you come from, girl?”

“Found ’er wanderin’ wet and skairt in the marsh, ’er ribs sticking up like fence posts.” Monarch reached for the dog but she snapped at his hand and he jerked back, embarrassed.

“She’s a good dog,” Jodhi insisted, wrapping a possessive claw around the dog’s frayed collar. “Trained to run and pull a sled. She knows all the commands. Watch.” Jodhi barked a series of commands that the dog followed with reluctant but instinctual obedience.

Soryk felt woozy and tucked his head down as he squatted on the floor, trying somehow to get his bearings.

“I’m afraid we can’t risk keeping her here. Whomever she belongs to will launch a search for her. If she escapes and is seen making her exit, our safety will be compromised. Even the beast won’t be protection against a legion of men determined to find us.” Sidra raised her voice to address those who lurked behind their doors, curious ears pressed against them to catch their conversation.

“You know this. Jodhi, Monarch”—Sidra spoke with more gentleness than was deserved—“she cannot remain.”

Jodhi, who had been salivating over the prospect of taking the dog to the open-air markets at Basalt (the trading post several miles north of Neubonne where the boldest and most mercenary of humans bought and sold contraband to somatics), stared at Soryk with clear malice.

"A dog is less trouble than some others with telling mouths and open eyes."

Less subtle than his wife, Monarch nodded and jerked his thumb at Soryk, kneeling beside a very contented sled dog receiving a good belly rub. "Who's this, then?"

"He's mine and he's welcome in the Erun. He has my full authority to travel here as he likes." Sidra planted her feet and commanded, "Ours is a peaceful city. I've given him my assurance that he will not come to harm here and I shall be very displeased if I hear otherwise."

Sidra stared down Jodhi. "Understood?"

Jodhi drew up her ancient hands and snarled. Monarch sighed and took Jodhi's arm, ushering her into their den while throwing reproachful looks over his shoulder in the hope that Sidra would catch one. The door slammed and Sidra shook her head.

"Badgers," she muttered. She smiled at Soryk and the dog, then bent to let the dog sniff her hand. "She's gorgeous. A bit thin but made from sturdy stuff, I think. What shall we do with her?"

Soryk shrugged and couldn't help grinning. "I'm to be yours now?" He was certain that Sidra blushed, or was it just a trick of the light?

"Come on." She brushed aside his question. "We have work to do. Places to go, people to see." She set off, her cheeks burning, Soryk and the dog happy to follow her.

14

BELOW THE ERUN

NIGHT CREPT THROUGH THE HOURS and lengthened the miles Sidra and Soryk spent patrolling the Erun tunnels. Sidra was an adept negotiator, settling minor disputes, redistributing funerary castoffs and surface-world spoils cadged from rubbish bins while tending to the occasional injury or illness. With gentle hands, she drew pain from tired limbs, coaxed peace into an unhappy babe, and cleaned festering sores, a smile ever-present upon her watchful countenance.

The somatics received them with gracious welcome, offering whatever was ready: scalded goat's milk with hot buttered toast, handfuls of roasted nuts, a ladle of soup, or a few licks of strong blackberry wine. Sidra always accepted, no matter that she must have been near to bursting toward the end. She introduced Soryk and the tagalong dog as her people, instituting some ambiguous claim of ownership and trustworthiness, a repeated ritual that eased much of the persistent wariness encountered in the dens.

At last, when Soryk thought he could go no farther, they reached a handsome metal grate emblazoned with a luminous brass wolf's head.

"Our last stop." Sidra smiled and squeezed his shoulder, aware of Soryk's fatigue.

This tree house was clean and spare, the wood stained in bright currents of honey and amber. A few elegant furnishings peppered the otherwise bare room. Sidra turned the wick on a low-burning oil lamp and golden light seeped across the walls and floors, illuminating a home that was welcoming despite its emptiness.

Soryk followed her directions to a high platform encircled by carved wooden arms that would catch the restless sleeper in their saving embrace. Soft furs lay heaped in its shallow, warm and inviting. Soryk dropped his coat and stripped off his boots, his relentless, jagged thoughts dulling in concert with his deepening breath. The green-eyed dog tucked herself into the pocket of his folded legs. Below them in the main room, Soryk watched Sidra lift the fawn-colored cloak, slowly unwrapping herself as if lifting an egg from its reed-bound nest.

Another voice, coarse and male, emerged to wedge itself between his lusty imaginings and thoughts of Sidra, shaking out her long hair as she peeled away layer after layer.

"When have you become so confident in your ability to judge the Others?" The voice held a hint of snarl. "Have you lost your mind, bringing a stranger here?"

"Mind your tone when you address me. You've always been far too familiar, Carac." Sidra's playfulness little dampened Soryk's mounting fury as he sat scowling in the platform overhead. He objected to this interloper's insouciant tone and tart manner, not to mention his rough disregard of Sidra's queenly rank.

"My lady." The voice softened. "I meant no disregard."

"As usual," Sidra laughed. "How contrite you are! All transgressions are forgiven."

Carac hummed with pleasure as Sidra stroked his grizzled head, reaching beneath his jaw to scratch his bearded neck and rub her fingers along the curve of his ear. She murmured something unintelligible and both chuckled.

Soryk leaned over the platform's edge, straining to catch the conversation played out in hushed and seductive tones. Trivial jealousies worried him, annoying as a persistent small dog, snapping at his ankles. Sidra the Lovely was not a woman bound by romantic conventions. Free with her favors and affection, she had transformed herself in the course of minutes from a cloistered, secret cove to a delightful, open meadow where any man might take his moment's pleasure.

Beside him, the red-furred dog opened a sleepy eye and gazed at Soryk balefully.

"Hush, you," he groused, cuffing the dog's ear.

Lamplight waned and darkness settled around his shoulders. Gentle murmurs accompanied the couple along the stairs as they ascended to a treetop loft. The sounds of their lovemaking pealed throughout the night as Sidra's cries of pleasure floated down like autumn leaves to litter Soryk's cold bed.

Quickly, now, quickly! The leaping sea bit at her hands and feet as she ran, hurtling over blood-smeared floes. Breath came hard, heart hammered. She felt small and weak against the elemental onslaught. The leopard seal was coming, thrusting itself onto the ice. Fear of death staked through her core and still she ran.

The spotted seal roared, its yellow teeth bared.

Something else was beneath the ice, a fish perhaps, swimming sluggish through the slush. On she ran as the volcano shuddered and burst, showering her with sparks and soot. Lava flamed and fell, marking the ice with great, steaming gouges.

There! The ice grew thin, she could just reach it. Sparks ignited her sleeve and she shoved it into the roiling grayness beneath her feet. Ice cracked and split. Something bobbed against its surface, threatening to break through, and she fell, slush blocking up her nose and ears and eyes. Some other thing swam sibilant around her, fish with soft, cherubic faces and skin in place of scales. Two of them circled and opened quizzical eyes. "Do you forget?" asked one. "Have you forsaken us?" queried the other.

Ice filled her mouth and she could not answer.

The fish turned to each other and said, "We are lost to her forever."

Their eyes opaqued, becoming colorless as white wine. Belly up they floated to the surface, the tiny, hopeful spirit lamps inside them winking out. Extinguished.

Soryk was in a foul mood. He slumped at the breakfast table, staring at a broken comb oozing wax-flecked honey in a dish. The dream lodged inside him, a choking burr. Fish like two dead babes, their carcasses adrift on the winter sea.

His thoughts were senseless and muddled. Uncharacteristically disinterested in food, he poked at the fruit buns and soft cheese on the table.

"I'm leaving the city today," Sidra announced, capturing Soryk's attention. "You are welcome to remain in any of the homes we've visited, including this one. Carac is here periodically, as am I. You would have the run of the place."

Soryk looked askance at the gruff par-wolf who'd introduced himself that morning in passing as he led Sidra from the high loft. Carac's fierce expression and wild hair, coupled with his bulging muscles and pointed teeth, little inspired warm welcome in his guest.

"Thank you for your offer but I think it best I be on my way."

Sidra and Carac glanced at each other and Soryk divined that he'd been the topic of an earlier conversation.

"How do you know the way if you don't even know who you

are or where you hail from?" Carac smirked in a deep, powerful voice that would incite fear among kings and warriors alike. Soryk raised an eyebrow. He didn't appreciate anyone questioning his motives. Carac's tongue lolled against his cheek as he guzzled from a mug and liquid coursed down his chin, wetting his shirt. Soryk was disgusted to imagine Sidra with this beast. What could she possibly find so alluring in an untamed par-wolf with his dangerous airs and nightmarish appearance?

"If you don't mind," Sidra inserted, amused by the tension between her paramour and the enigmatic stranger, "I'd like you to accompany me through the Erun. I can see you safely out of the forest, at which point you'd be free to make your way to Neubonne or Blundt."

"And if I remain?"

"I'll see you again in a few weeks, when I pass through." She grinned, flashing her dimples at him, and Soryk was stricken to imagine himself without her. He liked Sidra. She sat down across from him at the breakfast table, fully dressed and sporting her ridiculous antler hat. Her effusive good humor and sly feminine charm had an intoxicating effect on what he hoped would have been his otherwise good sense.

"Well," Soryk remarked, brimming with puffed-up, masculine bravado, "who can resist an adventure?" He returned her smile.

Carac growled under his breath and Soryk grinned in triumph.

"It's settled then." She clapped her hands with glee and helped herself to another bun slathered in honey. "We'll depart after breakfast." She tongued honey from the corner of her mouth and licked her fingers, oblivious to the two men eyeing her with lust.

Soryk excused himself to collect his belongings and prepare once more to greet the outside world. There was a yawning gap in his memory, but if he jumped it he could lose himself in a forest of ancient images, crowded together in his mind like tall trees. Feminine static filled his mind. One signal seemed to intensify and announce itself but would recede before he could identify its source.

He shook off his burdens; too many mysteries to sort out today.

He was troubled. It wasn't just the dream, or the strangeness of his situation, which he accepted with casual ease. There were gaping holes in his memory—he could live with that and with being the odd man out among the secretive denizens of the Erun city, but Soryk was a stranger even to himself. He yearned to dash the clinging sense of an assignment abandoned, to enjoy this new adventure, but worry persisted and he could make no sense of it. *Tick-tock. Time's on fire today.* He had to do something, but what? Soryk sat stone-faced, searching his memory. How could he arrive at adulthood yet not recall the journey?

They had chopped off his hair and he'd run away. Yes, that was right. He'd traveled to the city to join the packs of work-hungry men who lined the streets, waiting for passing construction crews to pick them out of the crowds. Buildings were going up all over the city then; Tirai Industries held a monopoly on development and owned virtually every tower, housing complex, rubble pile, and vacant lot in Neubonne. Work crews, swing gangs, and day and migrant laborers all thrived under TI's monstrous wings, working for cash and signing away all their rights in exchange for their cut of an exorbitant under-the-table trade.

He was seventeen and squatting in one of the rough, abandoned tenements allotted the day laborers. Hassle-free tenement living was another of TI's unofficial perks, like running water and the occasionally functioning electrical outlets that enabled the squatters to have light and hot food, and run their small, cantankerous heaters in defense against the seeping winter cold.

He'd liked the anonymity of being another faceless pair of hands, a simple corporate peon. At first he ferried bricks, rivets, and tools to the builders. As the youngest worker and most untried, he wasn't trusted to do much more than fetch coffee from the lunch caravan, but as the weeks passed and Soryk proved his competence, he was rewarded with increased responsibility.

The foreman assigned Soryk to the glaziers, and as he ascended from errand boy to apprentice, he finally felt that he had found a place for his exacting, intricate mind. The glaziers were artisans and held themselves to exacting standards. Though required to fulfill such quotidian tasks as setting all the thick, tempered tower windows, they also handled the finer details of decorating courtyards and common spaces with soaring sculptures of molten sand—ornate statuettes whose glass skin and veins glittered with gold and diamond dust atop nerve networks of hematite.

Soryk was startled to realize that he knew how to blow glass—could pluck a wad of melted glass from the inferno, coax it into readiness like a green fruit ripening in his hand, infuse it with spirit, and breathe life into a work of art. The memory of the warm pipe against his lips lingered like a lover's first kiss. He touched his mouth and smiled before growing aware of the tepid, infrequent conversation that stopped and started around him.

Sidra had given him a packet of clothing: long underwear, a gray homespun jersey, relatively clean brown trousers, a rough, knitted sweater of nubbiny wool, and a shapeless beige blanket, stained by years of use. He'd grimaced as he accepted the items, but knew that he could not travel with any semblance of pride dressed in the tight, torn thermosuit. He dressed quickly, self-conscious on the open platform and aware of the pale reediness of his body, slender and nearly as hairless as a boy's.

Carac paced the main floor, his muscles bunched beneath his shirt, his cruel face lean and hungering. He watched Soryk's descent with a blatant resentment he did not bother to disguise. Soryk swung his gaze toward Sidra, again oblivious to the tensions in the room. She strapped on her gear, tied her leather thongs, and arranged her fawn-spotted cloak over her shoulders. Then she smiled at each man in turn. (The word "man" was woefully inadequate to describe who these two were at heart; wolf and girl beneath their skins and neither much the wiser.)

Sidra embraced Carac and settled her antler crown on her head, transitioning from tender lover to brusque and businesslike ruler, once again becoming Sidra the Lovely, Queen of the Erun.

"Follow this newest lead and report back to me in three weeks' time. I cannot help but sense that Matuk is working some terrible new magic in that toxic lair of his. I doubt any will be left alive to tell their tales, but we must keep abreast of his dark dealings."

"And the children?" Carac asked grimly, his black whiskers twitching.

"A lost cause, to be sure. Fate has already snipped those threads. We can't undo what's already been done," Sidra concluded.

Soryk listened, rubbing the dog's neck and wondering what he should call her. He stepped back and gestured her forward "Come here, Red." Kika cocked her head, clearly confused.

"Come on, girl, come on." The dog sat on her haunches and gazed with interest at a passing dust mote.

"What are we going to call you then?" Soryk asked, stroking her thick fur.

Carac had been watching the exchange and growled as if to himself. The dog leapt to her feet and uttered a series of short, sharp barks.

"You can call her Kika," Carac told Soryk. "It's what she's used to."

Soryk shrugged, refusing to allow himself to be impressed by Carac's ability to understand the dog. "All right then, Kika it is."

Sidra smiled. "I like it."

Kika sighed in relief, glad that someone had finally gotten it right.

"Then let's away," Sidra exclaimed, restless within the tree's confines. "We have much ground to cover."

Carac watched his queen leave the home they had made together and strike out for the surface with the stranger by her side. There was something not right about him, something skewed about his appearance, as if he wore an ill-fitting mask. In his years with Sidra, he had encountered hundreds of bizarre and surprising mutations but never had he felt the way he did about this Otherman, Soryk. Carac resolved to keep a close eye on him until he was well away from the Erun. Should Sidra come to harm at this man's hands, he would have no one to blame but himself.

She had asked him to report on Matuk's latest acquisition but as she'd said, there was nothing left to do now but mourn for the passing of some unfortunate woman's children. His choice made, he would follow Sidra into the forest and let the damned rest quietly in their graves.

15

A BEASTLY ENCOUNTER

MIST SWIRLED FAST AND FURIOUS, spinning between the tree limbs as Sidra and Soryk walked. An occasional flicker of sunlight went its way through the thickets, illuminating the forest before fluttering away.

Sidra moved with casual grace and left no mark of her passing. Soryk stumbled behind her, unaccustomed to the wilderness and the murky quality of light. Silence pressed in from all sides, heavy and smothering, and he had to fight the urge to yell just to break it.

They walked for hours, made camp at dusk, and nestled into the brush after a supper of pressed mealie, boiled eggs, and cheese. Sidra didn't have much to say, and wrapped up in his own thoughts, Soryk respected her desire for solitude. Something rustled in the brush and he reclined warily, taking a cue from Sidra, who slept sitting upright, her blanket obscuring all but her face, blue in the moonlight.

He desired her. Wrapping the blanket tight around his shoulders, he considered Carac and decided that he did not wish to become the third wheel in a sordid love triangle between queen and par-wolf.

Still, his body was restless, hungry. When had he last possessed a woman? He recalled a few distant encounters with the White Lady, an angular, acid-tongued resident of the Tirai squats, so-called because she wore white every day and managed to keep it clean despite the squalor. She'd been a wire lancer who rigged informant lines for Tirai's secret infrastructure of company hackers and spies. She slipped behind wall panels and crouched in crawl spaces armed with her shiny aluminum toolbox and a look of icy concentration on her alluring face.

With brass-colored curls, olive skin, and kohl-lined black eyes, the White Lady was an exotic prize sought by many of the squat's laborers. She kept her own counsel, however, dwelling in an isolated corner of the abandoned penthouse among her spotless white bedding, white painted bureau, and stacks of stripped books, their colorful bindings removed to reveal blank spines. Soryk never spoke to her aside from the occasional mumbled greeting when they encountered each other in the squat's common areas but she'd kept a careful eye on him and his transformation from lackey to artisan.

Years later, the flowery taste of her mouth was still fresh in his memory. He could scroll through the moments, from when she had first peeled back her spotless clothing and revealed her lush form to the weeks of increasing debauchery that followed as they overtook the abandoned glassworks and converted it to their own private playground. She turned Soryk into a night creature like herself, secretive and paranoid, ever watchful and always, always filled with desire.

It might have lasted forever, but for the beating delivered by a tyrannical and obsessive squatter intent on possessing her. When Soryk woke from the attack and went to find his love, her nest was spoiled and dirtied. Blood, mud, and grease stained her once-white bedding; her denuded books lay shredded and broken, and a loose clump of golden hair twisted in the sour wind blowing through the shattered penthouse window.

Thinking her dead, he ran. He stored her tools in an electrician's cabinet, a tiny, locked room secreted between the elevator shaft and stairwell on the fourteenth floor, and it was there that he took refuge for the night. When Soryk awoke, He had become She. The adventure ended. Sorykah fled from the squat and walked back to her parents' house, some thirty miles and three days distant, though the memory of that journey lay submerged deep within the subconscious of her forgotten split soul.

If only he had looked! Soryk would've spared himself the changing pain had he seen that the body lying crushed into the pavement outside the squat was not the White Lady's but that of her attacker. He never knew that she had saved herself.

Winter clung fast with icy fingers, reluctant to relinquish its hold on the Erun. Spotty shafts of sunlight poked through the thick canopy of evergreens and cedars, deepening the shadows and doing little to dispel the constant chill. Frost crunched underfoot and frozen tussocks snapped apart as Queen Sidra led Soryk and his dog deeper into the primeval forest. The rain-blackened trunks of massive trees soared overhead. Soryk shivered to see claw marks raked across the bark, evidence of something fierce and terrible haunting the woods.

Soryk followed Sidra rather haplessly, entertaining the idea of a lengthy seduction and conquest, but the playful nature she'd displayed in the tree house was gone. Instead, she was somber and driven, picking a path through the loam and bushy overhangs, speaking little but smiling to silence his questions, reassuring him that she did indeed know where she was going.

Neubonne, was it? Headed to the charity hospital where he might lie in a clean, narrow bed and recover his sense of self. It sounded less appealing, however, the more time he spent in the wilds with Sidra the Lovely and the bright-eyed dog. The forest's sharp delineations and vivid geometries held him in thrall. He was fascinated by the weft of a sister tree's interlocked branches growing at absurd right angles to the ground, and awestruck by soaring, soldierly cedars and diamond-studded spiderwebs draping the leafy alcoves.

He was happy for no other reason than that he was alive and it was a revelation. Strange how this new sense of wonder and delight could coexist with the burdens he carried. No matter how he tried to shake it off and leave it behind, he was plagued by a nagging sense of anxiety, of some vital thing forgotten that nibbled away at the sweet and crunchy edges of his delicious joy.

Sidra broke her silence on the fourth day. They stopped at a lean-to to wait out a splashing downpour, and Sidra pulled out her single burner and kettle to brew up something with which to enliven the hours until the rain ceased. The Erun was rife with a network of strange shelters and haphazard hovels made of lashed-together twigs, slabs of bark propped on rocks, or hollows dug beneath dormant elderberry bushes. Sidra always seemed to manifest them as if by magic and Soryk had begun to appreciate her keen eye, because he never saw the shelters until Sidra had pulled him inside.

"I rather fancy a wee nip, how about you?" Sidra grinned and fished a flask from her bottomless bag, pulling out the stopper. "Go on, it's not natural for a man to spend five days in a row dry." She winked and urged him to drink.

Smoky, heavily spiced liquor inflamed his mouth and throat as he swallowed, choking on the homemade brew.

Sidra took a long draught, savoring the burn and sighing with contentment. Kicking out her legs, she lay back on her cape, fussing when the shelter's leafy walls ensnared her antlers.

Once he had his breath back, Soryk gestured to the awkward crown and asked, "Why don't you take it off?"

A kaleidoscope of emotions flickered across Sidra's face. She pushed her crown over her forehead as she took another swig from the flask. "I never take it off," she insisted.

Soryk raised an eyebrow, clearly recalling her bare head disappearing into the high loft with Carac. He inched closer, pretending to be intent on stirring the soup boiling on the little burner.

"Here." He reached for the queen. "You have leaves in your hair." She always had leaves in her hair, but it was a convenient excuse for him to touch her. Soryk plucked a small twig from the tangled ruins, certain that she reddened at his nearness.

Sidra offered him the flask. This time he drank without choking, holding it in his mouth until the burn spread into his sinuses and tears filled his eyes.

"It's good, isn't it?" Sidra laughed, the liquor already going to her head. It was strong medicinal stuff she cooked up at the tree house, its true application to render wounded somatics unconscious should they require rudimentary surgery. Two sips were festive, five were debilitating, and any more than that was downright dangerous. "I think you'd better wait a bit and let it do its work," she cautioned as he reached for the flask, emboldened by their closeness.

"Fine, fine," he murmured, reclining on a mound of leaves. Rain spit through the gaps but the little hot pot warmed the air inside the shelter and he was content. Kika nestled between them seeking warmth and Soryk stroked her fur, letting the day's torpor wash over him. He closed his eyes, pushing away the surfacing images of the drowned fish of his dream.

"Sidra the Lovely," he whispered, savoring the feel of her name in his mouth. "From acorn did you spring, in your gown of fairy fern, eyes alight like flaming stars, gossamer in your touch." The line of ancient poetry unfurled from the deep pockets of his mind.

"And how your wings did glisten, little ghost of mine, and fade beneath the waning sun, no longer flame but dun," Sidra concluded, a dreamy look to her eye. "I do so love the poets of the realm. Saint Catherine is my favorite. How did you know?"

Soryk shrugged, immensely pleased that she was moved by his speech and had not laughed at him. "A friend of mine taught me," he said, his mind filled with remembrances of stark black text leaping from the page of a spineless book. "And I in my simple white cap, did shun your cautious overture, because none would have believed, that simple grace would move me so."

Sidra rested chin in palm and raised a single eyebrow at her companion. "It's about a flower, you know."

"Or love. Or the Holy Mother. Depends on the interpreter."

"Yes, isn't it wonderful? But still—love, flowers, the Spirit are all one in the same, different expressions of the same energy." Sidra removed the broth from the burner and fished a carved wooden spoon from her pocket, stirring the pot and offering Soryk first taste.

He deferred to her, because she was both a woman and a queen, though not his own. Sidra nodded, pleased by his show of manners. She took a thoughtful sip and offered him the remainder of the broth still on the spoon.

He considered their tongues on the same utensil, the mealie in the pot a flirtatious intermediary between them. He watched her lick her lips and wished he was a spoon.

The next two days were sunny and dry. Persistent rainfall eased and the dense forest began to thin, admitting more light that bounced among shining green leaves. Soryk and Kika were well fed. The queen could manufacture a meal from scraps and air; the meatless stews and fry-ups she concocted on her burner were always tasty if a bit too light for Soryk's taste. He'd begun to daydream about meat and found himself recalling specific meals from days past, a garlicky roast he'd eaten at a tavern in Neubonne, a savory chicken hand-pie the White Lady had once brought to him when he was recovering from an illness. He longed for the taste of warm fat in his mouth and meat in his belly. Stray thoughts of catching and killing crept into the rear of his mind and loitered there, insistent in their bloody obsession.

Kika compensated by disappearing for a few hours every other day and rejoining them with a bloodied muzzle. Because Soryk had not seen any animals in the forest, he wondered what she ate until his curiosity and meat lust inspired him to track her.

An opportunity presented itself one evening when Sidra complained of lady pains and made camp early. She rolled into a ball with her flask and her skin cloak tucked tight around herself and slept. Kika took this as her cue and moved quickly, vanishing into the bushes. Stealing a wad of kindling lint and the flint fire starter from Sidra's cook bag, Soryk scrambled after her, clutching his small dagger.

Trotting with quiet purpose, Kika followed her nose to a heap of loose earth at the base of a rotted tree and began to dig, tossing soil into the air and forcing her muzzle into the soft spot. Excited, she lunged forward, snapping her jaws. Black soil flew into the air as her prey attempted to burrow more deeply into its lair, but Kika had already gotten hold of something brown and furry, dragged it from its home, and broken its neck.

Kika sauntered into the forest to consume her meal as Soryk examined the crime scene. There were a few discarded husks littering the area, grassy balls of what must be nesting material. He'd seen these little piles before but had believed them insignificant rubbish.

Scanning the area, Soryk proceeded from tree to tree, hunting for the detritus that would alert him to a potential meal. There: a mound of gritty soil patterned with discarded seedpods.

Cutting a long, stout twig, he sliced off its flimsy branches and whittled the end into a crude, efficient stake. He advanced on the rotting stump, weapon in hand. He intended to flush the creature out, catch it, and wring its neck as Kika had done; it didn't seem so difficult. The stick easily penetrated the burrow and sank into an underground hollow. Something moved and the surface dirt shifted. Soryk jabbed into it. There was a muffled squeal, thrashing beneath the earth and stillness.

Soryk withdrew the stick, stained with blood and fur, to push the hair from his eyes as he knelt, panting. He didn't realize how intensely he'd gone after the creature. Once he sensed that the animal was his for the taking, a noxious sense of power swept over him, emboldening him and making him crazed and reckless.

Scooping dirt from the mound beneath the tree, he reached into the darkness, touching something hot, hairy, and gummy wet. His fingers closed around a small, bony leg and he tugged the battered body free. His catch tumbled into his lap, a fat, round ball of red-saturated fur with tiny pink hands, a pointed nose and short stiff whiskers.

Soryk looked at the dead animal in his lap, at once guilty and triumphant. He'd killed this creature, and now he would have to eat it or suffer carrying the sin of death for pleasure. He would have to skin it, remove the entrails, and clean the carcass. Having never done these things, he was leery of his capability with the small, rough blade.

His skin pimpled in the cold as he stripped off his shirt, squatting near a fallen log, using it as a shield in case Sidra should waken and come looking for him. There was no need to be careful; time was the most pressing factor. Finding an open spear hole in the carcass, he inserted his knife and ripped open the skin, like tearing a burlap bag in two. A mess of intestines slithered over his hands and pooled at his feet. Soryk was horrified then by what he had done, shocked by the brutality that lay fallow within him, awaiting the awakening thrust.

He worked in haste, slicing around the neckline and forcing the skin back over the limbs. The meat was there, dark red and mottled with globs of gelatinous yellow fat, singing to him through the gloom. He would've put his teeth to it right then but for a rustling in the trees that drove him deeper into the forest, away from Sidra. In a darkened alcove, cloistered by ground-sweeping, ancient pines, he gathered the driest twigs and mounted them over a wad of lint, clicking the fire starter until flames swelled and the wood began to smoke. With bare hands, he wrested the small heart and other organs free and flung them far, wiping his bloodied hands on the leaves. There wasn't time to spit-roast the creature; it was too dense and round. Instead he sliced strips of muscle from the legs and sides, pierced them with his stick and held them in the flames, watching as the heat took hold, curling the flesh, browning it and filling the air with crackling beads of fat. Saliva pooled in his mouth and he could wait no longer, gnawing flesh barely browned and tasting of the woolly wilds.

Gamey and fatty, it was unlike anything he'd ever passed between his lips but hot and richly satisfying. He was piggish in the eating like a wild man, glad that he was alone to slurp the tiny liver down raw.

He finished and craved another. Wanted to boil down the bones and extract every molecule of nourishment from his small sacrifice, but he couldn't go back to Sidra with this kill as if offering meat for her soup pot, returning sheepish and bloodstained, some imaginary tail tucked between his legs. He rose as if waking from a fugue state, stared at the site of his butchery as if seeing it for the first time, blood and fur and skin splattering the hesitant winter green.

Guilt stung like nettles. He must disguise the evidence of his misdeed. Bury the carcass in a shallow grave, cleanse hands with mud and scrubbing pine, and rinse away the stains with snowmelt yellowed by fallen leaves. Something pricked the back of his neck. Eerie, how unholy quiet the forest could be.

Rustling, deep in the woods, a clumsy body lumbering through, much bigger than the red and cream dog of whom he'd grown so fond. Terror sparked deep within and his bowels seized.

The Beast. His blade was no match for the hideous creature he'd seen that first day when Sidra had treed him. He would have to run for it.

Soryk dashed the slaughter site and scattered wet leaves and dirt over the remains of his fire, pulling on his shirt as he darted between the tress, heading back to the camp and the welcome safety of Sidra's surety.

Sidra was sitting up, calm and alert, watching the forest when Soryk exploded from the trees with panic-glazed eyes. She raised a finger to her lips and gestured for him to sit beside her, then demonstrated wrapping the blanket around her body, covering her face, bowing her head. Soryk's heart pounded in his chest. Whether he was more afraid of being caught or eaten, it was hard to tell, but he followed Sidra's directive and huddled beneath his blanket, ears straining to catch the bracken-crashing Beast as it neared.

Stout tree limbs gave like dry twigs, snapping and shearing away from their trunks with clamorous cracklings as a whirlwind of destruction flowed their way. The beast roared, low and terrible, resonant as a thousand gongs simultaneously struck, and Soryk winced in pain. Hot drool dripped from the Wood Beast's grungy jaws, splattering the ground as it neared, snorting and sniffing as it nosed its way toward the meager camp. He could smell its foul stench of death and rot, feel the breath as it whistled between tartar-browned teeth and hear the labored grunting as the near-blind Beast rooted for food, its clumsy claws smashing the shelter to smithereens. Broken branches rained on their heads and still they sat unmoving.

Soryk was pinned by disbelief that stillness and silence should be their only weapons against such a monster. He thought of the carcass abandoned in the woods, the rich smells of seared meat that had roused this hideous creature and drawn it to them. All his fault then, should they be eaten.

The Beast hesitated, nosing around through the shelter's remains. It growled, snuffling and pawing at the food sacks with their bladders of oil, salt, and nut butters. The Beast bit through something that squeaked, popped, and ripped. Droplets splattered the side of Soryk's blanket. He began to shake uncontrollably. He thought he might leap up screaming just to break the terrible tension. When he thought he could stand no more, that he would have to take his chances and risk death, the Beast began to move away, drawn by something else in the forest. She lumbered through the bracken, leaving ruin in her wake.

The blanket peeled back from his face. Sidra peered in at him, her crown askew, her light eyes creased with both merriment and concern.

"Did she get you?" Sidra's wide mouth quirked into a smile.

Soryk threw off the blanket. "How you can be so damned jolly at a time like this, I'll never know!" His legs were shaking and he stamped his feet to disguise it but his ankle turned and he toppled over onto his knees, landing with his rear upended and an expression of comic astonishment on his face.

Sidra fell back clutching her belly. "Oh," she gasped. "That's rich! I haven't had a good laugh in a while." She wiped her eyes, grinning up at him and showing her teeth.

"I'm glad you find my antics so amusing," Soryk grumbled, but then he, too, smiled. She was so innocent in her humor and so caring otherwise, he couldn't hold on to his indignation.

"I'm sorry," Sidra patted his leg. "It's just that you're so afraid!"

"Shouldn't I be?"

"She's harmless."

"Harmless?" Soryk barked. "Ha!"

"The Wood Beast is one of the great secrets of the Erun. Even the somatics in the tunnel city don't know the truth about her. Do you wish to know the story of the Wood Beast?"

"I do," Soryk answered, and thus he learned the terrible truths of his formidable enemy's dark and secret heart.

16

TIRAI'S FORGOTTEN DAUGHTER AND HOW SHE CAME BY THE CHANGE: A TRUE TALE

"MANY YEARS AGO, men believed themselves invincible and could not fathom that they might slip from their place of power atop the animal kingdom's heap. But no place is assured, a dictator's least of all, and they were destined to fall.

"Oman was the first. They called him Oman Noman because it was said he forgot his identity with the change. Of course, a man is a man through and through and cannot be any other. The legend says that he lost his mind when his feathers came in, as well as his wife, lover, family, and business. Everything he possessed disintegrated and blew away, leaving him bereft. We tell of a journey into the night forest, where he vanished forever. Many assumed he had died from grief, or madness. His body was never found and thus he became immortal.

"But the Erun is an ancient scholar with her own lessons to teach and Oman learned how to survive in the wilderness. A foul genetic virus, the spreading change created legions of outcasts who sought refuge in the land of their hero. They too wanted immortality, because it's better to live forever as a villain in story than die unremembered.

"Oman took them in and taught them his ways, and they thrived. Oman took a wife who bore weird and wonderful children, and soon others in the Erun also paired and mated. Sometimes the children were born with obvious signs of the change, but others were completely ordinary and would always remain so.

"One of these everyday children was determined to leave the forest city and return to the world of men. A love of steel and glass burned inside of him. There was nothing to conquer in the Erun, no one to squash and destroy. This child, Daoud, returned to the city and became a terrorizing, mechanizing force that transformed the provincial town of Neubonne into a crowded and dirty metropolis.

"Daoud had many wives and allowed them their children, but a single son inherited his father's appetite for destruction tenfold. Matuk the Collector.

"When Daoud grew too feeble to run his empire, Matuk swooped in like a vulture with a bloodied beak to pick apart the carcass. Matuk's company swelled ticklike, glutting itself on smaller corporations.

"Everyone knew Matuk had a cold heart, but when he found Tirai in a brothel and rescued her from her life of sexual slavery, many were relieved by this rare show of humanity. Tirai and Matuk quickly married. Though well schooled in the manifold arts of the boudoir, she was an innocent at heart who still believed in love. It must have seemed like a miracle when Matuk brought her to his elaborate high-rise with its solid gold fittings, silk-paneled walls, and diamond-studded doorknobs. All he required of her was loyalty, that her yielding nature never be tainted or tried.

"She managed it, for a while, but disillusionment comes hard and fast in the city. Alone in her gilded cage, Tirai's soft heart grew querulous and when Matuk's beautiful sister Shanxi appeared, the seeds of Tirai's betrayal were sown.

"Shanxi was a backhanded seductress, feigning innocence even as she led her brother's wife astray. As Tirai's enchantment deepened, Matuk grew suspicious of her dreamy eyes and trailing sentences. To cement her fidelity, he impregnated her, keeping her home and bedbound until their daughter Radhe was born.

"The excitement of a new baby is no match for the intrigue of stolen kisses and even with her breasts dripping milk, Tirai still dallied. It might have continued this way forever, brother and sister quibbling over a delicate, milk-soaked bone but a heart of ice breaks more easily than one made of warm muscle. Matuk's simmering fury became an inferno. He burned down his sister's house with Shanxi still inside and Tirai vanished. Matuk claimed she'd moved to the country to live with family and none questioned him.

"He hired a nanny to raise his daughter Radhe, a sweet and doting girl, tiny and dark-eyed like her mother. In his daughter, Matuk found the devotion he had so craved from his wife. All he asked was that she never change and never betray him.

"Who can make such promises? Certainly not a child. Radhe was born of betrayal and it was in her nature to break her father's heart, just like her mother. Radhe was thirteen and just beginning to bloom when she caught the change. It started with her teeth. Grown large and pointed, they jutted from her mouth in all directions, making it difficult for her to eat. The change seeped into her bones and she grew deformed and nearly eight feet tall. Her eyes dimmed. She lost her hearing and strange wiry hairs sprouted all over her body. It was impossible to tell what she might become, even more difficult to escape the gruesome, stinking tumors that sprang up beneath her skin.

"Gentle Radhe lost the ability to speak. She could never settle her bones and rest in comfort; she could not eat. Unable to see or hear, Radhe stumbled around her father's extravagant penthouse, destroying all of his precious and expensive artifacts, bellowing incomprehensibly.

"Matuk was horrified. His compassion cooled and solidified into a core of iron. He couldn't leave his legacy to a monster. She was no longer his baby, with a candy heart and a voice like birdsong. All of Daoud's dark suspicions rose up in Matuk's memory, surfacing like drowned corpses from a pond—Daoud who had so despised his family, his raven-winged father, and clusters of strange, altered siblings.

"A tribe of somatics lived in the Erun—Oman's descendants and Matuk's kin—and there Matuk banished his deformed child, leaving her bereft and abandoned to fend for herself among the wilds.

"Here she staggers still, half alive, crippled and old, hideous and frightening. She bellows because she is an exile, forever hungry and cold. Stricken with the terrible burden of her loneliness and pain, Radhe the Wood Beast haunts the Erun, pining for her wasted life.

"What of Matuk, whose guilt now chews at him like a cancer? When a pragmatic man is visited by ghosts, he is forced to believe. Rumors insist that murdered Tirai returned from the grave to chastise the cruel man who destroyed her child, that her vengeance was the spur goading him to action on Radhe's behalf. Even at this moment, he attempts to make amends for his appalling transgressions by seeking a cure for Radhe, a magic potion that will render her human once more.

"Matuk shared his chemist sister's brilliance but his methods were crude, clumsy, and destructive. What began as a hopeful plan to isolate the mutation inside Radhe's genes devolved into a plot fraught with blood and torture as he sacrificed his somatic brethren to his mania for a cure.

"Perhaps Matuk is no longer able to see the villainy in his actions, for he believes he pursues them in clear conscience. Never his daughter's savior, Matuk has become the devil himself, ensnaring innocents in his web, capturing somatics for sport and experimentation, hunting them down for pleasure when their blood fails to yield results. His fierce and wicked henchman does all his dirty work; Matuk needn't soil his hands unless he desires the killing sheen.

"We are but fish in a net, hooked and destroyed by one who should hold sacred the utmost compassion for our plight. The man with the money and power to preserve this forest as a sanctuary chooses instead to capitalize on our weaknesses.

"What is poor Radhe to think, wandering naked and alone in these abandoned woods? She is friendless and forgotten. Years of near-starvation and isolation have chipped away at her unfinished adolescent self, until naught but a blurry streak of humanity colors her soul.

"Matuk grows more despotic as time wears on without him discovering a way to reverse the change that stole away his baby. His wrath mounts with each failure and the staked and severed heads of the somatics he has killed ring the grounds of the white manor, like a necklace of death.

"Matuk is the Collector because he keeps his finds. His is a domain of purgatorial suffering that grows more hellish with each passing year. Behind the walls of his impenetrable fort, the changelings of the Erun Forest linger and die.

"Dogs the size of small lions stalk the manor, their fangs running hot and wet, their muscled bodies and steaming, red tongues restless for a kill. They are loyal to none but their master, but even he must be careful, lest they take a whim and turn feral.

"The sights and sounds of Radhe's torment warn away any rescuers; harmless though she may be, none dares cross her. A meadow stretches between the manor and the woods, ensuring that Matuk can spy from his watchtower anyone who dares approach and the stench from the charnel house in spring sickens all downwind of its butchered, thawing horrors.

"If one could pass the Beast, the dogs, the mountains, and the

Gatekeeper, there would be no entrance into the manor itself, for the locks are welded and the single door requires a trick to turn it. Learn it, and the Collector would be yours, trapped like a rabbit in a snare, for that shriveled old man never leaves the tower and the years have not been kind. Weak and wasted, he rules by fear, not brawn, and would be an easy kill for one with a sharp eye and sharper sword. But until that day, there is nothing that can be done, save pray he doesn't catch you."

17

DEATH DEALS A HAND

WORRY NIGGLED AT DUNYA'S MIND as she perched on her three-legged kitchen stool, plucking a wild fowl Meertham had snared for the Master. The babes kicked and babbled on the grass mat she'd made in an effort to keep them from the hovering chill, their thinned legs thrashing inside their quilted suits.

"Me wee snow bunnies," Dunya smiled, tickling them each in turn with a short brown feather. She was pleased with how they were coming along, well pleased indeed. After her initial scare when she'd discovered their secret, she'd spent the day deep in thought. She had to get them away from the manor; that much was certain. Once the Collector tired of his honey-haired plaything, he wouldn't hesitate to dispatch that bonny pianist with her saintly, redemptive glow. Then he'd turn his devilish attention to her twin stars and commence to dabbling in his dark arts, committing any number of crimes against these fresh-faced two.

She worked the problem like a stubborn knot, trying and testing loose ends, looking for a way to unravel the loyalty that kept her bound. Faces floated in her mind: ravaged Soot, Chulthus, who'd passed last winter and whose flesh-spackled bones lay bleaching on the cold meadow, Dunya's own pups—faces blurred by time and tears—and endless legions of slain somatics, the dungeon inhabitants she'd cared for as they vanished, one by one.

Was it a matter of revenge? she wondered, lying in her sacking bed, listening to the damp boughs hiss and pop in the hearth's banked fire. She slept with the sewing basket beside her bed, one hand resting on the bundled babes all night. Trust was a commodity she could not parse with that lecherous old Gatekeeper slinking about the property. The bells might ring at any moment, summoning Dunya to the tower with an order to bring the babies trussed like roast piglets to be served and shamelessly devoured.

To be sure, it was a right crime how her Master had stolen her pups from her, the milk teeth still soft in their mouths, but it was an old trespass and she'd grown numbed to the constant ache she suffered for their loss. Although Dunya had served Matuk for many uncomplaining years (as a dog is wont to do for a treacherous master), malcontent brewed within her, a frothy and traitorous potion.

She knit her worries into the fabric of her day. Now that she knew what those children could do, there would be no saving them once the Master caught wind. He'd make mincemeat pies from their chubby limbs and leave them to the beast, grind their bones to extract their DNA, and concoct another of his miserable, antidotal tinctures with which to poison his daughter and bring about another sort of change.

"I know the truth," she said to the twins and to Matuk, in his far-off tower. "Don't think I 'aven't got wise to ye after these long years wiping up yer spills and burying that mess of bones come spring thaw. 'Tis the father that's the sinner, but 'e won't find no redemption by 'is ways, murderer and all. 'E's not getting his bleedin' little monster claws all over these two, even if I 'ave to kill us all meself, I'll not let another child suffer 'is fancies."

She could not feign their demise. He'd want their bodies. She might have a chance at a good life if she could escape the manor, but it would mean many days of preparation for the difficult journey. Dunya envisioned herself wandering in circles through the Erun until she and the children starved to death. That plan would only work if she were able to find a way out. Meertham and Matuk alone understood the secret workings of the unpickable lock. Dunya was imprisoned until one of the men (she shuddered to use that word, as it implied a much nobler fellow than the two wardens who juggled her fate in their hands) released her.

Meertham might be persuaded to help her. After all, he'd managed to care for the children long enough to see them through the forest; he could do the same in reverse and take them back to wherever he'd found them. Together, they'd venture into the wider world, released from Matuk's tyranny. Imagine, living free as one pleased, enjoying the company of others in a like-minded society!

Dunya shifted her weight on the rickety stool, her eyes fastened on the glowing orange grate of the iron stove. Why would he risk the only job, life, and home he'd ever known? He was as solid and unyielding as a stone slab. Not likely that a human heart beat anywhere beneath that cold, uncaring exterior. There had to be a way to access the inner sanctum of his shriveled soul. What would move him? Food? Money? Sex? She had very little to barter with, and nothing, including her own body, seemed a worthy reward.

Could she convince him to leave with her? Yes, she mused, returning her attention to her task and the denuded birds contorted stiff and lifeless in her lap. He should be as eager to break his chains as she. Whether together or apart, perhaps they could make a decent life for themselves. The dungeon dwellers spoke of a secret city buried beneath the Erun floor where somatics roamed free and lived inside great, hollowed primordial trees as big around as one of the white turrets that sprang from the manor.

Dunya rubbed a bird with rock salt, the only plentiful thing in that dire household. The meadow around the manor had once been a marsh and its rocky strata were rich with buried layers of a mineral-dense salt. Jagged crystals gleamed citrine yellow across the surface of the grasses, the piquant and brightly flavored salt mined and shipped to the cities to intensify the flavors on some rich man's palate. That was how Matuk had found this place, by visiting his mine for the first time, eager to rape the land and line his pockets with mineral plunder.

Matuk commissioned the manor, caravaning precious stacks of imported, baby-swaddled marble through the winding cavern connecting the meadow with the harsh, mechanized world beyond the Glass Mountains. One after another, the mountain's puking throat disgorged marble blocks that littered the grass. Matuk's insistence on building his summer playground with porous marble left him with a perennially frosty ice palace whose walls ran with water. The manor sank on its foundation until soil eclipsed the ground floor. Matuk had already taken up residence in the tower by then and watched the dirt creeping up to veil his windows, too stubborn to admit defeat and have the entire calamity razed.

Midway through construction of the ill-fated tennis courts and gazing pool, the tramway tunnel collapsed, burying alive a slew of workers and cutting off all contact with the outside world. Crafted from loose-knit slabs, the fragile and aptly named Glass Mountains could not support the wintry onslaught of snowmelt and crumbled atop the Tirai workers' heads, forever entombing them.

Matuk stayed behind then, having no immediate alternative but unprepared to live out the rest of his life in isolation. The manor teetered on a precipice at earth's ends, forgotten by all but storytellers and urban myth archivists. Dunya gazed at the babies asleep in their basket, and knew she hadn't the slenderest spider's hair hope of rescue. They might as well all be dead.

Nels knelt on the cold marble floor in genuflection, palms raised. She closed her eyes, fishing inside for that little comet tail of light hitched to the fast-flying star of the Mother Goddess, Blessed Jerusha. Nels had a direct line into the ear of her sainted protector and guardian. Her trust was absolute, her dedication unwavering. Whatever Jerusha chose for her, it was the right thing. She hoped that their desires might coincide.

Her prayer was just and vengeful. Jerusha did not suffer foolish women. Her attendants must be strong and resolute, just as the Holy Mother had been throughout her trials. Nels trusted her implicitly and would await her rescuing agent.

Holy Jerusha, Queen of Compassion, Light-Bringer, Guardian of Lost and Troubled Souls, hear my plea. Bless me with the gift and insight to right the wrongs visited upon me and liberate myself from that tyrant of a man upstairs. Show me the way! Cast your golden light into my eyes that I might see my salvation and live to serve you evermore. Bless and protect me, keep me safe. Watch over the twins, wherever they might be; shine on them and encircle them with your heavenly protection. Bless my lady Sorykah and ease her pain, that the loss of her precious babes not kill her as surely as an arrow to the heart. Bless and protect me. Show me the way to defeat my enemy. Keep us safe.

'Ere we go again, Dunya grumbled, the ringing bell insistent in her keen ears. *'E might as well come down 'ere 'isself and drive stakes into 'em!* She hated the plaintive, whiny tone of the Master's damned bell. Why hadn't she minded before? *S'pose because I 'ad nothing better to do. And now 'e takes me away from me babies* (her babies, now, since none had come to claim them) *and wants tea, piping 'ot with two cubes of sugar, no more no less, not that all the sugar in the world could sweeten that rotten soul of 'is.*

The tea tray was cumbersome in her hands; it was a long walk from the kitchens to the tower but she had to move fast—the tea would cool if she tarried and that would bode ill for her. Resting the tray on a sideboard, she lifted the ring of keys from her belt and unlocked the tower door. A gust of cold, musty air swirled down to meet her, setting the lamps to flickering as she ascended the stairway, careful to avoid the ice slicks that formed in the depressions on the stone steps and amazed again that a tower built of gleaming white marble could be so oppressively dark and chilly.

The sweet, melancholy notes of an ancient hymn floated in the air, faint as fairy whispers but growing in strength as Dunya rose through the tower. It was that holy pianist playing again, a sweet, sad-eyed woman with corn silk hair whose plump hands had grown thin with deprivation and left the skin between her metatarsals dipping like hammocks strung from tree branches.

Dunya entered Matuk's chamber and the music rushed out to greet her, a celebration of misery. The notes did not falter (how quickly one learns that missteps are not tolerated in death's workhouse) as the pianist swiveled slightly, gazing from the corner of her eye at the tea tray, gauging, no doubt, whether there would be enough left to appease her hunger.

Her eyes slid along the contours of the teapot in its handsome leather cozy, the little pitcher of warmed oil and vinegar for splashing across Matuk's dandelion greens. She could taste the sugar just by looking at it, heaped there so innocuously in its bowl, and the hot tea redolent of wild mint, rose hips, and juniper.

Dunya edged into the room, easing the tray onto the table in the reading alcove where the Master studied, poring over old newspapers and printouts, scanning collected Phantastics (lurid glossies detailing the somatics' bizarre transformations) in hope of some new clue that would rescue his demented daughter from her loneliness and put Tirai's ghost to rest.

"Make a sound, girl, and I'll slit your throat," he said as Dunya lifted the silver dome.

'ow long am I to suffer this miserable old goat's ill treatment? Dunya wondered as she laid out Matuk's supper.

Night came on hard and was bad for everyone. The approaching spring equinox ushered in the westerlies, violent gales that swirled around the subarctic cape and barreled overland through the Erun. Because the Glass Mountains formed such an effective barrier, katabatic winds pooled in the meadow between forest and mountain range, turning cyclonic and inciting madness in the dungeon dwellers. Radhe raged in the forest, her barbarous howls intermingling with the keening winds. Below the manor, the captured somatics screamed and beat the walls of their cells with cups, wings, and claws.

Dunya lay in bed, the babies' basket drawn close. Nights like this brought out the hunters. Gatekeeper would waken from his sleep and prowl the grounds in search of easy prey: burrowing grubbits stunned by flying debris or shell-shocked from their grainy tree holes into the whistling winds. Wouldn't be much of a stretch to come begging at her windows, to reach his long arms through the bars and use his bent walking stick to hook one of her children and force it from her grip.

Something sinister clacked and rattled beyond the water-beaded glass. A blurry shape shifted and moved as the wind whistled down the flue, like a wild bansidhe scratching its way into the manor. Fussy and restless, the babies squalled as Ayeda struggled to lift herself from the basket in search of Dunya's warm embrace. Leander beseeched Dunya, his bright black eyes wide with terror as the wind whipped through the trees. She pulled them to her, their soft bodies warm and pissy, smelling of sweet baby sweat.

Nights like this, the Master abandoned his sitting room to open the armory, taking with him hand pikes and blades. Morning's calm awakened Dunya's nightmares since it was she who would open the tower door to the hair-curling stench of clotted blood ripening on the chopping block and slicking the cold floors.

Westerlies could blow for days, each nightfall signaling the abrupt terminus of one of the dungeon dwellers' fragile lives. What would he do when he ran out of victims? Meertham might not appear for ages and then it would be her babes summoned into the tower, lured with poisoned lollies and split from their skins.

The summoning bell clanged, jarring Dunya from her thoughts. What could he want at such an hour? Chaotic winds had disturbed his routine; the Master was awake and restless. Dunya daren't leave the babes alone. Where could she hide them?

The pianist.

Such a pious woman would have charity for lost babes and keep them while Dunya attended the Master. There was a danger that Matuk would hear their cries, but between the raging storm, Radhe's howls echoing through the halls, and the noise from the dungeons, she doubted he'd notice their squalls. Gathering the sewing basket and a few dry rusks for chewing, Dunya wrapped the babies in tea towels and tucked them in. Lamp in hand, she crept mouse-quiet through the manor. Unlocking the tower door, Dunya hauled the basket upstairs, her arms burning with effort.

Alone in her blue room, the pianist slept off her hunger as she lay awaiting Jerusha's rescuing agent, clutching skeletal hands to her concave, empty belly. She stirred as Dunya entered, frightened but resolute in her determination to show no fear. Dunya held a finger to her drooping, furred lips as she approached the ornate, rusted bed frame. Dunya took the woman's hand in her own and caught her eyes, beseeching plain on her face.

"I'm trusting ye with what is most precious to me in all this world. By rights, I know they are not mine, but till claimed by life or death, they belong to me. Keep 'em safe while I go and see what the Master's on about."

The pianist nodded, wondering if she was dreaming as the wadded blankets rustled and a pair of short arms stretched forth, grubby fists shaking in the damp tower air, followed by a shock of spiky black hair as Leander wrestled his way out of the covers and stared up at his nanny.

Nels gasped and fell to her knees, biting her fist to stuff down the sounds threatening to alert her captor.

"Jersuha be praised, my little lost lamb! I'd given you up for dead!" Ayeda curled cozy in beside her brother, the bright golden feathers of her fine hair fanned across the pillows to fill Nels with unparalleled joy.

She fell weeping onto the basket, covering the children with dry kisses from her parched lips. Dunya recoiled, frozen by a mix of relief, horror, and resentment at the unanticipated, happy reunion. Although she was glad to have found a clue to the children's identity, she couldn't quite quell jealousy's rising surge.

A distant bell rang through the gloom. He was growing impatient.

"Not a sound," Dunya cautioned as she backed from the room. "Or . . ." and she drew a finger across her throat.

Buried in baby flesh and overcome with giddy relief, the pianist shrugged, too enraptured to care.

Upstairs, the library was a tumbrel of disarray. Books and papers strewed the floor; the rust-tainted tools of Matuk's butchery lay splayed and gleaming across the tabletop. Wind poured in through wide-open windows, frenzied the dingy curtains, and made the fire spit and gutter in the grate. Two enormous dogs lay panting before the fire, their pointed ears pricked high as their malevolent black eyes followed Dunya.

"Do you hear that?" Matuk said, leaning out through the window over the parapet below. Radhe howled in the distance, curdling Dunya's blood.

"Aye," Dunya answered. "She cries tonight. The cold will 'ave got into 'er bones and made them ache."

"Who remains in the dungeons? I must keep working!" He swatted at an invisible presence and grabbed his bone saw, stabbing it into the air. "Look! See how she hovers!" Matuk lunged toward his imaginary adversary, waving the hacksaw as if to cut her limb from limb. "You won't get me, woman! I am king of this house!" Matuk threw the hacksaw at the invisible invader and it bounced off the marble wall and landed on the dusty carpet.

Staggering from the window as Radhe howled outside, Matuk covered his ears with both hands, dropping to his knees. Pawing Phantastics, he shrieked, "I've found the clue. I can make the remedy this time!" Matuk ripped through them, muttering to himself as he snatched one clipping after another and just as rapidly discarded it.

"Ah-ha!" He crowed in triumph, gathering papers to his chest as Dunya watched, sickness brewing in her gut. She knew what this night would bring.

Matuk leapt to his feet, pointing at Dunya. "Prepare the table."

She curtsied, her fear overtaken by a cunning voice that insisted her escape was imminent. Whether it took hours or days for Matuk to create his potion, afterward there would be a foul and rotting body requiring disposal. Matuk would open the door, allowing Dunya to carry the remains to the charnel house. Perhaps she could secret the babes out with the corpse and make a run for the forest, but which way lay the Erun city? What of the wily Gatekeeper?

"Make haste, you lazy girl," Matuk snarled, gathering his fallen tools. "Go down to the dungeons and bring me the butterfly. Her wings will gift Radhe's disease with flight and it will leave her like a fly lifting from a carcass."

He pushed everything from the tabletop and kicked the clutter out of the way. Dunya darted from the room, fleeing down the steps without pause. The dungeon was a raucous place that stank of spilled urine and feces. Water beaded on the walls and puddled on the floor, forcing Dunya to wet her shoes as she slogged through inches of foul accumulated runoff.

The butterfly was a woman of indeterminate age who thrashed in the corner, flapping the tattered stumps on her back from which ribbons of torn flesh dangled. Dunya approached the cage filled with loathing for both Matuk and the poor, dumb thing destined to die beneath his blade.

She unlocked the cell, barking "Get out wiv ya, ya dirty thing!" The captured woman flapped in agonized silence, so thin and weak that she could not fight as Dunya wrapped steely fingers around her frail arms and dragged her from the cell. A dirty hood hung on a peg and Dunya placed it on Matuk's target, wrapping its long ties around the woman's arms and pinning her stumps to her back.

"March, girl!" Dunya growled, kicking at the poor butterfly's sticklike legs. She stumbled and jerked upright as Dunya hustled her through the hall, accompanied by the screams and moans of the other captives bearing witness to the executioner's parade. Dunya's heart was hard. She longed for the moment when the Master would become enraptured with his victim, and the untended hours she'd have to devise a plan.

Up they went through the icy manor into the tower, where the snick-snick of blades being sharpened rang down the passage.

The girl moaned and trembled. Dunya hoisted her up like a sack of potatoes, telling herself that it was better this skinny wastrel than herself. She had been too abused in her former life in the human world to find much sympathy for her kind—coarse crossbreeds doomed to mistreatment; spoiled, spat, and shat upon. Most of the city folk didn't believe the somatics had souls, or could feel or think with as much complexity as themselves, when in fact, because of their keen senses and sensitive natures, many were more attuned to their surroundings, thoughts, and emotions than the most educated and self-aware person.

Dunya had long ago compartmentalized her feelings. Each emotion was stored in its own neat and narrow little box. On nights like this, she made sure that all her boxes remained shut fast, that no stray wish or streamer of empathetic sorrow would escape and make her vulnerable to foolish fancies of liberation or retribution.

The wind raged and beat the tower walls. Radhe bellowed, the damp working into her arthritic, malformed joints as she lurked in the forest, rain splashing down on her bare back. Dunya glanced out one of the tall windows as they climbed the stairs, certain that the lightning flashes revealed a hunched and forlorn shape loitering at the perimeter of the meadow, its eyes upon the lighted tower room.

Matuk was already cursing her as Dunya entered the room, lambasting her for being slow, stupid, and miserly with her attentions. He barked orders and Dunya obeyed, fixated on the end of her imprisonment, when the door would open and she would taste freedom's air for the first time.

She stripped the butterfly and strapped her to the vivisectionist's slab, making sure that the gutters on the table's sides were aligned to drain into the buckets on each end, stuffed the girl's mouth with a dirty rag tasting of the previous victim's spittle, and backed from the room. Sometimes Matuk forced her to stay and attend him, but she intended to vanish with her babies before he had a chance to notice her absence. Immersed in his villainous preparations, Matuk was too consumed by the coming persecution to notice Dunya's disappearance. He would ring for her later, when he had finished and the room stank of blood and slit entrails, and gore coated the floor.

She would come with brush and bucket to scrub away the stains of his sin, package the remains, and cart them downstairs. That would be her chance; it was becoming clear now. Distasteful as it was, she would have to hide the babes among the refuse and sneak them out. Hopefully, there would be enough of the butterfly left to account for everything she spirited out. She'd have to be prudent, take no more than was necessary, line her underskirt with secret panels and fit each one with survival gear—a knife, flint lighter, twine for snares and hooks for fishing. The babies would have to drink a sleeping remedy to keep them quiet. She wouldn't be able to risk their discovery.

Yes, she thought with quiet glee, *it could be done.* If only she knew the secret of the lock, that she could open it for herself!

Here was one lock that she could open, however, and as she inserted her key into the pianist's door and turned the tumblers, she was pleased to see the blond woman rocking both babes and gazing into their eyes, rapture lighting her emaciated face.

"Well done, lass," said Dunya.

"I've asked the Blessed Mother so many times to bring me news of these two and though the days stretched on, my faith never wavered. See how she rewards me!" The woman, who now introduced herself as Nels, nanny to these two foundlings from the Sigue's singing sea, pressed her hands together and touched her forehead. "You are an angel, one of Jerusha's precious helpers."

Dunya cleared her throat, gruff and uncomfortable. Never in all her days had anyone likened her to an angel.

"Now that we are reunited, I expect you'll be leaving them with me?"

This had not been Dunya's intention. She stepped forward, her trembling hands already grabbing for Ayeda's blanket. "No! That's not the way it's to be at all!"

Nels recoiled and squeezed the babies to her once-ample bosom. "You don't mean to take them from me?"

"If they are to live, yes. D'ye think that man upstairs 'as their well being in mind? 'E intends to wring the genes from their blood and poison 'is nasty arrows with whatever gruesome stew 'e concocts. 'E's up there now, murderizing some dumb beast stupid enough to be netted by 'is bastard 'enchman."

Nels shrank back in horror, her pale eyes wide. "What nonsense you speak!"

"Do ye need to see the blood runnin' beneath yer door before ye believe?"

A gut-wrenching shriek stabbed through the floor and silenced the women's bickering. Several more cries, each weaker than the last, followed and then there was silence. Even wretched Radhe and the wild winds seemed to hold their breath.

Matuk's voice broke the hush as he cranked up the generator and blasted the electric klieg light's rooftop ray into the forest, pinning Radhe in its white-hot beam.

"Loose the arrows!" he screamed, as Nels thrust the babies into Dunya's arms and ran to the window to peer through the peephole she'd scratched in the painted pane. She saw Radhe fumble in the darkness, disoriented by the lights and desperate to find some solace among the trees and escape the volley of blood-tipped arrows poised to pierce her scarred hide.

Thuck thuck thuck! The arrows sailed through the driving rain and struck home. Radhe bellowed in mourning and dropped as if dead. Nels turned from the window, as white as chalk.

"What does he intend to do with us?"

Dunya shook her head. "Let me take them. They're safe with me as long as 'e's got a diversion—there's plenty o' fodder for the fires of 'ell in our dungeon."

"Then what? Look at me!" Nels pushed up the sleeve of her rank, greasy lace-trimmed gown and pinched the taut flesh on her arm. "There's nothing left of me! Would you leave me here to die?" She collapsed, hands clasped and murmuring prayers to her beloved goddess.

Dunya felt the words slipping from her mouth even as her brain fought to constrain them. "I 'ave a plan."

18

A KISS, A KISS, MY QUEENDOM FOR A KISS

"IF YOU SEE ANY OF THESE," Sidra remarked, tossing Soryk a large brown seedpod as withered and vile as a shrunken head, "pick them up. When we have enough, we'll have a delicious treat."

Soryk stared at the gnarly kernel in his palm. Sidra fed him all manner of unappetizing forest findings and her meals always turned out quite well. She'd trained him to collect silvery juniper berries, dandelion leaves and baby ferns, and the starchy roots that proliferated beneath the rich black Erun soil. There were fat grubs to be plucked from betwixt bark and hardwood and red, foot-long worms that proved surprisingly tasty when tossed in a hot skillet with handfuls of pungent wild garlic, salted mealie, and a splash of oil. Sidra waved away Soryk's questions about his hostess's hypocrisy. Hadn't he brutishly killed and devoured an innocent wild creature because she would not dirty her hands with butchery? And what about her lecture about life rights and passive vegetarianism?

When he broached the topic, she replied that insects and invertebrates were so abundant because they were intended to serve as food to support the broadest base of animals.

"Besides," she added, "they don't have eyes and they don't bleed. I don't have to see the reproach in their gaze when they slide into the nethers. It's the way of the Erun. We all do it. If Oman No-Man hadn't eaten bugs to ensure his survival, none of us would be here now." She popped a crisp, coiled worm straight from the frying pan into her mouth and chewed it, defiantly.

Soryk spent the day's remainder in a quiet state of unease. Some slippery thing glided round his mind's recesses, and he could not finger what troubled him so. He craved civilization. The tension and pressure of his own suppressed want began to take its toll. As much as he enjoyed Sidra's company and the pleasures of living in accordance with the land and his own whims, he knew he did not belong here.

Soryk was a man of the city. He felt unproductive in the woods, having no responsibility other than to tail the queen and scavenge seedpods and roots from the forest floor. The dream of the fish had mutated into a recurring nightmare that clouded the edges of his days and it seemed to him that the trees had grown even taller, more bent and oppressively twisted.

Sidra and Soryk waded through spongy loam that sucked at his boots as he walked and forced poor Kika to struggle along behind them, her legs blacked to the joints with mud.

Exhausted and cranky, Soryk snapped, "You said you were taking me to the city but you drag me deeper into this blasted forest. What sort of game are you playing at?"

Sidra turned, her eyes narrowed to angry slits.

"I'm not playing any games. You're running me far out of my way and I'm wasting days of travel escorting an ingrate through my forest! I should have left you in the woods when I first found you. Have you once thanked me for my efforts? Have you once done anything but tag along behind me, eating my food, sharing my blankets and shelter?" Sidra shook the tall walking stick she carried at him, as if to banish him with a wave of her wand.

Soryk balked at the outburst. Petulant and crabby, he kicked a clump of slimy orange toadstools that erupted in a gaseous cloud of black spores.

"Idiot!" Sidra lunged for his arm and dragged him away from the mushrooming fog. She covered her face with her cloak and motioned for Soryk to do the same as they dodged the eruption.

Soryk snatched his arm from Sidra's grip, annoyed by his clumsy stupidity.

"Stop where you are," Sidra insisted.

Soryk dragged his feet as he halted and stood fuming, sick of the damp and darkness and the suffocating Erun, pressing in from all sides like a living thing. "What now?" he snarled.

She stomped toward him and hissed, "You can be agreeable and travel with me for three more days until we break through, or you can blunder your way out on your own." She stood with hands on hips, the color rising to stain her throat and cheeks a vivid, mottled red. Given a choice between compliance and blatant rule flaunting, Soryk gritted his teeth and resolved to tough it out.

He was still brooding when they made camp and prepared dinner in tense silence. Sidra clutched twiggy greens and sat down opposite Soryk to strip leaves from stems. She spoke to him as if their earlier tiff had never happened.

"You'll like these." She grinned, holding a roll of leaves beneath her nose and inhaling. She offered it to Soryk, her elfin face suppressing a smirk as he sniffed the peppery greens and sneezed.

"What malarkey are you feeding me now?" He returned her smile. He had no need for misplaced anger when she gazed at him so fetchingly.

"Just you wait and see. Now fish out those pods you found so repulsive and we'll prepare a feast." Sidra took a knife and began slicing through leathery skins. She peeled them back, revealing a mess of long, thready white fibers. Soryk popped one of the hairballs into his mouth and gagged as the fibers clogged his throat.

Sidra heard him choking and looked up, her wide eyes crinkling with laughter. She stuck her dirty finger into his mouth, swirling it round to gather the hairs before removing the whole clump. She inserted the tip of her knife into the pod and cracked it open, revealing a lustrous red jelly speckled with tiny golden pips.

"Taste," she instructed, offering him half. Soryk followed the queen's lead, licking the fruity jelly from its shell. After countless days of boring vegetables and salted mealie, the mild sweetness was as intense as pure sugar and made his eyes pop.

They grinned like co-conspirators and all discord was forgotten.

"You know, if I hadn't dragged you away from those toadstools, your corpse would be feeding them now," Sidra remarked, igniting her burner and spooning oil into a pan.

"Why is that?" Soryk asked, savoring the feel of her finger against his tongue.

"*Amanita miasma.* Death's cloud spores. Inhale enough of them and the toxins will pollute your lungs and kill you almost instantly. You drop where you stand and the mushrooms grow on your corpse. It's a mistake that no one makes twice."

"You're very wise. How did you come to learn so much about this forest? Were you born in the Erun city?"

"Oh no, I come from Blundt. It's a horrible place." Sidra wrinkled her nose. "I left to study nursing at Neubonne University. Afterward, I worked at Our Father's Charity Hospital for eight years, caring for terminally ill infants. When Tirai Industries bought our land and demolished the hospital, many of the children were too sick to weather the move to a hastily constructed and inadequately equipped hospice. Tirai used a contractual loophole with the city to avoid restoring the hospital. The mayor of Neubonne took bribes and sold out our children in favor of a shaky deal with a hearty commission." Sidra's voice peaked with ire. "Greed killed those children. Tirai mistakenly expected that a tidy little settlement would appease bereft parents." She ground her teeth and adjusted her antler crown in what Soryk would later come to recognize as a nervous gesture.

His gaze ran over her like rainfall. She tensed at his closeness as he removed the red fur crown with its towering antlers. Her tangled hair stuck to the hat and pushed up from her head in funny peaks, rife with static electricity.

His fingers slid into the nest of her hair, smoothing it from smudged, familiar cheeks.

"Please, Sidra, meet my eyes," Soryk whispered.

Her eyes shone with want. Her lips parted as Soryk nudged closer, until his chest pressed against hers and she lay back against the leaves. Soryk lay beside her, enjoying Sidra's green smells of forest, rain, and wood smoke.

A lazy smile teased the corners of his mouth. "Are you free to give your heart away, or has some other stolen it from me?"

Sidra blushed. "Carac understands me, but his humanity has been partially erased by the change. It was capricious at best. His fidelity is a testament to the wolf in him more so than the man. Under different circumstances, I would not . . ." she hesitated and continued. "When he is rough with me and I taste my own fear, that's what is most exciting. Nothing more."

"Rough, tsk!" Soryk teased. "So, none can claim you as his own, then?"

Sidra shrugged and relaxed into his embrace.

"Did you know," he whispered, "that the first kiss sets the tenor for everything that follows?"

He pressed his mouth to her ear, whispering, "Shall it be rough and hasty, as you seem to prefer, or should I linger?"

Soryk grinned and bit the tender flesh of her neck. He rolled atop her searching for her mouth and then, *bliss*.

Mouths like honey melting and warm butter in their veins.

His hands traveled over her body, blanketed by layers of fabric.

Soryk leaned into Sidra and kissed her. He inhaled her breath and felt that he was falling into a deep, bottomless pool; rather than feeling suffocated, he became weightless. He fumbled with her clothes, seeking a path to her skin. The fabric opened as if enchanted, revealing warm flesh. Soryk groaned, sliding between thighs that parted to welcome him. After what felt like years of neglect, his senses roused, ferocious and demanding. He wormed a hand inside the queen's gown and found a small breast, just big enough to fill the palm of his hand. Sidra's breath was hot in his ear and she giggled in that innocent way of hers, so pretty and charming.

He thought he heard her voice, light and sweet, murmur, "Do you love me?"

His own voice, with none of the echoing strangeness he sometimes felt when he spoke, responded. "I love you my queen, Sidra the Lovely. My mayapple, my flower." Soryk was surprised to discover that he meant it.

"Clumsy prince, forgetful one," she teased. The light had faded and they saw little except the gleam of firelight reflected in each other's eyes. Soryk threaded a protective hand through Sidra's messy hair.

"There's something . . ." he murmured, his fingers testing the bony protuberances jutting from Sidra's skull.

She tensed, batting his hand away.

"No," he insisted, sending his other hand in search of the lumps. "What is that? Don't fear me, I won't hurt you."

Sidra pushed him away and sat up, bare breast peeking from her robe. "Stop touching me!"

"What is it, Sidra? What have I done wrong?" Soryk propped himself on an elbow, waiting for her senses to return and with them, Sidra into his waiting arms.

"Just leave it," she cried, clutching her wrap and leaping to her feet.

"Please tell me," Soryk begged. His neglected erection throbbed against his thigh. "Is it your change? Is that what drove you into the forest?"

But she vanished into the gathering gloom, leaving him alone and cold in the darkness.

19

SOFT FOCUS

I'M DYING.

It was a woman's voice, long unused but never forgotten, familiar as home and her own skin. She was crushed by the dense, humid air, rich with fragrance, and blinded by the bright colors hammering at her closed eyelids. Her heart and lungs seemed to function without synchronicity in the oppressive sensory onslaught.

No, not dying. Just not right.

Sensation flooded tingling, hyperaware limbs. It stretched and unrolled, spreading throughout her body, sought exit as if thrusting from an eggshell, breaking free from another type of little death.

What's wrong with me? Too hot, too cold, every little jagged grain of sand was a knife in her back. She focused her concentration in a beam, white light traveling her body's terrain, illuminating every nerve and corpuscle, searching. *There.* A clot of pain in her left breast, a buried sun burning within her flesh. Milk-clogged ducts, her sweetness having soured.

Sorykah cracked open an eye, scanning the immediate perimeter. She was in a forest, sheltered beneath a rocky overhang rife with tall, spore-speckled ferns waving in an early spring breeze. Sunlight spilled through the leafy canopy, splashing over mossy boulders and onto Sorykah's face and hands. Rising to confront this brash morning, she was conscious again of the uncomfortable fullness in her breasts and the urgency of her female body's needs.

Sorykah was shocked by how little she recognized. The rough gray blankets, the wooden dishes stacked by the fire, even the homespun trousers and knit pullover she wore were strange to her. The last thing she remembered was crawling into the cavity of a hollowed tree to outwait the hunters. Her hand flew to her waist, lifting her jersey, feeling the skin beneath and finding the closed wound, its scar still pink and seamed. She scowled, fingering the smooth, fleshy ridge. The wound had been repaired for days, if not weeks. How had she healed so quickly?

Jerusha, the pain! She rubbed the downy hollow beneath her arm, followed a trail of heat to a swollen breast both tight and hot to the touch. Running her fingers over the lumpy mass, she wished for her babies. Babies!

A lightning bolt of recognition speared her and everything came rushing back in a sickening tumult. Her breast burned and throbbed; her head felt that it would split open as a cascade of fragmented images and sundered memories assailed her. Her grief was unbearable. They were dead. Her delay, her hated, changing body, had killed her children as surely as it had brought them to life.

How many days had she lost this time? Recalling her lost babes and her thwarted quest, she broke down and sobbed, tearing at her hair, the strange clothes so plainly meant for a man. Misery condensed inside her throat and chest, barreling out of her body to erupt in a violent keening wail as she gave voice to her woes. Crawling along the Erun floor, Sorykah screamed and stuffed shreds of bark into her mouth to silence the cries that would not cease.

It was too much. Too treacherous, her shape-shifting soul. Trading he-flesh for she-flesh, lost deep in some alter universe where boundaries and distinctions were void. Cells transmutating, expressing their innate otherness as millions of microscopic chromosomes regained an atrophied leg, Y become X again. Most Traders could shift genders with little physical trauma and with memories intact. They suffered few ill effects, waking up groggy after a change, feeling a bit hungover perhaps, or as if recovering from a cold. For them it was a simple matter of switching clothes and names. Caution was their biggest concern, that they not change at the wrong time, or among the wrong people.

The Perilous Curse. Sorykah heard it referred to in passing—a scrap of urban legend, a street and playground rumor, nothing more. She'd never met anyone who suffered from it, and until she met the children's father, she'd never known another Trader. All she knew was that when she changed, she lost snippets of her life and woke to wander in a foggy fugue state. Her other gender's doings remained as slippery and elusive as a dream.

Every fetus began life as a female. An influx of active hormones later turned the genetic key, deciphering hidden code and releasing the chemical maelstrom that created a male. A bit of intrauterine spackle and paint, some minor plumbing changes, and circuits switched off or on and the change was complete. With her twins and their half-formed bodies of squidgy fat and rubber-tipped, cartilaginous bones, the change was easy. Fluid as blood. But for an adult long settled on her foundation, like an old house bearing down and wearing a depression into the earth, the change was a laborious and painful trial.

Sorykah wiped her face and took a deep breath. Someone had been taking care of her, or worse, she'd overpowered another and commandeered his belongings and possibly his life. That was too terrible to think about. She wasn't the type of man to kill a stranger for his few meager possessions. She glanced at her hands, checking for signs of violence. They were dirty, but no blood caked her fingernails. That was a hopeful sign.

Her unsupported breasts hung heavy with milk. A red streak flared like a fingernail scratch along the top of her left breast and the sight of it set off warning bells in Sorykah's head. Red streaks boded ill; they were the harbingers of abscesses and sepsis. She wanted to call for help but was afraid of who might answer. Perhaps she could scale one of the tallest trees and see her way clear of the forest, find a view of the Southern Sea or Blundt's telltale black smog but Sorykah's legs wobbled like a newborn fawn's when she tried to stand and she toppled to the ground. She felt hot and cold at once and thought she might be able to walk if she could just rest for a moment. The desire to flee was overpowering but she couldn't muster the initiative to move.

Invisible but audible, a man and woman argued in low tones, the man reluctant to surrender his position in favor of the woman's.

"My lovely, she is a Trader. I saw it with my own eyes. He lay down as a man and rose up a woman. Why do you find it so difficult to accept?" The male voice was gruff and rigid with suppressed emotion.

"Hsst! Don't be so contentious," the woman snapped.

Something growled in irritation, a dog perhaps. A very large dog.

"Look at her. She could be a spy sent by the Others. Did you not already reveal the location of two of the Erun city's main tunnels in addition to taking him belowground and exposing all our secrets? Secrecy is the only thing that protects us! You know that they have been trying to drive us into ruin for years. Why would you compromise our safety?" the male asked, his bitterness apparent.

Sorykah blinked bleary eyes and gazed up into the rough,

frightening face of a very coarse man whose wiry silver and black hair sprouted in tufts from his cheeks and pointed ears and trailed over broad, strong shoulders. His fiery yellow eyes burned with a wild light and when he opened his mouth to speak, rows of pointed teeth gleamed between his lips, stark against black gums.

Sorykah scrambled across the rocks, her heart thumping loudly in her chest.

"Carac, you've frightened her," the woman cooed, moving closer to rest a gentle hand on Sorykah's arm. "Darling, can you hear us?"

With mud-smeared cheeks and wide bemused eyes, the woman stared at Sorykah. She had a tumbleweed of snarly hair threaded with leaves and bits of twig and capped by a pair of tall gray antlers set in a furry hat that she bore regally, like a crown.

"What do you think?" she asked, pressing dirty fingers to Sorykah's forehead.

"Something's wrong with her. She was looking at her . . ." He gestured crudely to his own brawny chest.

"Your heart, darling, does it hurt? Are you having trouble breathing?"

Tears swelled in Sorykah's eyes as sickness and anguish invaded her. The stranger's kindness was doing her in. She had no resources left in her to remain stoic and impassive, a hard-hearted, vengeful mother intent on her mission. She had wasted too much precious time and her folly was responsible for the death of her children. Even if it was just to reclaim the bodies, she would continue to seek them . . . just as soon as she could stand.

"Lay down, dear." The woman motioned to the rough man and he wadded a blanket beneath Sorykah's head. Gingerly, the woman lifted the edge of Sorykah's jersey and peeked beneath.

"My lovely," the man admonished.

"Carac," she murmured, "leave us."

He did so reluctantly, melting into the trees.

Sorykah closed her eyes as the jersey was raised higher, revealing her bare flesh. Cool fingers touched her, feather light and cautious.

"I see the problem," the woman said after a moment of silence. "How long . . ." she cleared her throat and began again. "How long since you last nursed your baby?"

Sorykah moaned and covered her face with her hands.

"All right then, we'll have you fixed up in no time. You'll be good as new and ready to go home to your little one. My name is Sidra the Lovely, and I'm going to help you out of this jam you've found yourself in. I'm no ordinary lady-of-the-fens, I'll have you know. I worked for many years at the charity hospital in Neubonne. And," she added, striking her fire starter to ignite the kindling beneath her cooking pot, "lucky for you my specialty was caring for new mothers and infants. You see," she smiled, adding a few dried herbs to the pot and brewing up a strong-smelling concoction, "you're in good hands."

Once the pot began to steam, Sidra soaked a relatively clean square of fabric in it and applied it to the sore breast. "Hold that there," she instructed, and Sorykah obeyed. "You have a caked breast. We have to soften that up and then it will take some effort to work it out. It will be uncomfortable but we must do it before it abscesses. You're already running warm."

Sidra whistled quick and sharp and Carac reappeared, keeping his eyes averted.

"Bring me some wild garlic. It will be woody but take whatever you can find."

Carac backed from the clearing, aggrieved to have been cast in the role of errand boy. Though Sidra burned with unasked questions, she would have to wait until there was a suitable moment to talk. In the meantime, there was fever-reducing birch tea to make, a poultice of raw honey and garlic that needed mashing, and milking to be done.

Carac returned and thrust a handful of purple bulbs at Sidra.

Unused to his role as nursemaid, he shambled about the campsite until Sidra dispatched him to search for edibles.

"We don't need that man mucking about. He'll only distress you."

Fat tears dripped down Sorykah's cheeks as she watched Sidra grind and measure, adding a pinch here and a sprinkle there, applying muscle to her mortar and pestle. Once the poultice was ready, Sidra laid it on thickly over the infected breast, wrapped Sorykah in a blanket, and started on the tea.

"I've told you my name. What shall I call you?" Sidra held her breath, hoping that this was all some terrible mistake.

"Sorykah."

"Ah. From where do you hail? How do you find yourself in the Erun?"

Sorykah's feverish delirium acted as a truth serum, allowing Sidra to prise free the secrets Sorykah would have otherwise kept mum.

"I'm a submariner on the *Nimbus* and I hail from the wily singing sea." She sobbed, "My children were my twin stars and someone put their lights out!" She bolted up, cheeks and eyes blazing to announce, "When I find him, I'll chain him to a rock and tear out his liver!"

Sidra recoiled, clearly startled by the outburst. "Find who?"

"The Collector. Baby Stealer, Death Dealer. Him and his Snatcher-in-the-Night. They won't stay safe from me," she finished darkly.

Sidra pushed hot birch tea on Sorykah, who swallowed without remarking on its bitterness.

Intrigued, Sidra curled a hank of Sorykah's black hair around her finger. It felt just as it had before. The smattering of fine hairs on Soryk's chest was gone; the hands, while still strong, were slender and feminine.

"Sorykah." The name felt alien in Sidra's mouth. "It's true, then."

"What do you mean?"

"The good fathers at the Charity Hospital often said, 'Jerusha takes with one hand and gives with the other.' So the Blessed Mother has taken one and given me another. May it prove a fair exchange. Tell me. Do you remember the story of your birth? Was there anything unusual about it?" Tests had to be conducted, identities verified.

"I was in all ways, ordinary."

"Was, but are no longer," Sidra amended. "Will you tell me how you came into the world?"

"It was autumn. Cold enough to stay indoors but warm enough for open windows. That's how the bird got in."

"The bird?"

"'Blackbird, blackbird, eyes of gold,'" Sorykah began, "'ushers in the night foretold, stealing souls and drowning light, ravenous both in name and plight.'"

Sidra's hand froze in midair, kettle poised to refresh Sorykah's cup. "Saint Catherine," she whispered, pressing Sorykah to her chest. She squeezed Sorykah, who was too ill to be alarmed, but relinquished her at Carac's approach.

"Look who I found wandering the wood," he exclaimed with unusual enthusiasm, carrying the somewhat scruffy but always magnificent Kika in his arms. The dog slurped at Carac's face and he set her down beside the fire, scratching her neck and chest, tugging her ears and snarling. The false fight intensified and soon Carac and Kika were rolling together on the ground, growling and leaping with suppressed canine fury. They tumbled over the ground and tussled too close to the fire and sent ash flying. Carac and Kika sprang apart, panting but happy adversaries. The smell of singed hair enticed Sorykah from sleep and when she opened her eyes, the first face to greet her was Kika's, nosing Sorykah with curiosity and wagging her tail with great gusto.

"Kika, my brave girl!" Tears welled as Sorykah clucked her tongue, commanding the obedient dog into place at her side. The dog stretched beside her, licking Sorykah's hand.

"You know this dog," Carac stated.

Sorykah laid a tender but possessive hand on the sled dog's matted back. "She's mine. I bought her whole team from a musher in Ostara." With the birch tea working on her fever and the serendipitous return of her lost companion lifting her spirits, Sorykah was beginning to drift back down to earth, content for the moment to hover inside the mauve glow of her pain and drift among the wreckage of her recollections.

The late afternoon sun pinkened and droplets of mist filled the silvering sky. Sidra dismissed Carac from the women's company with instructions to resume his duties.

"He's off to man his post," Sidra smiled. "How's that dressing?" Sidra peeled back the blankets to slather more goop on the infected breast.

Sorykah wrinkled her nose and gazed into the shifting sea of gray paisley that swam in front of her eyes. "Where did you say we are?"

"The Erun Forest. No worries, darling; you're quite safe with me. None would dare touch us here in my domain."

"Your domain?" Sorykah raised an incredulous eyebrow.

"Indeed." The faintest note of irritation sharpened Sidra's voice. "I am Queen of the Erun and those who claim it as their home."

"Queen of the Erun and Queen of Hearts. By whose appointment?"

Sidra raised a single eyebrow. "Let's not bicker over political boundary lines and rules of primogeniture. It is understood that all who dwell in these woods accept me as their liege and are content to do so. Now, before you spoil the mood with any further rudeness, I insist upon your silence." Sidra threw her wrap around her shoulders and stalked from the campsite.

Twining her fingers even deeper into Kika's fur, Sorykah settled into peaceful abandon. Although heartsick and feverish, her brief lapse in resolve dissipated and she found herself on fire with a single-minded determination to heal and resume her quest.

There was no light save the campfire's orange glow, making a rather weak hedge against the oppressive night. Sorykah stripped back the blankets and the strange jersey. Her infected breast was rock-hard and swollen, but she recalled the way her midwife had kneaded out the milk-knots when she was so engorged after bringing the twins home. She would have to massage it out. Sorykah pressed into the milk-knot with the ball of her thumb, turning ashen, then red-cheeked from the exquisite pain and ensuing relief as she used the heel of her palm to break down the clot.

A kind voice materialized in the darkness and a reassuring hand lighted on her back. "Here, let me do that for you." The Erun Queen had returned.

Sidra instructed, "Get onto your hands and knees and lean forward."

Sorykah meekly complied and swallowed her pride as Sidra knelt beside her and commenced to milk her like a cow. Grainy, curdled milk was forced from the clogged ducts and a few sluggish drops splattered the leaves. The thin trickle strengthened into a stream as Sidra kneaded and squeezed, her mouth tight, her face stern with concentration.

Sorykah sighed as the pressure began to ease. Sidra rose, shook out her aching hands, and applied hot compresses. The routine continued unabated throughout the night, interspersed with sips of birch bark tea and fresh applications of garlic-honey paste to the softening breast. Although they'd begun the day at odds with each other, each minute was a thread pulling the stitches of a growing friendship closer together.

"I feared the infection could develop an abscess, requiring surgical care, treatment I am ill prepared to administer. I've asked Carac to fetch the infant of an Erun couple. The mum's hirsute, too hairy even for the coolest tunnels, whose scant heat makes her faint," Sidra said. "She lives on the edge of the forest with her man."

Carac soon materialized with babe in arms. The wee lad's strong sucking was much more efficient at releasing Sorykah's pent-up stores than Sidra's labored milking. Although quite surprised by his journey through the woods and the full, hairless teat thrust into his mouth, he was a strong, strapping boy and settled in happily, managing to empty both sides before falling asleep, milk-drunk and smiling at the corners of his cream-puddled mouth.

Carac dozed nearby, while Sorykah stroked the strange baby's lush, curling hair. The women made gentle noises and whispered about the child, chatting between themselves. Firelight and whispers encouraged Sorykah to break her secrecy. She spoke of discovering her ability to change and all the grief she'd suffered for it since: the theft of her babes, meeting Rava, and her sudden induction into the somatics' realm.

Morning brought new strength and a deepened connection. A restorative sleep and the baby's hunger had drained Sorykah of her infection. Handing the satiated boy back to Carac for the return trip home, Sorykah began to dress, tender with her still-fragile body. Sidra, who seemed to have little need for sleep and had awakened before her, pushed away Sorykah's hands and bound her breasts with strips of cloth.

"What woman warrior can fight with her ninnies flopping about in the way?" the queen jested, disguising her sadness. She'd return to it later, to pluck out that sticky-sharp thorn and lick her wounds in private.

"I must go. You understand, don't you?" Sorykah tried (and failed) to imagine that the man in her had been in love with this strange, albeit magnetic woman, that her lips, in guise of another's, had laid kisses on Sidra's brow.

They'd spoken of the affair during the still of the night while the baby slept beside a fire mist-doused into a heap of glowing ashes.

"Can you not bring him back, just for a little while?" Sidra wheedled. She was filled with regret and wished to make amends.

"I cannot," Sorykah lamented. "The change occurs of its own volition. I have never learned how to control it."

"Do you not remember," Sidra begged, creeping closer, "we spent days together! Recited poetry, spoke of castles, kings, and the minutiae of daily things. . . ." She trailed, flushed with shame, so different from the trilling, laughing queen Soryk had known. Now, unrequited desire and guilt had worked her into a declarative mood.

"I ran from him!" Sidra was so wrapped up in her own self-pity that she failed to recall that the man she pined for was buried in the shallow grave of Sorykah's female form. "We parted badly."

"You ran from him. From me, I mean," Sorykah had said, jostling the forest baby as she shifted on the hard ground. He fussed in his sleep, his irritated cry so different from Leander's. She could not imagine taking part in the scenario Sidra described and was quite appalled by Soryk's effrontery, climbing atop the Queen as if boarding a common passenger vessel.

Taking another nip from her flask, Sidra reached up with shaking hands. "Are you a trusted keeper of confidences, dark-eyed girl, with so many secrets of your own?"

Sorykah nodded. Sidra reached up to remove her antler crown and set it aside. The black pupils in her bright, pale eyes were as big as pennies. Sidra pressed Sorykah's fingers through her snarled hair and against her scalp, running them along two misshapen lumps, like knobs of broken bone beneath the skin.

Sorykah tested them gently, feeling the sutured scar tissue running like railroad tracks around a pair of low hills and the funny hairs that grew in all directions like tufty wild grass.

"You're one of them," Sorykah breathed. "But when did you change? What happened to your horns?"

Sidra shook her head. "Therein lies my deceit. No horns. No change, no gift. I am but a natural woman, human in every way. Will you hear my confession?"

Sorykah squeezed Sidra's hand, offering reassurance as she spoke.

"A cancer stormed my bones and tumors sprouted up almost

overnight, like poisonous toadstools after a rain. Raging cell growth gave me two hideous cactus-shaped horns. Their weight forced my forehead down over my eyes, creating a perpetual frown, wreaked havoc on my neck, and crushed my vertebrae.

"The Fathers at the charity Hospital took pity on their favorite and most loyal of healing servants, treating me to the best of their ability, but I grew so top-heavy that I had to spend all my waking hours in a recumbent position lest I break my neck.

"Surgeries were attempted. They cut the horns again and again. Willfully, I endured the barbarism of modern cancer treatments, but each remedy simply slowed further growth without retarding it. They offered me one final option, and I took it. They flushed out all my diseased marrow and replaced it with a synthetic substance that maintained existing bone tissue without generating new calcification. If I ever broke a bone, it would not repair itself. They would have to stabilize it with steel pins and braces, leaving me crippled and in constant pain.

"Suicide was contingent in my plans. Why break one bone and live, when I could break them all and die a pulpy mess, saved from a nightmare of endless suffering?

"Somatic activists latched on to my story. I stayed in a closed ward to minimize risk of additional infection, but outside appearances revealed a woman ostracized by society and quarantined while subjected to heinous and bloody attempts at a complete physical restoration.

"Somatics and their unchanged cohorts picketed the hospital, gathering in riotous groups of barking, braying, and roaring bodies, jostling for space before the cameras, attacking the surgeons and doctors who had effected my 'cure.' Fists and hooves flew as demonstrations became street brawls. I remember standing at the window, touching my stitched-up scalp and watching the mêlée below.

"I saw that the somatics were an unruly bunch, and that their fierce crusade would amount to nothing more than a campaign of terror. It was obvious that they needed a leader. A fire had been ignited within me. As I watched, torched vehicles burned in the streets, somatics ran amok through Neubonne's Lower Wards, culling their brethren from the masses and urging them to shed their human trappings. I knew that I could be their Light-Bringer.

"I would simply lift the window and step onto the ledge. I could see my gown billowing about me as I drifted to the ground below. The crowds would part for me. The surgeons would bow and scrape before their miracle, a woman wrestled back from the other side of death with her scars and saw marks and intact plastic skeleton. Somatics would gather together to bow before their queen, their forked and curling tongues twisting around my feet as I walked.

"Narcotics addled my brain. I left the hospital, my vision made clearer by the pain that burned within me like a banked fire smoldering inside my very bones. I threw myself upon the mercy of half-breed gangs and rejects who canopied me beneath fur and feather. They spirited me away with my decapitated horns still raw and oozing synthetic marrow; they brought me to the Erun tunnel city and I mounted the pedestal they erected for me.

"I admit that I have encouraged my own mythology. My adoptive family chose to believe me one of them, and I did nothing to dissuade their illusions. Gods are made, not born. They needed a leader. A queen. And I came."

Sorykah pitied Sidra. Polite but cool, she retracted her hands from Sidra's grasp as the tale concluded. *How could I love one as deluded as this, a monarch of her own making,* she wondered. *How could* he*?* Sorykah saw the gentle queen, full of mystery and power and ripe with her own desire to aid her kin and live a life of service, and thought *how could we not?*

We. Sorykah realized that she had referred to herself as a unit, two separate yet connected beings, and that was how Sidra began to cure Soryk/ah of the Perilous Curse.

20

LOYAL TO A FAULT

WHEN SHE DISMISSED HIM from the Erun city, Carac entertained the idea of following Queen Sidra's orders and venturing into Neubonne's Lower Wards to glean any facts about Matuk's evildoings from the gossiping somatics who lived there amid sloth and poverty: shysters and charlatans, false healers and prophets, and the streetwalking petty criminals cast aside like yesterday's garbage. The Others had categorized them as a seedy, corrupting element in a city that prided itself on its social programs, rehabilitation houses, and donations of reconstructive surgery for those who wished to shed their animal trappings and return to the world of men.

False, all of it.

Carac grimaced as he picked his way over the roots and fallen trees. He could not trust the strange man his queen had taken as her pet. It was more than simple sexual jealousy; though Carac was a loyal wolf, he was also a man, with a man's urge to spread his seed far and wide. He would not begrudge his queen her appetites. Still, a disturbing sense of concealment shadowed the stranger, and Carac was not fooled by his false mantle of harmlessness. Should his queen come to peril at the other's hands . . . Carac shook his head, overwhelmed by a sticky sense of dread as he watched his laughing queen depart with that trickster by her side.

He shadowed them, convinced that he would be errant in his duties as Queen Sidra's protector if he did not. Carac made his own choice, though it meant directly disobeying an order and incurring the queen's wrath. (Sidra was slow to anger, but once her rage was kindled, it could flare and burn out of control, a devastating force that destroyed everything in its path. Carac had seen this fury invoked but once; he had no wish to incite it again.)

He followed them day after day, gliding between the close trees like a wraith. He watched in silence as the heat between them grew and he bit his tongue when they kissed, both pleased and angered when Sidra ran from the thin man with fuzz on his chin. She did not know that he kept watch on the stranger. He alone saw the man lie down and rise a woman, reeking of milk and estrus. Carac smelled the change as it stole over the other man and robbed him of his sparse beard and his manhood. When Carac emerged from hiding, Sidra was not surprised to see him. Not glad, but not annoyed, either, and that was enough for him.

He'd done her bidding in the woods, fetching the child for the new woman in their midst and allowing himself to be abused as a mere lackey. What he could not abide was Sidra's dismissal of him, and they'd argued for the first time, their voices strained and hushed, barbed like arrows loosed and searching for their mark. Carac disobeyed a second time and followed them from the Erun, two females now, intent on a savior's mission. Their conversation was much different, less playful, more confessional, and Carac learned the way of women, who could reveal their hearts within minutes of meeting and forge a deep and lasting bond.

The relentless tumble of women's voices rang in Carac's ears. They argued about planes of existence, and if one type of dream held more weight than another. Sorykah described ice mining in the capricious Southern Sea while Sidra regaled her captive listener with lengthy political analyses.

Carac's heart was pity-stabbed by the Trader's sorry tale of her children's conception. It had been a brief, loveless affair, and she had taken no pleasure in it. Carac opened his mouth to capture the stranger's wind-carried scent, as tart and resolutely green as a crab apple. Odd that the man in her had smelled less of unreadiness, Carac mused, running his tongue over his pointed teeth. Still, he had the sense that both were rabbitty and cowed—waiting for the lid of some trap to be sprung without realizing that they could free themselves. Them, he snickered. Couldn't think of two people as one, couldn't scrub away breasts and penis to see some genderless neuter; instead, their faces slid over each other in Carac's mind, click-click, back and forth, like tiles being shuffled.

Once Sorykah had spilled her pathetic little pot of beans, Sidra followed suit, confessing the sordid details of her doomed and ruinous love affair with that rich dandy Chen (and here, Carac spat into the dirt) whose father, Matuk the Collector, was the very bane of their existence. Of course, she had left him when his treachery was discovered. Beat Chen about the face and neck with her strong fists and called him all manner of ugly names, accusing him of being a filthy traitorous liar, a brigand, and a Tirai Industries slave and whore.

"He was so beautiful," Sidra sighed to Sorykah, making Carac roll his eyes and growl, not enough to be overheard but just enough to let his disgust echo in his own ears, bridled by rage and leering, vengeful jealousy. How could he not sicken at the long lists of Chen's many exemplary traits—his wonderful smell of spicy plum and glorious blue-black hair, glossier than his great-grandfather's raven wings; his talents in the bedroom and the pretty verses he whispered as he moved within Carac's queen, filling both her ears and her body with his outpourings.

Even a novice to romance like Sorykah could see that Sidra still desired him. If rumors proved true, Chen still worshipped her although he made a grand show of despising her for rejecting him. Did not the grand bells in the manor's clock towers ring each day to mark the occasion of Chen's broken heart? He'd rechristened his island home the Isle of Mourning, and the waters dividing him from his beloved the Bay of Sorrows, and lived a wastrel's empty, sinful life.

"He awaits my return," Sidra confided. "He is mine forever, you will see," she insisted, making both Carac and Sorykah grimace.

Sorykah was easily bent and molded by Sidra's words. Her intellect was cool and rational beside Sidra's deep and watery passions, but she was untried enough to be gullible. The queen did not confess to having watched Meertham spirit some bundle into the manor. Instead she told Sorykah that the Collector's rube of a son would aid her if he knew she had been sent by his beloved. Chen and Sidra gamed with each other in this way, proving over and over their love, their superiority, their weaknesses and want.

"Chen will do anything for me. He'll give up the secret of the lock if you make me a promise."

Carac snorted at Sidra's confidence.

"Make him say my name. To drive the blade in a little deeper, to twist the knife. I'll take pleasure in knowing that he suffers." Sidra grinned, wickedness spread across her lips like fresh blood.

"Go to the House of Pleasure. Request an audience with him. He'll serve you a splendid dinner—he enjoys watching women eat. He says that the pull of our lips against the fork tines is suggestive. He garners as much thrill watching a woman tongue sauce from an eating stick as he would were she tonguing his own . . . well, the picture's clear, I'm sure." Sidra giggled and Sorykah looked somewhat cross. "The trick is simple enough but none would do it naturally. Once he begins to eat, do the same but do not gaze into your plate. Keep your eyes straight ahead, and by that he shall know you."

"Can he be bought for so little?" Sorykah asked.

"Never you mind, darling," Sidra said. "Trust in me and we will see that you have every opportunity to retrieve your children."

"Can no one come with me? I would relish the company and the extra set of hands, should the fight turn fierce," Sorykah ventured.

Sidra dismissed Sorykah's concern, keeping her voice light as she answered, "My duties here in the Erun are too great. There are many who need me. Who need us." Carac realized that Sidra sensed him following and was ashamed.

"This is your fight as well. The stories that spread"—and here the name stuck in Sorykah's mouth like a stout and many-pointed burr—"about the Collector's doings are filthy and unbearably cruel. It's in your best interests to dispatch him for the sake of your people."

"The tangle of plot and bloodlines that feed his villainy is far too complex for my unweaving. It's all I can do to keep my small band protected from those who are far less rich and powerful. The Erun city and our way of life are under constant threat. We must balance the good of the few against the good of the many."

The women broke free of the forest to emerge in a grassy plain where feathery grain stalks swayed in the peachy light and brushed their hips as they walked. Carac remained hidden behind the trees, silent and panting, his keen yellow eyes absorbing his mistress's every nuanced move and laden word. The Trader's gaze was desperate, her stance submissive, her voice imploring as she pressed the queen's hand to her heart, then knelt to wrap her arms about Sidra's knees, unmindful of the tears spilling over her cheeks.

"Sidra," Sorykah begged. "Please help me. Is there no one who can be spared?"

Sidra the Lovely, golden girl of the Erun, who shed tears so rarely that they were as precious as diamonds, pulled Sorykah from her legs, planted her on her feet, and urged her forward. She would not betray Chen, thus she could have no direct hand in his father's defeat.

"There is but one who can help, and it's to him that you must go," she replied.

Carac imagined his queen's words would sound cold and uncaring to Sorykah's ears.

The Trader would think herself unloved and Sidra would not dissuade Soryk/ah from the thought, the perversely practical queen believing it better to die broken-hearted than deluded.

21

THE ISLE OF MOURNING

SORYKAH LINGERED AT THE water's edge, boots in hands, her feet bared to the cool, sandy shore. The equatorial currents that warmed the southern bergs and caused their lethal calving flowed into the Bay of Sorrows, ushering in a false spring. Dew sprang up on the marsh grasses and weighted white blossoms that filled the air with fragrance. She turned to look over her shoulder to where Sidra lingered, almost beyond range of sight and hearing.

Sidra shooed Sorykah toward the fragile-looking reed boat that waited to shepherd her into the next phase of her ordeal.

Playful and welcoming, the water licked her toes. Sorykah did not consider the bay's depth or the voracious appetite of its seagoing undertow. She eased her weight into the rollicking reed boat and forced the flimsy craft into the current. Water curled against its sides and splashed away. A breeze played among the strands of Sorykah's hair, stroked her neck, and sang in her ears.

Cloaked by night, Chen's manor was little more than an inky

smudge against the sky. Sorykah wished for light to see where she was going but was glad that she could sail by unnoticed, slip into the trees lining the beach, and be lost among them.

Sidra advised abandoning the reed boat and letting the current carry her ashore, but the waves churned and plunged in a flurry of white foam and Sorykah feared being crushed, her head dashed against the rocks and broken like an egg. The boat thrashed and tipped; cold water spilled over its sides. Sorykah gripped the edges and cursed Sidra, certain of her death.

"When it gets too rough, close your eyes and jump," Sidra had winked. "Trust me. You won't be hurt."

Trust me. She hated those words. Wasn't that what that lying Trader had promised as he entered her body for the first and last time? *Trust me; nothing will happen that you don't want.*

She had trusted him and look what resulted. Yes, she admonished herself. Just look what happened. He had given her the children. Wasn't that what she had wanted, in her heart of hearts? She had traveled so far and yet was no closer to finding them. She hadn't been ferried all over the Erun, crossed mountains and wastes, and lost time playing queen's consort just to give up when faced with a little lukewarm seawater.

The boat careened dangerously; water rushed in and soaked her clothes. Not lukewarm, freezing! She sucked in her breath, tipping into the tide as water closed over her head. She sank into the cold, black water and damned Sidra to a slow and painful death followed by an eternity of fiery payback. Panicking, she opened her mouth and precious air bubbled out. A strong current thrust her to the surface, tumbling her over in its froth, sending her speeding for a shoreline barricaded by jagged rocks that gleamed like bloodied knifepoints. Gasping, she squeezed her eyes shut, loath to greet the firing squad with a smile. The waves thundered toward shore with gleeful abandon. Sorykah sailed past the rocks, bouncing over the splendid, buoying waves into a narrow channel where the ocean spit her onto the sand and retreated, leaving her whole and vigorously alive. She might have enjoyed the ride had she not been so terrified. Clambering to her feet and wringing the water from her clothes, she slunk along a stacked stone wall leading to the apex of the raked hillside.

Neat and well tended, the bountiful gardens heralded her arrival with scents of thyme, mint, marjoram, and sage. Night-blooming jasmine tangoed with a pungent ocean breeze. Short, broad trees staggered beneath their loads of fragrant blossoms and littered the path with a snowfall of pale petals. The full moon came into view, a golden goddess trailing diaphanous skirts across the textured sky. Chen's manor materialized in a sudden wash of buttery light, the delicate iron framework of its cathedral spires aflutter with billowing banners.

Bare feet noiseless against the still-warm path, Sorykah crept catlike toward the manor. She imagined how the sun would soak into the courtyard, how the heavy-headed rosebushes would droop in the heat, cicada song circling as lazy, pollen-drunk honeybees tottered between blossoms trailing chemical bliss to lure their hivemates to the spoils. She paused for a moment, sheltering beneath an ancient weeping willow that mimicked the sound of snakes on the move as its leaves twisted against the stones. Music filled the courtyard and light strained against colored panes, eager to find release in the night. She crouched spellbound and felt a nameless yearning stir within her, a deep and dark desire, a wanting. The song fragmented and female laughter found her hiding among the leaves. "Come out and play," it seemed to say. "We won't bite."

Eager for the company of people after so many days in the Erun, Sorykah was drawn forward as if enchanted; her feet and legs carried her where they would, bidden and answering.

She stumbled into a small orchard where cherry boughs, hung heavy with fruit, draped a fountain crowded with slender, sleeping koi. Turgid white lilies crowded the patches of earth tucked among pale marble statues of women in repose.

Horn and flute fell into a playful rivalry and skin drums vibrated beneath caressing fingers and palms. The open greenhouse door invited intrusion. Tables sagged beneath seedling trays where rich black soil lay heaped beside rows of plants that Sorykah was surprised to recognize as the daughters of Shanxi's alpine oenathe. These were larger, fleshier, and more dewy; their thick, spiraling tendrils ran juicy with sap. Sorykah was grateful that these sprouts were less animated than Shanxi's freakishly responsive children, who shivered with feeling and murmured among themselves.

Soaked through, she shuddered and sneezed three times in quick succession.

Silence throbbed in the air followed by the clatter of instruments thrust aside.

"They will receive you with grace," Sidra had said. "Accept their hospitality and enjoy it. They lead lives of endless pleasure while you are monastic in your deprivations. A change of routine will suit you all very well, I should think."

Sorykah froze, reluctant to be discovered, yet longing for the sight of fresh faces and the creature comforts promised by the lush gardens and fragrant scents.

A cluster of women materialized in the doorway, clutching one another's sleeves like a string of ducklings.

"Who's there?" asked one. "Show yourself."

"Show yourselves first," Sorykah retorted, crouching behind a sprawling oenathe.

A plump arm stretched forward to ignite a gas jet that flared and hissed, casting a glow over the tables. Five women stepped into the light—a quintet of curious cats licking milk from their teeth. Perfumed hair flowed to their thighs, curled and ornamented with fiery opals, gold beads, and tiny, jingling bells. Gold shimmered on bejeweled necks as the women tittered and craned their heads, kohl-lined eyes peering into the shadows.

"Step forward that we may see you," commanded a robust, silver-haired woman.

Sorykah forced herself from behind the oenathe, painfully

aware of her own sodden appearance. She pushed a lock of wet hair from her forehead and made a futile attempt to straighten her grubby jersey. Cooing like doves, the women surged forward en masse. Myriad hands floated over Sorykah's body, curious fingers like the beating of wings disturbing the surface of a calm lake. Someone picked a strand of seaweed from Sorykah's hair and giggled. Another hand encircled her wrist, measuring its slim width and clucking.

Shaking off her sisters, the matriarch stepped forward, folding plump, bangle-draped arms over ample breasts.

"It's been decided," she announced. "You shall have the Rose Room. I am Marianna, the matron of the House of Pleasure. These are my girls but all serve the master of this isle." Marianna curtsied and gestured to a petite brunette with sultry eyes and dimpled cheeks. "My charm-daughter Carensa will be delighted to serve you." Emboldened by her assignment, the pretty, smiling girl took Sorykah by the arm, pulling her close.

"You'll love it, you'll see! It's the nicest among the guest rooms; roses are his favorite. They remind him of *her*, you see. Oh! Don't shush me!" Carensa hissed to a tall woman with bright red hair, henna-stained fingers, and narrow, yellow eyes. "It's romantic! Wouldn't you agree?"

Sorykah shrugged, "I suppose." She had no idea where they were taking her. Sidra had been deliberately vague about proceedings at the manor. Her only advice: Savor it.

The redhead rolled her eyes. "She's hopeless, honestly. You've been out in the world; perhaps you can rub a bit of the shine off her apple. She thinks everything is honey and sunshine."

"Miss Doom and Gloom!" snapped Carensa. "Zarina insists that the world was formed in six days from bitters and rain clouds, and on the seventh we should all sit around beating our breasts in lamentation! Oh, do play us another dreary dirge on your lute while this funeral procession passes by!"

The redhead rebounded with an acidic reply and the verbal joust continued as they led Sorykah through the splendid manor.

Sorykah glimpsed decadent suites through open doorways, one decorated in white fur, another in crimson velvet, and another like a pasha's harem with mounds of gorgeous, tasseled pillows, its ceiling tented in gold silk. Sorykah followed the women up a central staircase and down a long, curving corridor to a pair of alabaster double doors.

Marianna said, "Pleasured guest, welcome to the Rose Room."

The fragrance rolled out like a wave to lift her up and carry her in. Roses—but fresher and sweeter, more delicious than any rose had ever been and virtually edible in their candy-scented glory. Sorykah squealed with delight, her toes sinking into the silky white furs strewn across the floor.

Bouncing on her toes, Carensa swept into the room, dragging Sorykah after her. "Do you love it?" Her dimples deepened. "Come and see the bath," Carensa trilled, leading Sorykah through an archway into an oceanic paradise. Gemstones in varying shades of blue, green, and gold inlaid each azure-tiled wall and a false wave of solid glass curled from the floor, forming a bathtub rimmed in milk glass. Silver dolphins cavorted in place of taps, and as Sorykah peered into the tub, she was horrified to see its clear glass bottom, through which the lower floors and several people were visible, milling about in the library.

She blushed and her escorts laughed wickedly.

The bedroom was yet more sumptuous, its pink-mirrored walls bare but for the reflection of an enormous bed inlaid with ivory and mother of pearl and canopied by a live rose trellis.

"Pink in summer, yellow in autumn, red in winter, and white in spring, this bed is the only clock we have. Without it, we'd never know what month it is." Marianna fluffed the perfect pillows and turned to Sorykah. "I expect you'd like to refresh yourself before dinner."

Sorykah nodded, delirious at the thought of a hot bath and the luxurious, downy bed.

"Everyone here is at your service, my lady. We exist to please you and, should you desire it, to pleasure you as well."

Sorykah gaped at the woman, certain that she was hearing things. "Pardon?"

"There's naught to do here but enjoy the finest gifts in life. We dance and sing, eat the most delicious food, drink the best wine, and indulge our every whim and taste. Each of your desires is to be satisfied. There's none that want, in this house. Is that not the reason you've journeyed here?" Marianna pursed her lips, vexed by Sorykah's astonishing naïveté.

Carensa squeezed Sorykah's arm. "Men have tried for years to get beyond the breakers but very few have succeeded. Once here," she giggled, "they have no wish to leave. Do you?"

Sorykah surveyed the gorgeous room and imagined spending the rest of her days in the beautiful manor, a pampered princess with nothing to do save please herself. No other company except these tinkling, giggling women. No sweet, pudgy children. No, it would not do.

"It's a kind offer but I'm afraid I have to be on my way. I'm only here to see your master." Sorykah grimaced at the title with its gruesome implications of ownership and submission. Were these women here of their own free will? Could they abandon the isle if they wished to, or was their allegiance purchased and contractually held in bonds of indentured servitude?

"He does not grant audiences to guests," said Zarina, "but we can relay a message for you."

"I'm quite certain he'll entertain my company." False bravado was one of the necessary skills Sorykah had acquired aboard the *Nimbus*. She was certain that her voice quavered as she spoke and she hid her hands in her pockets to disguise their trembling.

"My dear," said Marianna, leaning close to murmur in Sorykah's ear, "we deny ourselves nothing here. If that is your desire, then I will arrange it for you." She stroked Sorykah's grimy cheek and grinned.

"Girls," she purred, "see that our guest is well satisfied." Five young women giggled and fluttered coy lashes.

"Ask for anything you like, we have no shame here." Marianna squeezed Sorykah's hand and then she was gone, taking her trio of giddy blondes and leaving Sorykah with Carensa and Zarina, who turned the dolphin taps to run a steaming bath. Little Carensa took Sorykah's boots as solemn Zarina lit tapers and an incense coil and fed the banked fire.

Sand and seaweed spilled from her boots onto the rug and Carensa clucked her tongue. "It's always this way. Such a shame we can't have a boat ferry our guests from the mainland."

"Why not?" Sorykah asked, distracted by the gold-rimmed champagne flute Zarina pressed into her hand. Blackberry liqueur layered the bottom of the glass.

"The breakers, of course. There was a ferryman once but he wrecked like all the others. Now he's the head groom in the stables. Everyone who arrives does so by accident. They tumble ashore clutching a broken plank, fresh from a disaster at sea." Carensa's hands danced over Sorykah's clothes, fiddling with the fastenings that cinched her trousers. "Step out please," she ordered.

Sorykah did so, too tired to protest.

Carensa unbuttoned the woolen tunic and pulled it over her charge's head, leaving her standing in the homespun shirt Sidra had given her after her illness, its curious panels and ties offering meager support for her recuperating breasts.

Carensa raised her eyebrows but made no comment, unlacing the ties and tossing the shirt to Zarina, who left the Rose Room with the filthy clothes and boots.

Sorykah stood shivering and naked, her arms crossed over her breasts. The bath was ready. Steam rose and danced, mingling with incense smoke to blur the edges of the room.

"My lady," Carensa said, curtsying low. She offered her hand and Sorykah took it, struck by the thought that she had never held another woman's hand. Carensa's was small and soft, decorated with silver filigree rings and tattoos. She led Sorykah to the tub and nodded as Sorykah slid into silky, perfumed water that rose around her, the fragrance and color of violets.

"Oh my," she sighed, sinking low.

Carensa smiled and knelt by the tub, her fingers trailing in the water. "Been a long time, has it?"

Sorykah nodded, the hot water liquefying her frozen core. She had not been warm all the way through since leaving Dirinda, many weeks ago. How nice it was not to be cold!

Carensa poured Sorykah a glass of ruby port, which she drained in three swallows. She'd never been much of a drinker and the alcohol rolled in like a tidal wave to wash away her resistance and resolve.

"I'll leave you now. If you find yourself in need, there's a bell pull in every room. Should you require something that I cannot provide, well, I'll take care of that, too," she offered slyly.

The doors snicked closed. At last, Sorykah was alone. The wine muted her thoughts, offering a few moments reprieve from her endlessly circulating worries and woes. Were the children this well looked after? Were they safe, warm, and fed?

The previous night, she'd dreamed of finding them in a stony field, playing in the grass and conversing in some strange tongue. As she neared, she realized that they had stubby tails and woolly bodies beneath their clothes. Reaching for them, she stumbled and fell, crying out in horror as they rounded on her, bleating like lambs. Sorykah awoke, her throat thick with terror. The dream had been terrible not because her children couldn't speak, but because they did not recognize her. The difficulties of her journey and the necessity of keeping a hard heart left her too numb to succumb to tears. She would gift herself the selfishness of luxuriating in a hot bath and restorative sleep before stoking her worry to full flame in the morning.

Morning sun slanted through the leaded glass as Sorykah nestled into the feather bed, letting the struggles of her journey dissolve.

Carensa knocked and entered, balancing a demitasse on a saucer and looking as though she had slept in her clothes. She smiled, still sleepy and savoring the excesses of the night before. The whole manor had been pitched into erotic hysteria by the arrival of their visitor. They didn't know that she was a Trader; she was simply a blank canvas on which to paint their fantasies.

"Bottoms up. It's good luck." Carensa proffered jammy tartines and cocoa with chile, rich and spicy. "The master will take lunch with you. Consider yourself lucky. He does not take audiences with travelers. But first, you must demonstrate your worth."

"In what ways might I be found unworthy?" Sorykah smirked.

"Through an inability to enjoy pleasure. Because he finds no satisfaction in love, he has devoted himself and this house to sensual exploration in all its forms. You must prove yourself adept if you are to win favor with such a one as he."

Carensa drew gossamer sheers over the window and lit a winding spiral of incense. "Elu is extremely talented, in both the kitchen and the bedroom. I think you'll find him to your liking."

"And if I don't," Sorykah balked, not liking the conversation's turn.

"Consider it a test of loyalty. A few hours spent in the throes of *la petite morte* is a very small price to pay for the master's time," Carensa said. "You'll be in expert hands. Elu makes women's bodies run liquid beneath his fingers because in all matters sensual, he's the master."

Sorykah was robbed of speech. She was expected to perform like a trained seal to appease Chen's voyeuristic nature. His assumption that she would so easily surrender offended her sense of moral decency, but even worse than that, the thought of revealing her own lack of carnal experience to the stranger soon to enter her portals made her weak in the knees.

"You'll die a hundred times," Carensa advised, "but each death precludes a marvelous rebirth. You'll leave this house a new woman, I'm quite sure of it." She closed the door to the Rose

Room just as the bells in the tower clock began to chime, heralding the moment that Chen's heart had been cracked in two between Sidra's impartial fingers.

Upstairs in the Rose Room, Elu found his assigned conquest trembling and pacing. Lean and hardship-pared, Sorykah was uncomfortable wearing only a sheet to greet this stranger with smooth caramel skin and black curls. He smiled at her and paused inside the doorway to allow her to become accustomed to him. When he offered her a delicate pastry edged in gold leaf and layers of milk and dark chocolate, her eyes betrayed her tongue's desire. Sorykah was tempted though she knew the treat a transparent ploy. Would she allow herself to be bought for a trinket? The memory of a noxious meal of slimy snails and cold mealie made her reach forward and take the cake in hand. A spark leapt and burned in her black eyes.

"You win by sneakery," she said.

"Sneakery?" Elu rolled the word on his tongue, liking the feel of it.

"You place me at an unfair advantage." Sorykah swallowed, drawing Elu's green gaze to the movement of her throat. He raised an eyebrow. "You prey on my weakness. It's unfair."

"Life is unfair, pleasured guest. Who am I to disrupt the order of the universe?" He pulled Sorykah to him, enjoying her sudden startle, running strong hands over her long limbs.

Sorykah had not the reserves to resist such fine ploys. Her skin was alien to the sensations Elu coaxed from it, yet soon she lifted her arms about his neck in response, pressed her wanting body against his, and was taken against the windows with her naked breasts pressed to the leaded glass, arms stretched overhead as incense wreathed her dampened brow.

The rest of the morning passed as deliciously as Carensa had promised. Elu spoke little, but his few words were honey and treacle and all things sweet and good. Sorykah drifted in and out of sleep, waking to find herself safe in the tireless Elu's arms as he again stoked her passions to the burning point. When release came, wrapped up in a mess of snarled emotions that had entangled themselves over the course of Sorykah's search for her babies, it erupted from Sorykah's throat as a mournful cry that echoed the song of the Sigue.

The layabouts in the library below heard it and paused in their erotic storytelling to marvel at the sound. Elu's kitchen comrades slapped hands and chivvied up their bets. Engaged in a tryst of her own, Carensa merely smiled and yelped into her lover's ear, considering the myriad tricks her dear patissier employed to elicit such noise. In the women's private quarters, spurned Zarina twisted her red hair in her hands like a bright, bloodstained hangman's rope and plotted her revenge. And far from it all, Chen brooded atop the manor's high turret walkway, his eyes turned toward the Erun shore where his heart, Queen Sidra the Lovely, sat before her fire, a ferocious par-wolf nuzzling her neck while she gazed into the flames and pined for a life that could never be.

22

THE HOUSE OF PLEASURE

SEATED IN THE DINING ROOM with its handsome frescoes and gleaming French doors, through which the Bay of Sorrows was visible in the lingering twilight, Sorykah waited, biting her nails at the thought of meeting the infamous Chen, who so deeply etched his claim on Sidra the Lovely's heart that there was no untouched space left for any other.

A maid brought bread, butter, and salt. Another sauntered in and poured wine, catching a dribble with her fingertip and licking it off once she had Sorykah's eye. The two women giggled, and the wine bearer bent low, flashing her expansive décolletage as she spooned broth from a tureen into a shallow bowl and set it before her guest. Sorykah blushed and looked away, disturbed by the flirtatious tittering.

A portly butler followed the maids, pinching their cheeks and slapping their bottoms. A current of small talk flowed from the kitchen staff as translucent china plates were laid, dinner kept warm beneath shining silver domes while awaiting Chen's arrival.

Slathering butter on a broken roll, the man sprinkled salt across its yeasty rise and offered it to Sorykah, his merry blue eyes twinkling. Acute embarrassment ravaged her: She had no choice but to eat from his fingertips.

The broad doors parted and Chen strode in, cocky and overconfident, lithe and handsome in the way of rogues and scoundrels. His black leathers, jersey, and boots sucked up the available light; only the bloody red spill of his velvet robe kept the shadows from swallowing him whole. He nodded in her direction and seated himself at the table's far end, delving into his meal without preliminary.

Chen's obvious disinterest in her plight panicked her until she remembered Sidra's instructions: "Do not look at your food while eating, no matter what takes place or what he says to goad you into doing so. It's the only way he'll recognize you as my emissary, and he alone can reveal the secret of the lock. Should you fail in this, you will forfeit your claim to your children."

Sorykah used a pair of fiercely pointed, foot-long eating sticks to spear a chunk of something from her plate. Keeping her eyes trained on Chen, Sorykah struggled to not look down. Vague shapes danced on her plate's periphery, something like a colorful tangle of julienned vegetables and small cuts of sauced meat that made her think of tinned dog food. Chen was sullen, his handsome face drawn up in a scowl. A lock of black hair draped into his plate and curled in the sauce. He flicked it back and continued eating, washing down his food with great swigs of the heady red wine a serving girl constantly replenished.

The atmosphere was tense and silent. Although he had provided Sorykah with every luxury, Chen was a terrible host.

Sorykah found something solid enough to balance on the carefully suspended eating sticks, raised them to her mouth, and pricked the inside of her cheek. Wincing, she rubbed the sore spot with her tongue as blood welled against her teeth.

Chen glanced up, his eagle eyes keen.

Sorykah pressed a cloth napkin to her lips to stanch the flow, glad that they were a dark ruby red so that the blood wouldn't show. Chen did not inquire after her health nor did he rush to provide first aid for his wounded guest. Instead, he gestured for her to continue eating. His stare intensified as she blundered across her plate. Keeping her gaze trained on his scowl, Sorykah continued eating though her cheeks burned and her head swam with the effort of meeting his eyes.

Chen banged his fist upon the table. The vibration traveled the length of the wooden planks and Sorykah jumped, narrowly avoiding putting out an eye with her eating sticks.

"Where is she?" he snarled.

"I don't know what you mean." Sorykah attempted insouciance, but her voice faltered.

Wait for him to speak my name, Sidra had insisted. The whole charade would be meaningless otherwise.

"You bloody well do know what I mean! She sent you! You've given me the signal, enjoyed the extravagance of my hospitality, and now I want what's due." Chen strode down the table's left flank and closed in on her. Sorykah laid aside the beautiful eating sticks and folded her hands in her lap. Chen arrived like a smoking dragon, all fire and fury, spitting sparks and steam. "What does she want?"

Sorykah shook her head.

"Is she here then, lurking about in the gardens, enjoying a laugh at my expense?"

Again Sorykah shook her head.

Chen crouched beside her, softening his tone and stance. "You and I both know that she deposited you on my doorstep. Only the very foolish would dare to venture here unawares. You either have a mission or a message. Now, which is it?"

Fear percolated inside her and a lump swelled in her throat. Would this man help her? Sidra had seemed so sure, but Sorykah doubted him. A rich man living an indolent life, master of his own tiny fiefdom and intent on pleasure and sin, how could she persuade him to give up his father?

"You must say her name," she whispered.

Chen snorted and Sorykah smelled wine on his breath. He rubbed a hand though his thick hair and groaned. "By god, that woman loves to crank the screws. You wouldn't know that I have taken a vow never to say her name aloud. You don't, but she does. Spies in this house, no doubt. She forces my hand at every turn!" Chen paced alongside the table, his robe trailing the stone floor. "And if I don't?"

"Then she knows you no longer love her, and she will abandon you forever. She's said as much." Sorykah chewed the inside of her cheek. *Hold steady, you can do this.*

"Why should I care? Tell me, why should I care what she does? She'd sooner tend wild beasts than share my life here, being pampered and indulged, her every whim gratified. Doesn't she know I do this all for her?"

Sorykah thought he didn't understand his ladylove very well to think her so easily swayed by material comforts. "That's not what moves her. She has an extraordinary gift. She is a healer, a leader, truly a queen. Do you not see that? Don't you know that an idle life would be meaningless to her?"

"Idle!" barked Chen. "How dare you deem me so spoiled!"

Sorykah crumpled beneath his angry tirade and for the first time, looked down at the food she had eaten. Fragrant slivers of meat marinated in spiced gravy. Candied kumquats and star fruit fanned out along the rim of the plate, adding color and sweetness to a nest of shaved root vegetables. She had to admire the presentation. If nothing else, Chen and his staff had an adept and sensual eye for beauty.

"Bah!" Chen paced the floor and Sorykah recognized the same driven restlessness his aunt had displayed in the throes of her oenathe rapture.

"Oh for goodness sake!" She lifted her head, suddenly tired of his lover's theatrics. "She's willing to see you if you help me. If you aren't so foolish and addled to grant her wish then you should meet with her and resolve your dispute." Pursing her lips with a surprising new stubbornness that had gained ground over the course of her journey, Sorykah met Chen's challenge.

"Look," she sighed, "I need your help. I'm desperate. And I will do whatever it takes . . ."

Chen's smirking mouth quirked up in curious surprise.

"Anything," Sorykah amended, "that I can give with a clean conscience in order to secure your assistance."

Chen rubbed a long-fingered hand over his flat abdomen and considered Sorykah. She caught his dark, glittering eye and for the first time, stripped away her protective skin, revealing herself and her terrifying, wondrous secret. "My name is Sorykah Minuit. I am a Trader."

Chen shook his head in disbelief. He thought her joking but when he read the resignation etched on her face, he exhaled with a low whistle. "The stories are true, then."

She nodded. "All true. And more, I'm afraid."

Chen leaned forward to stare at Sorykah with liquid eyes. She reddened and looked away. His lean, brooding face and expressive brows were quite handsome. Black hair tumbled in lazy waves over his shoulders. His curiosity was a tangible thing vibrating the air between them.

"In all my years, I've never met one such as you," he murmured.

Here we go, thought Sorykah, steeling herself for the inevitable approach. The word *Trader* invoked a salacious reaction that conscientious people attempted to constrain, but there were always those whose lecherous curiosity required satisfaction. Sorykah had overheard some of the miners on the *Nimbus* describe a party where ordinary men and women mimicked her own natural ability, engaging in unconventional games of seduction and gender play. Ironic that they should regard her as the pinnacle of sensual desire and satisfaction when her own sexual experiences had been so unsatisfactory.

Sorykah forced herself to remember Sidra slinking through the Erun, her eyes upon this distant isle, awaiting the all-clear. Sorykah little doubted that Chen's sorrow made him a tempting challenge to the ladies of the manor. Many a maid had tried to woo him away from his lost love and might possess him for a night or two, but his heart would remain as steadfast as it was untouchable.

"Let's adjourn to the salon. We'll be much more comfortable there and then you can tell me your story without interruption." Chen rose and offered his arm.

Something (fear? desire?) fluttered in her throat as she threaded her hand through his arm, stepping close to the tall male body with its exotic scents of leather, wine, and spicy plum. Chen escorted her through the library (where she could gaze up through the ceiling glass of her bathtub into the candlelit Rose Room), past several whist-playing courtesans who nibbled chocolate truffles and watched them enter the indigo salon with a knowing gleam in their eyes and a smirk on their shiny lips.

"Please, seat yourself." Chen gestured to one of many pillows heaped upon the plush, carpeted floor. He settled near her, stretching out long legs, his hand settling on Sorykah's primly crossed knees.

"When's the last time you had a good meal?" His hot fingers roamed over the bones prominent beneath her skin.

She couldn't help laughing as she answered, "About five minutes ago!"

He grinned, the right corner of his mouth curling up higher than the left. "Have you enjoyed your time here? Found everything to your liking?"

She nodded, considering the hot, peppered chocolate served in bed, the violet foam baths, and the cloud-soft bed in the gorgeous Rose Room.

"I understand that you were most accommodating to my young patissier. He had very kind things to say about your"—Chen's smoldering eyes slid over Sorykah's frame with approval—"hospitality."

She blushed a deep rose, recalling handsome Elu in her bed.

"Word travels fast. We have so little new flesh to enjoy and gossip is one of life's spiciest pleasures." His smile seemed to melt by degrees as he rang the bell pull to summon a maid. As if on cue, she entered the room bearing an ornate glass tray laden with bonbons and petit fours topped with candied rose petals and gold leaf.

"A gift from Elu," Chen said, popping one of the tiny cakes into his mouth. "Mmm, if the taste is any indication of his affection for you, it seems that you enjoyed each other even more than I thought."

Sorykah's gaze floated toward the silk-tented ceiling, the lush white orchids—anything but Chen. His hand spider-walked from her knee to the dangling lacing string of her bodice. He curled it around a finger and tugged. The traitorous bow unfurled.

"A real live Trader, here in my house. How did I get to be so lucky? Do you know what a night with you is worth?"

She shook her head. She refused to learn about such things.

"The price of Trader flesh is very dear. Even with all my wealth," Chen swept his hand around the expensively appointed room, "I could not afford you."

Sorykah was astonished. She could not imagine her ordinary body being deemed such a treasure. If only she had the moxie to sell herself!

Chen wormed a finger beneath the hem of her borrowed gown. "It's no accident that the fates have delivered you to me. I believe someone has been kind enough to set the stage for a most delightful exchange."

A little ripple of heat bubbled, built, and spread, setting the blood racing beneath her skin.

"Each of us has something the other wants and if my instincts are right, you are willing to pay any price to take it from me. Am I right?"

Sorykah shifted on the slippery pillows, fanning her throat as she deliberated upon an answer. Chen pursed his lips, already keen to possess the prize he was certain was his for the taking. A rush of sensual energy invigorated him as he unlaced her bodice. Sorykah met his eyes, and he read the acquiescence displayed in her own dark gaze.

Here was a fruit ripe for the plucking, and him with his cherry picker at the ready . . .

Carensa arrived the following morning after Sorykah had finished her breakfast, her arms piled high with wads of fabric. She pushed a lock of brown hair from her eyes and sighed, shaking her head. "If your hair was longer, you could be spectacular."

"Am I not spectacular as I am?" Sorykah joked, crossing her eyes and poking out her tongue. Carensa indulged her charge with a smile, reaching for Sorykah's hands and pulling her from the warm bed. Nudity was so uninteresting and commonplace in the House of Pleasure that Sorykah was no longer shy about it. She shivered as the cool morning air struck her naked skin and stood as Carensa whisked the measuring tape around her body. Mulling over her fabric choices, she shuffled through bolts of velvet and satin, placing them against Sorykah's bare neck and frowning. "I'm making a gown for you to wear tonight when you dine with the court."

"I thought I would be alone with him." Sorykah frowned.

Carensa averted her eyes, her response deceptively casual. "Chen wants to prove you to the residents. It's nothing. An opportunity for you to perform and please yourself, that is all. Zarina will be back at eight to dress you. Until then, you are on your own."

Sorykah ran her hands over goose-pimpled arms and crawled back into bed, where she lay staring at the rose petals that had begun to drop with the season's end. Although she'd successfully pushed her fears to the back of her mind (Elu had served as a most helpful distraction), they clamored for her attention.

She had one chance to win back her children. Chen might despise his father but, like Shanxi, would not willingly sacrifice the man to Sorykah's killing stroke. Resentment simmered within her. How dare Chen ask her to trade her virtue for knowledge of her own offspring? What a pompous, self-aggrandizing bastard! She was disgusted by his willingness to sell out his father and by the misguided loyalty that drove him to cajole such a bargain from a hopeless woman like herself. A deal was made—Chen's pleasure for his father's secret. Despite all the rage and repugnance she mustered for the act she was about to commit and the man who had requested it, she couldn't quite suppress a fledgling, anticipatory thrill. Chen milked every ounce of acquiescence from her, his smooth-nailed finger stroking her exposed thigh, all the blood in her limbs attracted to that finger as if magnetized. His breath like trembling quills teased over her neck, the tops of her breasts, her ears. Sorykah shivered with a mix of intrigue and revulsion. She had remembered this as she moved beneath Elu, the black velvet whisper of Chen's promise inflaming her dreamy arousal, and she was consumed by desire, even though it offended her to want him. Now the whole day stretched ahead, empty and panting for want of play. She would dress and dine with the court, show herself with pinked lips and cheeks, made up like a porcelain doll, with gold dust on her eyelids and frosting the smooth ridge of her collarbones.

"Be a girl," Chen advised. "Pretty, polished, and flirtatious. It will make the transformation that much more stunning."

Besides Chen, who claimed deflowering honors, she was obligated to select four playmates. Elu and Carensa topped her list. (Sorykah blushed to acknowledge the wish for her male half to possess the pretty maid. The admission of desire was dizzying and caused her to redden in the girl's presence.) The others would be selected during the gala when the opportunity to win Sorykah's approval would dangle overhead like a tantalizing treat, causing all to rise, beg, and perform tricks to her liking.

The day passed slowly, in long, agonized stretches. Sorykah tried to read a novel and failed, forced food and drink into her rebellious stomach, and primped with the sterling tools of torture arrayed on the mirrored vanity. When Zarina arrived to take the tweezers from her hand and make brief sounds of annoyance, Sorykah was relieved to surrender control. The red vixen swiftly completed Sorykah's transformation.

As the sea extinguished the last crimson rays of sunlight, music commenced in the great hall below. Sorykah's breath hovered in her throat, trapped like a moth beneath glass. There were two components to her pact with Chen. He must say Sidra's name and pledge fealty to the somatic queen, thus satisfying Sidra's egotistical need to retain power and reestablish her claim on his heart. He had but to utter a single word and Sorykah's fate, like her naked body, was in his hands. Her mission was less simple: to change beneath his watchful eyes. Chen had little idea that what he asked of her was so absurd. He might as well insist that she rope the moon and harness the planets to it, so outlandish was his desire.

She worried all afternoon, her heart churning fiercely. What if she summoned the change and it did not come? She could not entertain such peevish, reckless thoughts. Could not dwell on the years and days lost, the forgetfulness of her blank slate upon awakening from her temporary hormonal coma.

Fear and sorrow triggered the change and nothing could be more sorrowful or frightening than failing Chen's task and forsaking her babes. During the few, restive moments when she succumbed to an uneasy sleep, her confidence was thwarted by visions of herself descending the grand stairs and opening her robe to find herself a woman, breasty and unmanned, deceived by an inner, unconjurable magick.

If she completed the transformation and coaxed Sidra's name from Chen's lips before he ravished her, she would rise from the bartering bed marked with the sins of her sale.

If she failed to summon the change at Chen's command, she little doubted that he would sweep from the room and vanish, leaving her to devise some ill-gotten ship to master the breakers and carry her back to the Erun shore. She foresaw herself trudging overland into the dark forest once again, fighting through the dense, primeval trees to reach the manor and almost certain failure.

Taking a final glimpse of her lavish finery—the stiff glittering ribbons threaded through her hot-ironed curls, her sumptuous velvet gown, and the bow-tied high heels on her feet—Sorykah took a mouthful of the omnipresent wine served at every occasion no matter how grand or insignificant, and began the descent to her final destruction.

Sorykah pressed a hand to her chest to still the restless wings fluttering inside. A masked stranger escorted her to a secret door in the frescoed wall panel, ushering her through a corridor that smelled of warm beeswax and incense, to the doors of the great hall. She followed with trepidation, wishing for more wine.

Music swelled like the bay's dismal tides and swept Sorykah up in its regal throes, so different from the playful tune that had accompanied her arrival. Bells rang and strings thrummed with increasing frenzy until a great cheer rose up from the crowd and the curtain began to rise. Broad explosions of lemony light from the diamond chandeliers zigzagged across Sorykah's vision, blinding her. She glimpsed an enormous bed stacked like a wedding cake and ringed by descending tiers of smaller mattresses, each sacked and tied inside its own silk bag. An elaborate framework of nimble, spidery stairs allowed access to each of the mattresses, where lacy pillows spilled, ostentatious with silk tassels and piping.

Mingled perfumes choked air thick with erotic excitement as the assembled crowd milled, splendid in the costumes of sleek leopardesses, leaping fauns, turquoise and ivory peacocks, and a whole menagerie of fantastic creatures, pointing gossamer fans and bejeweled walking sticks at Sorykah's skirt and petticoat hems, trying, perhaps, to lift them.

She hesitated, unsure of her role in this bizarre charade. Then the drums rolled, and a spotlight illuminated the main door. Excitement mushroomed and the crowd bustled and churned, heads swiveling to view Chen's entrance. The doors parted to disgorge Sorykah's adversary and future lover, his black hair shining, his olive skin well oiled and perfumed beneath his tight trousers, tunic, and black leather vest. He strode in, overflowing with the sensual charge of dominion, a cock-of-the-walk with preening head held high.

Sorykah wished to sail through the air above the crowd, gouge out his throat, and revel in the warm spray of blood as she vanquished him, and yet—as he moved through his flock of faithful admirers, drawing the ladies' hands to his lips, clapping a firm hand to men's shoulders in patriarchal camaraderie—he was somehow quite glorious.

The bed loomed between them, laden with portent. First, there were waltzes to be danced, champagne from the flowing fountains to be sipped and frolicked in, and pots of warmed chocolate that beckoned the dipping finger.

Full of mirth and saturated with his own masculine good fortune, Chen shouted, "Let the bacchanal begin!"

He wormed through an aisle of the partygoers, unmindful of the hands that reached out to trail their fingers through his hair. Standing before Sorykah he bowed low, barely able to keep the conquerer's grin from his lips. Chen offered her champagne and wild berries as they flitted from group to group, pausing to allow each its examination.

The panels of Sorykah's gown were tied to a framework of ribbon and as each new cluster of revelers viewed her to their satisfaction, Chen pulled a thread and released a panel, leaving strips of velvet in their wake. They made the circuit yet again; her sleeves disappeared and her full skirt diminished as she passed men and women clutching velvet scraps to their noses and crowing in triumph.

Perhaps it was the effect of the red currant cordial, but Sorykah's fear began to wane. Look how everyone smiled and bowed! How many, growing bolder and excited by her gaining nakedness, reached out to stroke her bare arms, or wind jeweled fingers along the dangling laces of her corset and tug her hair ribbons between their fingers.

"You must choose," Chen said, running his tongue along her ear's outer edge. "Pick one."

Sorykah found Elu dancing with a masked harem girl. Chen signaled Elu and he made his way to the bed, taking the second mattress from the top.

"You must select a woman to prove your change complete." Chen's hand was warm in the hollow of her back and he allowed it to slip onto her hip, where he untied another bow. Sorykah colored and swallowed, fanning her throat and gazing around the room. A few faces were recognizable beneath their paint and glitter but elaborate masks obscured others. She scrolled through the many women she had seen at the manor, trying to imagine how her male counterpart would choose and whom he would find attractive. She decided to please her feminine senses and select one whose aesthetics appealed to her. If Soryk was truly male, he wouldn't be too fussy about the warm, willing body beneath him.

Discarded veils, panels, fans, feathers, and lacings mounted like snowdrifts on the dance floor. Sorykah considered the women's costumes and the bodies inside them. Carensa's absence was noticeable. Marianna spun past in the arms of a one-eyed pirate and waved at Sorykah, who dismissed her from the task for being too matronly.

The ocean of whirling bodies parted, revealing a woman

whose shining ebony skin contrasted with her glittering gold gown. When she lifted her glass to her full lips, rows of gold bangles danced and jingled along her graceful arms like bells. Sorykah's hand tightened on Chen's arm and he followed her gaze.

"My, we do have good taste." Chen pulled Sorykah through throngs of drunken dancers to the golden woman's side.

"Kamala, I'd like to introduce our pleasured guest, Sorykah Minuit." Kamala fixed her black eyes on Sorykah and dipped low in a restrained curtsy.

"It's rare that a goddess will leave the heavens to frolic with mortals. My darling," Chen said, one arm tight about Sorykah's waist as he took Kamala's hand in his to kiss her palm, "might we entice you down from the skies for one night?"

She shrugged, tipped her head, and allowed her gaze to travel along the length of Sorykah's mostly unclad body.

"Are the rumors true then?" Kamala's voice had the velvety purr of a lazy lioness, well feasted and sun-warmed. "You have so teased us with this ploy of yours," she murmured, nuzzling Chen's neck.

"See for yourself." Chen lifted the hem of Sorykah's skirts, displaying her lacy knickers. Sorykah's cheeks flamed red and she pushed Chen's hands away, smoothing what remained of her skirt. "She is all woman."

Kamala shrugged and looked away, her interest waning.

"Goddess," Chen intoned, his voice edged with faint warning. "Our guest desires to pleasure you as a man."

Kamala raised an eyebrow and scoffed. "She will not be man enough for me."

"Let him decide that. Just lie back and enjoy the view. I am quite sure this little Trader will not disappoint her fans." Chen slid a hand beneath Sorykah's dress and cupped her bottom. She grimaced even as her thighs quivered at his touch. He gestured Kamala into the fray saying, "The second couch awaits your presence, my lady."

Annoyed at being removed from the party so soon, the golden goddess turned from her companions and strutted to the massive bed, hips swaying beneath her slinky gown.

Sorykah fidgeted with her lacings, awash in self-doubt. She had chosen to bed an earthbound deity for her first public debut as a man. Was it usual for women to have anxiety about their performance in the bedroom, she wondered, or was she channeling Soryk's dubious response to her selection?

"Kamala is a very wealthy woman, almost as rich as myself," said Chen. "She has gifted this house with many wonderful treasures, including her son, Elu."

Sorykah quailed at this news. What a talent for creating complications she had! Chen waved his hand to stifle Sorykah's moral quandary. "Mother and son are both quite libertine in their passions. I'm sure neither will mind sharing you. The bonds of pleasure are freely made and broken here; don't trouble yourself with artificial allegiances. Another," Chen urged.

Sorykah found a sprite with spiked hair and rich olive skin, who reminded Sorykah of the Siguelanders. Unlike imperious Kamala, this small, curvaceous woman was thrilled to have been chosen.

"And what of her," Sorykah asked.

"Less fortunate but no less attractive. Bai Liana is the granddaughter of an infamous madam. My father found his first wife Tirai in her brothel. We are cousins, of a sort. I consent to allow her to live here without duty," said Chen.

"Except for one," Sorykah riposted. "Is there no one here who is not related? Perhaps you can introduce me to them." She yearned for the night's conclusion. The tension and anticipation had risen to an unbearable level and the revelers grew wilder by the minute. Already, bestial sounds of drunken coupling issued from behind the silken screens fronting the shallow recesses lining the great hall's perimeter.

"Sorykah," Chen whispered, his teeth grazing her neck, "I'm

afraid the festivities have commenced without us. The ceremonial bed awaits."

Butterflies crowded Sorykah's belly and her bravery revealed itself as false. His chauvinism incensed her and she hoped that her anger would help fuel the change. Sidra must have been either very young, or very stupid, to be swayed by Chen's irritating overconfidence.

Chen shrugged and adjusted his breeches in a most ungentlemanly manner. The sounds of rutting filled his head and made him impatient.

"Come." Chen clenched Sorykah's neck in one strong hand and steered her toward the big bed where her partners languished among the gaudy pillows.

Chen clapped his hands and the music ended. Someone moaned in the quiet and everyone laughed. Chen grasped a hanging cord, vaulted onto a dais, and pulled Sorykah up the narrow stairs into his possessive embrace. The crowd pressed against the stage as if Chen were some sort of rock god, sans guitar and amps.

"The divine lords and ladies of pleasure have favored us well, my friends," Chen bragged. "We in this house consider ourselves artisans skilled in the medium of flesh. Though lauded throughout this country for our libidinous ways and spectacular talents in the bedchamber"—the crowd roared approval and Chen grinned, his lips like raspberries below his mustache—"there are still precious treasures yet undiscovered. New depths of debauchery yet unplumbed, fresh heights of ecstasy not yet scaled, and delicious fruits from the Tree of Life that have yet to be savored!"

A bawdy cheer erupted from the liquor-steeped, milling mass and Sorykah clung to Chen to prevent herself being dumped without ceremony into their midst.

"Behold, my darlings!" Chen bellowed, his eyes growing darker still but luminous with a wicked, lustful light. He reached into Sorykah's corset, wrapped a bit of ribbon around his finger, and yanked hard, with an obscene, theatrical flourish. Sorykah's dress melted away, leaving her clothed in stockings, garters, and white silk knickers. Horrified, Sorykah bowed her head and twisted away to hide her bare breasts from the cheering crowd but Chen held her suspended like a hooked fish.

"Is she not all woman," he teased.

"I don't believe you," shouted a gleeful male voice. "Prove it to us!"

The suggestion was met with another rousing roar and much laughter.

Sorykah's face was on fire and when she looked down, the blush had seeped onto her chest and arms, staining them a deep pink.

"See for yourself." Chen beckoned to the unseen man. He materialized out of the crowd, bare chest leopard-spotted and hair painted gold, and stood before them, his supplicating hand raised. "You are welcome to perform any necessary examination you like, my good friend."

The man unlaced Sorykah's shoe with his teeth and tossed her high heel into the crowd, a trophy for the minions. He examined her foot, ran a curious hand up her calf and thigh, slid his hand over her hips, and knelt, kissing Sorykah's hand. He smiled up at her, his liquid brown eyes friendly behind his cat mask, and she smiled in return.

"I believe!" the leopard-man shouted as he vaulted from the stage, his tail flashing behind him.

Chen continued: "We have all heard the stories. Perhaps we were told as children about the mysterious and mythical Traders, or perhaps our erotic imaginations were tantalized by a tale in some tawdry Phantastic, but we did not dare speculate, did not dare dream that such gifted beings could exist and walk among us."

Chen unhooked Sorykah's garter as he spoke and it slid from her waist.

"I myself have often wondered," he mused, pivoting Sorykah round, "how one would find a Trader, much less possess one. Tell me," he grinned, "do you know?" Chen laughed at his own wit as Sorykah burned with impotent fury.

"I said the gods have favored us, and here is the prize plum, offered for our delectation! Today she is a woman, curved and cleft"—Chen pressed his hand to Sorykah's heart to savor its dance beneath his palm—"and will grant myself and my brothers the kindness of her female form. But on the morrow . . ." Chen leaned in to hiss, " . . . if you wish to learn my father's secret . . ." then shouted to the assemblage, " . . . she will rise from her bed as a man—complete, intact, and functional!"

There was a collective intake of breath before explosive applause, whistling, and wild, rowdy laughter destroyed any remaining vestige of Sorykah's carefully hoarded secret.

"My brothers and sisters, it is my sincere joy to offer you this genuine genetic wonder, a woman of astonishing talent and the handsome fellow who resides within her. I present to you the gifted Trader, Sorykah Minuit!" With one last swipe at her clothing, Chen untied the sides of Sorykah's lacy knickers and they puddled at her feet, leaving her completely naked. The din from the crowd became a plastic thing that stretched and thinned in Sorykah's ears. Sorykah fixated on the memory of her twins for whom she was so willing to toss away her virtue and her soul. No sacrifice was too great. Any sorrow she carried over her temporary surrender to libertinism would be far outweighed by her grief at their deaths.

The musicians launched into a merry tune as Chen took Sorykah by the hand, leading her from the raised dais to the enormous bed. Flower petals peppered the silk sheeting beside handfuls of sweet herbs—lavender, chamomile, and fragrant mint leaves. Chen chewed a mint leaf as he propped himself beside her, scrutinizing Sorykah's face. She did not know that he was deciding his approach, much as an explorer would map the oceans and chart the stars before beginning his adventure. Did she crave tenderness and gentility, soft words and softer touches that would weaken her defenses and bring her to ecstatic tears? Perhaps this docile woman before him was the rare creature who could meet and match his own appetites. He was aroused by the thought of besting the man in her, of turning this changeling into a yielding, liquid woman who would cling to him and cry his name. He bent to rub his nose in the soft hollow behind her ear but she pushed him back, her dark eyes flashing.

"We had a bargain. I am sworn to uphold my oath." Her fingers splayed across his chest in weak resistance. His warmth radiated through his shirt and burned her palms.

"Did we?" Chen wiped the hair from her neck, one hand behind its slender column as he inhaled her fragrance. His faint exhalation tickled Sorykah's ear and shivers sprang up on her flushed skin.

"Don't be a fool," Sorykah said. "Say her name and let me go!"

"Let you go," Chen drawled, "and disappoint my audience? I think not. Look." He pointed to one of several white screens stretched in the ballroom's corners, upon which their images played, golden in the candlelight.

Sorykah gasped. "How are you doing it? Are there cameras here? I did not give my consent."

Chen's rude hand, hard against her mouth, silenced her objections. She felt her teeth biting into soft flesh and winced.

"You consent; you consent to everything. It is part and parcel of the bargain we have made. Would you forfeit the secret of the key to preserve your modesty? Would you disappoint my beloved queen with your shame?"

Sorykah struggled to push him off but he released her mouth and captured her wrists, running his pointed, berry-red tongue along her collarbone, swirling his tongue into her armpit, biting with satiny lips and gentle teeth as he followed the swell of her breast. Sorykah squirmed and thrashed as the scent of lavender and crushed mint rose from the bedding.

Chen reached down to part her legs and cup her roseate nether mouth. "A true male, you say. Where does your manhood hide? In here?" He slid his fingers inward, searching.

"Have you some boyish secret tucked up inside your slit? Are you true or are you traitor?"

Sorykah felt drugged, limpid, liquid. They were high above the crowd that surged in ecstatic waves around the cake-bed, embraced by the music's throaty, ringing din and the chandelier's diamond light. Chen's clothes fell away. His body was at once smooth and hot, brisk with a smattering of fine black hairs, coarse against the contrast of his plush skin.

His words rushed in tides through her ears, into her brain, to combat the image of sweet Sidra that waited there.

Sidra, my beloved, my darling. No, not her beloved. From what secret spring had that thought bubbled? Sorykah's head filled with visions of her friend but as though viewed through another pair of eyes, this new Sidra more alluring inside her aura of erotic mystique. But there were images that Sorykah could not recall. When had Sidra laughed at her for falling from a tree? She was confused. Her head hurt and tears squeezed from between scrunched eyes.

"Leave me to my death," she moaned. "I am too late. You toy with me and make my children suffer in their little graves. What a cold snake you are!"

A warrior poised to breach the gates, Chen radiated the heat of fire and fever. His breath was hot and his eyes were twin moons at once eclipsing the sun. Sorykah was wet against him and he smiled in triumph.

"Say her name," she begged. "Please, release me. Say her name!"

"Sidra the heartbreaker, Sidra the callous," Chen gasped as his precious Trader clasped him in her velvet embrace. He pushed himself in deeper, moaning, "Sidra, my Queen, my Lovely."

Thus the deed was done and the contract sealed.

Elu was next. When Chen tired of her and left the cake-bed, Elu mounted the stairs, a gentle smile on his handsome face. He cupped Sorykah's chin in his hand and she smiled weakly. He laughed, folding her to him, his familiar body a blessing. Being a man of so few words, Sorykah was always astonished when Elu spoke. His deep voice was a warm rumbly purr as he inquired, "Do you know what's coming next?"

She shook her head. Elu pointed to the dais where a domed glass box now lay wreathed in ribbons and flowers—a coffin fit for a queen. Lights played across the glass, refracting against its smooth surface and shining like the sea. The hall was a seething mass of bare and half-dressed bodies and the scent of sex was thick in the air.

"After I have raised my flag of conquest and proven your gender to his satisfaction, they will take you down to the box to watch the change progress." He gazed at her with epicene compassion. "There will be no privacy for you, no opportunity for deception. He watches always." Elu nudged his chin to the screens on which their faces were reflected, ten times larger than life.

Sorykah could only nod in mute resignation. Her time with Elu was brief, sweet, and poignant. If it ended too quickly, it was at least restorative. A fresh retinue of servants orbited the hall, balancing heavy trays of daintily rolled, dried leaves that the indulgent lit from small, smoking braziers. Other guests imbibed mouthfuls of steaming liquid to heat their tongues and melt the blue sugar cubes doled out on long-handled spoons. Ornamental jewel boxes circulated, their mysterious contents dipped by a wetted finger and rubbed into the membranes of eyes, nose, mouth, and under the skirts of the adventurous.

By turns and degrees, the party's fervent pitch escalated to wildness. Sorykah wondered just how closely Chen watched her. Aside from the mirror's tireless, unblinking eye, trained on her to splash her image across the viewing screens, she felt invisible. A horn blared and an unwelcome but familiar voice slurred through an echoing amplifier.

"No rest for the wicked, my darling!" Chen barked. The laughing crowd turned their faces to the screens. "Are your legs stuck together yet?" His malicious, self-congratulatory voice was poison-steeped. "Have you grown a third?"

Sorykah's face burned like a red-hot iron; she could fry an egg on her forehead. Sidra's darling was a cruel degenerate who heaped humiliation upon humiliation.

Chen emerged from the crowd shirtless, his bare chest marked with traces of lipstick, glitter, and tiny purple love bites, as if he'd been wrestling feral vixens. Beard shadow etched his chin and cheeks, giving him a piratical, sinister aura, and he leapt up the iron stairs, waving a megaphone. His face leered in across the bedsheet and his arm snaked out to snatch Sorykah's arm before she could flee.

"You keep us waiting," he sneered.

Crowing with maniacal laughter, the crowd surged around him like crazed circus folk, their fine face paint smeared into abstract whorls and lines. Clapping, braying, and shaking an endless array of fancy noisemakers, the revelers cheered as Sorykah was dragged from the high cake-bed by Matuk's heinous, spoiled son, who wiped a line of red saliva from his chin (the drugs he'd ingested caused him and many of the others to drool copiously) and yanked Sorykah over the mattress edge and into his arms. His skin was so demonically hot, it seemed to Sorykah that the Devil himself had captured her. Indeed, the hairs along Chen's forehead had peaked with sweat and stood erect like fine black horns.

Horns surged and drums thrummed while a passel of slurry drunks sung the lecherous "Folksong of Maiden-Taking." Chen's hot saliva ran uncontrolled over Sorykah's shoulder and dripped down her breasts. Distracted by a circulating tray of wine goblets, Chen released her and cantered into a gathering of half-naked women.

Carensa appeared at Sorykah's elbow to whisk her into a small anteroom and bathe her in rose oil and warm water, wiping the leavings from her thighs.

"Carensa," Sorykah asked, "what are the leaves and the powders? The liquor in little glasses?"

Carensa's broad grin melted across her face and puddled in her dimples. She waved her hand, entranced by its movement as she watched it pass. "Hallucinogens. Psychotropics, mood elevators, and thrill pills. Happy powder. Orgasm-in-a-glass. Do you want to know more?"

Sorykah nodded, enthralled. She had always been too timid to do much more than smoke a bit of hashish or sample the occasional liquor-tonic from Neubonne's Liquid Smoke bars. Her brush with opium at Pavel's bar had been a one-time accident, the product of despair.

"What's your poison?" Carensa pursed her lips and tried to focus on Sorykah's face.

"What does Chen like?"

"So you want to be a king among men, is that it?"

"I want to feel like someone else. I want this to be a memory that's more like a dream than a past reality." *I want to forget that my children are dead,* Sorykah thought bitterly. *For one night, I want to forget.*

"Let's see," Carensa tapped her brain as if nudging her thoughts into place. "There's Syrian rue and mimosa tincture—it's very bitter, so it's taken with a sugar cube saturated in sweet orange oil. Morning glory seeds are baked into the breads. There's also wormwood and sassafras liqueur, and damiana and passionflower cigarettes. Those are the tiny leaf rolls tied with purple. The ones tied in blue are ordinary bidis."

"Bidis?"

Carensa paused, one hand on Sorykah's hip. "Aromatic tobaccos. They're a good distraction if you've done too much of something else." Carensa sobered for a moment. "Chen's putting you on display in the box next. I can get you good and high. You won't care about a thing."

"He may as well have a little fun while he's here." Sorykah smiled sardonically.

Carensa wrinkled her nose in confusion. "Chen?"

"No," Sorykah shook her head. "Him," she sighed then, looking deeply into Carensa's glassy eyes. "Soryk. *Me*."

23

LITTLE LAMB LIES SLEEPING

A WELCOME LULL IN THE FIERCE, blowing westerlies allowed Meertham to exit the ruins of the half-excavated salt tunnel and venture into the Erun. He carried with him a burlap bag, this time stuffed not with somatic or human captives but a round, pregnant goat whose stubby horns and sharp hooves poked small holes in the dirty fabric, threatening to tear it open. She bleated pitifully until Meertham was obliged to free her head and feed her a few handfuls of grass.

It was at this moment, resting beside a mossy slag heap with the goat crunching leaves and Meertham's mind devoid of any thought at all, that the sound reached them. Though guttural and phlegm-drenched, there was no mistaking the Wood Beast's wretched, wheezing call.

The nervous nanny goat stopped chewing; grass slid from between her small, yellow teeth. Her slotted amber eye gazed at Meertham. Panting, coughing, and more bleating trailed the Beast's first cry. Meertham sat stonily, listening. Mist snaked between the cedars and cold gusts blew in from the coast to rattle the pines. He rose, shoving the grunting nanny goat back into his stuff-sack and slinging her over his shoulder.

It was an hour's trek to the manor and Meertham plodded steadily over the loam. Although he didn't fear the Wood Beast, he hoped that the path he'd chosen would steer him clear. Hard to tell, however, where she was. Sound hovered in every airy pocket between the trees. She might lurk in wait anywhere and would expect this nanny in his sack as an offering. Meertham was not in a position to refuse her, even if doing so meant arriving empty-handed and facing Dunya's disappointment, which he feared more than open combat with the dread beastie.

He had to admire the unflinching, dispassionate manner of Dunya's service to their Master. She had been at the manor as long as he could remember; it occurred to him that Dunya must not be much older than himself, for she was not elderly but a woman of child-bearing age, meaning she'd been but a girl when Meertham arrived. Matuk had always conspired to drive a wedge between them. Naturally, he would want them to be wary of each other, leery and mistrustful and beholden only to himself.

Why had Meertham never considered this before? Dark thoughts rolled through his simple mind. Pain struck—the wrenching knife twist in his gut that had begun to spoil his sleep of late. He folded, racked by coughing spasms as his innards tightened in agony. Something rose in his throat and he spat it onto the leaves, a ball of black grainy stuff like wet coffee grounds. He had seen enough injuries and deaths to realize that he was bleeding inside and terribly ill. It should not surprise him that his death would be hard. He had not been kind in his lifetime, and though he had enjoyed remarkable good health, it seemed fitting that he partake of his share of suffering. Queen Sidra the Lovely had magick and white light in her hands, but like him, she was only mortal, having neither the power of Jerusha or the old gods. Roots, herbs, and breathtakingly bitter tonics wouldn't drive the sick from him, just dull his pain. The pain itself . . . well, the knife that sliced into his belly at night also served to cut away the ties packaging his remorse and sorrows, now released to bedevil him and drive him mad with regret. Meertham thought little of his brief future, concentrating instead on the grievous past.

He stopped to catch his breath, wipe his sweating jowls, and spit out more of the gravelly blood flowing from his stomach. He retched hard, staggered a bit, and nearly lost the nanny goat when his sack glanced off a tree trunk. Bent double, hands on his knees, he was alarmed by the distinct sounds of labored breathing moving ever closer, huffing and wheezing in the fog. The frantic goat bleated, her desire to run overpowering her instinct to remain silent, and she fought desperately inside the dark sack, cognizant of the fetal kids distending her sides.

Alerted by the nanny goat's distress, Meertham roused himself from his own fixations to peer through thickening fog. His small, shortsighted eyes darted around the clearing. Something was out there. The Wood Beast lurched and crashed when she prowled; this was a different sort of presence, perhaps a runaway somatic seeking the Erun's mythical protection.

Although often beset by doubts and resentments toward Matuk, Meertham's first inclination was to track his quarry and discover whether it was something worth bringing to the manor. He hoped to deliver the goat to Dunya and vanish before the Collector learned of his presence, but Matuk had strange ways of knowing what Meertham did, and would as likely as not be behind the door to meet him when he arrived. Finding a wounded somatic in the wood would serve as a meager insurance policy. It was only because Matuk had need of his heft and muscle that Meertham himself had thus far escaped a knifing in the tower room.

Rough, uneven breathing sawed in his ears. Meertham moved toward the sound, his hand clenched to his gut. Even muted by the oppressive fog and immense trees glowering down upon his head, the cries unnerved him. He crept forward, his beady eyes straining in the gloom.

There. Beneath that lightning-split tree whose broken body

cleaved in blackened shards toward the mossy ground. He moved closer, the breath sharp in his throat. Something huge, and hairy, its hide blood-flecked and muddied, lay against a rotted log, wheezing jaggedly.

"Cursed Wood Beast. Someone finally got the best o' you, did they?"

The Beast barely stirred when he prodded it with a stick, but moaned, almost as a woman would, when he stretched a hand forward to poke at just one of the many broken arrow shafts protruding from the beast's back.

"Bloody Nora," he breathed, his fear and pain forgotten. "I know those arrows." Meertham shook his head. He'd passed racks of them with brilliant green-feathered tips on every visit to the tower. They lined the walls beside the large hunter's bow and Matuk's other assorted weapons. Had Matuk taken to sport-hunting the Beast? Meertham frowned and rubbed his bald head, creeping over to face the Beast and view the damage up close.

It was in pain; that much was evident. He wasn't one used to mercy but the thought did flicker. A quick jugular cut and the thing would bleed out in a matter of minutes. He was little aware of the hand reaching to unsheathe the serrated hunting knife as he kneeled and gripped the revolting, scab-splotched hide, searching for a fold of skin to grab and heft while the knife rammed home. The Wood Beast's skin had a disturbing quality to it, unlike any other animal he'd seen. Beneath the wiry hairs, old, half-healed wounds and the rough, lumpy patches, he expected that the skin would feel as coarse to the touch as his own. Instead, it was soft, vulnerable, and thin. Repulsed and confused, Meertham withdrew his hand. He'd never been so close to the Beast before. Reality had failed to meet his expectations. He faltered.

The Wood Beast moaned again like a young girl crying, and shivers traveled the length of Meertham's arms.

"Blessed Jerusha," he whispered, clutching his knife so tightly that his knuckles whitened. "What are you?"

It stirred with great effort, shifting its bulk with care. Meertham could taste its fear. Acrid, metallic chemicals flooded his mouth as the dread beastie clambered onto all fours (hands and knees, he thought), lifted the head tucked between the rotted log and its own limbs, and swiveled to gaze at him with a single, forlorn eye.

Meertham uttered a short, garbled scream and stumbled backward, away from the beast's bloodshot stare and the broken-jawed mouth that lowed, uttering a sad, steady vocalization that sounded most horribly, like a plea for help.

He tripped over a stone and scrambled to his feet, knife thrust out and shaking. The beast struggled to rise, one knuckle-dragging long arm pawing weakly at the ground. Meertham choked up a lump of bloody phlegm and spat, which the beast took as a personal rejection perhaps, for it rose up on two legs and roared deafeningly, bloody saliva spilling over its fractured mandible.

"Get back!" Meertham shouted. "You get back!" The beast roared again and Meertham had to cover his ears for the ringing. It raised a clumsy hand to its face and rubbed, Meertham was repulsed to note, like a small, tired child wiping away tantrum tears. The mouth gabbered and shook, strange sounds forced themselves out, and Meertham turned and escaped from the site, scooping up his stuff-sack and the nearly comatose nanny goat. He stomped through the woods, annoyed by his lapse in caution and judgment. Making a beeline for the manor, Meertham did not look back.

Radhe watched the mist swallow him up. She was used to being cold, but today it bothered her. She had lain for hours in a fog of pain and strange flashes of some deep, inner dread, dreaming erratically of the mother she had not seen for so many years. Odd, because she never thought of Tirai or the life she'd led before constant cold, fear, loneliness, and hunger became her sole companions. But she remembered her mother's small, oval face with its satiny golden skin and hennaed hair, and the scent of her body beneath the heavy perfume she always wore regardless of the situation or weather, the same way she always wore the flimsy, translucent nightgown with the flounced panties that Matuk insisted upon.

Radhe remembered the night that Matuk had entered the room while they slept, pulling Tirai from their shared bed and Radhe's pudgy embrace. How Tirai smiled reassuringly even as Matuk twisted her arms and dragged her squirming into the doorway, his face a mass of rage and Tirai's strained and sugarcoated whisper, "Go back to sleep my lamb, it will all be over soon."

That is what Radhe wished now, for it to be over. She had asked for help from the man with the knife. Had looked at him and said, "Take my life, I beg you," but he had spat his disgusting slime at her and run away. Pity, the smallest portion that one might dole out to a mouse caught in a trap, was denied her. Radhe thunked onto the ground. Something strange was happening inside her that she did not want to experience. She had already changed once. What additional sorrows might another change bring?

Radhe closed her eyes and tried to find a safe thought upon which to settle her restless mind. Ordinarily, when she felt afraid, she would loiter at the perimeter of the woods and gaze at the manor, hoping to catch a glimpse of her father's face, remind him that she was still alive—his daughter in the woods—and that she thought of him. Then he'd taken to shooting her full of arrows and macerated somatic DNA, punishing her for not having yet died, she supposed, so she preferred to stay hidden among the safety of the trees. It was the wind that drove her out, the fear that made the little girl surface inside the monster, only Tirai's lost baby, seeking solace in the storm, who came to haunt her father's realm.

Radhe opened her eyes and found an appealing emerald leaf,

veined in diamonds and buckling beneath the dew condensing on its face. Little pinpricks of ice sparked throughout her muscles and her organs fluttered in response. She thought that her body must be filled with fireflies, and the image of those tiny, friendly lights was as comforting as the stars that shone above each night, as constant as her mother's love had once been.

Go to sleep my little lamb, it will all be over soon.

OBLIVION

SORYKAH LAY ENTOMBED in a glass box lit from within like a flaming crystal. She was a chandelier crystal, emitting sharp prisms of light to dazzle and enthrall the viewer. She shut her eyes against the stabbing brightness and sought some tiny raft of inner peace to which she could cling like a drowning rat. Sorrow gripped her womb, twisted her heart, and wrung it dry as if seeking to tap her very essence. Sorykah wanted to sit up but she could only thrash helplessly.

Chen leered overhead, his expression one of mechanical curiosity. He was treating himself to a private show, too greedy to allow the others to witness her transformation. Distorted by the glass, his face stretched and distended with each word. His voice was muffled but the words rang clear, amplified by the drugs in her system, maybe the morning glory seeds, kicking in at last. "Don't fight your fear my darling! Or will it work in your favor?" he guffawed, wiping a runner of red spit from his chin as he inhaled from a bidi tied with a yellow string.

Why did panic always feel like drowning? Sorykah's heart pounded and she scratched at the glass, making Chen laugh.

"Let me out! I can't breathe!"

"Of course you can!" Chen's lips formed an O and he placed them over one of Sorykah's air holes, blowing smoke into the box. She coughed and kicked, banging her knees against the glass. "Better yet," Chen chortled, his voice clumsy with effort and drink, "a bit of Holy Roller smoke will walk you up the stairs to heaven. Sit at the right hand of the Sun God and drink the wine of ages!"

Sorykah kicked again, working herself into a heated sweat from the effort. *The key*, she admonished, *remember the key. He'll give you the secret, a secret that no other can possess and then, blade, gun, or stick in hand, I will find the man who took my children and slit open his disgusting belly.*

Chen lit one of the fat green damiana and passionflower cigarettes and inhaled luxuriously a few times before blowing great lungfuls into the box.

Shit shit shit! Sorykah hissed. Those three little words had proven themselves a reliable response to trouble. For such a prim, mild-mannered woman, cursing proved a rare and satisfactory allowance. *Prim and mild-mannered*, she though with a smirk, thinking of the bodies that had turned inside her all evening.

Gray and ropey smoke puffed into the box, invading her nostrils and throat. She inhaled legions of minuscule, venomous smoke-spiders as black ravens circled overhead, soaring between rainbow-rimmed starbursts spackling the interior of the glass box. The ravens wheeled around Chen's face as it pressed, smeared and wetted with crimson drool, against her coffin's flank. With hard black eyes, he watched her with a hand over his heart, shirtless and perspiring.

Showers of stars waterfalled over her skin and Sorykah began to float upward on buoyant lavender clouds skimming beneath her limbs. She was at once panicked and calm, watching herself twitch and flail from outside the box, standing next to Chen, one companionable arm draped over his shoulder. She strained through the light show strobing her eyeballs to examine the angular face that grinned back at her, neither sympathetic nor kind. She stared into her own eyes, muddy indeed, deep and feckless—was that the sort of man she was? Lanky and too cool, an effete, more youthful version of her host. Chen and Soryk could be cousins, with their matching peppered jawlines and black hair.

Soryk's soul was shaped by secrecy and defiance (she could see it, pulsing there inside him like an azure streak of twilit sky). *Still, he is a man, my man, the man I am,* Sorykah thought, for the drugs were working their glib alchemy inside her brain, loosening the tongue Sorykah kept so tightly tied. She transcended the glass case, a freed specter sailing through haze toward that familiar man beside Chen, with his flimsy, self-righteous smile. Tugged closer as some invisible line strung taut between them wound tighter, Sorykah flitted in beside him. She could see the memories that soft-faced stranger carried within, frozen in blocks of ice—Sidra's elfin face beneath her wild hair and antler crown, red-rimmed and pulsing like an animated heart. He was fiercely protective of his memories. There were so few! No wonder he hoarded them. Sorykah saw a woman with deep, olive skin and startling, brassy curls, this man between her legs and the woman's white shirted arms tight around him as soot and glittering glass dust lifted on a chemical breeze to embrace them. Sorykah rattled that man's memory as if it were a highball chilled by a few, thawing cubes, sorting through the meager selection until one leapt forward and stung her eye. Two faces—one fair, one dark—little blue-lipped mouths singing, "*Do you forget? Have you forsaken us?*" their fishy limbs stretching forth to break the surface of the water in which they floated.

Sorykah's mouth filled with ice and she could not answer these dying dream babies.

We are lost to her.

Chen's doppelgänger flinched.

You stupid, stupid man! Sorykah raged, sucked deeper into this half stranger's mind, a place of little light and long silences. Blackness swirled around her, rolling clouds that billowed and puffed, sharp pinpricks that stung bone and muscle. Cold fear flooded her body as hormones pumped and surged. She could hear the hair on her chest growing, rasping out of the follicles like hungry snakes slithering from their holes. Her female organs shriveled and dried. Her womb compacted into a tiny, shrunken walnut and crumbled.

Someone reached through the smog and grasped her hard, yanked her backward. The black smog snuffed out her breath and thoughts, leaving her inert, comatose, and male.

When Soryk awoke on a padded bench, his head was wreathed in shooting pains. He glanced around the unfamiliar room, trying to place the tacky gold wallpaper and overflowing pots of fleshy, thick-leafed plants. He blinked against the light and the hurt, wondering if perhaps he'd been injured in some sort of accident, for every molecule of his being ached. Coaxing himself to brave the repetitive pinging pain, he shifted onto his elbow and rose to a sitting position, allowing himself a moment to catch his breath before swinging his legs over the side and pulling himself upright. Still woozy from the change, Soryk rubbed his face with both hands, so caught up in his own drama that at first he did not hear the applause that greeted his awakening.

Chen clapped in genuine appraisal as he took stock of the man before him. Soryk met his eyes and scowled.

"My dear girl," Chen smiled and licked his lips, "or rather, fellow. That was extraordinary! I've read all the Phantastics on the subject but they were always so confoundedly unclear in their descriptions of the actual change. I'd begun to suspect no one had ever truly witnessed one. How is it possible that your kind could keep such a secret for so long?" He lurched sideways and righted himself, grinning. Chen wiped the hair from his eyes and crouched down, running his hands over Soryk's body. Coming to as if wakening from a lengthy anesthesia submersion, Soryk recoiled and pushed the stranger's hands away from his body, whose raw nerve endings still flailed and throbbed.

"Now, my good man. A thorough inspection is to be expected. I must satisfy myself that there's no illusion or trickery at work here." Chen kneaded Soryk's muscles, felt his bones, and measured the width of his shoulders and hips. The tone of his voice, overripe with malicious, prodding sarcasm, now changed to one of hushed, genuine wonder.

"Unbelievable! My god, you're *real*." Chen patted Soryk's absent breasts and the fine black hairs that sprouted in their place. "I admit," said Chen, "that I entertained the idea I might wish to possess you after the change but seeing you now . . ." He shook his head, his hands skimming Soryk's frame. Chen performed a rather perfunctory examination of Soryk's male parts: the scrotum was intact with two testes inside; the penis was normal and, presumably, functional.

Soryk shivered beneath Chen's caress.

"You should rest and recover before performing your duties." Chen twitched impatiently; he hated any lull in his parties.

Soryk stirred and opened sleepy eyes. "Where am I?" he asked, his voice more tenor than baritone but still, decidedly male. "What is this place?" Soryk asked, his monosyllabic words clipped clean. He wiped the sand from his eyes and scratched his balls, which caused Chen to shake with laughter. He clapped Soryk on the shoulder, swallowing the last of his chuckles. Soryk glared daggers at him as Chen reached out to ring the servant's bell.

"You have no idea what a find you are, my man. You'll be delighted to learn that you've arrived at my house during a splendidly debauched gathering of friends. I'm sure my offerings will brook no objections from a man of fine taste such as yourself." Chen squeezed Soryk's bare shoulder in a coarse, masculine way and turned him over to Carensa, who materialized wearing a spectacular, formfitting jumpsuit with strategic cutouts. She jiggled as she walked, and Soryk's eyebrows rose as he stumbled along after her.

Chen rubbed his hands together in a gesture of pure, unadulterated glee. There were still the uncut digi-reels to edit and much money to be made. He'd already decided to sell it as a three-part set, ending each reel on a cliffhanger, just at the moment when the first bead of sweat heralding the change broke out on the Trader's forehead.

Chen experienced a brief, uncustomary twinge of guilt that he soon suppressed. He had yet to make peace with the knowledge that he would soon sell out his own father, that pompous, senile old zealot. Sorykah had proved quite sweet, and he intended to use her most atrociously, all for the sake of money, that evil, weedy root. He couldn't keep his little pleasure barge afloat without his superfluous income. Matuk gave Chen full access to the company accounts and he took regular advantage of them, but the steady influx of sensation seekers to the Isle had twice taxed his funds nearly to the breaking point. The advantage of technology, he considered as he sparked up a fresh vanilla bidi, was that he needn't ever leave the comfort of his home to work. A few quick flicks of the tracking pen, a couple of keystrokes, and his product flooded the global market. Lo, how the money did flow!

The opportunity to preserve a real Trader's change for an eternity of Phantastics junkies and erotomaniacs was worth an uncomfortable minute or two as his conscience wrestled with itself, devil eventually pinning angel to the floor for the count. Chen pulled bidi smoke deep into his lungs and watched it sally forth again. He'd enjoyed the conquest. Sorykah was far less fetching than the women whose affections he usually entertained, but being a Trader added just enough exotic spice to sweeten the pot, sprinkled a bit of hot-pepper uncertainty and challenge into the mix. He felt like a game hunter, tracking and bagging the last of a species.

"What a bloody trophy." Chen leered, already looking forward to auctioning the soiled bed linens. He gave himself a smug little pat on the back. It had been a good day, and business had never been better.

25

MY SORROW, MY BITTERSWEET

SORYK WAS TREATED to a fine meal in the peacock salon with its gilded divans and wrought iron dining tables. He ate without speaking, desperate to remember how he'd come to this house. Sidra had abandoned him in the woods. He knew he'd been hurt, angry, and overcome by plaguing nightmares, but why did it all go black after that last snapshot of Sidra's departing back?

The people here seemed to know him and were not surprised to see him, so why could he not remember? Soryk concentrated on shoveling food into his mouth as fast as possible. It was so rich and hearty; he knew he hadn't eaten for hours, perhaps days. His stomach began to cramp and he had to slow his pace, even as his ravenous appetite urged him toward another helping of herbed rice, another ladleful of spicy yellow curry and more of the cool honeyed wine.

Carensa returned wearing a floating swirl of colorful ruffles.

"I liked your other outfit better," Soryk offered between mouthfuls.

She smiled, proving herself very charming, though her eyes held a spacey look and she had a slight tendency to drool.

"You would." Grinning, she sat down across the table and dipped a finger into his food. "Mmm, I love curry." She licked her finger and held it in her mouth for a moment before removing it, adding, "It's a gift from Jerusha. Wouldn't you agree?"

Soryk nodded, keeping his eyes trained on that impertinent finger once again swirling across his plate. "Little girl," he drawled, "if you do that again, I may have to bite it off."

Carensa laughed and ran a handkerchief over her lips, leaving a pink smear of saliva on the white cloth. "You're not the same person you were before. It's bizarre. I mean, you're you, yet you're *not* you." She grinned, flashing deep dimples.

"What are you on about?" Soryk asked, his irritation rising.

"So like a man, all cranky and impatient. Just like Chen."

"That smug bastard? You offend me."

She leaned across the table and tried to gaze into his eyes but failed because she could not focus her own. Despite himself, Soryk smiled. "Do I know you?"

Carensa rolled her eyes. "You did not jest when you claimed memory problems! We've spent much of the past week together. I tended you and bathed you. I even took the measurements for your peel-away velvet frock."

Soryk shook his head. "If that's true, it's all lost to me now."

"I am sorry," Carensa squeezed Soryk's hand. "I can tell you this much—that you arrived here as a woman in search of children abducted by the Collector. That Chen agreed to tell you how to open the lock on the door to his father's house in exchange for this"—she flicked her dainty fingers between them to indicate a shared rapport—"and what is to come."

Soryk stared at Carensa with such brutal intensity that it had the unfortunate effect of sobering her up. She shifted in her seat, betraying her nervousness with a furtive look at the salon's closed door.

"I arrived here as a *woman*?" Soryk's voice peaked, climbing high until it found its breaking point. Horror flowered on his soft-jawed face. "My children were stolen? I have children?"

"Two," Carensa whispered. "Twins. A boy and a girl. Traders like you."

Something wakened and stirred, a cold coil of apprehension slithering scale over scale. His ears began to ring and for a minute he was conscious of nothing but his own overwhelming panic. A ragged moan escaped his lips and he fought the impulse to sob.

Carensa watched Soryk drop his head on the table, his elbow yellow with curry and speckled with rice grains. She placed her small hands on his shoulders and held him, surprised at the way his slight shoulders sprang from his collarbone like wide wings and at the thickened ropey muscles lining the long bones beneath his skin. He even smelled like a man, but more so the savory sweat that flowed behind his change like a broken fever.

"What am I doing here?" he rasped, resting his head in one forlorn hand.

"This is the House of Pleasure. It is your duty to please Chen, its master, and to do so by granting your favor to the woman you chose for yourself while in your female form."

"You mean I'm to . . ." Soryk mimed something both juvenile and rude and Carensa smiled crookedly.

"Of course. Afterward, you are free to enjoy the rest of the party until its termination. Then my master will speak with you. He may be something of a bastard, but the man is true to his word. You'll have your secret."

Soryk sighed heavily, as if he'd just received an engraved invitation stating both the time and date of his own execution.

"Come." Carensa bade Soryk follow her. "Your ladies await."

Soryk freshened himself and donned a handsome suit of emerald velvet, a lilac silk shirt, and white spats. Carensa bent to screw on silver cuff links and Soryk took the opportunity to examine the breasts falling forward against her loose blouse.

"Did I choose you?" His lips quirked up at the corners as he stroked the top of her head.

"No, you didn't," she replied, rising to her full height yet still not meeting Soryk's shoulder.

"Pity," he murmured.

Carensa winked. "Now," she sighed, smoothing Soryk's green satin lapels, "you're a real gent!"

A distant bell chimed and Carensa took Soryk by the hand, gesturing to the grand hall beyond. "Chen has asked that you make your entrance on the stage. There is a special set already constructed for your performance."

"My performance," Soryk smiled. "That takes the romance out of it, doesn't it?"

"Be fearless. It's what Chen demands." Carensa led Soryk into a cavernous corridor where drowsy party makers slumped in red puddles of drool, wide, happy smiles smeared across their faces as they dozed.

"Lightweights!" Carensa sneered, tapping one of the men with her toe and snickering as he rolled over, exposing his open trousers and round, furred belly.

Soryk's gut tightened in apprehension as they neared the grand hall. The doors swung open as the gongs announced him. Rays of bright light in jeweled shades fanned the air as Chen played his treasured toy, the piano-like clavier à lumières. Brilliant sunbursts of daffodil yellow soared across the ceiling. Shimmering rays of inky purple and indigo throbbed in defeat as the light-song surrendered and Chen rose from the clavier, his expression rather wolfish as he pulled women from the crowd and thrust them toward the stage, where they clustered around Soryk, tugging at his clothes.

Muscular men, their loins draped in gold, paraded toward the stage bearing the regal Kamala on a tasseled litter. Chen went through his sideshow barker routine, granting permission for the women assembled onstage to strip the stunned Soryk and coax from him a demonstration of his prowess. Befuddled but willing (for he was a man denied years of experience; he would not refuse the fluttering hands that lit a hundred tiny fires within the pristine forest of his untouched desire), Soryk allowed the women their way.

Men and women reached to pinch any nearby bit of flesh, and it was like being nibbled by schools of hungry carp. He was glad when shown to a pile of soft mattresses to lie down beside Kamala, already fanning herself and bored by the proceedings.

Chen sat in a high-backed chair, eating cashews and stroking the hair of a maid who serviced him as he enjoyed Soryk's hesitant awakening.

Soryk shook with nerves as he knelt beside Elu's mother, but his confidence grew as hidden reserves of lust bubbled to the surface. Lofty Kamala mellowed as Soryk explored her body, savoring the sensations that lingered on his tongue and fingertips.

Giddy laughter and raucous music submersed Soryk in contagious merriment, but when Kamala sucked a crumbling blue sugar cube, washed it down with a thimbleful of syrupy, clear citrine liquid, and pushed the same on him, things began to go wrong. The walls melted and Soryk could not focus his eyes. Kamala's skin began to pull away in his hands like taffy as he reached for her, and he was held down and back by an army of black-taloned hands.

A regiment of ravenous, jet-eyed women, sharp of nail with lashing hair, pecked gobbets of meat from his flesh. The air stunk of sulfur as someone used a match to light a torch and Soryk believed that he walked the Devil's Playground in the volcano's shadow.

I have failed, he thought, as the children's sweetly cooing voices sawed at his conscience, severing Soryk from awareness. He tripped over a slack, reclining body and pitched off the edge of the low stage onto the feather- and sequin-strewn parquet floors, crashing headlong into a pair of slow dancers who cushioned his fall as he collapsed.

She was herself again. Whole and sound, blessed with breasts and bum and everything else that defined female physiology. Sorykah awoke on the cake-bed, where Elu and others had carried the unconscious Soryk after his fall from the stage. Amidst the wildness and kerfuffle, the streaking hordes drooling in the courtyard, blue-lipped from winter's last gasp upon the isle, and the heaps of dewy bodies collapsed against the cushions, the high bed was an island of tranquility.

Late afternoon light seeped into the room. Calm floated in her blood—the exhausted peace born of hundreds of hands and eyes on her body as receding waves of pleasure washed over and under her skin.

She feared leaving the relative safety of the cake-bed, although once or twice, she'd had to fend off a drug- or lust-crazed interloper, kicking them back down the iron stairs when words and pleas fell on deaf ears. She was hungry. She longed for a bath. Most of all, she yearned for the comforting, solid weight of her children's bodies in her arms. A jagged cry rose and caught in her throat.

Slumped over drawn-up knees, Sorykah hid her face from the crowd. Enraptured by their own minidramas and ecstasies, she doubted any of them watched but her sorrow was a private treasure, not meant to be quartered by the greedy.

"My angel, why do you weep?" A pair of slender hands and bare arms reached over the edge of the bed, silvery green as the birch leaves they had once steeped to brew a healing tea. Sorykah laughed and wiggled her own arms, beckoning.

"Come here," she laughed, lit by joy. "How did you manage it?"

Smooth-skinned and reptilian, her eyes paling to the nickel's metal gloss, Sidra raised herself to the mattress, agile as a gazelle, where she crouched, grinning wildly.

"What do you think of my costume?" Sidra preened, every inch of bare skin mud-painted and glistening. Mud-tamed into twisted ropey strands, her coiled hair wound around her head. Her birch leaf skirt was little more than a scrap of cloth anchored around her wide hips and her body was bare but for the mica-flecked mud, beads, twigs, and feathers arrayed as artful jewelry encircling her wrists and neck. Sorykah was too glad to see her friend's cheerful face to consider her dangerous crossing to the isle and subsequent trespass into the manor.

Sidra raised an ashen finger to her lips to silence Sorykah. "Jerusha is my name, and you do not know me."

"Jerusha, the universal mother to whom my nanny continually prays? Jerusha, the virgin goddess?" Sorykah coughed. "My dear, you are many wonderful things, but untouched by man is not one of them."

"Pah." Sidra's silver hand fluttered. "Petty semantic arguments." She settled onto the mattress, unmindful of the rubbed-in detritus beneath her. Sorykah flinched. Forest living must acclimate one to a certain acceptable amount of smuttiness, for indeed, they reclined atop a filthy mess.

Sorykah curled up beside her. "Why are you here?"

Sidra beamed with self-congratulatory excess. "Your tale of loss has haunted me, but even more concerning is the rift in self, the deep, impassable divide between your two, divergent lives."

Sorykah fidgeted on the mattress, wishing for more of Carensa's magical mind-wipe tonics so that she could avoid Sidra's lecture.

"Chen has an enormous library here at his disposal as well as an alarming collection of Phantastics and other writings about Traders. I broke in to do a bit of research." Her silver lips curved up with wicked pleasure. "Documentation about the fabled Perilous Curse is sparse, but I found two case studies in medical journals that detailed the disease's progression and treatment methodologies." Sidra leaned forward, the pupils in her pale eyes wide with intent. "Sorykah, I believe I can help you."

Resentful of the intrusion into her personal life, Sorykah turned away to survey the party, where dancers thronged the floor as a new cadre of servers circulated, offering trays with neat rows of colored tablets that disappeared like candies into children's mouths.

Sidra explained, "They'll want to stay awake now. None will leave until you do. It's a contest among them, to see who has the most stamina. When they wake up in two days, they'll gather to compare battle scars, see who has the most violent purple love bite, whose thighs or knees are most chafed. It's childish, I know."

"Is this why you and Chen parted ways?"

"Oh no." Sidra sighed, the old, familiar sadness leached into her flagging smile. "This is all done to spite me. He was a rich and handsome city boy when I knew him, set to assume his father's role as head of Tirai Industries. *That* is what drove me away, the tireless consumption, the casual disregard with which he conducted business. His unwillingness to right his father's wrongs, make amends to the Fathers of Charity. With a single signature, Chen could have authorized the construction of the new hospital we were promised but he found it fiscally debilitating." She set her lips in a grim line. "Love does not conquer all. Love cannot right the wrongs of the past, nor forgiveness erase them. It is to my eternal shame that he cares for me still."

Sorykah raised an eyebrow but said nothing. The queen put up a brave front; despite appearances to the contrary, it was still just a smoke screen.

"I have an idea," Sidra continued brightly. "One of the articles I read spoke about a case very similar to yours. The dominant identity, or primary in this case, was a man who changed about every twenty-one days or so. His alter tended to have her monthlies during the change and his bloodstained clothing and sheets confounded him. He lived alone, and so he hired an investigator to watch him for a month. You can imagine his reaction when he found out that he himself was the bloodletter."

Sorykah grew impatient. "How does this relate to me?"

"The investigator was the husband of a reputable psychologist who worked with transient-psychosis patients. She discovered a faulty connection between the brain's hemispheres within the longitudinal fissure. Normally, the membrane between them serves as a conduit—this is what allows us to have three-dimensional vision, for example. The hemispheres communicate via the corpus callosum, which is like a bundled cord or cable of axons. However, in the case of personality-disordered patients—"

"I wish you'd stop using those words," Sorykah interjected. "I am not crazy."

"No, of course not," Sidra amended. "I merely relay to you a factual study, and that is the correct terminology. By creating shared experiences between the divergent selves, the doctor discovered that new cerebral connections could be forged in the commissures. It's tremendously exciting!" Sidra's eyes lit up and her palpable excitement filled the air with electricity. She rested a silvery hand on Sorykah's thigh. "Don't you think it would be wonderful to achieve kinetic wholeness? To have equal access to both male and female aspects of yourself?"

Sorykah shuddered. The smoke-filled glass box and her journey into Soryk's dark and empty mindscape had left her edgy and disagreeable. Sidra was asking her to incorporate a stranger into her being, to dissolve any barriers between the two and allow them to exist as one. The queen assumed that Sorykah was as eager to get her hands on her male counterpart as she was, but to Sorykah, who considered her female form her true home and primary, the idea of some strange man taking up residence in her brain was overwhelming.

"I don't know him. I may not even like him!" Sorykah choked, angry to the point of tears and even angrier to succumb to such stereotypical female weakness.

"But I do," Sidra cajoled, her voice husky. She leaned in closer, her pupils so wide and inky that they subsumed the icy iris around them. Smelling of cedar smoke and pine sap, Sidra crawled closer, until her naked thigh rubbed Sorykah's and her arms rose serpentine to crush Sorykah in their grip. Sorykah squeaked as Sidra pushed her onto the mattress and straddled her. "What do you think you are doing?" she huffed, pretending insult.

"Since you left I've been racking my brains to find a way to connect primary and alter. I admit, my motivations are impure. As much as I enjoy your company, as much as you've proven yourself a true friend, my heart pines for another glimpse of Soryk." Sidra's hair curtained their faces and her presence became an inescapable spreading thing, a viral contagion of seduction and desire.

Sorykah squirmed and laughed in a deep, unfamiliar voice. *Shit shit shit*, she thought upon hearing it.

"I've missed him. I've been utterly repentant," Sidra continued, oblivious to Sorykah's discomfort, or perhaps continuing her pursuit despite it. "When we met, I realized that I'd been wrong to mistrust him. You showed that you and he were kind, trustworthy, dependable folk upon whom I could rely to keep my confidences, and it filled me with despair that I had rejected Soryk's advances."

Sorykah was astonished to hear the elegant and knowledgeable (if somewhat impish) queen wax rhapsodic about some thin sapling of a man she hardly knew.

"Yes," Sidra continued in a way that caused the hairs on Sorykah's neck and arms to rise in salute. "I refused him, refused *you*. What a dolt I was! It occurred to me that somewhere in my arsenal of healing talents, I should possess the means to restore you to wholeness." She stretched out on top of Sorykah, the whole silver length of her as supple as a strong birch.

"I asked myself, what are my best talents? What are my strengths as a queen, a nurse, and a woman? I confess, I've always considered myself something of a muse."

Sorykah laughed. "Is *he* gullible enough to swallow this tripe?"

"I'm quite serious," Sidra insisted, mica speckling the mattress and Sorykah's skin. "The healing arts are best practiced in an environment of total receptivity. When one is engaged in a sensual act, the body's energy centers open like sunflowers to soak up the solar rays. Each pore and cell exudes a unique chemical signature and the body is radically transformed by the interaction of these elements."

Gravely serious, the queen whispered, "I know a spell to waken the witch. Or warlock, as the case may be." Sidra's silver taffy body curved itself around Sorykah's. Her fingertips grazed Sorykah's scalp to shift and loosen the impacted and well-knitted bony plates of her skull, cracking her open by hand like a walnut clenched in a sturdy fist. Her hands were everywhere at once, it seemed. Sidra kept her chest pressed to Sorykah's to feel her heart pumping beneath her naked breastbone as their rhythms aligned, beat for beat. Unfamiliar with such close intimacy, and tossed among the new and disturbing sensations conjured from deep within her sheltered soul, Sorykah wrapped her arms around the queen. Blood ran molten beneath skins that merged as if growing together. The change was coming.

Sidra urged Sorykah to allow him exit. Her song was high and clear, then somber and impossibly sweet, and Sorykah responding by surrendering the man inside. Tiny tingles ran along her nerves, the sensation growing stronger and more insistent until her whole body was aflame. Her vision dimmed and she felt, for the first and last time, the queen's mouth (currant-sweet lips, breath cold and sharp as frozen juniper berries) on her own.

Sidra stroked the body beneath her as the muscles began to vibrate and shift, fleshing out the figure of a man. Sorykah's full breasts receded and Sidra put her mouth over her friend's and inhaled, drawing Sorykah's last breath deep into her own lungs. Sorykah felt herself pulled by some invisible hand, wrenched free of her body and rising above it. Now she could see how adeptly Sidra the Lovely—with eyes alight like flaming stars and gossamer in her touch—did caress and stroke and rouse to life the dormant alter inside Sorykah's body, coaxing him from the shadows. A flood of hormones razed the soft hills of her female hips and breasts, plundering her into the flat and narrow lines of masculinity.

"My sorrow, my bittersweet," Sidra said in farewell. "Bright are the coals in her heart, bright as the summer sea, but endless dark inside of her, are the things she keeps from me." She was sunlight upon the water, waking Soryk from his perpetual, sea-floor sleep.

Soryk stirred in Sidra's arms, his dark eyes full of recognition. His adolescent's beard rasped against the queen's cheek and she squeezed him in welcome, removing her costume and leaving herself bared to the world as she straddled the maleness rising beneath her. She coddled him, murmured sweet nothings in his ear, and stoked the fires of her delayed gratification, the little embers she'd nurtured with such tenderness in his absence.

Sorykah broke apart. An octillion atoms scattered and bounced, drawn back to the body on the bed like iron filings to a magnet. Sorykah was inside *him* now, surrounded by his deep and resonant pleasure, as Sidra made love to him. When Soryk released himself in the safety of the queen's embrace, Sorykah remembered everything. Soryk shuddered with pleasure and smiled, his strong arms wrapped around Sidra, her heart hammering, her brow damp against his chest. *This is it,* they thought.

"I will love no other," Soryk whispered aloud. Sorykah urged him, the pain so sharp as to be a fresh wound, still running with blood, *the children. There is no rest, no pause, until my children are safe in my arms.* His voice responded in kind. *Safe in our arms, or safe in the ground.*

26

THE SEED OF ALL OUR DREAMS

CHEN'S TOWER BELL GONGED the hour, resonant and melancholy. Carac sat alert in his reed boat, steady in the Bay of Sorrows. Dawn overcame the night and blossomed fickle and peachy against the earth's wide curvature, consuming the sea behind the House of Pleasure. Carac waited with thoughts idle and light, drowsy with cold and the earliness of the hour. The oars threatened to slide from his fingers into the depths, but each time he roused himself and held fast. A soft splashing broke the calm and Sidra, sheened like a silver trout, lifted herself from the water and slid wet and naked into the boat, splashing water all about her and lighting the fire in Carac's eyes.

Silently, he began to row as his queen skimmed the water from her limbs and wrung out her long hair, enlivened by the swim that drew the languor from her arms and legs. Her cloak lay folded on the narrow prow and she shook it out, wrapping its familiar, funky weight about her form, retreating into sexlessness and duty once again. Carac was disappointed but said nothing, rowing with his gaze locked on the advancing shore where Kika waited, prancing along the banks, kicking up clods of dirt.

Sidra was silent, too, not wishing to break the spell she had so carefully preserved over the hours since she slipped from Soryk's embrace to pick her way among the spent bodies discarded in heaps along the floor. The urge to creep and spy, oh, she'd pushed that away, reluctant to surrender to simple, maudlin curiosity and trump Chen by finding him still guilt- or sorrow-racked while she lived her glorious life as the monarch of her woodland empire. It was enough to tease Soryk from slumber and entertain her fancies upon the playground of his slender body.

Sidra stretched her legs and kneaded her bare toes against Carac's corded thigh. She could feel the coarseness of his body hair through the fabric of his trousers, and while it sometimes excited her, today she much preferred the seal-like sleekness of her new lover.

The shore humped its back beneath the boat and stilled them. Carac hopped out, dragging the craft and Sidra farther onto the black, crystalline sands where he offered her his hand. She was cool and regal again, wishing to visit the cold spring to bathe and rinse the salt from her hair. Carac remained behind to dismantle the boat and scatter the reeds along the beach. He would join her later at one of the camps within the forest; meantimes, it was privacy she sought and silence he would offer her.

Kika licked their hands in casual salute, returned from her foraging and happy to be among humans again, for they would share food with her and the woman would cosset the big dog like a pet, allowing her to rest upon soft blankets in the evening while scratching her behind the ears. Weedy seedpods clung fast with curved hooks and snarled themselves in her fur. Sidra crouched to pull them free as she rubbed her face against the dog's muzzle, yearning for closeness with the man who loved this proud animal as she did.

"Come along, pretty girl," Sidra murmured. "Let's you and I bathe in the Erun springs. Along with our dirt, we'll wash our woes away."

Deep within a rock crevice where the Glass Mountains had first pushed their way from the soil, the spring was Sidra's private haven. The rock, a deep, inky gray, thrust from the ground like a wisdom tooth, lodged crooked in the soil. Time and weather wear had split it into fragments, forging a path for the water that bubbled from an aqueduct, so pure that Sidra could drink it straight from the source, its sweetness flooding her mouth and restoring her tired body. She'd taken it upon herself to enlarge a natural depression and now she had a shallow pool for bathing.

She slid the wrap from her shoulders, knelt in the soft, black mud, and filled her hands with water. Frozen around the edges, the pool was bracing, cold and clear as she stood submersed to the waist, splashing and scrubbing the paint from her skin with a wad of soft fern. Soapwort grew wild here and Sidra could pound the lather from the stems and leaves using a rock as a pestle. She washed her hair and shook it free, bending forward to let it stream and swirl atop the water as she played mermaid. Her toilette concluded, Sidra would dress her clean body in her old clothes, the chamois wrap, the loose-knit jersey and layered skirts. She would don her antler crown and lose herself among the leaves to rule and administer healing to her loyal subjects.

She would return to this spring days hence, moved by an insatiable desire to taste its waters, which had wakened her from sound sleep, thirsting and obsessed. She would bathe again, conscious for the first time of her naked body's changes, revealed in the dappled light. She would marvel at the tenderness of her breasts, the gums that bled when she cleaned her teeth, the constant, dull ache in her womb. Sidra had never been a mother before and it would take time for her to recognize the signs in herself.

There would be worry, steady and unchanging, as she considered how her altered bones would fare. She would dream of a shattered pelvis, her womb broken apart like chunks of red mortar and brick beneath the wrecking ball, and the child that would heave itself, wailing, from the midst of her destruction. As the months progressed, she would imagine that she could hear her hips spreading, weakened by a hundred invisible fissures, and fear the loss of her mobility. Floating on her back, she envisioned Soryk's success. He would demand and claim his vengeance, and the shadows would lift. Regain his children, slay their mutual enemy, and banish with the stroke of a blade the dogging specters of violence and capture that made the somatics' lives so very bleak.

Perhaps one day, they might meet again. Sidra stared up into the sheltering canopy of trees, resplendent with hues of green, from the deep emerald of aged leaves to the pale, spring-green tips of the pines' new growth. She could not leave the forest. This was her home, the place that soothed her restlessness and silenced the seeking. The towering cedars were fragrant giants, watchful companions and friends. She could not leave them. The choice would be Soryk's, then, to abandon the ice mines and bring his family to dwell within the wide wood. They'd not spoken of it. Lips, tongues, and caressing hands told stories of love and pleasure, not future fealty or the chance for rare happiness.

Kika prowled restlessly, staring deep into the trees with her ears pointed high in alarm. She growled and shifted as if warning away an intruder.

Sidra rose up, prepared to assume a stance of regal authority. She moved toward her bundled clothes and the short knife hidden inside. Kika danced over the rocks, whining.

Sidra frowned. "Kika! What is it? What do you see?"

Kika tensed, the fur along her spine standing on end like a red Mohawk. She sprang into the air, wild with agitation. Crouching low, she shook her head, growled, and sprinted into the woods, tail flying behind her.

"Kika!" Sidra shouted, feeling very alone and exposed without the protective company with which she'd grown so familiar, but the dog was gone on an errand of her own, answering some canine summons only she could hear.

Carac appeared, his face placid, his observant eyes neutral and masking the lust that simmered inside him. Though he was not to interrupt the queen's bathing but on a pretense of urgency, he forgave himself this breach of etiquette.

"My lady, the little woodland boy runs a fever. His parents have requested your services." He dropped his gaze to the muddy ground. The smell of other bodies on his queen drove him berserk. He yearned to know the scent-stories of his lover, follow her into the House of Pleasure and sate himself with the fragrances of drunken couplings conducted among heaps of roast meats, nectar-heavy fruits, and yeasty, risen bread.

"Thank you, Carac." Sidra drew down her veil of cool superiority. Her servant bowed and departed to await her next command.

Sidra stepped from the pool, savoring the morning's icy breath upon her wet skin. She adored the cold and fragrant woodland air. Heat made her fierce and filled with angry, irritable fire. It made her bones ache and left her restless, fragmented. Although she sometimes entertained the idea of returning to the hospital in Neubonne to don the mantle of sister and midwife, she couldn't abide the stench of Chen's betrayal that saturated the city's very air.

Here she would remain in verdant quiet, a natural creature among moss-curtained rocks and autumn-gilded leaves—Sidra the Lovely, Queen of the Outlaws.

Saint Catherine dabbled in various poetic forms throughout her solitary life but the structural limitations of sonnets and quatrains proved too damaging to the lady's eloquent imagery. Among all her works, one stood above the others. Last to be penned, the holy sister wrote from her sick bed, her scapular, wimple, and habit exchanged for freed silver hair that wafted as frail as a spider's silk over a coarse linen pillow and homespun gown. She could not see or hear, but her nose was keen for it captured this fleeting tale of despair and love among the garden's sons and daughters:

"Rose, you are a cold mistress, forever luring the bee.
Petals dropt in secret, like maidenheads—they flee.
Hips rise hard and pollen weary, my venom-pluck'd workingman sings—
'Be the wildness in me, mother, or 'tis me the wilderness be?'"

27

FOILED AGAIN

THE SUMMONING BELL JANGLED, startling Dunya from sleep. Jerked from her cautious slumber, Dunya sat upright, her hand firm on the babies in their basket beside her. Images from the previous night swarmed inside her head like furious bees. Still, the roaring westerlies galed, whipping rain-hammered windows. Glancing at the neat pile of supplies on the marble counter, she sighed. Meertham had been away a month or so, judging by the moon's phase. He was due to return, bringing fresh victims to refill the emptying dungeons, his stuff-sack weighted with the crumpled body of a stunned detainee.

He would remain but a few days, checking the traps on the meadow before loosing Dunya to cart her barrels of sludgy body parts to the charnel house. She could tell him that she needed to gather salt. Yes, she nodded, rising on aching, unsteady feet. He hated to wait and watch during the long task's execution. It was slow work, creeping on her knees through the grass, painstakingly digging free the hard yellow crystals that studded the lawn. If she had warm mead or honeyed beer from the Master's private store waiting, perhaps she could lull him to compliance or sleep. If only she could lock him in the dungeon! But there was no conceivable way to lure him there or to drag his enormous, muscle-bound frame downstairs and into one of the cells. Even with the pianist's help, she doubted they could budge him from whatever spot he managed to land in.

The bell jangled its impatience. The Master expected her to anticipate his needs and flew into a fury if she guessed wrong. Dunya hesitated, eyeing the sleeping babes. She would have to bring them back to the pianist, but what if she was in the Master's room? Dunya wrung her hands as the rude bell tinkled. Saying a quick prayer that the babies remain asleep and that she not be gone too long, she locked the kitchen door and ran through the manor as fast as her short legs would allow.

Years ago, Matuk's world was comprised of neat ledger rows of figures, precise plans, and ruled charts, where both people and their ideas were tagged and packaged into efficient categories. Then, the binding strings that kept Matuk's madness strapped down had begun to weaken from the strain and loosen bit by bit.

The Collector prowled before the window, wearing thin the rug beneath his incessantly roaming feet. He did not even raise his eyes to his servant as she entered, wadding her apron in furry hands.

"I cannot find her." He gestured to the woods beyond the salt-speckled meadow. Dunya knew Matuk would never admit that Radhe was his child, would not give voice to his heinous mistreatment of Tirai's daughter and the lone witness to his cruelty. Instead, the beast was always "her," "it," or most unkindly, "that monster."

Radhe usually lurked around the meadow's perimeter, her misshapen hairy hide just visible among the rain-blackened trees. The weather had not turned; wind ravaged the earth, stirring up the smell of death and lifting the lid on a stewpot of olfactory horrors. She would wait still, even though her father had launched clusters of DNA-dipped arrows against her and plotted her eventual surrender to a change schemingly wrung from the blood of innocents.

Dunya peered out the window. Rain drizzled down and the winds rolled themselves across the meadow like invisible bowling balls to smash into the resistant cedars and sweeping pines. There was no sign of life in the wood. Beyond the wind's sorrowful soughing skulked a cavernous nothingness. No birds sang, no insects buzzed or churned, and the beast did not wail for comfort.

Matuk stepped close and it occurred to Dunya that he could push her from the window. He had the rank, greasy smell of an elderly, unwashed body, and his fingernails were caked black with blood. She put one hand on the window frame for support and said, "'Tis unusual for 'er to be gone so long when the weather comes on so savage."

"You know I cannot rest until I have measured the results and logged them in my book."

Dunya knew too well how he labored over those books, filling the pages from corner to corner with his observations.

"Find her for me." Matuk's voice was flat and cold. He'd never issued such an order before and Dunya could not begin to speculate upon its meaning.

She curtsied to hide her face and evaluate the vast realm of opportunity that dawned before her. It was like a gift from the Holy Mother, this answer to her furtive prayers, and her head swam with possibilities.

"'Ow am I to get out?" She could hardly keep her voice from trembling and clenched her fists to still their shaking. Dunya's mouth filled with saliva and her heart sang in her ears as her master fished beneath his food-stained jersey, lifted a cord over his dirty head, and showed Dunya the key hanging heavy from his hand. It was not a key at all, in fact, but a bone, slender and pared down to the marrow on one end, smooth, round, and polished on the other.

"The key alone won't turn the lock," Matuk said, his voice like molten lead. He bared his cracked yellow teeth in a salacious grin. "Tirai's bone, taken from the middle of her palm."

Dunya could not avoid wincing and this displeased her master. "Yours would work just as well," he snapped, and Dunya's cheeks blanched beneath her fur. Matuk strode to the bookshelf, and Dunya saw how his back had begun to bend, how his muscles had shriveled away in the way of the old who find themselves slow-dancing with death.

"Grease for the lock," he leered, tipping a vial into her outstretched hand. "Whorish witch that she is, my sister is more clever than any man. Her impartiality makes her easy to manipulate. She viewed my challenge to create an unpickable lock as a testament to her brilliance, silly cow." Matuk gripped Dunya's arms with cutting, bony hands.

"Those who betray me always get what they deserve," he hissed. "Don't you forget that." He waved her toward the tower stairs with a final warning: "I will be watching. Take too long and my arrows will make a home for themselves in your back."

Bold Dunya ventured, "I need salt. I'll just take a moment to collect me basket from the kitchens . . ."

Bristling with annoyance, Matuk waved her away.

Dunya ran for the stairs, almost howling with delight. Things could not have gone better had she spent weeks in the planning. She passed the tower chamber and hesitated, the desire for flight fluttering in her limbs, urging her to move. Was she beholden to rescue the woman? For Dunya knew the squalid depths of her master's moral decrepitude and of what he was capable. Would they fare better in the woods as a twosome, needing twice the food, making twice the noise, and leaving a double set of footprints for Meertham to follow when he tracked them?

"A burden shared is a burden 'alved," Dunya chided, and she unlocked the door, releasing Matuk's thousandth captive wife.

Nels lay prostrate on the floor, her eyes glazed with hunger and exhaustion. The bones of her wrist turned like fat marbles beneath her thin skin as she beckoned Dunya into the room.

"Have you any food for me? Water?" Nels's blond hair was the color of ash and her blue eyes were bleached and pale.

Dunya crept forward, all the while some infernal clock in her head ticking until she thought she would scream. "The key, lass! I 'ave the key!"

Nels was slow to comprehend, her mind dulled by too many sleepless nights. Dunya shook the woman; she could not wait for her.

"I'm taking the children. I'll leave all the doors unlocked; it'll be up to ye to make the most of it. Await me by the armory and together we'll leave this wretched place."

Nels nodded and Dunya feared that she would not survive long enough to take the stairs, much less reach the Erun's sheltering safety.

"The Master watches," she hissed. "I canna give ye any more time than this."

Dunya flew through the corridors, her slippers skidding in the wet. She careened into the kitchen and threw her supplies into an old flour sack that she tied around her chest. She'd wear her cloak and hope Matuk was too preoccupied to notice her hunchback. The twins fidgeted in their basket and Leander began to cry.

No time to measure. Dunya took a mouthful of the chamomile syrup she'd boiled down in anticipation of this moment. Bending low, she clamped her lips over Leander's as he squalled and forced the thick, brown syrup into his open mouth. She did the same for Ayeda, gave them each a hard biscuit to chew on and heaped clean but tatty kitchen towels over their faces to cover them. Matuk might wonder why she brought a basket of laundry into the wood but she'd tell him that she'd carried bandages and healing supplies for the beast.

Her dry tongue throbbed in her mouth and Dunya's entire

body trembled with excitement. She was running away from home, escaping years of hard servitude, loneliness, and grief. Running to a better life, she hoped, where freedom and hard-won happiness might finally be hers for the taking. Let Matuk believe that she'd been savaged by the Wood Beast, torn limb from limb and all the flesh sucked from her bones by his monstrous daughter.

The babies were quiet. Heavy, though—the basket must weigh at least thirty pounds. She would have to take care to avoid the appearance of struggling with her load. Dunya walked with quiet certainty through the empty manor and fleetingly considered the two captives left to rot in the dungeons: better to perish of starvation than a grisly dismemberment.

One of Matuk's enormous dogs appeared to slink beside her, sniffing at her skirts and the basket she carried, his red tongue dripping. His hot breath made great clouds of steam in the cold air as he buffeted Dunya's legs, his claws gouging the marble floors.

"Get away," she whispered, afraid to annoy him and raise the alarm. Matuk's dogs were well trained by their master and had a mean, frightening intelligence. This one had a wicked face and a sinister light in its eyes. Third in command in the manor's pecking order, Dunya leveled a slight authority over the beasts, tenuous at best and begrudgingly accepted by the pack. She fished in the basket. Leander had dropped his biscuit and Dunya took it, gummy and wet, to dangle before the dog. His nostrils flared and his black lips peeled from his teeth as he snapped the air. Dunya tossed the biscuit far into the main salon, where it hit the floor and skittered beneath a couch. The dog rolled black eyes and loped away, content with her bribery.

Dunya exhaled, shaking as she passed the main double doors, which had been sealed for as long as she could recall.

Quick as a mouse, me love, and just as quiet! She hustled through familiar corridors, marveling that white marble walls could exude such gloom and doom when they ought to shine with a soft, reflected glow. The armory tunnel's tiny alcove housed the lone door, crisscrossed with reinforcing iron plates and studded with black rivets. Nels was absent and Dunya shook her head, wishing that she had the time to hoist her downstairs, lash her to a sledge, and pull her to safety. She'd already removed the butterfly's body from Matuk's chamber, bundled it into a lined basket, and sealed the entire thing with wax. There would be no way then, to substitute Nels for the squashed and severed remains of the winged girl.

Carefully setting the babies on the floor (after peeping beneath the tea towels to find Leander sleeping and Ayeda staring into space, a chunk of biscuit propped between her gums making way for a stream of drool), she cocked her head to listen for movement behind her. The answering silence was deep—no bell rang to summon her, no footsteps shuffled down the tower stairs. It was time.

Dunya fingered the slender bone hanging from her neck as she searched the door for the keyhole. There was no handle or knob to pull, no latch to lift, nothing but a small metal square of overlapping tumblers rusted shut and caked with flaking black serum. There was no hole to clutch the bone and she prodded at the fixture, desperate to make it fit.

"Grease the lock," Matuk had said. Dunya gazed at the vial of blood, her stomach tight with apprehension. She abhorred the mark of this particular crimson stain upon her hands. Dusty wax sealed the cork; it crackled and flecked the stones beneath her feet as she peeled it away. Dunya eased the ancient stopper from the vial. Its contents, a deep burgundy and still liquid after the long years the vial had lain in wait, smelled of elemental copper and iron with a raw musky odor beneath unlike any blood she'd ever encountered.

What am I thinkin' standing here wit' me jelly legs full o' fright? Just pour the stuff out and turn the key, ye daft woman! She spilled a few drops as she dribbled the blood on the bone's knobby end and grimaced as she wiped them away with her apron. The viscous liquid clung to the bone with nauseating tenacity. Dunya edged the bone toward the metal lockbox, turning it with caution lest she snap its slender shaft, repulsed by the thin grating noise and slickery slide of bone in keyhole. The door sprang open on oiled hinges. Wind rushed over her face, sweet with the scents of rain on the meadow, and Dunya was so startled that she fell backward, clutching the door frame as it swept the passage.

Assailed by so many odors and their stories, Dunya's sharp senses were overwhelmed. She covered her nose to block the smells as she hefted the baby basket on her hip and tucked key and vial into her pocket. Casting one final, furtive look over her shoulder in hopes of finding Nels behind her, she walked into freedom.

What cosmic magicks are at work this day, she wondered as she stepped through the high grass, keeping her eyes trained on the sprawling Erun, which fluttered leafy, silver lashes and shook with spangled delight, rain-cleansed and fragrant. *I won't turn 'round for I know 'e's there, gaping out the tower window at me back and cursin' me with 'is every breath, the monster. I'll keep walkin' with me 'ead 'eld 'igh.* She moved with heightened awareness, knowing that Matuk watched her, hanging from the tower window with eyes like pickled eggs, clinging to his bow and arrows, licking the blood from their tips and anxious to retrieve his daughter and engage in another heartless round of target practice.

The Erun Forest loomed, ominous with possibility. How much ground could she cover, how many tense and spring-taut minutes could she afford to travel? Would he leave the manor, venture into the sparse and fragmented sunlight after years upon years of shadow-dwelling to pursue his fleeing maid? Matuk lived alone except for herself, Meertham, and the odious ruin of a Gatekeeper. But the dogs! Chulthus had been unique in her ease and lack of bite, but the same could not be said of her brethren.

Mean, nasty lot with ugly brindled coats, slob-caked hanging chops, and thick, brutish necks. Six of them in all, kept by the Gatekeeper but always one or two favorites in the Master's tower room, their red eyes full of demon fire, their massive paws clawing up everything in sight as their acrid piss stained the white marble walls and ate holes in the ornamental rugs. Those dogs would run forever in search of her. She had to find the Erun city before dark if the three of them were to outlive the night.

Dunya had been a hundred feet to the charnel house, but she'd never crossed the line dividing wild from tamed. Bent with age and wind, enormous cedars thrust into the sky, fighting the bowing, densely needled pines for sun and root space. Heavy boughs, saturated with moisture and weighted by fat cone clusters, dipped to meet her as she entered the forest. Dunya's thin slippers did not fare well against the prickling woodland carpet. She repeated to herself the stories she'd heard, all the rumors and clues gleaned from her years of deathbed confessional service. An old woman with a snake's shedding skin warned her of a forest path built to lure and deceive, a pleasant come-hither trail laced with enticements that drew wandering somatics ever closer to Matuk's realm with its buried tiger traps and snapping iron jaws that sprang shut on unsuspecting ankles and held captives until the henchman came to pry them free, reset the traps, and bear them to their doom.

East, Dunya thought, transferring the babies to her other hip as she walked, pulling the tea towels from their faces so that they might see the forest for the first time and admire its stern, unforgiving beauty. Her muscles stung from carrying the awkward basket. She longed to sit and rest but could not spare the time. Dunya set her mouth against the discomfort and slogged ahead, dogged in her determination to rescue these two.

The journey went well enough for the first few hours. She rested to shake out arms that threatened to lock and seize if not given a reprieve and pour a little watered gruel into the children's mouths. There was no sign of the Wood Beast or any other living thing. The only sounds were her breathing and the crackle of her feet upon the pine-cushioned forest floor. Inch by inch, Dunya's guard began to drop. A capricious lightness fluttered by and settled on her heart. She allowed herself the luxury of a daydream, a cozy tree hollowed by freed somatic hands, a place of comfort and warmth where a merry fire crackled in the grate and the teakettle sat hot on the stones, ever ready to pour and serve.

She was so wrapped up in her fantasy that the smothered bleating of a goat struck her as yet another fanciful element of her imagination, a colorful detail. *Indeed I'll 'ave a fine goat, milk for me kids* (and she smiled a bit at her own joke), *cheese for me. Fine silky 'air to card and comb and knit into sparklin' white nappy covers and jumpers.*

The goat bleated again and Dunya froze, blood thrumming in her head, the breath trapped in her throat. Not imagining it then: a dumb beast's pathetic, sorry cries for help. Rustling and rummaging, a low, muttering voice and a responsive goat, giddy for attention. Pines cracked nearby and Dunya hovered, swinging her basket to maintain movement and keep the children quiet, too fearful to even shush them or offer comfort.

Violent retching fractured the forest calm. Dunya whipped round, scanning the foliage for movement. Licking her teeth in anticipation, Dunya slipped her hand into her apron pocket, fondling the burlap-wrapped kitchen knife secreted there. The coarsely honed brown blade rocked loose inside its wooden hilt but it was sturdy and would master any task assigned.

She would face her attacker if pursued and trust that her instincts would prevail. Dry debris crackled beneath her heel as she turned, intent on fleeing the low, monotonous voice, like a walrus's roar drawn out over the minutes in a slow, steady grating that inspired unease and anxiety.

Meertham. It could be no other. She was trapped—well and truly sunk. Would she be bold enough to sink her knife into his ironbound muscular neck and drive home her blade until it pierced the rushing stream?

Dunya dithered, desperate to formulate some plan while she still had a few moments of invisibility. Meertham coughed, a wet hawking of phlegmy vomit followed by a grotesque spatter upon the leaves. She gripped the basket in furred hands, keeping her eyes on the hollows between the cedars, where freedom glimmered, fairylike and delicate.

Her heel left the ground and the toe anticipated following it, but in a millisecond stretched as tightly as Dunya's arch, the brush parted and Meertham stepped from the trees.

Meertham was a hulking slab of muscle and brawn but now, in his blood-spattered vest, stuff-sack slung over a hunched back, somehow diminished, as if boiled down to his essence.

They locked eyes. Dunya's widened in shock while Meertham's remained impassive. Neither was willing to make the first move—the dash into the woods that would excite Meertham's instincts and begin the chase, nor the capturing lunge as Meertham threw down the beleaguered nanny goat and dove for Dunya, knocking her basket to the ground, spilling secrets and innocent flesh.

Each of them weighed the other's intent. Loyalty tethered them. Fealty to the dread lord subsumed personal desire. It would be too coarse a betrayal should Meertham turn his back on Dunya's flight and allow her to leave. Doing so would render meaningless his years of service and make a mockery of his suffering.

Sickness broke the stalemate as Meertham heaved out his guts, barking up clumps of sandy intestinal debris. Death graffitied his flushed, crumpled face with bold paint. The henchman gagged and fell, allowing the stuff-sack to tumble to the forest floor. The pitiful goat bleated.

Dunya hesitated. She should have taken that second of opportunity to bolt into the shadows, but she did not.

Meertham was too far gone to challenge her, and his gaze transformed itself from cavernous vacancy to an expression of pleading.

Dunya smelt the rich milk distending the nanny goat's udder. She could make fresh cheese and butcher one of the kids to feed Leander its soft meat. She swallowed the saliva that filled her mouth and forced herself to concentrate on freedom.

Meertham hunkered against a tree to regain his breath after the coughing fit passed. Dunya took advantage of his distraction to set her basket down, creep to the stuff-sack, and loosen its tie. Greedy for air, the goat shoved her head out of the sack and licked Dunya's hand. Delighted with her liberty, the goat frolicked among the leaves, kicking up her stout hooves before selecting a particularly tasty spray of greenery and nibbling away with little happy sounds tucked between crunchy bites.

Meertham put a hand to his heart and wiped the spittle from his mouth.

"You can't leave," he wheezed, his voice clogged with foam. "He will find you." Dunya crept back to the basket, dragging the reluctant goat behind her. Ayeda stirred and reached for her, anticipating food, cuddles, warmth. Leander slept beside his sister.

"Matuk will find you," Meertham repeated. "I will find you," he added but offered it as an empty threat, generated by duty. His voice was drained of menace and he slumped over, staring at the grainy brown vomit on the leaves.

"I'm dying, I think," he mused aloud, almost as an afterthought.

Dunya crouched beside the goat and squeezed milk into a container. She had trained the babies to take milk from a cup. Leander, who had so much difficulty in the beginning with the sheep's milk, could now tolerate small amounts mixed with water and mealie. Ayeda would gulp it straight down and hold out her cup for more, which she did now as Dunya fed her, propped on her lap.

The manor was so cold and damp it made the babies cranky. She hated to see their red, runny noses and peaked faces, so Dunya had stolen a down comforter from an unused bedroom and cut and sewed it to make two sack-suits with arms. Pink, puffy and enormous, they looked ridiculous, but the down did the trick and kept away the chill. They'd slept much better in the suits and she was grateful for her industry now, as the shadows flickered among the trees like ghosts fleeing a graveyard.

Ensnared in some tense, temporary truce, both Dunya and Meertham were silent. She sensed that if she rose to leave, he would pinch her wrist in those manacles of his and drag her back to the manor and the beating that waited, curled up in Matuk's skeletal, old man's fingers.

"Dog-face," he hissed, his voice weak and thready.

She stiffened as she rocked the baby on her lap, smoothing the yellow hairs that waved from the edges of Ayeda's clumsily knitted hat.

"Fur-face," he repeated. "Do you hear me? I'm dying."

"I hear ye." What did he expect, hugs and kisses?

"Didn't think it would be like this, me being sick and all. I'm rotting from the inside out like a wormy apple." Full of grief, he sighed and tugged his jersey down over his knees as if trying to enfold himself in a cocoon.

"I suppose I don't deserve better." He stared at Dunya. "What does a body like mine do with all the misdeeds it's done? Stuff them down, coat them in something dark and slimy, to sit in the pit of me belly and eat me alive." He coughed, barking like a seal. "Do I?" He picked up a pebble and pitched it at Dunya, watching as it found its mark and bounced off her back.

"Do ye what?" she asked, not looking at him.

"Do I deserve this death?" His question was parenthetical inside its pleading, his tiny, bleary eyes alight with fevered desperation.

Dunya thrust Ayeda toward him. "Look at 'er!"

Meertham looked. Ayeda smiled around the spit-soaked fist

wedged in her wee rosebud mouth. He shrugged, uncomprehending. Dunya's ire began to rise and her lips curved into a faint snarl.

"This is not yer child! Not mine either, yet 'ere she is, snatched from 'er mum by *you*." She spat the word. "'Ow many lives 'ave ye stolen? 'Ow many bodies 'ave ye fed to the ground, ye dirty beast! Course ye deserve yer death!"

"Dunya," he whispered, using her name for the first time. His fat jowls quivered, the stout whiskers on his cheeks vibrating as he tried to suppress his anguish. "Time has passed me by, my whole youth gone in a flash . . . I don't even remember what it was like."

Dunya had only vague sensations of something that might have passed for happiness but she suspected they were culled from stories of other people's youths that she'd patchworked together into something resembling a past. Dunya had been at the manor since she was a girl, eight or nine perhaps. Matuk bought her to be a companion to his monstrous daughter, but even Radhe knew how hideous she had become and would not venture from her forested hiding place to greet her captive friend, so Matuk moved Dunya into the manor to serve him. At first, there was a cook, a butler, and a staff of groundskeepers, but in time, they quit. Then she was alone, and remained so until Meertham arrived, bound to a bounty seeker like the one he would later become, thrust into the doorway by a hand outstretched for coin. How they had changed!

She ventured, "It's all 'is doing ye know," and raised her eyes to the manor, scratching its thin white fingers between the trees.

"'Twas the Master's fault I lost me pups . . . 'is fault that I even 'ad 'em." But she could say no more because that story was too terrible to repeat. Meertham would remember, she knew. Dunya cleared her throat and continued, attempting to soothe him so that he would not rise as she did and strike her down. "We were but children, wee ones sold like meat to the king's butcher. What could we've done?"

Meertham opened his mouth to speak but when it filled with

bloody bile, closed it again and swallowed. "I've never known a woman." He stared at the ground, poking through the pine needles with a stick. "Never even been kissed, not once."

Dunya raised her eyebrows but remained silent as she heard Meertham's confession. She was not one to absolve him of his sins, could not allow him to transfer his burdens to her.

"Don't even know how long I've served him. Thirty years? Forty? Don't even know how old I am. Couldn't go home if I tried." He bowed his head.

Dunya, a sweet girl at heart (somewhere deep below the bitterness that encased her soul like a hard, glossy pearl around a sand grain), found that she could not look at him. This conversation stirred up too much misery, yanked the careful, homemade bandages from gaping wounds and left them to fester in the rank air. She carried Ayeda back to the basket and tucked her in, smoothed sleeping Leander's hair, admired his black brows, inked in with a calligrapher's artful stroke, and wrestled the nanny goat from a patch of nettles.

Meertham's voice droned on as he ticked off a lengthy list of misdeeds inflicted in his employer's name. She could not listen. Instead, she tied the nanny goat's rope around her waist and checked the ground to make sure she'd taken everything that was hers.

She stole a glance at him slumped there, shivering and mumbling. She hoped he'd not be so thick as to go back to the manor. The Master, vile soul that he was, would just put him to work, most likely to track down his fleeing housemaid.

"Meertham," she called. He dragged his gaze from the forest floor and searched for her, his futile, clouded eyes scanning the trees. She realized that he could no longer see. Whether from fever or age, he was going blind. Against her will and wishes, it softened her, led her to kneel beside him, one hand gentle on his own cracked, sandpapery skin as she spoke in whispers.

"Ye know the way to salvation. Can we not go there together?"

He raised his face to her voice like an old dog, hungry for affection, much the way Chulthus had done before she died.

"Salvation?"

"The forest city, filled with them like us," Dunya pressed. She'd take him along, find a quiet place for him to spend his last days away from the Master's urgent toil.

"Girl, I can't show my face there! Who would have me, knowing what I am?" He shook his head ruefully, wiping away the beaded sweat that glinted on his forehead.

He was right.

"I won't find me way in the dark," she apologized, in farewell.

Meertham's hand snaked up to grab Dunya's ankle, wrapping his fingers around her furry leg so that she could feel the hindered blood pumping in her veins above.

"There is a room on the third floor of the east wing where the morning sun drifts in as white as snow. It's quiet there. I'll be able to see the ocean."

Meertham yanked her down and she dropped hard on her rump. They scuffled, Dunya's body weighted by Meertham's massive frame as he leaned against her, crushing the air from her lungs. *Jerusha, I can smell the death on 'im.* The rank odor of his bloodied, rotting innards made her gag.

"I did a favor for you once, fur-face," he panted, "because we are friends, of a sort. Because we are too much alike not to help each other when the situation demands it. I know that you remember."

She shook her head. "Leave me be, ye great monster!" The territory inside her heart was a cemetery pocked with mounds of dirt and studded with remembrance stones. Too many deaths and one in particular that he drew from her memory.

"You begged me to do it."

She had.

"Still bleeding from the birth when you got down on your knees and begged me to do it."

She turned away, staring into a gentian evening sky bitten and bruised. "Me own wee boys! Should I 'ave left 'em to the great evil that spawned them? Better to be dead than suffer our fate!"

Meertham had taken pity on her that day, methodically breaking the necks of Dunya's strange babies, with their canine bodies and human hands, their smooshed-in faces and silky furred skins soft against his rough fingers as he dispatched them one by one. He wasn't quick enough, though. Appearing to view the results of his handiwork (with sick glee burned into the corners of his mouth), Matuk had flown into a rage and beaten Meertham with a pair of red-hot tongs from the fire, burning off half an ear. The remaining live children were confiscated while the dead ones . . .

Meertham had tried. She would have been the last in line but he'd have done the job, if she'd asked it of him.

"I want to die in peace," he said, releasing his hold. "The devil may take my soul but at least I'll cross in silence."

Dunya stood and brushed the leaves from her gown. Her heart was filled with lead, her wings clipped like the battered butterfly she had carted in buckets from her master's tower room. She looked around as if seeing the forest for the first time, the last time. The air would never smell so sweet again.

"Well then, we'd best get back. The Master's going to 'ave a right fit when 'e sees the pair o' us staggerin' out the woods. Come on now, ye'll 'ave to walk, I've already got me 'ands full."

Resolution set her lips, barring the way for the tears that threatened to spill. *I am stronger than this,* she consoled herself. *Ain't I?* But she could not answer.

"Come on then," she said, her cheerful voice masking falsity and lies. "Rest yer hand on me shoulder an' I'll take ye 'ome."

28

THE MOON IN HER MOUTH

SORYKAH'S EYES FLUTTERED OPEN, admitting the morning's pink glow. Languid with a soft joy that left her lips curved in a smile, Sorykah slid from the Rose Room's huge bed, shedding flower petals upon the tiles. The night's tale was printed across her body in trailing purple love bites, red scratches that lined her back like a new-planted field, and the shadowed bruises on her thighs.

During the night, Chen had whispered, "Stay with me and I'll make you mistress of this house." Like a wolf, he'd run his adept tongue over the soles of her feet, the creases of her palms, the cleft between her legs, and murmured, "*You'd* be content to stay. I can taste how much I pleasure you, my little Trader."

And then, from behind, her breasts leaking milk, her hair wound tight around his fist and her neck arched over his shoulder, he asked, "Maitresse, duchess, queen—which title do you like?"

Sorykah could not shake her head to decline, but he knew that she refused.

"Are you not my girl?" he'd insisted, pushing her over the peak of her arousal, clapping a hand over her eyes to blind her like a horse.

"Are you not my girl?" he'd asked again, his hair curtaining their faces from the voyeurs gathered before the silken screens. Beauties and pleasures aside, she was most definitely not his girl.

Marianna appeared and interrupted Sorykah's reverie.

"If there's a time for tears," said Marianna, "it's now. The yard boys are readying your vector. You'll be gone this time tomorrow, unless you choose to stay." Marianna smiled, creating a radiant spray of wrinkles at the corners of her eyes. "He quite fancies you, I think. It would be good for him to have a companion, and one such as yourself, well, you'd do double duty, wouldn't you? Riding and hunting by day, the pair of you young lads, but a woman at night, like a warm homecoming for the weary soul. What man could ask more? He'd have the best of both worlds."

Sorykah was brusque. "I've lingered too long already." The roses on her bed had begun to shed their petals with greater frequency; the season was turning. She pressed her hands to the breasts less heavy with milk and wondered how much longer it would last when motherhood, like infancy, could be so fleeting.

Chen barged in wearing pressed new clothes, wet hair slicked over his head.

"We have business to conduct. You made a promise to me," she said.

"And you've fulfilled your end of the bargain, most wonderfully, I might add," he murmured, tilting her embattled face to his and kissing her overworked mouth. She resisted him and he collapsed into one of the gilded armchairs flanking the fire, rubbing his hands over his face. When he looked up, it appeared that he had wiped away all of his carefree youth and joy, revealing an embittered, hard-hearted man.

"Word has reached my ears that my *father*"—and he said this wryly, the word loaded with numerous, unflattering implications—"has claimed several captives from the streets of Neubonne. This is nothing out of the ordinary, for rumor has always swirled about him. They call him the Collector and not without reason. The difference this time, is that he took people. People, do you understand? Not somatics."

Sorykah became conscious of a teardrop falling from her chin and splashing onto her clasped hands. "What does that mean?"

"It means that my father has completely lost his mind. He was a brilliant businessman in his day. He built an empire, turning my grandfather's single seedling into a mighty forest, but his is a dark and depraved heart."

Chen's eyes glazed with ill-disguised horror as he continued: "I refused to believe the vicious stories that always circulated. I turned a blind eye. Sidra showed me that."

Turning from the fire, his face appeared scored with deep lines, but this revealed itself to be a trick of the light when he came forward to sit on the bed beside Sorykah.

"You have given me much happiness and for that I thank you."

Happiness that you forced from me, Sorykah thought bitterly, *your own pleasure taken in exchange for mine. You fucked me while you withheld your secrets, uncaring that your dalliance may have cost my children their lives.*

Another tear splashed onto her hands.

"Just tell me what you have to say, so that I can leave this place."

Chen's mouth hung open, waiting for words to fill it. When he found his tongue, he said, "There is but a single door leading to the interior of my father's house. To reach it, you must first pass the Gatekeeper, a disgusting creature who is ashamed of nothing, as his appetites reveal. If I were to visit my father, I would need only to show this ring"—and Chen flexed his fingers so that his ruby signet caught the firelight and winked at them—"and he would let me pass." Chen pulled the ring from his finger and slipped it onto Sorykah's; it was still warm from the heat of his body.

"He is old and often drunk, but he's not so far gone that he'd mistake a woman for me. If you cannot change in time, then you are lost. It will be up to you to decide how best to dispatch him. Once you have reached the inner courtyard, you'll see the twin portals of doom, immense oaken things that have been barred and locked for years. The true door is in the west tower, above the dungeons. Here's where it gets sticky."

Chen eyed Sorykah as if weighing her worth. She hoped that he was a more noble man than his mad, demonic father and was heartened to discover that indeed, by a very slim fraction, he was.

"There is a trick to the lock. It cannot be opened by any key, nor picked nor broken. My aunt, who is something of a technical wizard, devised it for her brother many years ago. I assume that she meant it as a joke, something that he would never construct, much less use, and yet it exists. Even I am unsure how to turn it."

The little flickering flame of hope that had rekindled in Sorykah's breast again sputtered out and died.

"Don't give up yet, my little chickadee." Chen offered rare encouragement.

"I've seen your aunt," Sorykah confessed. "She took me in. In fact, hers was the first place I ventured for help when I left Ostara. The somatics there seemed convinced that she alone could aid me in my search."

"In that they were correct. My father has been both cruel and kind to Shanxi, and now she can no longer fend for herself. She seeks atonement for her sins but loyalty to her brother prevents her from forsaking him. She speaks in riddles and fairy tales. If you have seen her, then she will have given you the key."

"She gave me number of things, but a key was not among them." Frustration grew as Sorykah realized that Chen had forced her to trade her virtue for something that he did not even possess. "You mean that I bartered my integrity for a riddle? Gave myself to you and your minions for nothing? Nothing!?" Sorykah snatched her hands from Chen's and slapped him away from her. "Sidra was right about you. You have but a single layer that is as shallow as topsoil!"

She could not have imagined that it was possible for him to look so wounded.

Chen rose stiffly, drawing his jacket closed. His handsome face hardened, and their sibilant connection, like a river of singing Sigue Sea flowing between their souls, was silenced.

"Your transport is being readied. You may depart first thing on the morrow." He strode from the room and slammed the door as the chimes in the clock tower began to sound, and Sorykah realized that she was perhaps the second woman to have broken his heart at that particular hour.

Light burst across the fresh-scrubbed sky, signaling Sorykah to rise and depart the Isle of Mourning. This was the last leg of her journey and she would win or lose as wit and courage dictated. Drawing on her trousers, boots, and the Company coat that had been cleaned for her, pulling all her goods into the pack she prayed would stay with her this time, and tucking Sidra's short blade into its sheath at her waist, Sorykah examined herself in the Rose Room's pier glass.

Worry and hardship had carved new lines into her brow and a telling hollow lingered in her cheeks. Her eyes were even darker and murkier than usual, sentiments echoed by her own heart as she prepared herself to take lives, one or many if the situation called for it. She had no worries for her eternal soul if indeed she had one; the man and mother in her demanded justice. The meting out of punishments and suffering little plagued her conscience. She'd not waste time quibbling over the finer theological points of retribution, whether or not she tinkered with some vast and infernal universal scorekeeping machine. She'd storm the manor and wrest control from Matuk's gnarled hands, do what needing doing and be done with it.

Sorykah was surprised to realize how deeply Sidra had touched her. Sidra was the first friend, the first lover to know both halves of Sorykah's fractured soul. The memory of Soryk and Sidra's lovemaking resonated deep within Sorykah's subconscious like an intoxicating witch's brew, working its magic from the inside out. Sidra's sex cure. Would the shared experience of their only night together be a powerful enough remedy to unite her divided brain and finally allow her to be whole?

Sorykah opened the French doors and stood on the balustrade. Across the Bay of Sorrows, the Erun Forest stretched like an immense green band encompassing the Glass Mountains' stark, funereal peaks. Would she ever see Sidra again? She had melted from Sorykah's embrace and vanished with no one the wiser. Those who watched thought Sorykah had merely been taken with the spirit of the house, grown playful and experimental with another of the costumed inhabitants; they didn't know Soryk frolicked with the somatic queen, the woman responsible for Chen's dramatic and well-documented suffering.

Perhaps when everything was finished, Sorykah could seek her out. However, the idea of Sidra in Ostara, walking among secretive locals and dispassionate Company men, seemed weird. Sorykah could not imagine her dressed in ordinary clothes, roaming the little burg's narrow streets with nothing to do but barter sled dogs and drink in Ostara's many taverns. Sidra wouldn't be satisfied to remain housebound with two babies and a pious nanny for company. Nor could Soryk dwell in the forest or the Erun city. He was bred of the cities and needed the press of bodies and voices, the sooty gray challenge of the streets, to enliven his imagination.

Sorykah considered the verdant, frost-laced wood that waited, holding its breath for some unspoken threat to pass. She clearly recalled the close, warm tunnels in the Erun city and Sidra's tree home, its astringent, sap-stained curves splendid and breathtaking. She'd not leave behind faithful Carac, the cloistered couple in the wood who had entrusted a stranger with their precious child. Queen Sidra had wandered too long inside her dream. To awaken her now would be tantamount to murder, a malingering illness that would trample her bright spirit.

Below her in the courtyard, the baggy skin of a hot-air balloon plumped toward fullness. *Good God,* she fretted, *is that what they intend to send me away in?* Did they honestly expect her to fly the cumbersome thing? Her stomach catapulted in her belly, a little bird beating its wings and failing to achieve flight.

"I have come this far," she consoled herself aloud. "I'll not let a little ballooning divert me." With that, she steeled herself for farewells and the dangerous airborne journey to Matuk's palace of sin.

29

CONQUERING THE SUN

DARK HAIRED, DARK HEARTED, *the evil Other woman.*

Red-haired Zarina watched from her bedroom window as the tethers lifted and the sandbags dropped, a sudden flaring explosion of fire inflating the bulbous envelope of the cream and turquoise paneled balloon. Marianna took Sorykah's hand in her own and squeezed, making Zarina grimace. She disliked Marianna's ease with strangers, especially those who landed like zealous conquistadores to stake claim on a native woman's paramour.

Kneeling before the carved wooden trunk at the foot of her bed, Zarina used both key and combination to free the locks, lifting the lid on her treasure store. With tender hands, she extracted a wrapped bundle, clanking and heavy in her arms. Zarina stripped the bundle of its covering to lay out the assorted disassembled pieces of a long-range air gun. She worked with quick surety, relying on the nights of repetitious study that enabled her to click all the pieces into place without guessing or hesitation.

Zarina had no knowledge of this particular gun's history, but she knew how satisfying it was to pull the trigger, to hear two or three seconds of faint, high-pitched whistling as the fun-gun's mini-missile launched itself into open space and the resultant splatter as it split heads like melons from three hundred feet. Noiseless and devastatingly precise, it pierced feathers, hides, and bones, but left behind no bullets or powder.

Zarina supposed it had been used by poachers traveling through the Bay of Sorrows. Shipwrecks and the debris they left behind were common. Novice sailors, unused to the precarious waters and the wind's capricious temperament, often foundered and smashed against the rocks. Zarina patrolled the beaches, picking through the wreckage in search of interesting finds. Much of it was junk by the time it reached her, damaged beyond use by the churning waters, but on occasion there was a spectacular prize—like her air gun.

It had arrived intact, a bit rusty, its barrel sand-caked and sticky-triggered, but Zarina meticulously restored it to full working order. She stalked the rocky shore, first shooting branches from shrubs, followed by a clump of leaves, a single leaf, and tiny triumvirate pollen buds as faint as pepper grains. For a girl like Zarina—exacting, restless, quick to anger and easily incited to senseless, passionate jealousy—the plotted execution of defenseless shrubbery was faint reward. There had to be better targets, bigger challenges to master.

Butchery was permitted on the isle. The kitchens and the appetites of the residents demanded it. Domestic birds were cooped behind the kitchen gardens, along with a series of plump sheep and goats, and cold canals nourished the isle's fisheries. Confident in her abilities, Zarina began to hunt: wild rabbits, squirrels, fat pigeons, and once, a glistening black raven, plucked from the bright blue sky as he rose, cawing out his ebony-throated glories.

Zarina wiped the body of her gun and considered for a moment her striking absence of remorse; there was none and it did not disturb her calm.

The rules of the isle were few. There was no tie, no allegiance that could not be undone. Hearts and the bodies that they governed were subject to many whims, and Chen inculcated his residents to construct an attitude of indifference to possessiveness, envy, and spite.

Handsome Elu had flirted with Zarina during the weekend of the Spring Rites, when the pleasure makers resurrected forgotten goddesses and paraded their effigies through the structure gardens as the residents danced and drank in celebration of the season. But while Zarina had lost her meanly hoarded heart to the pastry man, his remained untouched. Still, the affair continued, Zarina besotted and savoring her own good fortune, Elu content to amuse himself. Then Carensa arrived, a mainland seeker whose talent with a sewing needle purchased her admission to the manor. Elu's visits to Zarina's room diminished, but she had no foil for the desperation boiling inside of her until she caught the lovers in an overgrown arbor, Carensa's legs wrapped around Elu's waist as he contorted above her. She would later remember the incident as if viewed through a blurry lens, the ferocious shrieking that rent the air, waking later with long, shiny brown hairs clenched in her fist, the roots intact on the strands.

Checking her target through the sight, Zarina assumed a marksman's stance, the air gun's barrel wedged against her shoulder, polished and ready. She took stock of the swelling blue envelope in the courtyard below her, keeping a yellow eye trained on Sorykah amidst the pompous spectacle beneath her window. Horns blared and bells rang raucously as spent partyers circulated and offered their farewells.

She slid her gaze back to Sorykah, her fate stamped with Death's unbreakable, scythe-imprinted seal the moment that she'd first raised a hesitant finger and selected Elu from the crowd of a hundred willing men. Her Elu. Zarina's precious baker boy. Not Sorykah's. She frowned, felt her temperature rise as she pushed away the memory of Elu's body crouched over Sorykah, their grinning, wicked laughing faces ten times larger than life and splashed across the screens as if designed to drive Zarina to the brink of madness.

His duty done, for a single penetrative event was the quota for such parties, Elu defied convention by taking her again, supine and lazy beneath the traitorous, sex-changing guest. Zarina snarled and rapped her forehead with sharp knuckles to drive out the memory.

The yard boys loosed the lines and freed the sandbags. The exqusite balloon—with its panels of blue and ivory, its drapery of shining silver tassels and stiff, glossy bows—seemed to take a final deep breath before it began to lift on the air.

Zarina's finger hovered above the trigger, awaiting the nerve impulse that would free her restraint, pressing the trigger home with killer surety. She held her breath and closed one eye to aid her concentration.

"One shot," she breathed, finger poised and itching to pull.

Sorykah raised an arm in farewell. The crowd jostled and a figure burst from its ranks, his startling green eyes fixed upon the departing craft. Elu sprang for the basket and Zarina watched the whole thing in aching horror—Elu gripping the gondola's rim and pulling himself up to join the treacherous, two-faced Trader. (*Neither woman nor man, how could Elu have soiled himself with such a dirty creature?* Zarina puzzled.) Sorykah fell against him, laughing like a simpleton.

The balloon floated over the Bay of Sorrows. She faltered, for one potentially fateful moment. It had not been her plan to take down any but the Trader. *Trader, traitor,* she mused. Yes, Elu had betrayed her, and by leaving the isle and the women who loved him, he had betrayed them, too. It was right that she dispatch him along with the other. What difference did it make to Zarina if he lived or died? He would never be hers anyway.

She took a deep breath and leaned forward, again testing the gun's fit against her eye and shoulder. Shivers ran over her skin; she began to pant. The onyx pupil in her yellow eye widened with anticipation, revealing the tiny reflection of two happy lovers, sailing into the future with their arms wrapped about each other. The itchy finger caressed the trigger's short, smooth length, then arched, flexed, cracked, and pulled.

30

FALLEN

WHITE SUN FROSTED THE SILVER SEA. It seemed wonderfully portentous that Sorykah's venture should be heralded with such optimism. Elu cranked the gas jets and the steady fire flared and soared, lifting the balloon higher into the gaining winter currents to send it floating away from the Isle of Mourning. Sorykah bent over the basket's rim to gaze at the ocean below, churning sluggishly in its bed like a sleeping woman wrapping herself in white-fringed blankets.

"It's so pretty, isn't it?" she breathed. Elu wrapped his arms around Sorykah and nodded. "Thank you for coming with me, I need a good friend." The admission was difficult but she was glad to test her nerve by admitting her loneliness aloud. "The task ahead is daunting, to say the least."

A tern swooped by, black beak sharp around a dangling fish.

"Signs of life," Sorykah murmured. Her face darkened. "It won't last. The Erun is silent as the crypt." Elu gave her arm a reassuring pat, a silent affirmation of their togetherness. His eyes spoke of allegiance and his lips of desire, and Sorykah understood that he was hers for now, though not always, and she was pleased. Together they watched the sea roil below and the malachite trees draw closer. Sorykah thought she saw the bony white spires of a distant castle appearing through the mist, but when she looked again, the vision had gone. Massive, foreboding, and impenetrable, the Glass Mountains unfurled across the horizon, an endless angry pencil scratch marring the Erun's peaceful green.

Elu stretched toward the hand valve to crank the gas jets. He made a strange brief noise and Sorykah turned to find Elu wearing a peculiar expression as his hand dropped from the valve. Bringing it before his face, he gaped in astonishment at the hole in his palm. Blood had not yet begun to seep from the deep wound but Sorykah saw shock creeping over him. Sorykah stepped forward to catch Elu as his knees buckled and gave way. His weight upset the gondola, and it rocked nauseatingly. The balloon buckled and flapped, and the descent began. Air sang in their ears as Sorykah struggled to rouse the rigid Elu, who stared over Sorykah's shoulder. The envelope had torn, and the rapid loss of altitude sent the balloon careening toward the sea. Sorykah pushed Elu into the corner of the gondola while she cranked the hand valve, trying to gain enough levity to carry the balloon to shore before they plunged into the ocean that rushed up to meet them. Flames leapt high, soaring into the flailing balloon's slashed envelope. Fire licked its collapsing skin and ignited yards of cream and turquoise fabric. Sorykah watched in horror as elegant bows and swags burst into flame.

The gondola skipped over the waves as Sorykah hastily ejected food sacks, clothing, and bedrolls, almost slinging her own bag over the basket's rim until instinct told her to keep it. Fiery streamers, sparks, and blackened ash exploded overhead. Seawater soaked the gondola's bottom and leached into the basket, wetting Elu, who lay shaking and pale-faced.

"Come on, come on!" Sorykah screamed, urging the balloon a few more yards toward shore. They scudded over the water and bounced across the rocky beach, leaving a trail of orange embers, burning balloon chunks, and sparks. Coughing and clutching Elu to her chest, Sorykah braced for the impending, brutal landing. Glancing off a jutting rock formation, the balloon gave a final, valiant heave and launched itself skyward before the wetted, flaming basket gave way in a glorious orgy of fire and gushing black smoke.

Sorykah and Elu pitched free and flew across the beach, Elu bouncing with rag-doll limpness against the rocks, Sorykah thrown clear but landing hard on her back with a loud crack. She fluttered in and out of consciousness as flaming shreds of ruined balloon rained down from the smoke-veiled sky.

My back is broken, she mourned as she came to, the sickening snap of breaking bones still pulsating and raw in her memory. She collected her thoughts, blown to bits along with everything else, and began to assess the damage. Elu's safety was foremost in her mind but she could do nothing for him, save wish him well. A scrap of fabric lay smoldering near her right shoulder. She managed to turn her head a few painful inches and watched as the damp grass soon dried, ignited, and began to burn. The fire was contained for the moment, but soon it would lick its way across the foot of kindling between itself and Sorykah. Soon the entire meadow would burst into flame.

"Elu!" Sorykah's voice was hoarse from the fall and the smoke. "Elu!" She screamed again, her call a kitten's weak mew.

A spark leapt up from the little fire and bit her on the cheek. Sorykah involuntarily jumped and found that her legs responded. Testing her limbs with a cursory wiggle, Sorykah rolled to one side and heard another loud crack. She'd broken the arms of a twiggy, fallen branch, not her own bones. With a splendid joy tempered by the numbness and shooting pains in her back, she stood to search the meadow for signs of Elu, everything crackling and popping as her skeleton realigned itself.

Debris and wreckage lay strewn for yards. Aside from the drifting ash and smoldering piles of balloon skin and basket, the meadow was empty. Sorykah shielded her eyes against the morning sun, searching the yellow grass for signs of Elu, but he eluded her, as if he had deliberately hidden himself and now dared her to discover him.

Sorykah was too distracted to dwell on the accident's cause, if indeed it had been an accident. Elu's injuries and their subsequent plunge to earth were too casual to have been incidental. Something pierced Elu's hand and damaged the balloon, but what, and from where? Perhaps Matuk's guards spied their approach and plucked them from the sky as easily as one would drop a duck in hunting season.

Her head throbbed under the noxious weight of the acrid, burning fuel and a large, throbbing occipital bruise. She touched it and winced, wishing for ice and pain pills.

"Elu!" Sorykah moved with a growing sense of urgency, studying the grassy flats lumpen with sleeping gray giants, offspring of the Glass Mountains.

She limped back and forth, stamping out small fires before she spotted him, a lifeless bundle abandoned on a low rise. Sorykah ran, ignoring the throbbing insults her body hurled at her as she screamed his name. A gummy line of blood decorated his forehead where his skull had cracked. Sorykah wormed her hand inside his jersey and felt the warm, muscular contours of his familiar chest. Elu's heart beat weakly. Even if she managed to bandage his head, there were likely broken bones and internal injuries, bruised or lacerated organs bleeding into his body cavities. In the wilderness, the gaping hole through the meat of his palm would grow septic and poison him. Sorykah lay beside him, pressing her face to his chest, wrapping her free arm around him.

"Elu, I fear you haven't got much time left. I can't help you. In fact, I don't even think the Queen of the Erun could help you and she is a healer with true magick in her hands. Your body is broken, though I hope that your spirit is intact."

She thought he made the faintest whisper of acknowledgment, but his face was waxen and unmoving.

"I do not think that I told you," she continued, her voice cracking. "I don't think that I told you how much you have meant to me." She stifled a sob and hugged him closer. She felt the heartbeat beneath her palm grow fainter, the pauses between beats lengthening.

"Thank you Elu, for gifting me with such brief happiness." Sorykah held her breath and began counting. By the time she got to twenty, his heart had ceased to beat.

Elu's skin was chalky in the gaining sunshine; he'd already forsaken his body for the nethers. She had to remain rational. Sorykah decided that she had neither tools nor time to dig a grave and would instead construct a cairn and leave his decomposition to the elements. Small gray stones were plentiful but scattered; she would lose the day to this task, but they existed outside of time. Though the sun traversed the sky and the moon tugged the tides closer to its bosom, the surreal day was a dream, a fiction.

I will gather stones.

Sorykah stacked precise rows along Elu's form and blocked all the cracks and spaces so no birds or beasts could make a supper of him. When the last stone was in place, Sorykah paused inside the fading sunlight to admit her thirst and fatigue. She'd collected a few scattered parcels from the balloon as she picked up rocks for the cairn and now she made camp beside Elu's grave and sorted through the wreckage.

One bag contained mealie cakes, jam, some hard cheese, and a wineskin filled with watered red wine—a feast fit for a queen. Sorykah decided against starting a fire. Besides the fact that she'd seen enough of it for one day, she was also leery of discovery by poachers now that she was on the mainland. Although it seemed like another lifetime, the near miss with the lascivious blond hunter and his impartial companion remained in her mind, etched in vivid ink.

She'd lost track of the days but guessed that she had left the *Nimbus* over a month ago. Blank spots gaped in her memory; she had no way to judge their length so perhaps there were additional days missing. She considered the children. Gray zone. She had to stick to safe subjects when thinking about them. Remember Ayeda's smile, the curiosity that shone from her silvery eyes and made them flash like polished nickels. Sweet Leander! Already Sorykah sensed that he was the fragile one, the sensitive child who would require a buffer zone between himself and the world. How would she protect him?

Her thoughts began the precipitous slide into the realm of terror so she distracted herself by aligning her body against Elu's cairn, searching for comfort atop the rocky ground and tucking her coat over her legs to wait out the night.

Even though Elu was nothing but a corpse beside her, Sorykah was glad for his company. He could not speak, of course, but she was used to his wordless yet steadfast friendship, and so felt his presence hovering above the wide strip of grass edged by sea and stone and the Erun trees whispering beneath the dimming sky.

Morning came and Sorykah ate sparingly, filled with resolute determination to find and kill the Collector. She'd endured legions of trouble—attack by man and beast, cold and starvation, a wandering fugue state, the loss of her faithful dog and sled team, and now a suspected attempt on her own life. If all the drama hadn't yet stopped her or convinced her to abandon her mission, neither would the crash or Elu's death.

The shore curved inward, spooning the rushing tide between pools and packed sand, littering the beach with debris and bits of humanity pilfered by the spring floods. She skirted a heap of washed-up garbage, broken branches, leaves, sand, and stones, but slowed to study the rubble as she neared. Something blue and flapping caught Sorykah's eye and she moved closer to investigate. Buried among the detritus, a tattered coat waved its lone sleeve. Where the sea had deposited its findings, there were broken glass jars worn smooth and clouded by polishing sand, glimmers of metal, beads, coins, and an abandoned shoe.

Kicking aside broken ship's planking, rusted metal plates knobby with orange, crusted rivets, and an endless variety of junk, she picked through the rubble, her curiosity aroused by the occasional useful item—a roll of fishing line still wound tight, a tarnished silver fork, a dented, locked metal box with something rolling inside—marbles perhaps? Thrusting her hand into a slimy bundle of tangleweed, her fingers closed around the hilt of a blade that perfectly fit her grip. She ripped away the kelp as she tugged it free, a blade that after a long overland voyage tumbling through murky floodwaters, had come to rest here to await exhumation by its rightful owner.

"My knife," she cooed. Sorykah's hands trembled as she brushed away the last of the mud and polished the blade with her sleeve. Nels would pronounce it a miracle, a sign from the Blessed Jerusha that she should pursue and slay the Collector without remorse or hesitation. Nels's Holy Mother very conveniently agreed with whatever Nels insisted to be the goddess's own truth at any particular moment, but Sorykah would not object. Protected by eons of warmongering Magar craftsmanship and her own righteousness, she would swiftly dispatch her enemy.

Armed with knowledge and secrets gleaned from Shanxi and her devious nephew Chen, and with the forest wiles pilfered from Queen Sidra, Sorykah possessed the weapons and torches with which to slay her dragon.

She whistled as she wrapped her sash around the hilt and strapped it to her belt. Now she was ready. Turning once more to the forest, Sorykah peered through the thickets and realized that although she had seen her course from the air, once on the ground she was lost. The forest stretched for miles in all directions. Should she veer north, east, or west? Plunge herself into the forest like a diver into a pool and strive with all her might toward the other side? Worry plagued her.

Sorykah sank to the ground, heavy with defeat and thinking of Nels, that fervent follower of Jerusha, the Blessed Mother. Nels had been horrified to learn that Sorykah's children were unblessed heathens. She took it upon herself to procure a temple priestess to issue the twins a "magic sprinkle" guaranteeing their welcome into the Great Mother's aerial home upon their deaths.

"Jerusha turns away none," Nels consoled Sorykah before the big event, "but it's always better to attend a party that you've been invited to." Nels's stern but gentle attempts to convert Sorykah to the true path often enticed her employer into metaphysical discussions about universal law and order.

"Believe, and you will see evidence of her existence," Nels asserted, countering Sorykah's equally adamant "Show me proof, and I will believe."

Sorykah's insistence on physical fact had served her well enough so far, but she'd never been lost to the mercy of greater forces like this. Perhaps it was the thought of Nels, or the powerful presence of the Holy Mother herself, peering down from the heavens to gaze upon her lost child's plight, that moved Sorykah to request divine intervention.

I will follow any cue; I will take any path shown to me. She bowed her head against the old feelings of panic, rising and staking their conquering claim on her brief peace. *Breathe*, she urged herself and willed her mind to calm. *I will not be afraid of my own fear, not after everything else. I am stronger than this. Stronger than you*, she insisted, addressing it directly.

"Ayeda!" Sorykah bellowed, summoning every molecule of the fading yet resolute tie that forever bound her to her children. "Leander!" she screamed, her voice raw and urgent with despair. "Show me the way! Answer me!"

Her cry rang out across the lifeless meadow, and she sat awaiting a response, her heart thundering with expectation, her breath coming hard and fast. The meadow sprawled colorless beneath a gray sky; thin clouds hid the sun. As she waited, the impatient wind pushed them on and the clouds continued their journey. The sun revealed itself and cast bright rays across the yellowed grass. A series of shallow pools as bright as mirrors caught the light and reflected silver and brilliant blue, a trailing ellipsis diminishing on the horizon like a stone-cobbled path leading to the forest's core. The sea keened behind her, mourning the loss of another dismal day. The pools glimmered and faded as the Erun's shadows subsumed them, but the light lingered, beckoning her forward. *Follow us*, the pools seemed to say.

Sorykah leapt to her feet and began to run.

31

DANS LA FOSSE AU LION

AS SORYKAH SET FORTH once more into the trees, she was alone with her thoughts. Without furred or feathered distraction, she could begin to digest the bizarre events of the previous weeks. The certainty of rescuing her children had served as her North Star, but as she drew closer to the grim manor, she struggled to keep her hopes alight.

Sorykah plowed through dense underbrush and clinging gloom, blind to everything but thoughts of her children. If any poacher dared to accost her now, she would turn on him with a bright and terrible fury, Magar blade in hand. Should the beast approach her, she would bow in deferential silence and let poor, ruined Radhe pass unmolested.

Three days, three nights. The fourth morning broke with reluctance, dragged lazy and glassy-eyed from its black, starry bed. Slow to rise and hoarding its warmth, the sun made a laborious trek over the horizon, its weak white rays unable to penetrate the dense mist shrouding the trees. Slivers of fear needled her heart, but Sorykah had no time for doubt. There was only faith to be clung to, faith to save her from complete madness and panic at being alone and childless in the unwelcoming forest, lost and alienated from everything dear and familiar.

She ignored her hunger because she would lose time if she stopped, lose moments that might mean life or death to her two, had they survived this long. She hadn't even wasted time to consider the absent Wood Beast, whose dreadful presence so filled these woods. After hearing her sorry tale, Sorykah could no longer think of her as just a mindless, flesh-eating monster. Radhe was quiet. Strange really, because Sorykah had encountered her on each of her forays into the forest. And while the Erun was spooky as a crypt on All Hallow's Eve, it was lifeless.

Was it her imagination or was it growing a bit brighter? Yes, the spaces between the trees were broadening, revealing larger patches of silver sky and slate clouds. The air here blew a bit more freely and she quickened her pace, every thought and emotion muffled by her urgency. She leapt fallen logs, her boots crackling on the crisp pine, the small white clouds of her exhalations leaving a steamy trail behind her as she darted beneath the trees.

She slipped on something wet and careened into a heap of bracken, her legs pulled out from under. She reached down to wipe the mud from her boots and discovered a viscous red smear on her hand. Horrified, Sorykah leapt to her feet, examining the ground beneath her. There—a gelatinous pool of blood on the loam, red at the center but ringed in black. Not too fresh, then. She turned, following the tracks with her eyes, seeing the broken bushes, the disturbance that led her to a fallen log where a heap of something hairy and altogether hideous lay convulsing. She stepped quietly, making a gentle sound in her throat, a low warning of her approach. Although she knew a tormented child was trapped inside all of that cruel deformity, she was wary of getting too close, having her fingers bitten off by a wild thing driven mad by pain and despair.

This beast turned tender eyes to her, shifted its head, and parted a mouth whose long, jagged teeth jutted around a flapping, speckled tongue. Sorykah inched closer, humming all the while, her head filled with pictures of the little girl who watched from the bed as her mother was dragged into the night, never to return.

"Oh, you poor girl," Sorykah murmured, shielded by compassion. Arrows sprang from Radhe's back and sides, buried in her lungs, liver, and kidneys. Sorykah knelt, overcome with sorrow and stretched out a hand as one would to a stray dog. Radhe panted and shifted a bit closer, dragging her bulk over the hard ground, reaching forward with one curled limb. Her swollen knuckles, the hands that were more like claws, were gone. The arm that Radhe extended was a woman's, with scabby elephantine but human skin between patches of hairy hide and large, quivering tumors. She had broken, dirt-caked fingernails, and open sores on her joints, the half-healed remnants of her years dragging along the ground.

Sorykah collapsed, all the starch in her backbone dissolving. Radhe gazed with searching, clouded eyes and Sorykah realized that she could see very little; variations in light and color, nothing more. Kneeling close, holding her breath against Radhe's rank, unwashed body and the sharp tang of her clotting blood, Sorykah gripped an arrow shaft in her right hand while pressing with her left on Radhe's back to steady her as she twisted a bit to dislodge any sticky bits of meat embedded around the arrowhead. One quick, sure tug and the arrow slid free, loosening the clots that kept Radhe from bleeding out. Fresh blood coursed from the open wound but Sorykah kept to her task, extracting each stubborn point with maternal patience and skill. She sang as she worked, a little ditty she had taught herself when her own twins were newborn, and the softness of her voice as it skimmed over the lullaby's soothing notes gentled Radhe. She did not flinch or gripe when Sorykah caused her pain, and the Trader knew that the beast was nearing her end.

"Can you turn?" She pressed on Radhe's shoulder, the skin slack and unexpectedly soft, grizzled hairs springy beneath her palm. Radhe obliged, moving as if trapped in the syrupy sea of nightmares. One of the arrow shafts was broken and Sorykah had to push her fingers into the cut to get a better grip as she slid a finger around the arrowhead and worked it free. Radhe didn't seem to notice the operation that the Trader performed with surgical precision but emerged from her silence, tongue straining to form sensical words. Sorykah talked between the verses of her lullaby, urging her to rest while reassuring the dying woman with her presence. A pool of blood crept across the forest floor, saturating Sorykah's trousers.

"I am sure that your mother wouldn't want you to be alone," she said, "so I will remain with you until the end."

Radhe made a gurgling, choking sound: a lament or sigh of relief.

"I know your story," Sorykah continued, removing her packs and setting them outside the bloody circle. She spread fallen leaves across the soaked ground to make a mat for herself, then settled in beside Radhe's deformed bulk to take her human hand and press it between her own two smaller ones.

"You have been bereft for so long that sorrow is your calling. Poor misunderstood girl! Just a baby, weren't you, when he took her away."

Radhe grunted and closed her eyes. Water ran from beneath her lids and trickled over the folds of her wrinkled cheeks. Great strings of spittle spilled from her open jaws as she wheezed and slobbered. Sorykah held the beast's human hand as she ruminated on the years of neglect and starvation Radhe had endured at her mad father's hands. Monstrous Matuk was the beast in this wood, not his daughter.

Radhe growled in response to some inner torment while the foreign bodies in her bloodstream continued their reconstructive work. Whatever Matuk had done to her this time, it was working. Lumps of tissue began to seethe and bubble beneath Radhe's skin, making her moan. Sorykah watched in horror as she turned her head, scraping it against the side of the fallen log and peeling off wide swatches of flesh like skin from an orange. Half of Radhe's face hung from a splintered knot, while underneath, red muscle gleamed bright and taut. There was a human face there, or part of one.

"Little girl," Sorykah urged, willing herself to steady, remain calm while terror stamped itself upon her very soul. Even as the teeth dropped from Radhe's massive, low-slung jaw and tinkled onto the grass, she held firm. There would be no fear, no disgust or rejection allowed. Her life had been such a godforsaken misery, innocent Radhe deserved to die in peace.

"Little girl," she began again, finding her voice. "You can let go now. Go and join your mother. I am sure that she waits for you."

Radhe moaned through the liquid that filled her throat. Bit by bit, Radhe was yanked back into humanity, her flesh cracking, splitting, peeling open in gory red crevices. Enormous tumors dropped like autumn apples too long on the branch, pulpy yellowish masses that rolled out from between Radhe's beast hide and her emerging human frame to burst upon the forest floor, revealing sordid, blackened centers. A foul stench of sickness and putridity soiled the air. Sorykah coughed and turned her head to hide her revulsion, but still, she sang.

Radhe was comforted at the last, when she most needed it. Death was the one thing of which she had been most afraid. The old gods would not set a place and welcome her to their table. No, if indeed there was an afterlife, she would be the scrap cleaner and scullery maid, a kick-around loiterer condemned to begging and thieving.

Radhe deemed her purgatory just. She crawled into the woods to await her fate while the change picked her apart with stabbing little icicle fingers. Radhe knew angels could fly like the birds, but they could also walk and that is how this angel approached her, on two feet.

The woman unlocked all the doors in Radhe's mind. She

turned on the taps and let the sadness flow, seven thin waterfalls that pulsed and ran red to the ground. She had dark hair, like her own mother, and could sing with two voices at once, the milk-sweet warm echoing the dulcet tones.

Sorykah smoothed the slime-caked black hair now shot with gray that she found beneath the other portion of Radhe's falling flesh, Radhe's head smaller and reassuringly egg-shaped inside the carcass of the Beast.

Radhe sobbed softly, rubbing together raw, angry gums. She was as toothless as a baby swaddled in the skin of a monster. She shivered and groped toward Sorykah, lips trembling, desperate to speak. Sorykah bent low as Radhe reached out and made contact, her icy fingers fumbling over the contours of Sorykah's face, feeling her arched brows, her smooth cheeks, and the locks of loose hair tucked behind an ear.

Small and perfectly made, Radhe was a girl again. She had spent years suspended inside another, encased in an inescapable, organic torture chamber. Her enormous dark eyes were those of a child haunted by ghosts. Bloody, naked, and red, Radhe curled in on herself, a bud that would never open.

"It's all right, little girl," Sorykah whispered. Radhe placed her hand on the side of Sorykah's face, her thumb pressed against Sorykah's lower lip to better understand the words: "You can go now."

Radhe's hand tightened on Sorykah's face, gripping her skull bones as if to anchor her against the darkness of an unwelcome night. She managed a word before going limp, her life evaporating on the breeze. It wasn't until much later, when Sorykah had broken through the forest onto the vast field surrounding the Matuk's manor, that she could decipher Radhe's word. Yellow and dry, the flat meadow rolled in grassy waves toward five ivory towers. Shielding herself in a copse of trees, she summoned all her rage and fury, calling the change to her as if hollering for a mean and errant dog. As the change boiled inside of her and snuffed out the light, she heard Radhe's voice as clearly as if she'd been standing before her.

"Mama," she'd said. "Mama."

Sorykah stroked Chen's ruby signet ring, turning it on her finger so that it caught a bit of light and glinted with a deep inner fire. He had traded his father's life for his own pleasure; this ring was Sorykah's payment for her performance at Chen's ball. Sorykah had been a bought bride, abandoned on the dirty cake-bed. Memories of Sidra elicited a potent mix of longing and regret. Sorykah shared Soryk's emotions, and knew that the change had already begun. Fiery pinpricks of light washed through her veins as if she'd swallowed a thousand burning stars. Waves of blackness pitched and heaved, seeking to drown her in a sea of forgetfulness. Sorykah struggled to imbed her mission deep within her shared consciousness, planting it squarely in the wasteland of her Trader's mind, where both of her selves could find it.

She fought the sleep but it was too powerful. Her skin crawled with a million scurrying ants who rebuilt her, molecule by molecule from the inside out. She rubbed the ruby ring with numbed fingers and heard her own voice, deep and masculine, cry out, "Remember! Find our children."

Yes, she thought, her mind-voice softer, wispy-edged, and female. *Save the babies. The rest is frosting on the cake.*

32

UNANSWERED PRAYERS

MATUK'S DOGS LURKED BEHIND THE DOOR, noses twitching and snuffling the scent of Dunya's betrayal. One of the beasts stood on hind legs to lick the blood from the lock and got a bone key in the snout when the housekeeper returned. Meertham and Dunya staggered through the door, poor Dunya's legs bowed and back buckled from the strain of supporting the ailing Meertham and carrying the baby basket. He'd said nothing to her about Sorykah's children, mewling and kicking off their tea towels as the chamomile's effects faded and restlessness set in. Fixed upon his impending death, Meertham yearned for the quiet peace of that small white room with its sea view and air of abandonment.

"Back off, ye wretched 'ounds!" Dunya groused, emboldened by Meertham's presence. The dogs had instructions to bring Dunya to their master upon her return but were confounded by the appearance of the burly henchman, a creature strong enough to wring their necks should he so desire it. Prancing and rolling her slotted eyes, the little nanny goat shook her tiny horns at the enormous hounds, more courageous than Dunya would ever be.

Slinking along the ground, Matuk's dogs growled deep in their throats, a sound so viscerally disturbing that it made Dunya's bowels weaken. She knew their purpose: to wrap their slavering jaws around her limbs and drag her up the tower stairs.

Meertham chucked up stinking gouts of blood. He spat upon the wall and the dogs barked, frenzied by the smell as they leapt snapping at Matuk's servants.

"Shut your great yaps, you damned dogs!" Meertham lunged, delivering a stinging clout to the alpha dog's wiry black snout. Deferential and cunning, the black beast wavered, its red eyes locked on Meertham's.

"Where is he? I'll beat the mean from him!" Meertham lunged into the prowling pack, snatching one dog by the ears and another by the scruff to dash their heads together.

Temporarily repulsed, the dogs hung back as Meertham and Dunya staggered from the armory tunnel into the coolness of the main hall. Click-clack went the nanny goat's hooves, a sound of penny nails being hammered into tile.

"Let me lay me burden down, so's I can better 'elp ye," Dunya murmured, edging toward the security of the locked kitchen and dragging the goat along the slick floor.

Hungry and soaked, the babies were sullen after their aborted rescue. Fearing a sudden crying jag, Dunya deposited Meertham on a cobwebbed couch and dashed downstairs. Her kitchen was familiar and welcoming, even as she prayed to abandon it forever. Dunya deposited the baby basket and tethered the goat to the table leg, tossing her some wrinkled old cabbage leaves that the nanny goat nosed and began to nibble. She'd also left some greasy sausages in a pan on the stove in an attempt to feign her return and now she sliced one in half, pushing meat into the babies' fists and praying for temporary contentment.

Fastening the door behind her, Dunya ran on trembling legs to

Meertham's side, lifting one of his massive arms and tucking her small frame beneath it to better guide him upstairs. He felt different, both lighter and heavier at the same time. Dunya considered his imminent death and realized for the first time that without his infusions of food, supplies, and new victims, Matuk would turn to the babies to slake his thirst for blood.

Perhaps she could delay a bit longer, pretend that Meertham still walked the Erun, threatening its residents with his presence and the filthy sack slung over his shoulder. At least she would have the kids to offer once the goat birthed them, the cycle of depravity widening to suck another innocent into its whirling vortex.

"No, I'll not 'ave it, ye wicked plonker!" She hadn't meant to speak aloud but there was no one to report her treason.

"Who's a wicked plonker, then?" Meertham smiled faintly, more grimace than grin.

"Och, ye know 'im. 'E what yanks our tethers and sends us scurrying!"

Together they limped up a twisted stairway, its water-warped frame bent and misshapen. Dunya never ventured above the sunken first floor and the stairs groaning beneath them worried her nerves.

"Keep on, another level. Turn right and go to the end of the hall," Meertham instructed as they ascended the high reaches of the manse.

Dust poofed from their feet with each step upon the carpeted floors. The silence was a tangible presence, a shroud upon their heads. Water dripped in the distance and the smell of rot evidenced structural damage, revealing the white manor's disease.

Dunya wrinkled her nose, covering her protruding, hairy snout with her hand.

Meertham panted and coughed but refused to rest until he located his sanctuary; once safe behind the small, plain door, he fell from Dunya's grasp to topple upon the single, narrow bed.

She sighed, rubbing her strained arms as she gawked at

Meertham's treasures. It was obvious that he'd used this room for years, perhaps since first arriving at the manor, and years of accumulated trophies cluttered the floor, pushed up against the baseboards in orderly rows.

There was a small doll, her plaster face cracked but intact. A ring of keys, assorted feathers stacked in jars and cups, clothing neatly folded but clearly not Meertham's, some of it pink and printed. Glass marbles bright with winking lights, a hairbrush, a golden tube of something red and waxy that twisted up at Dunya's command and captured her fancy.

Books, spoons, tools, scissors, eyeglasses, a holey wooden bucket, and a muddied icon of the Blessed Mother Jerusha, her graceful hands holding a white rose as her eyes gazed lovingly at her swollen womb, lined the walls.

Meertham struggled to remove his clothing. Dunya knelt without thinking, reaching for the buckles and pulling his rough, club-shaped feet from worn and patched boots. She stripped him of his leather jerkin and turned her back, staring out the small round window as he shimmied out of his trousers and crawled into bed.

The sea was a skinny gray line behind the Erun's tall pines.

"Hmph! Ye can see the ocean, after all. Fancy that!"

"Did you doubt me?" Meertham wheezed, closing his eyes.

"Never." Dunya crept to the bed, staring at her friend. He was her friend, she supposed, after all that they'd shared and the things he'd done for her. The killings had been an act of kindness and wasn't charity love's merciful root?

She leaned closer, staring at his crinkled brown face with its tough leathery skin and the ivory whiskers that poked from his cheeks as broad as blades of straw. His lashless eyes drowned within pools of wrinkled folds and his tusks, thicker than Dunya's own slim forearm, glistened in the light.

"Meertham," she whispered. She reached forward with shaking hands.

"All right, me bird," he muttered, astonishing her with this deceptive glimmer of affection.

"Truly, ye've never been kissed?"

He shook his head, his breathing heavy.

"By a human woman, ye mean." Dunya moved closer, pressing her weight on his chest. It felt as though she rode the planks of a vast beer barrel, Meertham some practiced seafarer bearing her through the worst of a storm. She'd never been to sea, nor dipped her hand in its waters, and she imagined a cold, foamy, and effervescent blue.

Meertham grunted something in reply.

"Am I woman enough for ye?" Her own boldness surprised her. She'd never had a kiss either. Beatings o' plenty, babies begot by force and the Master's wickedness, long, lonely nights in the embrace of some imaginary lover also a dog-face, but as she pictured him, tall, smiling and dressed in shining brown short hair, a handsomer version of herself perhaps.

The dying henchman turned his head to cough while Dunya rode the broad chest that vibrated beneath her like a beehive.

She waited, smelling the death creeping over him, doling out draughts of sickness and taking bets against his dying hour.

Meertham broke the silence. "Am I man enough for you, fur-face?"

She frowned. It was an unexpected question.

Though rheumy with cataracts and steeped in milk-clouds, his gaze was steady.

"Go on then," he gasped. He attempted to pucker but failed, his fleshy lips too muscular and overstretched by his handsome tusks to achieve it.

Dunya wiggled closer. His breath was tangy-sweet but not bad. He was a solid and comforting bulwark beneath her and she wished he would put his arms about her and pull her closer still. He didn't.

"If I kissed ye, would it count?" she asked, hesitant fingers reaching up to touch the wide expanse of his split lip. It huffed and quivered and Dunya grinned.

Meertham shrugged minutely. They both held their breath.

Dunya kissed him. Her droopy mouth spread itself over his in a haphazard fashion. She wasn't sure what she was meant to do and tentatively extended the tip of her tongue to his upper lip and gave it a little swipe.

Meertham sighed deeply and shuddered; Dunya scuttled backward, wiping her mouth with the corner of her apron to cover her embarrassment.

"'Twas nice, that," he murmured.

Speechless, Dunya curtsied and trembled. Both feet touched the floor, and she was upright and walking before she could speak.

Truthfully, it had been an awful kiss, sloppy wet and stiff, but gentle enough and warm enough to satisfy them both.

"Now I can die in peace," Meertham said, settling with finality into the pillows.

Far away, Dunya thought she heard the ringing of a bell and the sinister thump of heavy paws plodding along the floors.

"Yes," Dunya agreed. "Same for me." She backed toward the door, filled with an urgent desire to retreat to the safety of her kitchen and leave Meertham alone with his treasures and his sea view.

"Take something to remember me by," he offered. Without hesitation, Dunya secreted the golden tube of red wax in her apron pocket. She didn't know what it was for, but she wanted it anyway.

Meertham shifted in his bed, the rattle of his stricken lungs loud in the quiet room.

"I won't forget ye," she whispered, but he didn't answer.

She opened the door. Matuk waited, leering and shriveled like some hideous monkey-man, a laboratory experiment gone horribly awry.

"What won't you forget, Dunya dear?"

Matuk dug bony, sharp-nailed fingers into the delicate skin of her ear and yanked. Lightning bolts of pain lanced Dunya's head and she whined as he jerked her downstairs toward the armory. Two dogs materialized at her master's side, their sharp canines dripping hot, sour froth as they nipped her heels in a halfhearted attempt to sever her Achilles' heel.

"Did you believe that you could steal into my house without my seeing you? Do you think that anything happens here without my awareness and consent?"

Dunya whined, a steady, pathetic, and irritating sound.

Matuk dragged her through the dusty, abandoned hall and up his tower stairs. Even when she slipped on the worn, icy steps, he did not release his hold and the pain brightened like an iron in the blacksmith's fire. Stars blipped and flashed before her eyes.

The tower was the manifestation of chaos. Matuk had lost his battle with Tirai's raging, vengeful ghost, and disorder blew out the tower door to meet them. Phantastics pages and glass shards swirled windborne but Matuk did not cover his face as Dunya did.

He tugged her ear and literally lifted her up the stairs, hurling her into the room with such force that she slid across the floor and cracked her skull against the far wall.

"Where is my daughter?" Matuk advanced, wielding a thin scythe already caked with blood.

Dunya couldn't help herself. She folded her body into a ball, preparing herself for the scythe's stinging bite.

"Speak when I address you!" Matuk slammed the curved blade against the wall above Dunya's head and she quailed.

"I've frightened you," Matuk whispered, giving in to one of his rare but dreadful fits of kindness. The gentle voice, the stroking hand, and soft, liquid eyes heralded burgeoning explosions of rage. He knelt beside her, rubbed his bony, clawlike hand over the silken ears he'd so crudely manhandled just moments before.

"Let me take away the sting," he cooed, his rubbing growing more purposeful, more sinister. His hands slid over Dunya's furry face, along her neck, and over her thin shoulders as he abandoned the scythe and reached into the neckline of her blouse.

Bile rose in Dunya's throat.

"I need to know if my treatment worked, sweetheart." Matuk dropped the scythe, both hands now roving like five-fingered invading armies come to conquer and claim her soul. "My wife insists that I see for myself. She assures me that Radhe has been cured and I must"—he stuttered for a moment, distracted by some vision in the corner of his eye—"yes, I must know, you see? She rides me *like a fucking demon*!" Matuk showered spittle into the air, his ancient breath rotten and foul in Dunya's sensitive nose. One hand still lodged deep within Dunya's sparse décolletage, he snatched the scythe, and waggled it in her face. Dunya flinched and struggled to swallow the great knot in her throat.

Matuk screeched and pressed the scythe to Dunya's throat, the blade curving along the underside of her jawbone, the blunted, starred tip digging deep into fragile tissue where blood began to well and stain Dunya's fur.

"I had forgotten how soft you are." His fingers wormed between Dunya's small breasts and she held her breath and her tears, thinking of the twins and how she must not allow them to be damaged in this way, their bright futures dimmed by the smelly, ruinous Master.

Blessed Jerusha, save me, Dunya whispered, though none could hear her voice.

"So very soft." The scythe dropped and Matuk scooted closer, heaving his scant weight upon Dunya's smaller frame. He lifted one of Dunya's stiff arms and held it to his chest, where Dunya felt the sharp outline of his ribs through his dirt-roughened jersey. "I think you might be ready to breed again. Eh? What do you say?"

Dunya thought she would urinate upon the stones if he did not stop.

"Please," she begged, her frail voice muffled within her malformed mouth.

"Please Master, do breed me! Is that what you say? Yes, sir, make my doggy belly swell with gruesome little puppies, please! Please do it now, sir, please sir, might I have some more?"

If ye come, do it now! Blessed Mother, Dunya repeated the prayer she'd so often heard the nanny intone, rocking on her knees, hands raised to the blue room's artificial sky. *'Oly Jerusha, Queen o' Kindness, Light-Bringer and Way-Finder, 'ear me plea. Rescue me! Tie me legs! Spoil me womb and make it fruitless. Show me the way! Cast yer golden light into me eyes that I might see saving and live to serve ye forever! Ahh! Feck! Feck! Bless and protect me, keep me safe.*

Dunya curled into a quaking ball, resisting in her small way, the intrusion of her master's skeletal hands, his ferocity as he tugged the ties of her blouse, the breath panted hot and moist in her ears, a sound like the roaring of the distant, unvisited ocean.

Blessed Mother, Dunya whispered, *oh gentle lady o' the night, wiv the stars in yer eyes, 'elp me!* She squirmed from beneath Matuk and scuttled along the wall. The open window yawned an invitation, but should Dunya plunge from it, the children would die of starvation, or cold if the nanny goat ate their tea towel bedding.

Dunya's hand found the wax tube in her apron pocket and she clutched it, possibly believing it to be some sort of talisman of female power with its lucky colors of gold and red.

Matuk got to his feet, sweating visibly.

"Up on the table, my dear." He patted the gore-streaked vivisectionist's slab with its runners caked full of blood, fat, and strips of skin. "Let's make the most of the impulse, shall we?"

Dunya's sorrowful brown eyes widened, showing their rare whites. She'd grown up wild and heathenish, giving little thought to prayer after her first few desperate attempts yielded no results. Dunya's mother had beseeched the sky and the punishing gods who'd turned their backs on them to reverse her daughter's cruel change. Her prayers were too faint and uninteresting to be heeded by fickle deities with more important things on their minds. Dunya prayed for a speedy death when her monthlies stopped and her womb bulged with ill-gotten offspring, but she lived and her tentative faith wavered.

Since the arrival of the twins, Dunya added her pleas to the pianist's constant invocations though none had yet generated a response, but that was before she had the tube, hard and shiny on the outside, creamy satin on the in. All Dunya desired was time to retreat to her kitchen and explore the possibilities of Meertham's gift. Clenching it in her small hand, she began to sense that it held a mysterious power that she might be able to absorb or somehow turn to her advantage. She pondered its sleek beauty; maybe the tube was some sort of weapon or communication device.

"Up on the table, Dunya. I know that you heard me." Matuk advanced, his lined face menacing in the half-light.

Dunya pulled the cylinder from her pocket and aimed it at her employer, hoping that it would launch itself, ignite, explode, or otherwise reveal its potential.

Bewildered, Matuk stared at the tube thrust toward him like a laser. Dunya's hairy face was expectant but her anticipation quickly changed to disappointment as the tube lay solid, warm and inert in her hand.

Matuk's legs went wonky and jerked to the side. His face contorted as horrible choking sounds forced themselves from his turkey-gobbled throat. Dunya froze, pinned by her weapon's latent power, convinced that she'd caused the Collector's spasm.

Shocked by her newfound authority, Dunya thrust the lipstick toward her victim and waggled it menacingly. This caused an even more appalling show of noise and hysteria as Matuk staggered against the table, clutching his stomach. Water ran from his eyes and his jagged teeth bared themselves to the firelight, hard yellow kernels as raggedly uneven as a dried ear of Indian corn.

Firelight burst from the grate, illuminating Dunya's fierce countenance as a steady hissing sound filled her ears. She thought that a black rain cloud coalesced beneath her feet and lifted her up.

This is it! Me prayers 'ave been answered. I've been blessed with the power to command the devil 'isself!

The rain cloud was just one of Matuk's stinking hounds come to knock her off her feet and savage her with its fangs. The Master ceased laughing, wiped his cheeks, and gasped for breath. Dunya fell beneath the woolly hound and sensed blood seeping from the punctures on her thin arms. The impotent tube toppled to the rug and rolled silently away.

Still chuckling (the sound of a cantankerous outboard motor churning up sludge from a lake bed), Matuk took the floor in two great strides and heaved Dunya onto the table. He smiled as he strapped her down, ha-ha-ha'd while she began to weep, clapped her furry shoulder in praise of her joke while wrestling a pair of stirrups from beneath the table.

"Ankles up!" Matuk patted the stirrups. "By the gods, I didn't know you were capable of humor, you hideous sexless beast!"

Dunya searched the floor for her treasure. Her keen ears strained to catch the returning Radhe's bellow from the wood, a savior sound that would draw Matuk's attentions from her, but there was only the steamy gurgle of panting dogs, Matuk's insane giggling, and the snapping, sparking fire.

Matuk belted Dunya's ankles and reached to lift her skirts.

Double and triple feck! Who's going ta 'elp me now?

"Dog-face!" Meertham's voice sailed up the tower stairs, as welcome as an approaching Viking ship to one previously left behind.

"Dog-face!" he hollered again. Dunya recognized the effort it took to raise his voice and force it up the stairwell, but Matuk's hearing was less acute and he did not hear the strain belying Meertham's cry.

Matuk paused, one finger on his chin in a gruesome parody of thoughtfulness.

"I think we'll try something different this time. You and Meertham are both getting old. Should either one of you disappear, well, well, I'd have no one left to attend me. Imagine the sheer brawn and servile nature of your offspring!"

Matuk whistled two notes and one of his dour hounds slunk out the tower door, and melted down the stairs. Matuk rustled through his notebooks, collecting his equipment.

He addressed Tirai's ghost as though she stood before him in her pink peignoir, smelling of perfume, tiny and radiantly alive. "How would you like a new baby, my loving, vengeful harpy?"

Meertham climbed the stairs by lifting one sluggish leg at a time, nipped into action by the devil at his heels. The henchman dragged himself into the Master's apartment, swallowing the blood that welled in his throat.

Dunya quivered on the table. Meertham wanted to laugh and cry. His enslaved friend was such an unlikely heroine; brown and furry in her antiquated gown, apron, and lace-edged cap, like a costumed Labrador at a child's tea party. He'd stupidly assumed that Dunya would be safe while he lay abed waiting for death to take him, surrounded by trash and treasures. Then he remembered that Radhe's earlier disappearance sparked the housemaid's first breeding. Matuk's daughter had been caught in a poacher's trap. She'd worked at the trap for days (after inadvertently killing the men who arrived to claim her), finally managing to bend metal enough to free her mangled leg and limp back to the manor, where she prowled the perimeter of the meadow, crying like a puppy for days on end.

Meertham's slow brain began to see that she was not safe.

Radhe's absence left a gaping hole; Matuk's parasitic sickness required a host. Dunya's body was smaller and more frail than Radhe's; she could endure much less torture. So Meertham heaved himself out of bed, barking up his guts and wiping away the sludge that trickled from the corner of his mouth. He lurched downstairs, tracing the well-worn path through the great hall and past the armory door.

He called her as he staggered through the manse but she did not answer.

Standing now in the presence of his master, Meertham, drained of strength and drive, felt it rewarm and stir, churning like lava in the bowels of the Devil's Playground.

"How perfect. You arrived just in time to partake of a tasty bit of crumpet, or should I say dog biscuit?" Matuk laughed vilely. "Right you are, my dear. They do make a handsome couple." Matuk stood ready, his notebooks heaped on the table around Dunya's bum.

"Will you perform on command?" Matuk's eyes slid over Meertham's wasted body in a way that set his henchman's flesh on fire. "Or shall I take your seed by force?"

The scalpel in Matuk's hand glinted in the firelight and Meertham saw the arrows, lined up and ready, each one tipped, no doubt, in organic, slow-acting toxins that would draw out his surrender and eventual death with agonizing sloth.

The fire's yellow glow also illuminated the long-handled poleax clenched in Meertham's fist, its sharp hook keen for the feel of ripping flesh.

"A battle to the death, then," Matuk leered. He sought and easily found an old aerosol can of the etherine he used to subdue uncooperative captives. He advanced fearlessly, bloodlust in his eyes and predicted: "You'll go down quickly after a noble fight."

Meertham clenched his teeth to keep the pain at bay while he stood his ground, enormous and threatening, the poleax swaying in his hand. Hook or blade, he pondered. First, he would release Dunya.

Inch by inch he shuffled toward the table. Matuk lay in wait with a cobra's calm, a wicked smile spasming across his lips. "Mount your bitch, good man."

Meertham's emotional register had few notes, but warning tones blared within his head. He could barely coordinate the muscles required to remain ambulant, much less devise a strategy to free Dunya without getting himself sprayed with arrows or chemicals in the process.

"Master," Meertham lied, "there's fresh catch in the sack." Grainy vomit roiled in his gut; he could not spew in the Master's chamber without risking his neck and Dog-face's, too. Meertham swallowed, groping for the lurid details to beguile Matuk's black heart.

"Pretty wee lass. Brown as a berry with a voice from the doves. Me, I could roll her into a ball and tuck her under my arm."

"You don't require this creature's help for such a tiny treat," Matuk scoffed, rolling the hem of Dunya's gown between his fingers.

Dunya whined; she could not help it.

"Aye, true enough." Meertham's gaze was riveted by the Collector's thumb, stroking the scalpel's face. That he did not bleed signaled a dull blade. The cuts would be rough and require a sawing motion—no clean sweep here.

"Looks like she's swallowed a sackful of angry cats, though. Big belly out to here," Meertham feigned ease, though the effort of it sent sweat galloping over the crease in his fat neck.

Matuk's eyes enlivened with glittering black flame. "I ought to snip one of the plums from your ballock sack," he mused, though Meertham sensed his Master's lust for breeding waver.

"Still"—he rubbed a spidery hand over Dunya's exposed, furred knee—"there's little reason to rush your pleasure. If you can find it in all that hair!" He flicked Dunya's leg and she flinched, expecting blows.

"Come now." Matuk advanced, etherine and scalpel at the ready. "Take your bride."

Meertham let swing the poleax. The blade hissed whisper soft to land before Matuk's left foot, poised to rise from the dingy rug.

"I think," Meertham wheezed, "that I've need of help. T'is not my job to wrestle snakes and bulging bellies."

Matuk paused, steadying the impulse to raise the canister of etherine and saturate his henchman's brutish face. Meertham had never once challenged him, even though he held all the power and could snap Matuk's neck as easily as he'd snap his fingers.

"You dare to contradict me, boy?"

"Aye," Meertham said. He hunched his shoulders, curving his neck and spine to diminish himself before his lord. "But only for want of saving your prize."

Spots swam before his lowered eyes. A chunk of phlegm lodged in his throat, stealing his breath. If he coughed it loose, a river of blood was sure to follow. Now that he danced along the void's edge himself, the stench of his dying thick in the air, he too could hear Tirai's voice, crying out from the grave.

"She calls you," Meertham muttered.

Matuk's withered body tensed; his eyes darted through the shadows in search of his wife's haunting specter.

"Tirai?" Matuk quivered like a lapdog.

Meertham lifted his head and dropped the poleax. This was to be his one moment of bravery in a lifetime of cowardice. He sidestepped Matuk and placed a heavy comforting hand on Dunya's arm as he fumbled with the wide belts and freed her.

"Dog-face," Meertham urged, his red-rimmed eyes fastened firm on her own. "Go downstairs." Dunya obediently slipped from the room, Meertham's gaze locked on her departing backside.

Matuk gripped his head between his hands and shouted, keeling away from the window and toward the fire as if to sear Tirai's voice from his mind.

"I am lord and master of this house," he shouted into the leaping flames.

Tirai's ghost billowed around him, her milky hair streaming, the coals of her dead eyes burning with unearthly fire. She had a hundred flailing arms and beat her husband with fleshless hands, yowling with rage and sorrow, "My child is dead! My child is dead!"

Meertham limped from the room and took the slick tower steps one by one. He heard Dunya's voice whispering behind a closed door and the other, soft and concerned, that answered it. He felt the gust of cool, fresh air that swirled up the stairwell and gauged from the advancing footfalls that a stranger had arrived.

There, he could just make it round the bend and disappear into the darkened hall. The shadows were legion and welcoming, blanketing him beneath their black skirts, dousing the fading light in his small eyes. The cold marble soothed his fevered skin. There was no view of the sea from the unused hearth and the cobwebs were thick and choking but it was a hidden place, safe and tucked away.

Meertham coughed once; the great clot flew into his mouth and he spat upon the stones. The blood was hot against his lips as it spilled from them, steady and pulsing onto the white marble. Dunya's kiss still lingered on his mouth. Even the gushing blood could not wash it away.

He pressed clumsy, rough fingers to his lips and smiled. "Dogface," he whispered, and then, said no more.

33

LIBERTÉ AND VENGEANCE

SORYK LEAPT FROM THE GROUND where he'd fallen, his nerves tingling and raw. The woman had urged "Save the babies," instilling his mission within him. He would not be afraid, he scolded himself, even as his heart banged against his sternum.

Now he faced the enemy. Someone so villainous that he would slice up his kin, use their bones to prettify his lawn, and savor the stench of corpse flesh wafting over the meadow. Weatherbeaten pikes ringed the meadow, each one topped with a somatic's severed head. Distorted by time and sun, the faces of the dead contorted in pain. Some had bits of shoulder or bared bleached collarbones hanging below the severed vertebrae. One was the top half of some half-human creature, its barrel-shaped ribs naked beside the twisted long bones of its remaining arm.

He untied the sash at his waist and gave his blade a few experimental swings, getting used to the feel of his hand upon the hilt. Soryk traversed the broad meadow in a matter of minutes, translucent yellow chunks of salt crumbling beneath his boots.

Naked of bell, knocker, chain, or window, the closed gate repelled intrusion. A serpentine crest of lichen-splashed stone and pointed iron spikes, the fence loomed and was upon him. A garish interpretation of a medieval castle, the Collector's manor sprawled as repulsively lovely as boiled and polished bones.

"Gatekeeper!" he bellowed in pitch-perfect emulation of his pimp and benefactor, Chen. Imperious, sneering, saturated with privilege, Soryk rattled the gate, demanding entrance. "Open for me!" A frightful creature limped to the gate, peering between the bars with suspicious eyes, his wrinkled lips white with scum. Soryk seethed with impatience as the old monster fussed with his ring of keys, chomped spongy gums, and cranked the winch to lower the gate.

"Crick-crack," sang the odious being, his voice warbling like an old woman's. "Buying or selling today?" The drawbridge sagged and the Gatekeeper shuffled forward, scanning the air with ancient eyes, his stringy hair brushed from his face as if readying for a visit from a good-looking guest.

"Neither," Soryk replied. "Walk closer, so that you may know me."

An unholy stench met Soryk's nostrils as the Gatekeeper eddied forward, his lumpy limbs dragging the paving stones that marked Matuk's inner sanctum.

"Cripes," Soryk coughed, covering his nose with the back of one hand, the wine goblet of the ruby winking in the light.

"It's you, is it? Come to see his papa after such long years. He'll be in want of money for his dirty pictures."

Soryk grimaced; the nasty beast was not just filthy, but strapped-to-the-table mad in the bargain.

"Let's have a look then." Gatekeeper was drawn to the ruby, which so looked like fresh blood it made him smack his lips. He took Soryk's hand, his skinny anteater's tongue flicking over the surface of the jewel, tasting treasure.

"What did the Master name this gem when he bought it from the pasha?" His eye swiveled loosely in its socket; liquid pooled in the hanging pocket of his drooping, red lower lid. Gatekeeper's tongue swiped the back of Soryk's hand, drenching it in stinking, carrion-scented slime.

"Urgh." Soryk withdrew his hand, repulsed.

"It's Tirai's Heart you wear on your hand. Tirai's Heart, bought for a song from her madam. Ring more dear than girl!" He laughed as if sneezing into a bucket of water. "Your mum came even cheaper! Cheaper chippy!"

"Let me pass." Soryk glowered, his fingers hovering over the cool blade.

"Hasn't seen his mum in a leap year of blue moons, buried beneath the blue room, she is," the creature snuffled. "Crick-crack," he jibed, grinning to show the broken brown nubs of his few remaining teeth.

"Let me pass!" Soryk hissed.

Suddenly, the fulsome Gatekeeper was upon him. "Password! The master insists. What's the magic word?" His hot breath punched Soryk in the face and he recoiled, brandishing his Magar blade.

"You dare to challenge Matuk's heir?" The knife met resistance within the seething folds of the creature's oatmeal-textured, dirt-spackled neck and Gatekeeper withdrew, nattering under his breath as he slunk off to the gatehouse.

Soryk sped past the creature's smutty hovel and through a tunnel shot through with murder holes. He faced massive double doors bolted and rusted shut beneath a lintel carved of flaking stone. Stone roses climbed the frame, pricked with petrified thorns while dwarves mined a miniature region of Glass Mountains. Upon closer inspection, he could see that the roses wore animal faces and the dwarves carried enormous pruning shears with which to clip them. Soryk shuddered and tried the door; the heavy planks did not give.

Lacking any tool with which to inflict major damage, he ran the manor's perimeter, his gaze flowing over the windowless white marble pocked and stained by sun, salt, and wind. The entire ground floor was sealed in, the windows small, round, and caked with a cushiony accumulation of grime.

Neglect had served as gardener and wilderness as groundskeeper. Discarded, half-chiseled marble blocks spilled across the high, rough grass. Stagnant fountains ran green with algae and crawled with massive, amber snails. The seasonless gray day stretched timeless and deceiving. Whether it was noon or nearing dusk he could not be sure, but it felt as though each minute that he delayed—running his fingers along the veined stone looking for chinks or traps to be sprung—was struck as though upon a great gong.

There! A narrow path snaked, the grass worn thin and broken beneath the weight of trudging boots. A small mound of broken marble too imperfect for use in the manor had been roughly mortared together to make an igloo for corpses. The stench from the charnel house drove him on, coughing and enraged, to the small wooden door imbedded within the white marble. No means of entry here either. Soryk stood panting, hands on his knees as he muttered, "Shit, shit, shit."

There was no keyhole through which to peer, just a depression like an inverted, metal pyramid—the all-seeing eye. Fine layers of hammered steel were locked in an intricate embrace, sticky with a dense coagulation of unknown origin. Soryk ran his hands along the wood, searching for a place to pry. He wedged his knife into the hairline seam between door and frame and almost bent his blade trying to jimmy it open. Soryk kicked the door, a surly gesture, and withdrew to consider his options. The woman-voice in his head yammered constantly, nagging him as he scanned the area for clues.

"Argh!" He dropped to his knees and clamped hands to ears, which only amplified the sound and made it worse. "Shut up!" he screamed. "I'm doing the best that I can!"

You must do better.

"I am handling this," he insisted aloud. "Let me work." *She* responded by flooding his mind with the old, persistent nightmares. He felt a strange tingling in his chest, *in his breasts*, and his hand gripped the blade so tightly that it lost sensation.

Clouds swirled frothy overhead as the failing light further diminished. Soryk had the sensation that he was trapped within the twin lobes of an hourglass, the trickling grains about to loose their load and bury him. He crawled through the weeds blindly. Something hard snapped beneath his knee and he reached into the dirt, withdrawing the desiccated shards of a small bone. Feeling through the close-knitted grasses, he found others, all broken, all stained and each of them identically severed. Mesmerized by the shard of bone in his hand, a vague thought flickered in the back of his mind, a memory itch needing to be scratched. The solution was hidden somewhere in the real world, and he could not reach through dreams and ether to access it. A riddle, a story—the conundrum of the unkey for an unpickable lock. He turned a bone shard in his hands, smooth and globular on one end, rough but clean cut on the other, the exact size of his pinky finger. Was it a finger bone? He held it against his hand and compared the two. Indeed, it was a small, fine-jointed bone, axed off the hand.

He stared at the door frame, rough cut, not pretty like the lintel over the main doors. This one was crudely carved—practice work for a mason's apprentice still years from mastery. A ceramic picture tile was mortised between the stones forming the stiles alongside the door. Soryk peered closer, straining his eyes in the waning light.

A little girl stood in old-fashioned peasant dress, her head covered by a kerchief, her skirt and kirtle patched and torn. She held a half-eaten bread loaf, a jug, and the slender frame of a small wooden chair hung over her arm. Seven birds circled overhead and a small pair of scissors and a needle trailing thread bordered the picture.

Puzzle pieces shuffled themselves and clicked into place. He frowned and thumped his head to jog them into rightful order, recalling those little toys with the interconnected tiles that had to be shifted within a frame to make a picture. *The problem with those,* he mused, *is that's there's always a missing tile. The picture can never be complete for its design does not allow it.*

So where's the missing tile? The woman voice was irritated, insistent. Desperation clawed up Soryk's clothes like some skittish wild thing. A wan light caught and flickered in one of the high tower windows where the vague outline of a pacing form filled the frame before passing on.

Come on now, so close I can taste the wine in the golden goblets, feel the air moved by the ravens' wings as they brush by my cheek. Finding the memory was like hunting for a grain of sand in a bucket of mud; Soryk gnashed his teeth in frustration. His brain hurt.

The pictures dredged themselves from the pit of his subconscious. One by one, they slid and snapped into formation, and the answer revealed itself. He did not think, did not pause to moan or marvel at what he must do. There was no time for hesitation. The chopping stone sat low and innocuous on a weedy hillock, its surface scored with cuts.

He'd take the left because his right was stronger, more accurate when doing the dirty deed. A rational man and one disinterested in appeals to foggy, foreign, or forgotten deities, Soryk had never once prayed. Rolling up his coat sleeve and spreading his fingers across the cold stone, the words "Jerusha, protect me" formed on his lips as he raised the Magar blade high overhead. It had to be taken in a single strike. He curled up his thumb and four fingers, leaving the pinky exposed.

Then the finger was still and pooling ink in the twilight. Soryk saw stars. Keeping his hand high overhead to slow the copious bleeding, he rooted through his rucksack until he found a cotton shirt to tie around the wound. He thought he might vomit from the pain setting his nerves alight like strings of roadway flares.

He picked up his severed finger, bile roiling in his gut, and swore vengeance upon the cosmos if this did not work.

The lock was caked with blood; he could smell it now, peering into its steely heart. Like butter and silk and all things effortlessly smooth, he slipped the flesh from his finger bone, exposing the bone's rough-cut end. Urgency screamed in his head, rattled his bones, and convulsed his bowels. Blood greased the lock, the bone gripped and held, infinitely fragile. A series of hollow tick-tick-ticks and the door popped open with a sigh, as if rigged on hydraulic hinges. Frosty, damp air rushed from the corridor, a collection of runaway phantoms.

Clutching his severed finger and its loose sheath of skin, Soryk wedged a stone beneath the door to prop it open and edged into the corridor. The dank, musty air smelled of wet and rot. Condensation gathered and ran. Everything was quiet but for the sputtering oil lamps dotting the hall and the sounds of his breathing as he attempted in vain to control his shaking with slow, measured inhalations.

The corridor split into two directions. One branch veered off down a few steps to what looked like the main house. He glimpsed cavernous, dim rooms and the hesitant flicker of distant lamps. Winding stairs lured Soryk into the tower, intent on finding the occupant sequestered in that high room he'd glimpsed from the outside.

Hurry, hurry! The woman-voice buzzed inside his head, high-pitched and desperate. *Find them!* Soryk passed several small doors, each closed and barred from the outside. What began as the occasional splatter upon the white stone became a series of steady drops; something brown and staining, splashed here, smeared there. Advancing up the stairway, Soryk's anger reawakened.

He has my children. Those two that haunted his waking hours and colored his days with deep remorse. The dreams, the nightmares, and voices in his head: false memories that proved real. They were his children, too.

Rage stoked itself into an all-consuming fire, filling him with its heat, reddening his vision until like a mad bull, he readied to charge the door, break it down, and destroy everything on the other side. The beautiful Magar blade slid from its sheath into his waiting palm, warm and gleaming with death's urgent promise.

Wait. A calm voice, redolent with surety and passion filled his mind. He tossed his head, shaking free the cloying, insistent word.

"This is my fight," Soryk hissed. "I will claim my prize."

No, this is our *fight. Bred and birthed of my womb were they, flesh of* my *flesh, not yours. I will take him. It is my right, and my duty. The prize will be mine.*

Fire engulfed him in waves. Darkness mottled his sight as he staggered backward, tumbling down the tower stairs. Pressure built in Soryk's heart and organs as an influx of hormones flooded his body, sending chemical destruction to his male tissues, softening his features and erasing his masculinity. *I will not succumb,* he insisted as the heavy, obliterating sleep rolled in to suck him into its depths. Soryk collapsed on the landing and dragged himself into a small alcove, arms and legs splayed and bruised.

"I will not give in," he moaned, and the Magar blade clattered from his fingers onto the stones. Feeble lamplight waned as he spiraled down a black tunnel, away from the sweet voices that materialized in the gloom and hovered above him like bees enticed to honey, and the gentle, female hands that took his arms and dragged him, unwilling, inside the tower room.

Sorykah woke crushed to a skinny bosom smelling of mildew and spilled tea. She was in a powder blue room that looked as if someone had regurgitated rococo curlicues over every surface and her left hand throbbed in pain. She gaped in astonishment at the crude bandage on her pinky finger.

"What in hell has happened to me?"

"I knew you'd come! I knew it! Didn't I say so, Dunya? Didn't I tell you that faith would work its miracles and bring us relief? Praise Jerusha!"

Sorykah pushed away clinging fragments of change-sleep and tried to speak though muffled by a pair of pythonlike arms that squeezed as if to press the life essence from her.

"Ye'll crush 'im to death that way, then 'e won't be any good to us at all," complained a gruff sort of woman's voice.

The arms released her and Sorykah sat up, rubbing the sleep from her eyes.

"That's no man, Dunya dear. This is my mistress." For the first time, Sorykah took in her nanny's beaming face, thinned by hunger and pinched with suffering, but beloved all the same. She smothered Nels in a long hug and the women laughed and rocked back and forth, pulling back at the same moment to exclaim, "I thought you were dead!"

"Ye thought her dead?" Dunya was irate. "I built me faith on ye and ye lied!" The dog-faced girl huffed, crossing furry arms over her chest.

"My child, faith is never a lie. Belief can't erase truth. As Brother Halloran, the highest-scoring pitcher in the Fathers of Charity Hospital baseball league famously said, 'I cover my bases, that's all.' " Nels smiled again but her eyes were watery and the apples in her rosy cheeks were absent.

"What happened to me?" Fireworks of pain sent showers of brittle, white-hot stars through Sorykah's arm.

"Ye picked the lock, ye bonny soul!" Dunya crowed.

Nels took Sorykah's good hand in her own. "You did the right thing, my friend. It was a small price to pay. Naught but pennies!"

Sorykah grappled for a hold on her memories, catching the tail of her arm raised high, the crunch of cut bone, and the ting of her Magar blade against the chopping stone.

"I did this?" Her face crumpled in shock.

"You did, praise Jerusha. Look." Nels brandished a gold needle and a snippet of red thread. "I found this in your coat. It was just threaded through your hem, waiting to be found. Whoever put it there expected you to use it."

Nels tenderly unwrapped Sorykah's bandages. Her pinky jutted at an odd, cadaverous angle. Lavender beside the other fingers, it wore a collar of neat red stitches.

"I thought it might grow back," Nels said in apology. She

looked at Dunya, poised on tiptoe behind Sorykah. "Go on," she urged, "it's your story."

"Now, Mistress, I suppose ye'll be wanting to know about those babes o' yours." Dunya's voice was low and rough with a suppressed territorial growl.

Sorykah's heart skipped a beat or three, jerking her out of her body and the present before it jump-started with a healthy kick and slammed her back into reality. "Yes, please" was all she could muster.

Nels's thin face was fearful. Dunya stamped her foot and thrust out her deformed jaw in defiance, but for all her bravado, she could not quite disguise the panic skittering across her features.

Sorykah heard it—the faint, high ringing of a bell, tinkling with annoyance. "What's that sound?"

"The Master calls me," Dunya whispered as if entranced.

"It's *him*, isn't it?" Sorykah cut her eyes at Dunya. "Minion of the devil that left a trail of destruction from here to Neubonne!" The Magar blade rose of its own accord to dance in the air between the women.

"Sorykah, she is our savior. She's the one that kept the children safe from him, waiting for you to come and fetch them home. Blessed child, she is a good egg, this one." Nels pressed Sorykah's arm to her side and held it firm.

"My children," Sorykah choked on the words.

Dunya said, "Locked in the kitchen where I left 'em. 'Ole and 'ealthy."

Sorykah pulled Nels to her feet and squeezed Dunya's shoulder in silent thanks. "Go there and wait. If I succeed, I'll come for you. If the bell continues to ring, take the children and go. I left the door open." Sorykah worked Chen's ruby ring over her joint and offered it to Nels. "You can use this to bribe the Gatekeeper. I have a feeling that he wants it very much. Go to the Erun city, and Queen Sidra the Lovely will take care of you. She is a gentlewoman; she won't turn you away."

"What are ye going to do?" Dunya said.

"I intend to extract my payment from your master. And then"—she dropped the bag and coat that hampered her, and rolled and flexed her shoulders in preparation—"we are going home."

Nels made a sign of blessing in the air over Sorykah. Dunya visibly quavered. She'd sacrificed her own freedom to care for Meertham. Now Sorykah was here, wiry and dirt-smudged from her travels, the righteous fire of retribution blazing in her eyes. Dunya could brave the tower stairs, face her master alongside this fierce woman, and release years of pent-up rage to aid in his destruction, but dogs are loyal even to those who beat them. Dunya had unearthed a wide streak of cowardice by returning to the manor. Nels termed it compassion and lauded her for her empathy but Dunya knew herself a weakling. She would return to the kitchen with Nels to cower and outwait fate and she hated herself for it. As much pain as Matuk had dished up and stuffed down her throat over the years, as much wickedness and murderous evil as she'd played accessory to, she did not want to be an accomplice to his death.

"Take the tower stairs," she whispered, her brown eyes liquid with pity. "The Master is old and slow but the evil in 'im is enough to ruin ye in one stroke. 'E's got 'is dogs up there for company. Take care o' them first or ye'll have no chance. They'll tear your throat out as soon as look at ye." With this, she clasped her skirts in furry hands and was gone.

"Nels, follow her. Hurry now." Sorykah shoved her nanny out the door. Her mouth was full of injunctions, orders, wishes, and prayers, but she bit them back. Nels paused in the doorway, a twinkle in her eye, and Sorykah envied the certainty of her faith.

"Into the fray, then," and she too was gone, chasing Dunya down the stairs, invigorated by hope.

For the second time that hour, Sorykah climbed the tower stairs, Magar blade thirsting for a bloodbath. A torch burned outside the door and she took this in hand, pausing to press her ear to the wood and listen to the silence on the other side. *It must be done.* Soryk's voice resounded inside her head, grave and certain.

As she clicked the latch, she heard the dogs rise to investigate, their great chops whuffing. They smelled an intruder and as soon as she was through, they were upon her—two enormous brindled beasts, their clanking jaws foamy with hanging runners of spit. Teeth clamped down on the soft meat of her calf and Sorykah plied the torch, firing up one monster until it ran howling, smoke curling from its charred pelt. Leaping and growling, the second dog knocked Sorykah on her back and dived for her throat. She raised her left arm to block it and curled up to protect herself as the right hand jabbed upward, slicing into the animal's shoulder. She cut through to the bone, and blood sprayed them both as they tussled but the dog was undeterred, snapping its jaws, trying to get them around Sorykah's head and bite down as if popping a large rubber ball. Teeth sheared across her scalp as the dog straddled her, gnawing at her head.

Tingling starbursts that signaled the change began to bubble in her blood. *Not now!* Sorykah heaved against the dog's enormous, muscled frame and managed to free her arm just enough to raise her blade and pierce the dog's side. Yelping, the dog gave Sorykah's head a final desperate shake and collapsed, panting heavily.

"You're quite the fighter." Matuk the Collector spoke. Sorykah rolled onto hands and knees, blood pouring from her lacerated scalp.

"I would go so far as to deem you a worthy adversary, but we're certainly not on equal terms." The shadows formed themselves into the outline of a man as he stepped into the firelight. "Still, you've come this far, and that's a feat of which to be proud." Matuk crouched just beyond reach of her blade and for the first time, Sorykah could finally see the face of her tormentor.

He stood, gesturing to the wingback chair beside the hearth. "Come and sit a moment. Let me have a look at you."

Sorykah rose with caution, every nerve and fiber in her body burning. She'd managed to control the change enough to keep it at bay for the moment, but it lurked within her tissues, restless to assert itself.

Matuk peered from the window into the deep forest. He was

several inches shorter than Sorykah, thin and hard looking, as if the skin rode too close to the bones beneath. His greasy black hair was streaked with gray and his back was bowed.

Sorykah limped to the chair, needing a minute to recover from the attack. Blood trickled steadily down the back of her neck and slithered beneath her shirt collar. One of the dogs menaced her from the far corners of the room but Matuk waved his hand and it grew silent. Sorykah surveyed the chaos in the tower room. Broken glass showered the rugs; newspaper clippings and pages torn from books lay strewn across the floor beneath shelves crammed with hand-bound journals. Discarded dishes were heaped on Matuk's dining table and the mushy carcass of some large bird lay abandoned beneath it. The feathered arrows Sorykah had plucked from Radhe's back were bundled into wide metal quivers mounted alongside the open window and an enormous crossbow rested against the wall.

Worse than those was the stained, narrow table with its gutters and buckets, the assortment of knives and steely cutting instruments lined up and ready to flense Matuk's next victim. Cobwebbed laboratory equipment crowded the room, untidy tangles of electrical cabling and wire, outdated, dusty machinery and teetering stacks of Petri dishes. Sorykah guessed that Matuk had dispensed with the rigors of research when madness took over.

"You're injured," Matuk announced, his back to her. He was so filled with hubris that he did not believe that she would attack him.

Sorykah's hand throbbed. She stared at the clumsily repaired finger, a bony twig and its fleshy sheath. Even if the muscles and tendons managed to repair themselves, she could do nothing about the haphazardly cut bone. Grimacing, she yanked the finger from its stitches and tossed it into the fire. The smell of burning human flesh filled the room.

"Tell me, who have you come all this way to avenge? Your sister? Your father? Are you one of mine?" Matuk tittered, as if the whole charade of niceties was endlessly amusing. "Did I bed and abandon your mother years ago and now you've come to claim what you believe to be your rightful inheritance? My children are many but only my son Chen is heir to Tirai Industries and its holdings."

"And your daughter?" Sorykah asked, holding her left arm upright to further slow its oozing. The torch she'd lost in her scuffle with the dogs lay smoldering and now the rug beneath it had begun to blaze.

"My daughter?" Matuk placed his hands along the windowsill and leaned out into the night. Sorykah moved toward him, her hands outstretched. She could already feel his small shoulders beneath her palms as she gave one good push and sent him flying. Matuk whirled and delivered a solid uppercut to her jaw. Sorykah fell back, clutching her mouth. No one had ever punched her before and it stung both her face and her pride. She rubbed her cheeks and spit out a couple of broken teeth.

"You bastard," she snarled through a mouthful of blood.

Matuk grabbed his bow and notched an arrow, aiming for her heart. "My daughter is an aberration, like all of her kind. It is my duty to cleanse her of disease, to ensure that my line is free of my grandfather's sickness. Monsters will not run my empire into rack and ruin." He launched the arrow.

Sorykah scuttled to the right and the whistling arrow snicked across her bicep and snapped against the hearthstones. Agile and quick-moving for a man of his age, Matuk reached for another arrow. In books and films, the villains and heroes always wasted too much time with final explanations and reasoning, but this was no movie. Sorykah wasn't going to dillydally around, entertaining the ramblings of a madman. She leapt forward, body extended as she sailed into him, knocking him flat. Matuk tried to stab her with an arrow point but Sorykah grabbed his wrist, diverting his attack. Her body was tingling and she fought hard against the change but lost. It happened so quickly that she was awake as Soryk emerged, giving her the added strength and power needed to slam Matuk's head against the dissection table and wrestle the arrow from his grasp. Together, Matuk and Soryk/ah rolled toward the open floor-to-ceiling window, struggling for supremacy.

The sleep hovered like a first-time referee ready to yank one of the players out of the game. Sorykah couldn't see, but she felt Matuk's hands against her and heard Soryk's deeper voice, snarling and angry as he goaded the old man closer to his death.

"Wait," Matuk hissed, cuffing Soryk across the ear with his ringed knuckles. The jewelry sliced open more flesh and in the millisecond that Soryk took to acknowledge his pain, Matuk had bested him.

The Collector slithered from beneath Soryk and snatched a knife, holding the triangular, serrated blade mere centimeters from Soryk's eyeball. "What's happening to you?"

Soryk said nothing.

"God's teeth," Matuk breathed. "Look at you."

Soryk wanted to crawl away and reclaim the blurry stretch of time between his tumble down the tower stairs and discovering himself here, bleeding and battered within the Collector's lair.

"You are a Trader." The old man's voice was thick with want.

"Tried and tested," Soryk replied, knocking away the scalpel poised in Matuk's grip as he scampered away to catch his breath and regain his senses.

Matuk frowned, his calculating eyes watchful. He was already salivating over the prospect of getting this invader up on his table, exploring his capricious organs. Better yet, he'd drain the body of blood to concoct an endless series of potions and steal its precious secrets.

"Why are you here?" Matuk mused, as if he had all the time in the world. Didn't he sense the scissors closing around his thread? The Collector's life was about to be cut short.

Soryk snarled in reply, cagey and watchful, awaiting the triumphal moment.

"The winged girl?" Matuk surveyed his attacker with gleaming eyes. "No, she doesn't seem like one of yours. Have you come to reclaim one of my impaled friends out on the lawn? You can take your pick," he laughed. "They're all equally dead."

Soryk growled but held his ground. If he went for the old man now, he'd lose the advantage, might wind up slashed and bleeding to the death at that monster's feet. Soryk's fingers tightened upon the hilt of his Magar blade. The woman-voice urged him forward with fatal intention. *Kill him kill him kill him.*

Soryk presumed that he was a man of peace. Death was not something he took lightly. He would get what he came for and get out, leaving this madman to his amusements. He'd leave Matuk alive and preserve the unblemished patina of his own nonmurdering soul. If only that damned voice would leave him alone . . .

"The children," said Soryk.

"Children?" Matuk spun from the window. "Ahh," he purred with an almost sexual satisfaction. "My boy found them for me. Fine, fat lads they were. One fair, one dark." Matuk sucked his lips as if tonguing the flesh from a roasted capon.

Give him to me. She was insistent, unrelenting.

"I was waiting for their talents to reveal themselves but now that you're here, I think you'll be very intrigued by my work. Perhaps you'd like to have a seat and watch?" Matuk grinned, moving toward the dingy bell pull dangling beside the autopsy table.

Give him to me. Kill him. Now now now!

Soryk crumpled. Lights pulsed before his eyes; the change surged through him like a lightning strike, sure and electrifying. His heart throbbed with effort, consciousness danced before him, taunting and elusive as he fought for control. Something, *someone*, was rising inside of him, unfurling enormous wings, a dreadful lamia trumpeting its battle cry and veiling the light with spreading shadows as it silenced him.

Sorykah pounced upon Matuk and knocked him to the floor. They flipped and fought, Sorykah maddened by rage and slashing at any portions of the Collector's flesh that her blade could reach. She punched him three times fast and felt his jaw splinter around her fist.

"You will not take my children from me," she spat, clocking him again in the soft parts and delivering a great blow to his temple with the hilt of her knife. She would not pummel him to death like some immoral brute. Sorykah crouched panting near the fire, hands on her spine. Matuk wormed across the floor as her back was turned and pushed her into the grate. She took a faceful of hot, smoking embers but shielded herself from the worst of it. Searing pain blazed from her bitten arm, extinguishing the last of her reason and sanity.

Blinded by ash and fury, Sorykah threw down her blade and snatched up an iron poker. She javelined it across the room to impale Matuk where he stood, gloating in sick triumph. He folded in two and toppled to the ground, blood spilling out to soak the carpet. Sorykah collected her knife and wiped the ash from her eyes. She stood over him, peering down at the miserable wreck of something that had perhaps once passed for a human being. He spluttered in astonishment, his eyes wide within a mass of crinkled skin.

"Why did you come here? Who are you?" Matuk rasped, the death rattle already gurgling in his throat.

Sorykah grasped the handle of the Magar blade, muscles taut, beaded sweat and blood glistening on her forehead and splashed across her bared arms. Smoke and soot blackened her face and the jagged edges of her broken teeth shone wet with bubbling, bloodied saliva.

"I am vengeance," she spat and slit his throat, grunting with effort as the blade sliced through bone and ancient, fibrous tissues. Matuk shuddered beneath her, foam gurgling from his repulsive mouth.

Radhe and Chen's father, and Shanxi's brother, emperor and master of the industrial Tirai giant, lay dying. Sorykah slipped her sword from Matuk's sundered viscera, remorseless. She'd kept the blade all these months, saving it for some imagined exercise in medieval chivalry or self-defense. A pretty gift given to her by the amoral Trader man who had fathered her children. He'd been a collector of sorts, too, moneyed and careless. The Magar blade, several hundred years old and worth its weight in gold, meant little to him; he already had so much. It was a token payment for her body, her time, her willingness to disappear from his life.

Matuk's body had already begun to crumple and settle into lifelessness. He'd died and she hadn't even been paying attention. Sorykah found a grimy rag and attempted to cleanse her hands of mortal wrongdoing. Though she culled fierce satisfaction from the sight of the Collector's blood beneath her nails, she did not want to frighten her children by appearing as a sin-soaked murderess, dressed to the teeth in their captor's blood and guts.

She prodded Matuk's body with the corner of an old book.

"My friend," she addressed her adversary with ironic satisfaction, "you are well and truly dead."

Sorykah wiped her Magar blade on the tatty rug and glowered at the bested dogs crouching in the corners. She stalked the narrow white corridors of the manor, noting the faded grandeur of the dust-coated furnishings and the odd beige material papering the walls between the cathedral ceiling's soaring ribs.

She smelled him before she saw him. A noxious odor of decomposition announced his presence before he lurched into the corridor, drawn by the open door that beckoned him into the forbidden house of his master.

"Oi!" Gatekeeper shuffled into view, waving a stout stick, his face contorted with rage. "You're a liar! A liar!" His high, feminine voice was shrill and terrible.

Sorykah resumed her fighting stance, hoping that her appearance would frighten him into submission, but they both knew which of them was the more dangerous.

Gatekeeper bared rotten teeth, advancing on Sorykah and swinging his stick with a clubbed arm. "You sneak! You lied to me, you lied!"

Sorykah was speechless. The cannibal had ethics.

"Come on, then," she goaded, "I'll kill you like I killed your master. We'll see who sings tonight!"

He hurled a handful of stones and caught her on the forehead. She staggered and fell against the wall, wiping the blood that dribbled from the cut into her eye. As fierce as a rogue wolf driven from the pack and forced to hunt alone, desperation and desire emboldened him.

The smell of him was awful—rancid grease, old blood, and shit left to ferment beneath layers of grime on his never-washed body. Bile rose, bitter in her throat.

Her lips parted to scream but Gatekeeper suppressed her cry and she felt that skinny licking tongue green with plaque and disease against her teeth. She heaved the contents of her stomach against his mouth, but he was undeterred. Over seven feet tall, he had an advantage and used it to press his prey to the cold wall.

"Think I wouldn't smell you, woman? Crick-crack! Confused me with the dazzle of his ring. Bright berry, red blood, Tirai's heart! I tasted it! I know!"

His fetor, combined with the smell of dog and her own vomit, was so powerful that she couldn't concentrate on anything else. The smell of dog! She feared the return of Matuk's hounds, hungry for another taste of her.

She heard deep growling and tensed, thrusting her shoulder into the fetid old monster and clenching her teeth against the onslaught of his vile, wormy tongue.

Gatekeeper was torn between biting into the false-Chen's throat and slurping the blood from her open vessels or wringing her neck and leaving her to rot for a soft and sludgy feast at a later date. His hesitation cost him.

Kika sprang from the corridor where she had crouched growling, and jaws locked around the shriveled, stinking skin of the Gatekeeper's arm. He shrieked and tried to shake her off but Kika dragged the old fiend to his knees, lowering his neck for the executioner's strike.

Sorykah's arms were strong, but not enough to lop off the Gatekeeper's head.

Give me your strength, she begged. This time she would allow Soryk the pleasure of revenge. He surged through and brought down the blade.

Then he was gone and Sorykah was whole again, awed by the speed and intensity of her change. Her body shook, cold and hot together, the sauna and the icy plunge taken in one system-shocking breath.

"Sweet Jerusha," she gasped.

Kika dropped the odious monster's limp arm and shook herself briskly. She sniffed once at the head dangling by a few slippery tendons and trotted over to Sorykah, nosing her and savoring a good scratch beneath the chin.

"Ah, my girl," Sorykah crowed. "I am so pleased to see you!" She rubbed her face in Kika's dirt-dulled fur, the dog straining toward the manse's gloomy interior.

"Yes, you're right. Let's find the babies."

Together they found the kitchen. Sorykah paused against the gray-veined marble wall, slick with condensation, before pushing open the door and taking in the welcome sight of Dunya, Nels, and, squished between protective bosoms in their much-abused and worn basket, Ayeda and Leander, wide-eyed and startled.

Sorykah choked back sobs as the women rushed to catch her in grateful embraces.

"Oh mum, I knew ye'd be the one! Never did I 'ave a doubt!" Dunya beamed, her sorrowful eyes shining.

"Holy Mother, you've done it!" Nels chimed in. "Is he gone? Are we safe?"

"'Course we're safe, ye skinny nun," Dunya snorted. "Would she be standing here, coated wiv slime and looking like the Devil's own sister, if she hadn't taken 'im out?"

Sorykah staggered a bit, pushing the women away from her. Their hands and noise were too much an intrusion on this perfect, private moment. Dunya and Nels, the grimy kitchen, the whole world, in fact, fell away as she moved forward, weightless and open.

The children goggled at her as if she were a clown who measured his success in terms of nightmares delivered to the enfeebled. Ayeda opened her mouth (new teeth, Sorykah noticed) and released a loud cry of astonishment or recognition; startled by his sister's noise, Leander burst into frantic, hysterical tears. Even Kika howled with brief solidarity.

Sorykah moved toward her children, her emotions frozen like her heart had been during weeks of travel beset with nightmares and anguish as she fought to keep images of their deaths at bay.

"Shhh," she whispered, reaching out to stroke Ayeda's cap of wheat-colored curls. Insulted by his mother's choice, Leander wailed even louder and Sorykah scooped him up, the ice in her veins cracking, melting, and dripping away. She squeezed her son, lifted Ayeda by one arm, and crushed her to her breasts, laughing and giddy with relief.

"You don't remember me, do you my dolls," she announced, as if by recognizing it, she could alleviate her pain. "It's all right," Sorykah insisted as Ayeda pleaded with Dunya over her mother's shoulder and Leander struggled to escape the rank, dirty stranger holding him captive. "It will all come back." Sorykah graciously allowed Nels to pluck Leander from her arms and collapsed on a wooden stool, her head in her hands. On an intellectual level, she understood that eight-month-old babies would forget a face they didn't see every day. Still, she'd hoped for some form of recognition, a smile of welcome, chubby arms reaching out to her.

They were alive, hale and hearty thanks to Dunya's vigilance. Nels's thinness was shocking, but as Sorykah watched her, she was pleased to see that some of the color returned to her nanny's cheeks. She shivered and wanted very badly to go home. The Quonset waited silent and vacant, in need of a joyful family to enliven it with voices and laughter. Even from this distance, Sorykah believed that she could hear the Sigue lullaby, morbidly beautiful and sharp with longing.

She hoped to have a job waiting for her. She assumed that the Company had reported her absence, dutifully completed the requisite forms in triplicate, surrendered them to the authorities, and replaced her with some fresh-faced academy lad, but none of it mattered. There were new choices, new options. Sidra's giggle danced through her mind, leading a vision of warm silver thighs clenched around her hips, *his* hips, the queen gilded by fine clay, her half-closed eyes liquid with lust. The women waited and watched, each bouncing a baby on her hip. Suddenly radiant with the pleasure of her success, Sorykah said, "He's done for, you know. I dispatched him myself."

"Jerusha will forgive you," Nels asserted, worried for Sorykah's soul and possible repercussions in some foggy future afterlife.

"Ye did the right thing, miss," Dunya added. "'E deserved it. Ye've done this wood a favor and none o' us can pay ye back."

"I have no need to be absolved of sin. That said, I thank you both." Sorykah's voice wavered, and she cleared her throat again. "I've not done any more than was due. But you," she said, "you saved them." She placed a hand on Dunya's shoulder, looking her squarely in the eye in a way that Dunya was unused to. Dunya could not remember having ever been thanked for anything that she did, was certain that no other woman had gazed at her without flinching or bearing such an expression of warmth and welcome. An unconscious whine seeped from the dog-faced girl's throat; had she a tail, it would have been wagging ferociously.

Dunya, prepared to claim the babies even if it meant stealing them from their mother, felt something shift within her, as though some foreign splinter had been dislodged or a cankerous sore drained of its poison. The prospect of her own future opened itself, tentatively.

"Now," Sorykah said, "we leave this house of death and distress and return to the sea."

"Agreed!" Nels grinned, her smile horsey in her now-bony

face. "All I want is a hot cuppa, a few wee chockies, and a good book. I've been dreaming about it for days!" Sorykah laughed. Dunya's face clouded with confusion. She had never read a book or tasted chocolate, and the idea of lying abed with either of those things seemed an appalling show of laziness. Still, she had no master to please, no ringing bell jangling angrily to call her to task and keep her slaving deep into the night.

"What shall you do, Dunya?" Nels asked.

"Set fire to this place," she answered immediately. It sounded like a good idea and so she would do it.

"And then?" Sorykah inquired, soft-voiced and smiling as she ran hands over Ayeda's body, feeling how much her daughter had grown during their time apart.

"She comes with us, of course," Nels insisted, mother-henning her friend.

Dunya declined before offering somewhat shyly that she'd always wanted to visit the Erun city. She fancied a tall tree house with a cozy kitchen and a fireplace, somewhere warm, dry, and quiet.

"Don't know what I'll do wiv meself, all that time on me 'ands," she said, hiding her face so that the women would not see her tears.

"We will take you." Sorykah pressed her nose into Ayeda's hair, bliss erupting like a fountain within her. From within the safe haven of his nanny's arms, Leander offered his mother a smile and she thought *You melt me, little boy.*

Dunya smeared fat across the wooden tabletop, the stools, and her broken-down bed. The fire spread like a bright, poisonous rash as Dunya touched her torch to the lard-caked table. Fat popped and hissed, transfixing the women as the fire began to eat away at the wood. They could already see how it would leap from stool to cabinet, gobbling up everything in sight, spilling cinders from its mouth.

Leander said "Ooh," reaching for the leaping orange streamers that danced before him and Sorykah laughed. "Yes, my darling, it's all going up in a cloud of smoke. That nasty man won't bother you anymore, isn't that right, my dove?"

Dunya considered Meertham, alone with his panoramic ocean view in his far-off room. Smoke would snuff out his guttering candle before the flames came and hammered down his coffin nails. Maybe he was already dead. At any rate, it was what he wanted. Nels could add him to her prayers.

Smoking and curling, the skin-covered walls peeled like bark from paper birch trees in the sloughing season. Sorykah and Nels followed Dunya with stoic reverence.

Dunya ushered the group into the far tower and the armory. With a nod, she dashed upstairs to dispatch the autopsy table, the towering bookcases heaped with collected Phantastics, watching with satisfaction as the flames set to work on the armchair and bloodstained rugs. Matuk himself was little more than a heap of rags turned tinder. His dogs had fled. Dunya tossed her torch behind her as she descended the stairs for the last time, her spirit so light that she felt she would lift from the ground and take wing.

Because of her deformed jaw and loose jowls, Dunya's smile looked less like a grin of pleasure than a grimace of pain, but her voice was cheerful and she brushed the dirt and soot from her hairy hands. Freedom flew in giddy circles inside her body like the wheeling seagulls she had once watched from the tower window, swooping effortlessly over the open ocean.

They stepped gingerly over the Gatekeeper's headless body, as if afraid they might rouse him with the sound of their soft breathing. The door was closed; Gatekeeper perhaps, had shut them in.

"The lock," Sorykah moaned, fretting over the sacrifice of another digit.

"Yer fingers and toes are safe wiv me." Dunya produced Matuk's bone key and the vial of blood. The lock sucked up its offering and turned without complaint. The women crowded through the door, eager to be away. Nels and Sorykah threw their torches into the open doorway behind them, and Dunya closed it with ringing finality.

Moonlight glowed faint and creamy between the trees, but the sky was already gray with early morning haze. Sweet cedars perfumed the air and dew weighted the meadow grasses. Sorykah pulled the new day deep inside her. The waking forest cocooned her in its noise, birdsong, insect buzz—the woods in vocal rapport. The Erun had recovered from an infestation of fear and now its evicted tenants had come to reclaim their homes.

Ayeda squawked and pawed Sorykah's breasts. The warm burn began as her milk ducts awakened and let down. Sorykah waved her companions to the meadow's far side and the quiet, sheltering trees. "Let's find a spot to rest over there. I need to nurse this baby."

At the mention of nursing, Leander wrinkled his brows and smacked his lips. Weeks of goat-flavored mealie and cold bacon rinds had not dulled his appetite for the sweet, warm goodness of the milk in his fuzzy infant memories.

Sorykah kissed his downy forehead, her eyes shining. The baby stared at his mother with somber, dark eyes, each like the light of a star burning from the depths of a black well.

"No worries, my lamb," she said. "There's plenty to go 'round. Though days and miles separated us, I did not forget you."

PHOTO: MELODY HUFFORD

KIRSTEN IMANI KASAI, a native Coloradoan, has lived in places as diverse as Newark, New Jersey, East Hampton, New York, Bradford and Penzance, England (sadly devoid of singing pirates), and a windowless cubby beneath the stairs in a San Francisco flat crowded with ten roommates, four iguanas, three cats, two German exchange students, and a bald illegal Irishwoman, none of whom possessed a front door key. Before having children, she moved to a new city every six months, indulging her taste for novelty. She currently resides in Southern California with her husband and children.

www.icesong.com
www.redroom.com/author/kirsten-imani-kasai